THE
CROWN'S
FATE

EVELYN SKYE

BALZER + BRAY

An Imprint of HarperCollins*Publishers*

Balzer + Bray is an imprint of HarperCollins Publishers.

The Crown's Fate

www.epicreads.com

Library of Congress Control Number: 2016962059

ISBN 978-0-06-242261-3 (trade bdg.)

ISBN 978-0-06-266695-6 (int.)

Typography by Jenna Stempel

17 18 19 20 21   PC/LSCH   10 9 8 7 6 5 4 3 2 1

First Edition

To Mom and Dad—

For the time Grandma fretted that I wouldn't be able to do anything with a degree in Russian literature and history, and you told her, "Don't worry, Evelyn will find a way."

And for all the times you loved and believed in me, before and after that.

The Crown's Game is an old one, older than the tsardom itself. But it is not the only game.

There are games of love, played by boys and girls. Games of deception, played by gamblers and thieves. Games of war, played by generals and kings.

Then there are the games that combine all three, played only by those with nothing to lose.

But if the player has nothing to lose, then nothing remains . . .

Except to win.

CHAPTER ONE

Vika Andreyeva was a confluence of minuscule bubbles, streaming through the wintry dusk. For a few moments, she gave herself up to the thrill of the magic, to the escape of evanescing. *I am the sky. I am the wind. I am freedom, unleashed.*

As soon as Vika rematerialized on the Kazakh steppe, though, solid reality replaced the joy of being everything, yet nearly nothing. She was here to work, to carry out an official assignment as Imperial Enchanter. She sighed.

Only half an hour earlier, she had appeared at the royal stables, where Grand Princess Yuliana Romanova had been grooming her horse. Or rather, a stable boy was grooming her horse, brushing its chestnut mane, while Yuliana pointed out every tiny knot.

The boy didn't see Vika appear in the corner of the farthest stall, but Yuliana's sharp eye missed nothing.

"Leave me," the grand princess said, shooing the stable boy away. He jumped and skittered off, well trained not to linger against Yuliana's wishes.

When he was gone, she turned to Vika and said, "Baroness Andreyeva, it would be preferable if you entered the room—or the stable—the proper way, by being admitted and announced by the guards. Like everyone else."

Vika cast Yuliana a sideways glance. "My apologies, Your Imperial Highness. It's just that, you see, I'm *not* 'like everyone else.'" She crossed her arms.

Yuliana huffed.

"I'm here because your messenger said you wished to see me?" Vika curtsied with more than a touch of sarcasm. Hay clung to the hem of her dress as she rose. She noticed but left it there. Vika had grown up in a forest; it seemed strange, almost, *not* to have bits of mud and leaves clinging to her.

Yuliana arched a brow at the hay. "I need you to do something."

No *How are you?* Or *Thank you for coming.* Not that Vika was surprised.

"What is it?"

"Manners, *s'il vous plaît*," Yuliana said.

Vika dipped her head and allowed it to bob down heavily. "Of course, Your Imperial Highness. I am at your service."

Yuliana rolled her eyes. "My brother and I need you to go to the Kazakh steppe."

"Pardon?" Vika jerked her head upright.

"Are you deaf now, too, along with being impertinent? I said, we need you to go to the Kazakh steppe. The last time Pasha was there, talk of another rebellion was underway. We need to find out if their plans have developed any further, but our traditional means of gathering intelligence via scouts is slow. However, *you* could evanesce to the steppe and come back all in the same day. We've never had information so fresh."

But Vika was hardly listening. She couldn't go. That was where Nikolai, Russia's only other enchanter, was from, and now he was gone because he'd lost the Crown's Game. . . .

How can I possibly walk through the steppe, as if it were just another place? Vika's heart stomped to the beat of a mazurka, painfully aware of the wrongness of each solitary move without Nikolai as her partner.

She shook her head. "I don't want to go. You can't send me there."

Yuliana had marched up to Vika, kicking hay in every direction. "I can, and I will. You're the Imperial Enchanter. Do your job."

Which was how Vika found herself on the steppe now. She gave herself another moment, not only to recover from evanescing—it always took a few seconds to get reoriented—but also to brace herself for facing this place that reminded her too much of what—*whom*—she'd lost only two weeks ago.

She took a very deep breath. *This is part of my duty. All my life, I've wanted nothing more than to be Imperial Enchanter, and this is what it entails. I can do this.* But it was a victory tinged with bittersweet.

She took another long inhale.

Before she left Saint Petersburg, Vika had transformed her appearance to blend in more easily with the Kazakhs, changing her hair from red to black, and her clothes from a puff-sleeved gown to a tunic-like *koilek*, a collared dress, and a heavy *shapan* overcoat made of sheepskin.

A few paces from the dark corner where she hid, the tented

marketplace bustled. There were tables piled high with nuts, and bins of spices. Stalls selling fur-lined boots, and others boasting silver jewelry, all intricately patterned and inlaid with red, orange, and blue stones. There was a table that specialized in all manner of dried fruit, and everywhere there were people, smiling and inspecting goods and bargaining.

A girl walked by, carrying a tray of enormous rounds of bread. They must have just come out of an oven, for their yeasty warmth filled the air. The smell, which reminded her of Ludmila Fanina's bakery at home, comforted Vika and pulled her out of her brooding.

Besides, brooding didn't suit Vika. It was more Nikolai's disposition than hers, and she was actually incapable of being melancholy for long before something inside her itched to move along. The one time she'd submerged herself in sorrow, after Father's passing, she'd come out of it more agitated than ever, and she'd nearly destroyed Nikolai's home in response, only to become mortified with regret halfway through. Vika would not make the mistake of wallowing again for too long. She clenched her fists and stashed away the swirl of emotions that surrounded her thoughts of Nikolai, as hard as putting away those feelings could be.

The bakery girl set down the tray at a stall a few yards away and began unloading the loaves onto the display. A crowd of women immediately surrounded the table, drawn to the fresh bread like garrulous seagulls to a picnic, and started yammering for the girl's attention.

Ludmila would love to try Kazakh bread.

Brilliant! Vika's eyes brightened. It would give her something to focus on other than Nikolai.

She conjured a few Kazakh coins in her palm. Then

she evanesced the money into the bakery girl's till and in exchange, evanesced a round of bread all the way back to Ovchinin Island, where both Vika and Ludmila Fanina lived. The loaf would arrive at Cinderella Bakery, Ludmila's shop, still warm and steamy. Vika sent a brief letter with the bread, even though she was quite sure Ludmila would know who'd sent it.

And now back to the task at hand.

Vika left the bakery stall and walked around the perimeter of the marketplace. The only flaw in Yuliana's plan was that unless the people were speaking Russian or French, Vika wouldn't understand what they were saying.

But why can't I?

Being the only remaining enchanter in Russia did mean Vika could ask more of the empire's magic, since she no longer had to share it. And she'd always been able to understand animals, like her albino messenger rat, Poslannik, by casting an enchantment over them. It had simply never occurred to her to translate another human language, because she'd needed only Russian, rudimentary French, and the speech of wolverines and foxes on Ovchinin Island.

As Vika walked, she began to conjure a dome, of sorts, to surround the entire marketplace. The enchantment began on the ground, like a shimmering veil of liquid crystal rising from the dirt. At least, that was how it appeared to her, for Vika could see the magic at work.

The enchantment trickled upward toward the sky, flowing as if it were not subject to the rules of gravity. It climbed the outside of the marketplace, then arched over the tops of the tents, enclosing the shoppers and vendors and their goods inside.

But not really. The dome wasn't solid; the people couldn't see it or feel it, and they could enter and exit as they pleased. Vika's magic would only capture the scene, and then she'd be able to take the enchantment back to Saint Petersburg to replay it for Yuliana and Pasha, who could walk through the memory dome as if they themselves had been here.

It also included an enchantment to allow Vika to understand Kazakh. Or an attempt at an enchantment like that, anyhow. If she could listen in, she could better root out whether there were any new developments in the region's unrest.

She smiled grimly at the marketplace before her. *I hope this works*, she thought, for if it did, she could capture scenes in other places, like the borders where the Russian and Ottoman empires chafed at each other. Such information would be invaluable.

She also hoped it failed, because spending the rest of her days alone, spying at the edges of the empire, would be no life at all.

The dome enchantment glistened lazily under the winter sun, its liquid crystal walls ebbing and flowing as the magic soaked up every word and action taking place within its confines. Vika picked up bits and pieces of the conversations. "Two pairs of boots . . ." "That's too expensive for a leg of lamb . . ." "But Aruzhan hates dried apricots—"

But then there was a lurch at the top of the dome, and Vika gasped as ripples stuttered over the surface of her enchantment, and a hole broke open into a jagged crack. Her power stumbled, as though the flow from Bolshebnoie Duplo—Russia's magical source—had suddenly been blocked. The sparks that normally danced through her fingertips were snuffed out.

What?

Her chest tightened, as if the air were being wrung from her lungs. The ripples threatened to build into something more, to cascade down the sides of the dome, undoing it all.

Vika opened her arms to the air, palms up, and labored to catch her breath while attempting to control the enchantment. She pulled on the magic that already existed, attempting to draw it up and over to patch the crack at the top of the dome. It was like tugging on fabric that was already stretched too tight; there wasn't enough of the magic to go around.

But then, as quickly as it had hitched, the power flowed smoothly through Vika again. She was almost certain it wasn't her doing—the magic had hardly budged when she pulled on it—but somehow, the ripples on the dome flattened into a serene surface, flowing over the crooked tear at the top to make it whole.

She dropped her arms by her sides, sweat beading on her forehead. What could have possibly caused a hitch like that in the magic? Her power had never faltered so completely before.

Fatigue suddenly trampled her, like being run down by a carriage pulled by half a dozen spooked horses.

And Vika laughed at herself, for in her head, she could hear what Ludmila would say, what she *had* been saying: *Too much work and not enough cookies. You need to take care of yourself, my sunshine. Rest and eat more sweets.*

Rest. Vika shook her head. There was no such thing as

rest for an Imperial Enchanter, certainly not one at Yuliana's constant command.

But that doesn't mean there can't be more cookies. Vika's stomach growled.

She evanesced a few more coins to the nearby bakery stall. A moment later, a *chakchak* cookie appeared in her palm, a cluster of fried dough piled together with syrup and walnut bits. Vika took a crunchy, honeyed bite.

She smiled. Popped the rest of the cookie into her mouth. And sent money for a handful more.

Being Imperial Enchanter wasn't all bad.

CHAPTER TWO

Once she finished capturing the scene on the steppe—and having heard nothing that would imply an immediate threat from the Kazakhs—Vika evanesced back to Saint Petersburg, to the banks of the frozen Neva River. Behind her, an enormous statue of the legendary tsar Peter the Great sat atop a bronze horse and watched over the capital he'd built, this glorious "Venice of the North." The city's bridges were dark at this hour, their holiday garlands that sparkled in the daytime now swallowed by the night, with only an occasional streetlamp casting ghostly halos upon the snow-covered cobblestones. And all the people of the city were fast asleep. All but Vika, of course.

To anyone else, midnight was silent. But to Vika, who could feel the elements as if they were a part of her soul, the darkness was full of sound. Water beneath the thick ice of the river, sluggish and near frozen, but still stirring. Winter moths flitting through the chilly air. Bare branches, bending in the wind.

She wouldn't be able to sleep for a while, if at all, not after spending the last few hours immersed in the steppe. Heavens, how she missed Nikolai. For a brief period of time during the Crown's Game, there had finally been someone else who could do what she could, who understood what it was like to be one—or two—of a kind, who knew who she truly was.

So instead of going home, Vika looked out at the frozen river in front of her, in the direction of the island she'd created during the Game. The people of Saint Petersburg had dubbed it Letniy Isle—Summer Island—for Vika had enchanted it as an eternally warm paradise.

But she shuddered as she remembered the end of the Game. Nikolai had attempted to kill himself, but the knife Galina gave him was charmed to "never miss," and by that, she'd meant "never miss the target that *Galina* intended." So when Nikolai plunged the dagger into himself, it had actually pierced through Vika. And to keep her from dying, he'd siphoned his own energy to her.

Vika closed her eyes as the echo of both Nikolai's and Father's deaths reverberated through her bones. Two incredibly important people had given their lives for her. She was unworthy of the sacrifice.

I would have stopped them if I'd known what they were doing.

But that was why neither had let her know.

The wind nipped more bitterly around her. Father was gone for good, but Nikolai . . . Well, she'd seen him—or a silhouette that looked like him—in the steppe dream. There was an entire series of enchanted park benches on Letniy Isle; a person need only sit on one of the Dream Benches and he or she would be whisked away into an illusion of Moscow, Lake Baikal, Kostroma, or any of the other dozen places

Nikolai had conjured. Each bench was a different dream.

Was Nikolai still there now, in the steppe dream? Vika had gone back every day since she'd seen him that single instance last week, but he had not reappeared. Yet the benches themselves still existed, which meant his magic hadn't been extinguished. Perhaps that meant Nikolai was still, somehow, alive, too.

Then again, Vika could feel the old magic inside the statue of Peter the Great behind her, and that had been created decades ago by an enchanter who'd died in the Napoleonic Wars.

But hopefully the shadow boy Vika had seen was a scrap of life that Nikolai had managed to hold on to for himself. Not quite enough to be real, but enough to be more than a dream.

"If you're still in the bench, I'll find a way to get you out and make you yourself again," Vika said.

As she uttered the promise, her chest constricted. But it wasn't the invisible string that tethered her to Nikolai as enchanters; this pull on her chest was a different sort.

Vika pressed her gloved hand to her left collarbone, where the scar of the Game's crossed wands had once burned.

Before the end of the Game, Nikolai had said he loved her.

It was possible Vika loved Nikolai, too.

But she didn't have much chance to contemplate her feelings, for behind her, heavy footsteps approached the statue of Peter the Great.

Vika's pulse sped up. Had someone seen her evanesce here? Ordinary people couldn't know about magic. A long time ago, they had believed, and there had been witch hunts.

Hysteria. Not to mention that the more people believed in magic, the more power Bolshebnoie Duplo generated, which in turn meant that enchanters were a greater threat to the tsar because they could possibly usurp him. It was why the Crown's Game and its oath had been conceived, to ensure that any enchanter would work *with* the tsar, not against him, and why common folk's belief in magic had to be suppressed.

After all she had survived, Vika didn't want to meet her end on a flaming pyre.

The footsteps drew closer. Vika darted away from the embankment and ducked behind the Thunder Stone, the massive slab of granite at the base of Peter the Great's statue.

A minute later, a young fisherman stumbled into view. He was singing.

No. Slurring.

Thank heavens, Vika thought as she relaxed against the Thunder Stone. *He probably didn't see me anyway, and even if he did, he won't remember in the morning.*

But then the boy reached the statue and stopped.

Oh, mercy, she thought. *Anyone but him.*

Vika lightened her steps as she inched around the Thunder Stone to a spot where he wouldn't see her.

Because he might have worn a fisherman's cap, but he was no ordinary drunk.

He was Pavel Alexandrovich Romanov—Pasha— tsesarevich and heir to Russia's throne.

CHAPTER THREE

It was too late to be evening, yet too early to be morning, when Pasha tripped his way into Peter's Square. There was nothing princely about him at the moment, for he hadn't shaved in the fortnight since the end of the Game, and he wore a tattered coat and a threadbare fisherman's cap, which had come from the secret chest where he stored his disguises. There was also the matter of the entire bottle of vodka he'd gloriously—or perhaps, ingloriously—drunk on his own, and as he came to rest against the base of the statue of Peter the Great, reality was a bit slippery for Pasha to hold on to.

"*Bonsoir*, Your Imperial Majesty," Pasha said from the Thunder Stone. Towering above him, an enormous bronze Peter looked out across the dark river, while his horse trampled a serpent, symbolizing the enemies of the tsar and Saint Petersburg. Legend had it the statue was enchanted, that it would always protect the people and the city.

"Quiet out tonight," Pasha said. "Looks like it's just you

and me, tsar and . . . future tsar." He'd hesitated because he'd almost called himself a tsar, too. But Pasha was technically still only the tsesarevich, the heir to the throne, until the official coronation in Moscow next month.

This felt right, though. *Tsar and future tsar.* Pasha laughed and lowered himself down to the snowy ground. He rested his head against the Thunder Stone.

"Do you ever wish you could go back in time and do things over?" Pasha asked the statue. He tilted his head farther back until he was looking up at the underbelly of the horse, as well as in the general direction of the bronze tsar. Snow fell into Pasha's eyes. The horse snorted.

Pasha startled. "Did your horse just—?"

But after a few moments of definite silence (he must've imagined the horse making a noise—damn it, how much had he drunk again?), Pasha returned to leaning against the stone. "No, I suppose you never felt that way. You're Peter the Great. You're great by definition. Whereas I will be, what? Pasha the Unshaven." He waved his arms dramatically in the air. "Pasha the Unprepared. Pasha the Dreadful, who never apologized to his best friend before sending him to his death." He exhaled loudly. "I just wish I could have a second chance. I would . . . I don't know what I would do. But I know I wouldn't demand the end of the Game. There must have been some other way."

"Be careful what you wish for, Your Imperial Highness," a voice said.

Pasha jumped to his feet and whirled. He looked at Peter the Great, eyes wide. "Did you say something? O-or . . . was it you again?" He shifted his focus to the horse.

A girl came from around the other side of the Thunder

Stone. Her red hair flamed beneath the dull brown of her fur hat. "Are you talking to the statue?"

Pasha blinked at her. It took a few seconds for his addled head to process what had happened. Of course. The voice had belonged to a girl. And not just any girl. To Vika, his Imperial Enchanter.

"I'm not talking to the statue," Pasha lied. How long had Vika been there, on the other side of the Thunder Stone? Might as well add "Pasha the Insane" to his list of illustrious monikers.

Vika came closer but stopped several yards away from him. Ever since the end of the Game, she'd maintained her distance. Pasha winced at the memory that the girl he'd once almost kissed now despised him.

"I mean it when I say you ought to be careful what you wish for," Vika said.

"Why? What could happen?"

"Anything. Or nothing. I don't know. But I've told you before, magic comes tied with many strings. Wishes, I'd imagine, are a bit like magic. Don't say I didn't warn you."

But Pasha smiled at her admonition. She could have left him here, babbling to Peter the Great and possibly making a grave magical mistake. *But she took the time to intervene. She actually talked to me, voluntarily.* That was progress. He thought back to the last time they'd spoken, a week after the end of the Game. She'd been in the steppe dream, and Pasha had come to find her, to apologize. She'd dismissed him.

And then another week had passed and he hadn't seen or heard from her at all. Now here she was, in the middle of the night, watching over him like an Imperial Enchanter would. Or perhaps even like a friend.

Pasha looked at the expanse of snow between them. Maybe the distance could be shortened, both figuratively and literally. He took a step toward her and tripped in the snow.

Damn alcohol. It was probably closer to *samogon*—homemade moonshine—than real vodka. *That's what I get for drinking in an unfamiliar tavern*, he thought. But he couldn't go back to the Magpie and the Fox. Too many memories of him and Nikolai there.

When Pasha got up, he held on to the Thunder Stone for balance. "To what do I owe the pleasure of your company?"

"I was out for a stroll, Your Imperial Highness."

That was also a post-Game development. Vika refused to call Pasha by name. He tried not to wince again—at least, not too visibly. "Out for a stroll, at this hour?"

Vika furrowed her brow. "Since when do you have the right to judge my comings and goings?"

"I was only curious—"

Vika held up her hand. A cold wind, colder than the one that already bedeviled Saint Petersburg, swirled around her. "You've had too much to drink, Your Imperial Highness. I hope you pull yourself together before the coronation. The people will only tolerate the grand princess running the empire for so long."

Pasha's insides flared. Perhaps it was indignation. Or perhaps it was the *samogon* in his stomach. Either way, it was enough to fuel him to stand up straight, without the Thunder Stone's help.

But it's true what Vika said, isn't it? Pasha's sister, Yuliana, was keeping the country going, attending Imperial Council meetings and receiving ambassadors, while he, the tsesarevich, was sneaking out of the Winter Palace in shoddy disguises and drowning himself in self-pity.

I can act like a ruler, too. The thought sloshed through his head, splashing against the inside of his skull.

"Vika," he said.

"What?" Her fiery hair whipped in the wind, like a solitary flame in the middle of the snow of Peter's Square.

She was *his* flame, though, wasn't she? She was *his* Imperial Enchanter.

A sloppy grin plastered itself across Pasha's face. "I order you to conjure me a midnight snack."

Vika scowled. "I beg your pardon?"

"You were right, I've had too much to drink, and I need some food to soak up the alcohol. And a fire, too, because it's a bit chilly out here, don't you think?"

"No, I don't." She stomped through the snow until she was only a few inches away from him. She was much shorter than he and had to look up at him, but somehow, she managed to make Pasha feel like *he* was the one who had to look up at *her*. Vika had a way of commanding more space than she occupied. "I know that losing your parents must have been traumatic—God knows I understand that firsthand—" She paused, but she gathered herself in a fraction of a second. "Yet I'm still me, even after Sergei died. You, on the other hand . . . I don't know what happened to change you, to make you demand the end of the Game like you did. What happened to the tsesarevich who was so sweet with me, and who was inseparable from his best friend? And now this, ordering me around like a mere kitchen servant . . ."

She glared at him even more intensely, her eyes like emeralds on fire. "I may be your Imperial Enchanter, but I refuse to use magic for inconsequential rubbish like fixing you a snack. Try it again, and I'll quit. Let's see how you do on charm alone, without any magic by your side."

Pasha's mouth dropped open.

But at the same time, Vika shrieked and grabbed her left wrist. She fell against him, and Pasha caught her as they both stumbled backward, braced by the Thunder Stone.

"Vika, what is it?" All thoughts about himself vanished. She didn't cry out again, but her entire body shook so hard, the tremors traveled through Pasha's hands where he held her, into his bones.

Pasha pried her gloved fingers off the left sleeve of her coat. She sucked air through her teeth. He pushed the wool up and away from her wrist.

A bracelet—no, a cuff, a filigree of metallic vines—was wrapped tightly around her and burned and glowed orange like embers against her skin. Atop the cuff, the Russian Empire's gold double-headed eagle watched her with fiery ruby eyes.

Pasha gasped. He'd been here before, almost like this but in a carriage, with Vika by his side as the scar on her collarbone glowed menacingly bright. And now this bracelet.

"Where did you get that? What is it doing to you?"

"It appeared just now," Vika said through her teeth. "And it's burning me, can't you see?" Her eyes watered as she bore the pain. But she wrenched herself away from Pasha's grip.

And fell immediately to her knees in the snow.

He moved toward her, arms outstretched.

"Stay back," she snapped.

He did as he was told. Her tone left no room for debate.

18

Vika muttered something under her breath. A moment later, a platter of black bread and smoked herring appeared in the air in front of Pasha's nose. The bread was steaming hot, as if it had just come out of the oven, and the smell was enough to make his *samogon*-soaked stomach growl. He leaned instinctively toward it.

Then the platter unceremoniously dumped its contents onto the dirty snow at Pasha's feet. Some of the herring landed on the toe of his boot. *"Sacré bleu!"* He jerked away, and the herring slid onto the ground, a slimy trail remaining on his shoe.

Vika exhaled, and the tension in her body melted away. The bracelet stopped glowing and turned an innocuous, ordinary gold.

An immediate reaction to her obedience, Pasha realized. He'd ordered her to conjure him a midnight snack. She'd refused. The bracelet had appeared and punished her, but had relented as soon as she complied with his request. Well, technically complied. He hadn't said anything about the snack being clean.

She looked at him from where she remained kneeling in the snow. "Are you happy now?"

Pasha shook his head. "I . . . I'm sorry. I didn't know that would happen."

"You seem sorry quite a bit lately, but only *after* being horrible." She climbed to her feet, still glaring.

Since it was the truth, he didn't try to defend himself. He pointed at Vika's wrist instead. "Are you all right now?"

"As all right as one can be, I suppose, being literally cuffed to Your Imperial Highness's service." She bit her lip, but ferociously, not at all in the coy manner that girls of the court ordinarily bit their lips in Pasha's presence. "It was foolish of me to think I could simply refuse you or walk away from being Imperial Enchanter."

"If I had a choice, I would release you from your obligations." Pasha took a step toward her.

Vika scowled. He didn't move any closer.

"But you don't have that power, Your Imperial Highness. The bracelet ensures that I stay. I swore an oath of loyalty to your father at the beginning of the Game and promised to abide by all the rules and traditions that had previously been established."

Pasha's brain was still soaked through with *samogon*, and drawing logical conclusions took great effort. He spoke, but the thoughts came slowly. "And since you won the Game . . . you're bound by the ancient magic of the oath to serve the tsardom?"

Her shoulders sagged then, as if sadness suddenly weighed her down and crushed her anger beneath it. "Apparently, if I can't be trusted to act in the interest of the crown, then there are safeguards to ensure that I do so. The roles of tsar and Imperial Enchanter have not survived for centuries by chance." She transferred her gaze from Pasha to the bracelet on her wrist. Then she yanked her coat sleeve down over the cuff so she couldn't see it.

Pasha leaned back against the Thunder Stone. Part of him was relieved Vika couldn't just leave him. He needed her. But part of him hated that she stayed only because she was compelled to, not because she wanted to.

"Well, then, Your Imperial Highness, now that you have your midnight snack . . ." Vika paused, as if to allow Pasha a moment to look at the bread and herring scattered (and now frozen) in the snow. "I should probably be going. As you mentioned, it's quite late."

She curtsied. It was terribly formal, with an emphasis on the "terrible" part.

"Wait." Pasha moved forward, undeterred this time by her glare. "I mean it when I say I'm sor—"

"Don't bother." Snowflakes began to spin around her, and within seconds, Vika had dissolved herself so that she, too, was a part of the flurry, and then the wind whipped and carried her off.

Pasha was alone again with the statue. He fell back against the Thunder Stone and ran his hands through his mess of blond waves. His fisherman's cap fell to the ground—appropriately, into the herring—but he didn't care enough to pick it up.

"Now I truly wish I could have a second chance," he said.

Pasha immediately slapped his glove over his mouth. For he'd made another wish, even after Vika had warned him.

And yet, I'd do anything for it to come true, he thought. The *samogon* made him both wistful and reckless. But why not? There was no risk, not really. Nikolai was dead. Vika hated him. Pasha was not getting a second chance with either.

He kicked the loaf of bread across the square, hung his aching head, and trudged through the snow, back home to the lonely halls of the Winter Palace.

CHAPTER FOUR

Vika rematerialized in the birch woods of Ovchinin Island, her home in the middle of the Neva Bay. Yuliana had wanted her to move into the Winter Palace, but Vika had refused; she would not be a dog at the grand princess's constant beck and call. Besides, although Saint Petersburg was stunning in its cosmopolitan way, it could not compare to this: logs and boulders covered by thick blankets of pristine snow. Dense, wild forests sparkling with icicles beneath the moon. Preobrazhensky Creek sleeping peacefully under a layer of crystal-blue ice.

And yet, despite the beauty surrounding her, all Vika could think of was the bracelet. It was no longer hot, but she could still remember its burn.

"Get off me!" She dug her fingernails beneath the edges.

The bracelet did not budge. But the eagle's ruby eyes flashed at her.

Vika glared right back at it. And she remembered the challenge Father had set up for her, before the Game, with the lightning and the ring of trees. She'd had to fight fire with fire. *Could it work now?*

She focused on the bracelet and thought about heating it. Melting it.

It heated. But not because of Vika. She yelped as the gold glowed orange and the cuff tightened around her, the filigree digging in so that she could feel each curling vine of its pattern searing into her skin.

"All right, I give up!" she shouted.

The bracelet wove another inch of gold around her wrist, as if to emphasize that Vika's fate was not her own. Only then did it cool.

But the smell of singed flesh lingered, and Vika gagged. She smothered her nose and mouth with her right hand, the uncuffed one that did not stink of charred skin.

In that regard, the bracelet was very much like the Game's scar of wands, which could also cease burning at a moment's notice, yet still leave pain lingering long afterward.

She thought of Nikolai, and for a moment, she forgot about the wisp of smoke that still rose from her skin.

If only he were here right now. He might have an idea for how to evade the bracelet. Or at the very least, Vika would be with someone who could commiserate. Nikolai had shared similar suffering. He would understand both what an honor it was to be Imperial Enchanter and what a burden it was, as well.

The need to see him suddenly consumed her, a silky, warm yearning like the all-encompassing feel of his magic.

To Letniy Isle, she commanded silently.

Please, Nikolai, she thought as she began to evanesce. *Please be there tonight.*

CHAPTER FIVE

Nikolai sat astride a black mare, both he and the horse watching a golden eagle soaring above as it scanned the Kazakh steppe for prey. *Everything is always the same*, he thought. Endless sky. Hunting. Breeze rustling through the tall grass. He sighed.

Of course, Nikolai could change small pieces of the scene if he wanted to. He could make his horse dappled gray when he fancied it, or paint the sky in sunset or storm, for none of it was entirely real. This place—this junction between fantasy and reality—was a magical dream he'd conjured back when he was alive.

Not that he was dead now. He was something . . . in between. The end of the Game had made him like this, neither corporeal nor mere spirit. He was a literal shadow of himself. Which also meant that his ability to enchant was a shadow of what it used to be.

The wind around Nikolai gusted, heralding the arrival of someone else on the steppe. He paused to look over his shoulder. *Who has come now?* This scene was accessible to anyone.

Whoever you are, Nikolai thought, *welcome to the nightmare bench.* "Nightmare," because he hadn't been able to escape the dream no matter how ferociously he tried to wake up, and reality marched onward everywhere else, without him. It was as if his state of in-between-ness had condemned him to existing in a place of in-between-ness, too.

Still, he watched the visitor as she materialized into the steppe dream, and when he recognized her, Nikolai's entire body went to pins and needles. Her red hair flamed in the sunlight, broken only by a single streak of ash black. Even though she was tiny, she stood proud and powerful, as if she were twice her size. And she wore a green gown, years out of fashion, the same one she'd worn at the very beginning of the Game. It could still be improved by a yellow ribbon.

"*Bonjour*, Vika," he whispered to himself, as he shifted his horse and his shadow-self into the shade of the mountain nearby.

Vika squinted at the vast horizon before her, in his direction, as if she could hear him, even though he knew she could not. But then again, they'd always had an undeniable connection. They'd been the only two enchanters in Russia. Destined to come together. Destined to tear each other apart.

He slouched a little at the last thought.

"Nikolai! Are you here?" Vika called into the never-ending sky.

The golden eagle wavered at the sound of her voice. Because Nikolai faltered at the sound of it, too.

She'd come in search of him, and he couldn't bear it.

Not when he looked like a shadow. Not when he loved her but couldn't have her. And most of all, not when he felt both glad that he'd sacrificed himself at the end of the Game in order for her to live and resentful that he'd ended up in this nebulous state of ante-death.

Vika pushed through the tall grass, clearly not caring a whit whether burrs scratched and clung to her gown. But Nikolai wouldn't allow her to reach him. For every foot that Vika marched forward, he extended the dream's landscape another foot. It was the least—and the most—his magic could do.

And yet, slowly, Vika began to make progress toward the base of the mountain where he sat on his horse.

But then she stopped. She was close enough that he could smell the honeysuckle-cinnamon scent of her magic. Close enough that he could feel the wildness and warmth of it. Yet still far enough that he could remain hidden.

She frowned. "Why won't you show yourself to me?"

The sad edge in her voice was a chipped blade, still sharp but no longer whole.

"I just . . ." Vika sighed. "It's been a long night. Although I suppose it's daytime here. . . . You *are* here, aren't you?" She looked around her, at the grass and the sky and the yurt village in the distance.

Nikolai closed his eyes.

"You can't stay here forever. You have to come back."

Give me a reason, he thought. Because at the end of the Game, Nikolai had confessed that he loved her. But Vika hadn't said it back. Was she here because she wanted *him*? Or was she here out of guilt that he'd funneled all his energy into her and was left but a dark-gray echo of his former self?

"Pasha is a mess," Vika said. "Not that you should forgive him for what he did to us. I certainly haven't." She scowled, took several deep breaths, and continued. "But even though I'm furious at him, I feel for him, too. He's lost his sense of self. Yet flickers of it still appear every now and then. You should have seen the elaborate memorial he held in your honor, and he even made public that the tsar was your father. I'm sorry . . . I didn't know. But if you came back, you would be royalty, Nikolai."

His eyes flew open. He'd known before the Game ended that his mother, Aizhana, had been spreading word throughout Saint Petersburg that he was the tsar's illegitimate son. But he hadn't realized the news had reached Pasha, and that it had been made official.

I could be royalty. Nikolai laughed quietly to himself, in part because it was what he'd always wanted—as an orphan from the steppe, he'd never quite fit into Saint Petersburg society, no matter how hard he tried—and in part because it was cruelly ironic that his acceptance into the nobility's ranks came only when he couldn't enjoy it.

"And perhaps," Vika was saying, "Pasha's guilt would be alleviated with your return. Maybe he'd be able to find his old self again."

Nikolai sighed and looked away, even though she couldn't see him. Of course she hadn't actually come for him. It was about Pasha. Everyone was always so concerned with Pasha. Was that the only reason Vika wanted Nikolai to return?

It's not enough, Nikolai thought. He had loved Pasha like a brother, before they knew they were actually brothers. In fact, he still loved him.

But did Pasha love *him*? For with a single twist of fate,

Pasha had cast aside their entire history and demanded the end of the Game. It was because of him that Nikolai was here. That he was a shadow.

Nikolai's heart ached.

"Is it that you *can't* come back?" Vika asked.

Nikolai turned toward her voice again, unable to stay away from her for long. He was like a black lily that craved the sun.

"If you would let me," she said, "I could try to help you."

Say it, he thought. *Say you want to help me because* you *want me back. Not because Pasha needs me. Because* you *need me.*

But she didn't.

Nikolai stayed in the black shadow of the mountain, his own darkness rendering him nearly invisible. He willed his horse to stay silent.

Vika looked up at the eagle still circling in the sky. Then she sighed, shook her head, and woke herself from the dream. Nikolai watched as her body faded till it was nothing. Nothing here, anyway. She'd be solid outside of the Dream Bench, on the island in the Neva where reality existed.

"For the record," Nikolai said aloud, even though there was no one to hear him, "I don't regret for an instant giving my life so you could live."

Because the truth was, if Nikolai had died, Vika would have been all right. But if *she* had lost the Game and he had survived—if the crossed wands that scarred their collarbones had incinerated *her*, with his dagger in her heart—Nikolai could not have endured it.

And yet, although he regretted nothing of giving his life for her, his horse now took several steps toward where Vika had stood—which meant it was actually Nikolai who did so, for it was his will that created and directed everything in this dream. It was as if an unseen force kept him and Vika tied to each other, and wherever she went, he wanted to follow.

His sacrifice ought to have been reward enough. But it wasn't, and now he wanted not only for Vika to survive and win the Game, but also for himself to be able to live a life with her afterward. Nikolai frowned. *I'm not as noble as I'd thought.*

Or perhaps nobility was overvalued.

Then again, if there was anyone who could make more of the cards that life had dealt him, it was Nikolai. He'd always been resourceful. He'd always found a way.

His golden eagle swooped down and perched on his arm. It tilted its head, as if asking for Nikolai's thoughts.

"I'm going to free myself from here," Nikolai said. He would not remain trapped in this strange purgatory between wakefulness and dream forever. "I'll get out. I swear it."

CHAPTER SIX

Later—or was it the next day? it was impossible to tell—Nikolai hovered in the shade of a yurt as a young couple strolled by. In reality, they were sitting on a Dream Bench. But here, they were touring the Kazakh steppe in summer, arm in arm as they gawked at the colorful zigzag patterns on the wide, round tents and licked their lips at the *zhauburek* kebabs roasting over the fire. The tribe who populated the dream could not see them; it was, for visitors, like walking through a museum exhibit. A moving diorama.

And so, because they had no expectation of being seen, the couple did not notice that Nikolai had noticed *them*.

He had an idea about how to escape the bench. Nikolai's mother had resurrected herself from ante-death by leeching energy from maggots and worms belowground. Nikolai was not as badly off as Aizhana had been, but his state was a variation of ante-death nonetheless. Perhaps he needed more energy if he had any hope of returning to his former self. *At the very least, I want out of this damned steppe dream. To be in the same world as Vika.* He slunk up behind the visiting couple and reached in the man's direction.

And yet Nikolai hesitated before he actually touched the man. It wasn't as if he would hurt him. Nikolai would take only small quantities of energy from each visitor, and they would simply feel like they needed a nap upon returning to reality. (Which was a bit ironic, given that they were asleep while visiting the dream.) But even this harmless act of siphoning off the slightest energy reeked of dishonor. There was something filthy about it, like Nikolai was stealing. And even worse, it pricked at his pride that he couldn't fix himself on his own.

But it must be done. Nikolai swallowed his distaste and rested his fingers on the nearest visitor's back.

The man didn't even flinch, for Nikolai's touch weighed nothing. The man's energy, though, was more than nothing. It was a thin rivulet of richness straight into Nikolai's core. He let out a quivering breath as the infusion of energy radiated inside him.

This, the man felt on the back of his neck, like a wisp of a breeze. He twitched away and looked over his shoulder. But there was no one and nothing there, only a yurt half-hidden by shade. He and the woman left soon after that.

Good riddance, Nikolai thought, although truth be told, he knew it wasn't the couple but that filthiness he felt that he wanted to be rid of. As if the man and woman disappearing would mean Nikolai's memory of how low he'd stooped would disappear, too.

Obviously, it did not. Nikolai leaned a little more heavily against the side of the yurt.

"Don't look so grim," a woman said as she materialized in

front of him. Or what had been a woman, eighteen years ago, before she'd been buried in that damnable state between life and death. Now resurrected, she was more walking ghoul than human.

"Aizhana," Nikolai said. She hadn't visited him before, but he purposely kept his surprise out of his tone. He didn't want her to think he was excited to see her when he was, in fact, quite the opposite.

Click, click, click. She clacked her long fingernails together. "When will you start calling me Mother? Or Mama?"

Nikolai cringed. "Never."

She grimaced, exposing yellow teeth and rotten gums. Her black hair was missing in places, and the rest hung stringy and limp around the sallow skin of her face (where she *had* skin). And she'd stunk of week-old fish and putre-fied flesh before Nikolai had surrounded her in an invisible bubble, back when he was still whole and had complete use of his magic. Nevertheless, her stench remained contained. *Not everything about me has been consigned to shadow*, he thought. It was some consolation to know that the enchantments he'd cast in the past still existed.

The only thing remotely human about Aizhana was her eyes, which glowed golden and defiantly alive. "I thought you were capable of looking beyond the superficial," she said.

"I am," Nikolai said. "It's not because of your appear-ance that I refuse you. It's because you killed my father."

She flashed him a ghastly grin. "I'm glad you have come around to believing that the tsar really was your father."

"A lot of good that information does me." Nikolai turned and began to walk away from the village, back to the open grassland where his eagle waited.

Aizhana limped straight through the fire over which the villagers cooked their dinner (it was only imaginary fire, after all) and followed Nikolai. "You would be back on the reality side of the Dream Benches by now if you would just kill the visitors who come here. You would have a great deal more energy that way. Taking the tsar's life—as well as those of his guards and a few others along the way—is how I am so strong."

Nikolai glared over his shoulder at her but kept walking. In fact, he picked up the pace.

For a barely living woman with one crippled leg, Aizhana was awfully fast. It was, as she'd said, the energy from the lives she'd stolen.

And perhaps it's also that, as a shadow, I'm awfully slow. Nikolai frowned.

Regardless of the reason, Aizhana did not fall too far behind him.

Finally, Nikolai stopped pushing his way through the waist-high grass and whirled around. "What exactly is it you want from me?"

Aizhana stopped as well. "*From* you? Nothing. But *for* you? Everything. That girl should not have been the one to win the Crown's Game. And the so-called tsesarevich should not be the one to ascend to the throne. You have as much claim to the crown as he does. More, actually. At the time he would have been conceived, his mother had a lover. Alexis Okhotnikov, I believe. So your precious friend is really the bastard product of the tsarina and a mere staff captain."

Nikolai crossed his arms. "Don't say that about Pasha."

33

"You still defend him? After he all but shoved you to your death?"

Nikolai rubbed his eyes with the heels of his hands. It was true, what Aizhana said. Pasha had forced the end of the Game, knowing that meant either Nikolai or Vika would die. And of course Nikolai was angry and heartbroken over it.

But Pasha had also just lost both his parents. And Nikolai understood Yuliana well enough that it was clear her hand had more than guided Pasha's decision to declare the violent finale of the Game.

It was difficult for Nikolai to know which was worse—that he still loved Pasha, or that he still felt betrayed.

"The rumor about the tsarina and her lover is unsubstantiated," Nikolai said, avoiding Aizhana's question—her *accusation*—about coming to Pasha's defense. "Besides, if you call Pasha a bastard, then I am, too. The bastard product of the tsar and his murderer."

Aizhana cackled. If the birds in the steppe dream had been real, they would have startled from the grass. "Call yourself what you want, but that still makes you first in line for the throne. You are older than the tsesarevich by a year, and you are a direct descendant of the tsar."

"Right. And Russia wants a walking shadow for their leader."

"Russia wants revolution, Nikolai. They don't want the old ways, and they don't want the tsesarevich, who is merely his sister's puppet. Listen to me. All you need to do is kill a few people, and you'll have the energy you need to be whole again, and more. You could make yourself indestructible, and with your magic, no one could stop you."

Nikolai spat in the grass. "When I figure out how to

make myself whole again, it will have nothing to do with killing innocent visitors to this dream."

Aizhana shrugged. "Your misguided sense of honor holds you back. But remember this—the crown can be powerful yet as fragile as paper. Right now, Pasha is only a boy playing at becoming tsar. You could take advantage of that, my son." And with that, she bit on her arm to force her body awake, and she vanished violently from the dream.

Nikolai shuddered. Then he pressed on through the grass toward the mountainside. But he couldn't shake the black stickiness that lingered in the air, like humidity of the foulest kind.

Unfortunately, Aizhana always left an impression.

CHAPTER SEVEN

Vika waited just outside the door of Madame Boulangère, a snooty French bakery on Nevsky Prospect,
the main boulevard through Saint Petersburg. She was there
to intercept Renata, a servant in the house where Nikolai
had formerly lived, because Renata could read tea leaves and
might be able to see what was happening with Nikolai. But
Renata thought Nikolai was dead, and Vika couldn't simply
appear at the Zakrevsky house and talk openly about what
had happened in the Game, for other servants might hear.
Not to mention that Galina Zakrevskaya, Nikolai's mentor
and the tyrant of the house, hated Vika.

So here Vika was, hovering by Madame Boulangère,
where Renata was inside, picking up Galina's daily order of
baguettes and *pains au chocolat*. (Funny, in a way, that Galina
was like her brother in that sense; Sergei had also had a
standing order at a bakery for bread every day. Although
Father's preference had always been hearty, practical Russian fare, not extravagant French confections.) While Vika

waited, she watched the people around her scurrying up and down Nevsky Prospect with brown paper parcels full of Christmas cakes and boxes with new suits and hats for holiday fetes. She wondered for a moment what ordinary life would feel like, the kind where days were filled with mundane concerns like what color ribbon to wear in her hair for Christmas night.

But Vika did not want an ordinary life.

Finally, the bell above the door to Madame Boulangère tinkled, and Renata hurried out with an armful of baguettes wrapped in old Parisian newspaper and a box presumably full of sweets. She stopped short and nearly dropped the bread when she saw Vika waiting.

Vika shot a quick charm to keep the baguettes cradled in the crook of Renata's arms.

"*Privet*, Renata."

Renata clutched the bread tightly again. Too tightly, in fact. The crust of the bread crackled under her hold. "*Zdravstvuyte*," she said, returning the greeting but using the formal form of hello.

Renata looked mostly the same: a gray dress with a white apron, and intricately woven braids swaying against the nape of her neck. But there was no spark left in her eyes. Even near the end of the Game, Renata had been a candle flame of bravery. She'd leaned against the bars of the cell in which she was trapped and wished Vika well.

No trace of that courage remained. Nor was Renata's telltale kindness present. She merely looked at Vika blankly. "How can I assist you, Baroness Andreyeva?"

It was the same way Vika acted toward Pasha. Detached. Reluctantly dutiful. Using her official title, not her name.

"I need to talk to you. Can you spare a few minutes?"

"I don't think I have a choice." She looked at the snow at her feet.

Vika gritted her teeth. She knew what it was like not to be permitted choices. She would not impose the same on Renata. "You always have a choice, at least with me. But thank you. Come this way, please."

She led Renata off busy Nevsky Prospect onto a quiet side street. Vika looked up at the snow drifting from the sky. She issued a silent command, and the snowflakes began to flurry in a protective cylinder around them. "There," she said. "Now no one will be able to hear or interrupt us." Any passersby would simply see a heavier burst of snowfall.

Renata forced a smile despite not wanting to be there, the learned reaction of a servant, born and bred to be polite. "That's a pretty bracelet you're wearing."

Vika glanced down at where the sleeve of her coat had shifted when she'd conjured the flurry. "Oh. Um, thank you. It's from His Imperial Highness."

"The tsesarevich?" Renata's eyes widened.

"It's supposed to mean I belong to him. To the extent I can ever belong to anyone." Vika snorted, which actually showed a great deal of restraint, considering that every time she looked at the bracelet, she wanted to punch the tsesarevich and the grand princess in their haughty faces.

But Renata didn't laugh, either because she was too well mannered or because she was too entranced by the gold and the rubies.

"Anyway," Vika said, shaking the sleeve of her coat down to cover the bracelet, "I wanted to say I'm sorry. I should have come to you as soon as the Game was done. I was distraught and confused, and . . . It's no excuse. But I'm here now, because I wanted to tell you—"

"You don't need to." Renata stared again at the icy street beneath her scuffed boots. "I know . . . I know it's not your fault how the Game ended. Nikolai had said from the start that you were more powerful than he. And someone had to die. But I had still hoped he would win, that somehow, he'd find a way to defeat you and survive. It was naive of me. I'm sorry, because I know that means I was hoping you would die."

Vika swallowed a dry patch in her throat.

But she forced away the hurt of Renata's comment, because if Vika had been in Renata's place, Vika would have hoped the same thing. She shifted her focus and snapped her fingers at the street.

A sofa and a table, both made of snow, sprouted from the cobblestones, like mushrooms do from the forest floor. "Please have a seat," she said as she took the bundle of bread and the box from Renata's arms and led her to one of the chairs. "Don't worry, the sofa is warm."

Renata gaped.

"Magic, remember?"

"Oh." Renata nodded slowly and sank into the seat. The snow was fresh, soft powder, and its cushions were airier than goose down. Renata let out a little sound, something between confusion and pleasant surprise.

Once she was settled, Vika sat down, too. "I came to you because I need your help."

Renata looked up at her and blinked.

"You see, Nikolai didn't exactly die at the end of the Game—"

"What?"

Vika had to pause. It was harder retelling this than she'd anticipated. "He didn't defeat me, but he defeated the Game, in a way."

Renata paled. "Nikolai is alive?"

"In a manner of speaking."

"I—I don't understand."

Vika frowned. "Honestly, neither do I." She took Renata's hand and began to tell her everything she knew, from how the final duel had concluded to the shadow boy who'd appeared. Renata trembled the entire time.

The snow flurried a bit more fiercely around them.

Renata pulled at her braids. "But if he's a shadow, how do we know he's alive? Can Nikolai touch things, and can he feel them? Does he eat and drink and breathe like a real person? Does he even know who he is?"

Vika clutched the snowy armrest. "I don't know. I saw him only once, and that was a week ago. I've tried to find him again since but haven't been able to. That's why I sought you out. Perhaps your tea leaves will know what's happened to him."

"The last time I read your leaves, I was wrong." Renata frowned. "I prophesied that either you or Nikolai would die soon, but if what you're saying is right, then my reading was not, because neither of you died."

"Your leaves only predicted that death would come. They didn't say for whom. So they were accurate, actually, because the tsar and tsarina passed, as did . . . Sergei." Vika plucked at the sofa. A thread woven of snowflakes came out between her fingers. But the thread dissolved, seemingly as quickly as Vika was losing those she loved. She looked away from the droplets of water on her fingertips. "I just want to know something, *anything*, about Nikolai. Will you do it?"

Renata nodded slowly. She rose as if to fetch tea from the kitchen but then stopped as she saw the flurry of snow around them. "But, uh, where do we—?"

Vika held out an open palm, and a single steaming cup of tea appeared on it. It was a simple blue cup and saucer from her own table at home.

What if Nikolai did not appear in her leaves? What if their fortunes had crossed only in the past, but were no longer intertwined in the future? If so, then asking Renata to read these leaves would amount to nothing. And yet there were no other prophecies to read, because Nikolai was not around to drink tea and offer his cup.

Vika swallowed the tea as quickly as she could. She ignored the fact that it scalded all the way down. When all that remained were spindly leaves, she set the cup on its saucer.

Renata steadied the quivering in her hands and leaned forward. She pursed her lips as she studied the leaves, which clung to the inside of the cup with no discernible meaning. At least, nothing discernible to Vika. But that was why she had come to Renata.

"Is he in my leaves?" Vika asked.

After a few more seconds, Renata leaned back into the sofa. Snow puffed up around her. "Yes, he's there," she said.

Vika smiled.

The Game might be over, but their story was not.

But Renata coughed and wrapped a braid tautly around her finger, and Vika's smile vanished in an instant. "What else is in the leaves?" she said.

Renata sighed. "You're fighting over something again. And this time, death isn't a small presence."

"What do you mean?"

Renata released her grip on the braid and pointed to the black tea leaves, twisted and splayed from the bottom up to the rim. "Death is all over this cup. Whatever you're fighting for, it will affect more than just you or Nikolai."

Vika sank deep into the snowy cushions of the sofa. Her heart sank with her.

"I don't know what to do," Renata said as she stared at the cup.

Vika sat up. "We have to tell him."

"What?"

"About the leaves. We didn't last time, and it was a mistake. What if things could have been different if Nikolai had known?"

Renata hesitated but finally nodded. "You should go see him right away."

But now Vika froze. Because she hadn't been able to find him in over a week.

Perhaps the problem is me, she thought. Perhaps he'd appear for Renata, though. After all, he had kissed Renata right before the last duel of the Game.

Something fluttered inside Vika, something not entirely pretty. It was not butterflies but more like bats, jealous that Nikolai might be more amenable to seeing Renata than her. After all, Vika had been in his life mere months. Renata had been in Nikolai's life for years.

But Vika pressed her palm to her chest and quelled the bats inside. *I may have known Nikolai only a matter of months, but our relationship was far from shallow.* Besides, this was not the time for something as petty as jealousy.

"No, it should be you who goes to the steppe bench," Vika said, her voice tight. "Nikolai won't show himself for me, but perhaps he will for you."

Renata's eyes lit up at the suggestion. "It's worth a try. Ludmila would tell us to be optimistic, right? She'd say the glass is always half-full."

But Vika didn't respond. She merely bit her lip and hoped, but not too much. For when it came to her and Nikolai, optimism was made of warped glass.

CHAPTER EIGHT

The smell of laundry soap floated across the steppe dream. Nikolai would know that scent anywhere. Renata.

He scrambled to his feet from where he lay in the brown grass. He wouldn't hide from her, for he knew Renata was here for *him*, unlike Vika, who seemed to have come for Pasha's benefit.

As soon as Renata saw him, she cried out and ran, alternately tripping in the grass and shoving it away.

"Oh, Nikolai, it's true, you're alive!"

She opened her arms as if to embrace him, but Nikolai stepped back.

"Careful," he said. "I'm alive, but I'm not quite solid. You'll fall straight through."

Renata stopped, arms still outstretched. "I don't understand."

"Nor do I." He exhaled loudly. Nikolai was accustomed to knowing the answers, and if he didn't, to being able to reason them out. But his current predicament didn't appear to care for logic. "I seem to have some substance, but not much. I'm a bit of a conundrum."

Renata smiled. "You always have been."

Nikolai made a small sound under his breath—something akin to laughter, but not quite—and dipped his head to concede the point. Then he stepped forward and wrapped his arms around Renata, loosely, so that his shadow would not blur into her.

As soon as he had her against his chest, though, Nikolai relaxed. "Thank goodness you're alive, too." He hadn't realized until that moment how worried he'd been about Yuliana keeping her promise to release Renata and Ludmila after the conclusion of the Game. But here Renata was. Whole, and streaming tears down her cheeks, and very, very much alive. "You're all right."

"I'm all right now that I know you're here." She looked up and smiled, wiping away her tears with her sleeve.

"My being a shadow doesn't frighten you?" Nikolai asked.

Renata shook her head, and the ends of her braids whipped against her neck. "You're still you. I'm so glad Vika told me you were here—"

"Vika told you?" Nikolai's voice cracked.

He turned slightly away from Renata. How embarrassing to wear his hope so plainly.

She noticed, of course. "Yes, but . . ."

"But what?"

Renata reached for one of her braids. Nikolai recognized the movement, a tell for when she was nervous. She'd always been the lousiest of the Zakrevsky house servants when it came to lying or hiding things.

"Say it," he said.

Her fingers tightened around the braid. "I . . ."

"Renata, please."

"I think there's something between Vika and Pasha." Her words came out in such a rush, Nikolai could hardly understand them. And yet he caught the essence of them.

His silhouette felt suddenly heavier. "I beg your pardon?"

Renata looked everywhere but at Nikolai. "Vika wears a bracelet Pasha gave her, made of rubies and gold."

"But—"

"She said she belonged to him."

"As his Imperial Enchanter, perhaps—"

"Nikolai." Renata ran her hand gently down his arm. "We thought you were dead. She had no reason to wait for you."

"But I haven't been gone very long." He shook her off and started scratching at the back of his neck. "Damn Pasha."

Renata pressed her lips together.

"If it weren't for Pasha demanding the end of the Game, none of this would have happened."

Renata shifted away from Nikolai. "The Game was going to have to end no matter what."

"But he didn't have to callously send us off to kill each other, as if our lives meant nothing to him at all."

"Would you not have made your fifth move if he hadn't?"

"Perhaps I would have let the wands burn." Nikolai touched his frock coat where his collarbone was. "Perhaps I would have chosen to be incinerated, and then I really would have died."

What little energy Nikolai had seemed to drain away, and he lowered himself onto the ground, resting his head on top of his knees. The grass was so tall, it thrashed in the wind against his face.

Renata crouched at his side. "You're upset. You have every right to be."

All the muscles in Nikolai's shadow body tensed, and when he spoke, every word was equally tensed. "Pasha and I were like brothers. Do you know what it's like to have someone you love—someone for whom you would lay down your life—betray you? It's like having my heart scraped out of my chest with one of Galina's caviar spoons, bit by excruciating bit. I wander alone in this steppe dream day after day, replaying my friendship with Pasha, and whenever I think of the first time he foolishly stepped into Sennaya Square to play cards with us, or of how it felt when he and I would abandon a hunt to spend hours climbing trees and fishing in streams and laughing about nonsense together, it gouges my heart to pieces all over again."

And yet I still miss him, Nikolai thought.

Renata inched closer. "I'm sorry. But the tsesarevich is, too. If you could see it for yourself—"

Nikolai sighed. "Yes, well, I need to get out of this bench first."

"You need to rest."

"No, I need to gather more strength." Nikolai rose to his feet. It was better, anyway, to shove away the discomfort of his myriad feelings about Pasha, to bury them deep inside himself to be dealt with at another time. There was plenty of other suffering from his lifetime crammed in the depths of his heart.

"Where are you going?" Renata asked.

"To the yurt village."

"May I come?"

Nikolai looked down at where she still crouched in the grass. "You really want to?"

She nodded. "I'd go anywhere with you."

I'm a fool for not loving her, Nikolai thought. Renata had always been there for him, even when he was terrible. *It's just that Vika—*

But Nikolai shook himself out of it. There were more important things to think of right now.

"Thank you," he said to Renata. "I have a new idea for getting out of this bench. Come with me to see if it works."

Back in the village portion of the dream, Nikolai explained, "I'm repossessing some of the magic I used to create this scene. I can't seem to get enough energy from the people who visit, so I need to find another source. I thought I might be able to erase some of this dream and absorb the magic I originally used to create it."

"You're going to take all this away?" Renata looked at the villagers, who were gathering around the fire for dinner. She smiled sadly.

"They're illusions," Nikolai said. "Don't lament their demise."

He focused on the horizon, where the sheep were led each day to graze. That part of the dream began to shimmer, as when heat hazes the skyline, and then the scene seemed to dissolve slowly. Nikolai gasped as the fields vanished for good and the magic that had once created it found its way back into his body, like liquid sunshine trickling into his veins.

Only a blur of nondescript summer color—yellow and green and blue—marked the new border of the steppe dream where the fields had once been.

The children watering the sheep were the next to go. One, two, three of them vanished midstep. The men relaxing by the fire went next, disappearing as if evaporating. With each subtraction from the scene, a tiny burst of energy flared within Nikolai.

He erased the women preparing dinner. For a few seconds, a knife continued slicing onions. Then Nikolai absorbed that image, and the rice pilaf, too.

Renata blinked at where they'd all been a moment ago, mouth slightly open.

He watched her. He'd forgotten the glow that shone about Renata whenever she saw him conjure—or in this case, vanish—something new. Her awe was its own kind of magic.

After watching her a second more, Nikolai began to wash away the yurts. They faded slowly away, like watercolors diluted too much. All the while, his body temperature rose.

Oh! He hadn't realized it before, but he hadn't been hot or cold or anything in between since the end of the Game. In ante-death, it seemed, certain sensations were suspended.

But now I can feel warmth again.

All that remained of the steppe dream was where Nikolai and Renata stood, the grassland, and the mountains in the distance.

"I feel more alive than I have in . . . wait. How long has it been?"

"A fortnight since the end of the Game."

Nikolai frowned. It seemed both much longer and shorter than that. The passage of time must also be something that

49

got lost in ante-death. Especially when paired with an endless dream.

Still, he felt more himself now than in the past two weeks. Nikolai reached up out of habit to adjust his top hat. His arm passed in front of his face.

His arm—no, all of him—remained entirely shadow.

"No."

"What is it?" Renata asked.

"It can't be!" Nikolai checked his other arm, and his legs and his torso. Black and gray, here but not here, real but entirely imaginary. "It was supposed to work! Why aren't I solid again?"

Renata sighed. She cut it short, but not before Nikolai heard.

"Maybe you'll be visible when you're no longer in the dream," she said hastily, as if to make up for letting her disappointment slip. "You just need to leave this place first. Come with me. Let's try."

Nikolai clawed at his sleeve. It didn't even feel like wool, not really. Just . . . air. Slightly soft, black air. His pulse raced inside his shadow heart. And who even knew if that pulse existed or not?

"Nikolai." Renata pried his fingers off his sleeve and squeezed them with her own, although she did so lightly and did not close her hand all the way. It worked, and her fingers didn't pass straight through his, but rather rested around where his shadow was, like she was holding on to nothing.

I am nothing.

Nikolai couldn't move.

"Wake up with me," she said with more force in her voice

than usual, as if she knew where his thoughts were taking him. But of course she knew. Renata knew him almost as well as he knew himself. "Breathe," she said, "and let's pull ourselves away from here."

All right. Breathe. I can do that. Nikolai inhaled.

"Again," Renata said.

He took another, deeper breath. Then he squeezed Renata's hand gently, and she must've felt at least *some* pressure from his touch, because she smiled. It was a small measure of comfort, knowing that he did, in fact, exist.

Renata shook her head to jostle the dream out of her mind. Within moments, she began to fade.

But Nikolai remained rooted in the steppe.

Renata frowned. "I'll be back in a minute," she said, her voice already distant, halfway back to reality. "I'll wake, then fall back asleep to return."

"Don't," Nikolai said. He dropped her nearly transparent hand from his.

"But—"

"No! Leave me. I want to be alone."

Renata's mouth opened as if to say something, but no words came out. Possibly because her ability to speak had already returned to the other side of the bench.

But more likely because she didn't actually say a thing. For when she had disappeared completely, she did not return.

Nikolai looked at the empty space where she'd been. "Thank you," he said. He had truly meant it when he said he wanted to be alone. And Renata had understood that.

He walked a few paces in the direction of the mountain, the only thing left besides the grass here on this illusory steppe. Then Nikolai fell to his knees and bowed forward until his head pressed against the dirt. His hat tumbled off. A single despondent sob racked his shadowed body.

The long grass cut tiny scratches in his skin, as the wind whipped the blades at his face. He was not whole, and yet he could still be wounded. And the barrenness of the plains stretched into an empty, blurred horizon, promising an eternity of loneliness and confinement and misery.

"I'll find another way," Nikolai said. "Because, devil take me, I cannot stay here."

CHAPTER NINE

At the same time, Pasha was walking through the center of the ballroom, where Vika's Kazakh dome had been set up behind locked doors so the palace servants wouldn't stumble upon the magical scene. He shook his head as he and his sister, Yuliana, wove in and out of the marketplace stalls for the umpteenth time this morning, listening to the conversations for any hint about a threatened rebellion against the Russians.

"There's nothing in here about Qasim or his revolt," Pasha said.

Yuliana crossed her arms and kicked the edge of the dome. "Vika didn't do her job."

"Actually, she did what we asked of her, only you're frustrated it didn't turn out as you'd hoped." Pasha winked, a small dose of teasing to ease the truth. "Perhaps there's no information because there's nothing happening in that part of the empire right now. Have you considered that you might be looking for trouble where it doesn't exist?"

"Looking for trouble where it supposedly doesn't exist is precisely what a good tsar needs to do. If you see it only when it's obvious, then it's already too late."

Pasha's stomach plummeted, and he stopped midstride next to a vendor selling silver earrings. Here it was again, the truth that he was not ready or fit to be tsar, that his sister was the one really keeping the empire afloat. Pasha's major accomplishments for the day only included shaving (finally) and turning up in this ballroom when he was supposed to.

Yuliana cut across the dome to his side. "*Mon frère*, I didn't mean to imply—"

Pasha held up a hand. "It's fine. You spoke the truth."

"It's a particular flaw of mine."

"No, it's a relief to know you'll tell me what's real rather than kowtowing at my feet like everyone else in this palace. It's a relief someone capable will be by my side to care for the empire."

"You're more than capable," Yuliana said. "You have remarkable instincts about people. I'm good with hard facts and figures. We simply have different strengths." She stood on her toes and pecked Pasha on the cheek.

"Do you think so?" he asked.

"I know so." She smiled, which she did so rarely that it made the gesture worth all the more. Pasha's stomach settled. Mostly.

"On that note," he said, "I actually have another meeting to attend."

Yuliana quirked a brow. "With whom?"

"Major General Volkonsky. He requested an audience."

"Do you—"

"No, I can handle it," Pasha said, for he already knew what his sister was about to offer. "Besides, it will give you more time to go through this dome at your leisure."

Yuliana looked around the Kazakh marketplace, which had restarted itself from the beginning of the scene Vika captured. The conversations were commencing again, like actors rehearsing from the top of a play.

There really was nothing here. *But Yuliana won't let it go until she's been through it a dozen times more*, Pasha thought. He knew his sister well.

Just as Yuliana knew him. She nodded, agreeing to let him see Volkonsky on his own, because she understood that this was something Pasha needed to do to prove his capability to himself.

He gave her a cursory smile—although he was sure she could see his anxiety, only thinly veiled—and hurried out of the ballroom.

"His Imperial Highness, the Tsesarevich, Pavel Alexandrovich Romanov," the young guard Ilya announced as Pasha arrived in the throne room.

Volkonsky was already there, standing at attention. He was only thirty-seven, but his military experience and fame gave him the gravitas of someone much older. His brown hair was neatly combed, his sideburns fashionably long yet tidy, and his dark-blue uniform was perfectly pressed. Medals clinked against one another on his chest as he bowed.

Pasha ascended the dais and sat on the throne. The velvet cushion beneath him was plush, but the gold armrests—sculpted as screaming eagles—were cold, even through his gloves. He tried not to look too uncomfortable.

"Please rise, Major General," Pasha said.

Volkonsky stood upright. "Thank you for agreeing to see me, Your Imperial Highness."

"It's an honor to have you in my court," Pasha said. The major general was one of the most admired noblemen in Russia, and the Volkonskys were a dynasty descended from fourteenth-century nobility. "What can I do for you?"

"My men and I are looking forward to your upcoming coronation. And it is because of the changing of the throne that I've come today. I would like to propose that you reconsider your father's policies regarding serfdom."

Pasha tilted his head to indicate that he was listening.

Volkonsky nodded and continued. "Serfdom is essentially indentured servitude. England stopped the backward practice centuries ago, but here we are in 1825, still forcing peasants to work with no prospect of freedom. I've fought side by side with noblemen and serfs alike, and we are, at our core, the same. Serfs are men, passionate Russians, and they are as much responsible for the defeat of Napoleon and the continued greatness of our empire as I am. So why, in times of peace, do we not accord them the same respect?"

Pasha clutched the screaming eagle armrests of the throne as he tried to get comfortable with being in charge. But then he reminded himself that his father had lectured him on the issue of serfdom; it was not a subject that Pasha knew nothing about.

"I sympathize with your compassion, Major General. But the solution cannot be as simple as abolishing serfdom. It's an issue that my father studied, and it is incredibly complex. Where would the serfs live, and how would they provide for their families, were they given their freedom from the nobles they serve? They would not be able to afford to rent the land they work, and therefore would not be able to generate enough income to feed their families and pay for the roofs above their heads. And there are so many more complications."

"So you mean to do nothing?" Volkonsky asked.

Pasha frowned. It wasn't that he wouldn't attempt to make changes. But he couldn't commit to anything because he knew there was more to this conversation that was being left unsaid. The Imperial Council had warned the late tsar that some of the aristocracy returning from the Napoleonic wars had, despite fighting for Russia, been seduced by the democratic philosophies of the West. They didn't like Russia's autocracy, and abolishing serfdom was only one of their requests. They wanted to get rid of the monarchy entirely.

Pasha ran his hand through his hair. He couldn't help it, as unroyal as it may have seemed. "How does this fit in with what men like Pavel Pestel have advocated, namely revolution and assassinating the tsar?"

Volkonsky bowed his head. "I swear on my honor that I do not subscribe to Pestel's radical solutions, Your Imperial Highness. If anything, I am partial to the idea of a constitutional monarchy. We would work together with you as the tsar, not against."

Pasha didn't even need Yuliana here to know that was a lie. A constitutional monarchy would make the tsar all but a figurehead. Of course, that was preferable to Pestel's desire to have Pasha dead.

"I will consider carefully every possible path for the future of our people and our empire," Pasha said as he straightened on the throne, trying his best to respond the way his father would have. "But I ask that, as someone with long-standing ties to the imperial family, Major General, you convince those who share your views to be patient and give me time. Let me be clear, however, that there will be no constitution. The tsar is the tsar."

Volkonsky stiffened. Then he dipped his head. "Of course, Your Imperial Highness. I am, as always, at your service."

Pasha nodded and dismissed him. His guard, Ilya, showed Volkonsky out of the throne room.

When Ilya returned, Pasha beckoned him.

"You're the best of my men at tracking people," Pasha said, for Ilya was the only one of his Guard who had any sense of where Pasha was (approximately a quarter of the time) when he snuck out of the palace. The rest of the Guard were helpless in the face of Pasha's knowledge of secret passageways and disguises. "Whenever you're not on duty here with me, will you keep an eye on Volkonsky for me? Report to me anything he does that is contrary to the tsardom, and don't let anyone else know I've asked this of you." It was the best Pasha could think to do, strategically. Act like Yuliana. But he had to force himself not to squirm in his throne, for acting like his sister was uncomfortable to say the least.

Ilya hesitated for a second. Probably because it was no small task to spy on a man like Volkonsky. But then he saluted. "Yes, of course, Your Imperial Highness. I'll tell you everything you need to know."

When Ilya was gone, Pasha jammed his hands back into his hair. He hoped he'd done all right with this meeting, because for once, he'd wanted to attempt something like this on his own. Perhaps all the constitutionalists needed was the sense that the crown was listening and would work on improving things. There had been too much stubbornness and enmity between the tsardom and the constitutionalists in the past.

Pasha might never have been good at strategy and war, but he was, as Yuliana had pointed out, adept at understanding and charming people to his side. At persuasion and compromise.

I hope Yuliana is right, he thought. *Because I'm not just training to be tsar anymore. I actually* will *be tsar soon. And I can't muck this up.*

CHAPTER TEN

Aizhana looked down at her son, asleep in the grass and dirt. She'd once curled in despair like that, too, when she had been abandoned by her lover, left unwed and pregnant, utterly ruined.

But this was Nikolai, and though she hadn't known him for long, she had observed him enough to recognize that this was not like her son. Was the weight of the Game and antedeath finally too much for him to bear? It was a great deal to handle, even for a boy as strong as he.

And yet, ironically, this sad turn of events—Nikolai's inability to save himself—could be the opportunity Aizhana was waiting for. *He needs me now*, she thought.

Aizhana lowered herself gently to his side. She smiled and brushed a lock of hair out of his face. Even as a shadow, his features were elegant and refined. "What a beautiful boy you are," she whispered.

His principles held him back, made him think it was wrong to murder for his own gain. But he shouldn't have to be relegated to existence in a dream. Nikolai deserved more.

He could be tsar.

I have energy to spare, and no qualms about obtaining more. Aizhana watched her sleeping son. Sometimes, the young did not know what was best for them. But that was what mothers were for. Aizhana lifted her hand and placed it on the back of Nikolai's neck. She was careful not to scratch him with her brittle nails.

He stirred but did not wake.

Good. Sleep, and soon you will feel stronger. Better. Aizhana closed her eyes, too.

But she did not rest. Instead, she felt the current of energy inside herself, some of it gray like the beetles and maggots she'd siphoned it from, and some of it black from the people she'd killed to obtain it, for she'd slaughtered them out of anger and vengeance. Her methods stained the energy with their darkness.

Just a little bit of my energy to sustain him, she thought. *He won't even notice.* She smiled. *I'm doing what a mother ought to do.*

Then she sent a trickle of energy from her own body, through her fingertips, toward Nikolai. His shoulders tensed around his neck where she touched him. There was opposition, and Aizhana's energy pooled at her fingers like a funnel that had been stopped.

"Shh," she said. "It's all right, my darling. It's only a little, until you get more of your own."

Nikolai's shoulders remained taut for another moment, and then the tension released, as if the muscles, like the rest of him, were too fatigued to fight back.

The gray-black energy in her fingers burbled as Nikolai's

resistance disappeared, and it dribbled into him like a liquid parasite, pleased to find a new host.

"There is too much of Saint Petersburg and its rules about honor in you," Aizhana said. "But this is good, for my energy will give you more of my spirit, my fight. You should be tsar, my son. Pasha sent you to your death and tried to take away all that mattered to you—your magic and the girl you love."

Thinking of the wrongs heaped onto Nikolai roused her. She abandoned her plan to share only a little energy, and instead sent a surge of her black power into his veins.

"I'm giving you this energy so you can be strong, but also because I hope you will see that I am right, that you will exact revenge, just as I did with your father," Aizhana said. "Take from Pasha what matters most. And make him suffer while you do it. That is the Karimov way." She shot her appetite for vengeance into Nikolai, straight to his heart.

He took in a pained breath and reached in his sleep for the back of his neck. Aizhana jerked her hand away.

Nikolai rubbed his skin where her fingers had just been. Then he sighed—contentedly, Aizhana liked to think—and let his hand drop back to the grass.

She smiled her broken-toothed grin. It was gruesome, and yet laced with affection. The kind of twisted smile only a mother could give.

"You see, my son? I can tell you feel better already."

CHAPTER ELEVEN

That evening, Vika dreamed of being on Letniy Isle again, at Candlestick Point at the end of the Game. Nikolai stood before her, pacing. He twirled in his black-gloved hand the dagger that his mentor, Galina, had gifted him.

"I've never wanted anyone but you," Nikolai said.

Vika felt herself tugged forward, closer to him, by the invisible string between them. And yet he continued to spin the dagger.

"Then what is the knife for?" she asked.

"To end the Game." Nikolai tightened his hold on the handle. The sun reflected viciously off the blade.

"You love me, so you're going to kill me?"

He smiled reluctantly, the corners of his mouth weighted with regret, then shrugged. "Yes."

She tried to throw up a shield to protect herself. But the enchantment would not appear. She couldn't even feel the magic in her fingertips. Another hitch in Bolshebnoie Duplo's power?

Vika frowned. This was not how it had happened at the end of the actual Game.

But it didn't matter, for this alternate version barreled along regardless of accuracy, and Nikolai strode up to her, embraced her, and slammed the dagger into her heart, hilt to her chest and blade protruding out through her back. She cried out and collapsed into his arms.

"I didn't intend for it to turn out this way," he whispered, even as she felt her life and her magic bleeding onto his coat, soaking into the wool, seeping into his skin.

Vika gasped. But not only from the physical pain. She also realized Nikolai was extracting the magic from her on purpose.

"Then why?" Vika managed.

Nikolai paused and looked at her. His eyes, though always black, were now bottomless, like a chasm too deep for the sunlight to penetrate. A moment later, he turned away and resumed taking her energy.

"Because this magic never belonged only to you," he said.

"Nor to you." She sagged farther into his arms. "It's meant for us together."

Nikolai frowned but nodded. Then he jerked the blade from her body and stabbed himself, too. "Us. Together."

Vika gasped and startled awake.

CHAPTER TWELVE

Nikolai groaned as he woke in the steppe dream. His neck was stiff, damn it, probably from falling asleep curled up on the hard-packed dirt. And it was dark now, with no moon in the black sky—the very *limited* sky, since he'd gotten rid of the majority of the dream. He groaned again.

But then he stretched his limbs, and they weren't creaky like his neck was. Rather, they felt almost normal again.

Nikolai conjured a lantern so he could examine his body in the dark. He held his breath as the light flickered across his arm, and . . .

He let out all the air in a single puff, because he was still composed of shadow.

But nevertheless, something was different. It wasn't warm, as his energy usually felt, but it was *some* kind of strength. Dark, like his shadow form, and a bit cold, like a trickle of ice water in his veins. How strange. He furrowed his brow. What was it?

And yet the feeling was not unwelcome. Nikolai climbed carefully to his feet, brushing off the bits of grass that clung to him. He pulled his shoulders back and rotated them several times. Shook out his hands. Twisted from side to side.

Yes, he was definitely stronger than he'd been a few hours before. Perhaps all he'd needed was sleep, and some time for his past magic—that which he'd repurposed from the dream—to reinvigorate him. But was it enough?

It had better be. He didn't want to think about what it meant if it was not.

"Shh," he said to the uncertainty trembling inside him. When it stilled, Nikolai tried to imagine waking, to stir himself from the dream. He yawned. He stretched. He shook his body in inelegant ways that would have embarrassed him had anyone else seen.

But nothing changed. He remained firmly surrounded by the steppe. The golden eagle landed beside the lantern and cocked its head at him.

Come on, damn it. Nikolai rubbed at the back of his stiff neck. Using magic had always been second nature to him; it had always been there whenever he needed it. But it was as if magic had forgotten him now that he'd lost the Game, lost his body, lost his grip on reality.

Or was it that *he* had forgotten magic?

Nikolai concentrated on the memory of it. When he was a small child and just discovering his abilities, he'd delighted not only in the tricks he could play on the other village children, but also in the sensation of magic itself.

Yes, Nikolai thought. *That's what I need. To recall the feel of it.* That silken quality of its ebb and flow, the heat of its power, the subtlety of its butterfly kiss. He remembered how magic could buoy him like a rising tide, and how it could wash over him like a crashing wave.

He was not only a shadow, but a shell, without it. The longing for that missing, essential piece of him ached as badly as the Game's scar had once seared.

That was not the only feeling that haunted him, though. For some reason, there was also an echo of Aizhana's voice, her exhortation from the last time he saw her in this dream: *The so-called tsesarevich should not be the one to ascend to the throne.* Because Nikolai was first in line.

He shook his head, trying to jostle away the thought. Thinking about Pasha risked opening Nikolai's most unbearable memories and emotions, for his heart contained a roiling cauldron of sadness and injustice and anger, and if he did not keep the lid secure, the pot would boil over.

When he was younger, Nikolai hadn't known how to keep his feelings in check. He'd been mistreated as a child on the steppe and then grown up under Galina's tyrannical rule. He used to hurl daggers through projects of his that failed, and he would sometimes sew his own mouth shut— magically, of course (real needle and thread would hurt too much)—when he was upset but wanted to keep inside what he felt were inappropriate sentiments. But as he grew older, Nikolai figured out how to bury his past under gentility and grace, even though it was still there, just beneath the surface.

Now, however, he gasped as iciness spread inside him, like spindly tentacles, reaching for that secret cauldron in the depths of his heart.

"No!" he said.

But he was powerless to fight it, for that very energy

was the only energy of substance that Nikolai had, and all he could do was double over in horror as it lifted the lid on everything he didn't want to feel.

Nikolai tallied his brother's wrongs in his head. Pasha's betrayal. The apology that meant nothing because it had come too late, come at a memorial service after Pasha thought Nikolai was already dead. And the fact that Pasha could continue to live his gilded life, with Vika by his side, while Nikolai was stuck in ante-death as a shadow . . .

Had that been Pasha's hope all along? That by forcing the end of the Game, Vika would prevail? She'd been the stronger of the two enchanters. And with Nikolai out of the way, Pasha would be able to swoop in on Vika, taking advantage of her grief.

Damn you, Pasha. Damn you to the ninth circle of hell.

Nikolai shivered, but the chill simultaneously steeled his muscles.

And then a new idea pushed its way forth, growing quickly, like fractals of ice on a frozen windowpane. If he escaped from this dream—this nightmare—he could make Pasha suffer. He could claim the crown for himself.

But a spark of light within Nikolai pushed back. *I once loved Pasha, and he loved me. . . .*

And yet men declared duels for insults far less than what Pasha had committed. So why shouldn't he suffer consequences for his actions? Dante's ninth circle was too good for a traitor like him.

I deserve to be tsar as much as Pasha does.

And as the idea of wearing the crown settled into Nikolai's mind . . . there it was. Magic. Like a cold flame, flickering inside him. He seized it and felt it swell.

"Yes . . ." Magic had not forsaken him! It had not abandoned him because he'd lost the Game.

His golden eagle landed beside him in the grass and nodded at him.

"You're right," Nikolai said. "I need to go."

He did not take in his surroundings one last time. He did not bid them farewell. For if he never saw this steppe dream again, it would be too soon.

"Wake me up," Nikolai whispered.

The stars above him blurred, like specks of salt dissolving into the imaginary night. The scent of grass was replaced by the smell of maple candy and oak.

He was still a shadow, but it didn't matter. He was sitting on a bench on an island in the middle of the Neva.

Sitting, firmly rooted, in reality.

CHAPTER THIRTEEN

As night settled in, a sparrow pecked at Pasha's ante-chamber window at the Winter Palace. Pasha frowned from where he sat in his armchair. "What is this?" he said as he rose and crossed the room.

He slid the window open, and a gust of snow blew in. The bird darted in as well. It flew so fast, it nearly clipped Pasha across the nose. *"Zut alors!"* He jerked out of the way.

The sparrow careened across the antechamber and smashed itself into the opposite wall. The bird shattered on impact, and Pasha cried out again. But it wasn't a live bird at all; it was made of stone. Shards of sharp gray rock rained down onto the burgundy rug.

A small, rolled sheet of paper tied with a black ribbon lay in the bird's remains.

Pasha walked slowly across the rug to retrieve it. He brushed away the rock dust and untied the ribbon.

The paper leaped from his hand and flew into the air,

unrolling itself in the process. It floated directly at eye level so Pasha could read.

Meet me at the statue of Peter the Great at midnight.

The handwriting was ornately elegant yet as precise as a British timepiece. Pasha staggered and braced himself against the wall. He inadvertently crushed the letter in his hand.

It was from Nikolai.

Pasha's knees gave out, and he crumbled to the rug like rock dust.

Nikolai is alive.

CHAPTER FOURTEEN

Vika lay in bed, her dream about Nikolai hovering over her like an uninvited ghost. She'd been awake several minutes now, but she could still feel it, his knife in her chest, his greedy, tragic claim on some of the magic.

If only Father were alive and here to comfort her, as he used to do when Vika had nightmares and would crawl into his bed and his warm arms in the next room. But now that room was empty. Vika curled into a ball beneath the covers.

It was not easy to discern what was real and what was a dream. As Vika blinked the sleep from her eyes, her body actually did feel lesser than it had before. Was it the cuff that was draining her?

But that didn't make sense, for she wasn't doing anything against Pasha or Yuliana's orders. If the bracelet was supposed to help the tsardom, it wouldn't weaken her while she was asleep.

Actually, it wasn't that Vika felt weaker. It was more that, with all of Bolshebnoie Duplo's power, she'd recently

felt like a snake, poised to strike, able to accomplish anything. Now, however, she felt more like a coiled spring, still
full of energy and potential but considerably less formidable.
Why?

Vika bolted upright in bed.

What if . . .

She recalled the snag in her magic in the dream. And the
real hitch when she'd conjured the dome over the Kazakh
steppe. She hadn't understood what could have caused it if
all of Bolshebnoie Duplo's magic was hers.

Unless it wasn't.

"The magic is meant for us together," Vika whispered,
remembering her dream.

It was Nikolai. It had to be. He was reaching for a share
of the magic again, extricating himself from the bench. She
knew it like she knew herself, because she could feel him on
the other side of their invisible string now, tugging even if
he didn't mean to, tied to her because they were the sun and
the moon, always together yet always apart.

The tea leaves.

Always fighting.

The magic pulled. Vika leaped out of bed.

She evanesced to where it was calling her.

CHAPTER FIFTEEN

At midnight, Nikolai arrived. Pasha was already in the square, standing a few paces away from the statue of Peter the Great. His blond hair was damp from the flurries around him, his entire body tense as if ready to either pounce or flee, whichever the situation called for.

Nikolai approached with slow, measured steps, his boots making little noise on the snowy cobblestones. The sky was gray with clouds that parted only for the moon, and the few streetlamps around them were decorated in silver garlands for Christmas. But these decorations that used to bring Nikolai joy now elicited nothing within him; the lamps might as well be choked with black vines.

Pasha watched, his eyes widening as Nikolai drew near and yet remained a shadow under the moonlight. Or perhaps he was simply surprised to find Nikolai truly alive.

Pasha bowed slightly, attempting to hide his shock. *"Bonsoir, mon frère."*

"I do not think that greeting is appropriate," Nikolai

said as he came up to the Thunder Stone. "It is not, in fact, a good night."

At that moment, a gust of wind and snow blasted through Peter's Square. Another moment later, Vika appeared.

Nikolai's silhouette lungs forgot how to breathe. He stared at her, and it was as if time had been suspended in the square, the falling snow the only indication that the seconds continued to march on.

Despite the painful tightness of his lungs constricting for lack of air, Nikolai began to smile. Here they were. All three of them, together again. This was not supposed to be possible.

"Thank goodness you're here," Pasha said to Vika, breaking the quiet.

She gave him a quick nod.

Nikolai choked. *Deuces, she's here for* Pasha? Air rushed back into his lungs, and his shadowed chest expanded again.

"Is it true that you're here for him?" Nikolai tried not to glare at Vika, but he couldn't help it. All he felt was a swell of cold inside him, much like when he'd escaped from the Dream Bench, and the chilly sensation washed over him so completely, it subsumed him.

"I'm here for myself," Vika said.

Nikolai laughed mirthlessly. "Of course you are."

"But the question is, why are you and the tsesarevich here?" she asked.

"Because I want the crown."

"What?" Pasha and Vika said at the same time.

Nikolai shrugged. "You heard what I said."

"On what basis do you have a claim to be heir?" Pasha's voice was steady, but he pressed his hands flat against his coat. Nikolai recognized the gesture, a method for producing outer calm that Pasha had used for years to deal with the pressure of being part of the imperial family. His need to employ it now made Nikolai smirk.

"The tsar was my father," Nikolai said. "You made it official by bestowing upon me the title of grand prince at my memorial service. But it's unclear whether the tsar was *your* father. I hear your mother rather enjoyed the company of a certain staff captain. Alexis Okhotnikov, was it?"

"How dare you!" Pasha's illusion of calm evaporated, and he advanced toward Nikolai, while at the same time beginning to remove his glove, to throw it down as a challenge in a duel.

"No!" Vika started to run between them.

Nikolai snapped his fingers. A dozen sabers appeared in the air and flew at Vika, surrounding her, their sharp tips gleaming and pointed at her.

She skidded to a halt. Snow piled around her boots.

"What are you doing?" Vika said.

Pasha stared. "Release her!"

But Nikolai was paralyzed by his own warring thoughts. What had he done? Vika wasn't supposed to be his adversary anymore; they'd joined together at the end of the Game. And yet here they were again, one against the other.

"I'll release myself." Vika frosted the ends of the swords, encasing the tip of each blade in a block of ice. They tumbled from the air and onto the cobblestones with a dozen heavy thunks.

Her ability to free herself so easily shook Nikolai out of his stupor. He might have returned to reality, but somehow, the lion's share of magic from Bolshebnoie Duplo seemed to remain hers, as if his shadow self couldn't quite hold on to power. They were not as evenly matched as they'd been in the past.

"Are you all right?" Pasha asked Vika.

She ignored him and turned to Nikolai. "Don't do that to me again." She picked up one of the swords, melting the ice so that the water dripped down the blade, and brandished it in the moonlight. It was a haunted echo of the end of the Game, when the sun had caught on Nikolai's dagger.

He did not miss the reference, and an unseen band tightened around his shadow heart.

"Neither of you are thinking straight," Vika said. "Your Imperial Highness, you cannot challenge an enchanter to a duel. He'd kill you on his first turn. And as for you, Nikolai . . ." She whirled to face him, although she lowered the sword before she spoke again. "You're better than this."

Am I?

But what was greatness? Was it constantly accepting second place? Nikolai had spent his entire eighteen years coming in second. He'd merely been tolerated in his village on the steppe. In Saint Petersburg, he'd been permitted only to skirt the outer edges of the nobility. And he'd conceded the Crown's Game. Whether by Nikolai's doing or not— usually *not*—first place seemed always just beyond reach, taunting him.

Now, however, the throne was right there for his taking, and that same cold flame that had flared to life when he escaped the Dream Bench burst forth again. What was this chill, and where had it come from? And yet Nikolai didn't care, for the possibility of finally reaching his potential sent a thrill and a surge of strength through his veins.

I don't want to be second to Pasha anymore. I won't.

Vika stood waiting for him to respond to her.

Nikolai shrugged. "Things have changed. And what I used to be doesn't matter."

CHAPTER SIXTEEN

If Vika had had any hope for Pasha and Nikolai to make up, to shake hands and be friends again, it died with this declaration. And it seemed there was no need now to tell Nikolai of Renata's prophecy, for it was laid out here, as clear as ice. Or as murky as ice. The analogy worked either way.

Vika shook her head. Nikolai had always been ambitious. He hadn't taken it easy on her during the Game. But this sort of ambition was different, driven by malice rather than self-preservation. This wasn't the Nikolai she knew, the one she might have loved. Had turning into a shadow done this to him?

Did I do this by condemning him to ante-death at the end of the Game? Her arms, which until then had remained outstretched to keep Nikolai and Pasha apart, fell to her sides.

Meanwhile, Pasha simply stood staring at Nikolai. Pasha's hand remained on his other glove, but rather than tearing it off, his fingers now pinched the edge of the leather tightly.

"Why are you doing this?" Vika asked Nikolai.

He laughed, its ringing laced in black at the edges, like a funeral ribbon, pretty but mournful at the same time. The sound tied itself into a hard knot in Vika's chest.

"Pasha demanded our deaths without even flinching."

"I was irrational with grief," Pasha said.

"And he regretted it," Vika said, her defense of Pasha spilling out and catching her by surprise. But despite her anger at him, she knew commanding the end of the Game had not been without consequence for Pasha. "He apologized."

"After the fact," Nikolai said. "It doesn't change what he actually did. He was supposedly my best friend. And he claimed to love you. Yet you forgive his betrayal and cruelty so easily?"

Vika looked at the statue of Peter the Great. She couldn't look at Nikolai. She couldn't look at Pasha, either. *Because Nikolai's right.*

Pasha advanced, his hand no longer holding on to the glove. "I inherited the Game. I had to do it."

"No, you didn't," Nikolai said. "You could have just let it play out. You could have expressed sadness, regret, at the Game's very existence. You did *not* have to force an ending."

"I . . . I know that now." Pasha averted his eyes to the snow at his feet. "Are you going to kill me?"

"Eventually," Nikolai said. "But in the meantime, I'm going to make you wish I had done it quickly." He opened his arms and swept them around him, as if encompassing all of Saint Petersburg. All of Russia. "To start with, I'm going to turn the people against you. You may not always have cared about being tsar, yet you've always been Russia's golden heir, their beloved prince. But by the time the coronation takes place next month, the empire will loathe you. And it will be upon *my* head that they set the Great Imperial Crown."

The moonlight cast a white glow upon everything beneath it, but Pasha's face paled even more at Nikolai's threat.

"Is this what you really want?" Vika asked Nikolai. "To rule an empire? To take on all the responsibility that comes with it? Your life will no longer be your own."

Nikolai paused. But a few seconds later, he looked away from Vika, and it was clear whatever internal argument he'd had was done.

"My life was never my own anyway," he said. "It was Galina's, and then it was the Game's. If you think about it, my life always belonged to the empire. This isn't much different. My decision is made."

Nikolai reached out to touch the Thunder Stone and looked up at Peter the Great.

"What are you—?" Vika began to ask.

But she stopped, because the massive statue shifted on his saddle. The horse came to life beneath him, the corded muscles flexing like living bronze.

"Nikolai . . . ," Vika said. "Don't."

Pasha gaped. "What do you intend to do?" he whispered, the question nearly lost under the stamping of the horse's enormous hooves.

Nikolai dusted off some snow that clung to his shadow coat, his movement casual, as if it were an everyday occurrence that a statue came alive beside him. "Legend has it that Peter the Great guards our city from the enemy," he said. "As such, he's going to warn the citizens that an enemy walks among them. And this is the story he will tell: the tsesarevich discovered that his brother was the rightful heir to the throne, so he attempted to have his brother murdered, in order to secure the crown for himself."

"That isn't true, and you don't have any evidence of it!" Pasha said.

He hurled himself at Nikolai before Vika could do anything to stop him.

But Nikolai had a shield around himself, and Pasha rebounded off it and fell backward. He landed on the snow-covered cobblestones with a hard smack.

"It doesn't matter," Nikolai said. "Once the story is out, it's out."

"Don't," Vika said. "Not only because of His Imperial Highness, but also, you'll expose *us*. You'll expose magic, and chaos will ensue."

"That's part of the point." With that, Nikolai waved a shadow finger in the air, like a conductor's baton, and the bronze horse reared and whinnied. Peter the Great shouted, his voice as low and sonorous as cathedral bells. His horse leaped off the Thunder Stone, and they charged out of Peter's Square, toward the rest of Saint Petersburg.

"Vika, please," Pasha said, staring after the statue, which kicked up snow and chunks of stone as it galloped away. "Do something!"

Nikolai leaned against the Thunder Stone, watching them. Vika recoiled. This cruel, detached boy was nothing like *her* Nikolai, not even when they'd had to fight each other in the Game.

This is my fault, she thought. *He gave me his life and became a shadow.*

But I can't watch him lose his soul. She'd have to save Nikolai from himself.

Beneath her coat sleeve, however, the bracelet had begun to heat. She had to obey Pasha, to stop the statue of Peter the Great. Although there was no way of knowing whether Pasha or Nikolai was the rightful heir to the throne, Pasha was still the one officially next in line. Vika's loyalty was bound to that.

She curled into herself for a moment, as her soul seemed to tear itself in two. How could she be Imperial Enchanter when she had to fight Nikolai to do it? How could she be true to herself when a vow required one thing of her, but her heart tugged her toward the only other person like her?

What is it that I truly want?

But the cuff didn't care. It seared into her skin. Vika inhaled a sharp, strangled breath.

Debate later. Action now.

She whirled to Pasha. "You, back to the palace." Vika raised her arms, dissolved him, and evanesced him to the warm confines of the Winter Palace, all before he could utter a syllable of protest.

"And you." She spun toward Nikolai, who still leaned against the Thunder Stone. He cocked his head at her expectantly. "As Imperial Enchanter, I'm sworn to the tsesarevich. Don't make me fight you."

Nikolai shrugged. "Our fates are already in motion. We cannot stop them."

"I don't believe you," Vika said.

He hesitated. "If only you were right," he said quietly.

For a second, Vika thought she could hear the old Nikolai in his tone.

But then he secured his hat and shrugged again. "Too bad you're wrong."

Vika's heartbeat stumbled, like it had momentarily forgotten the steps to the mazurka. But she shook her head. Their fates had been in motion during the Game, and they'd averted that end. She had to believe they could do it again.

"We aren't finished," she said.

Then she dissolved herself and evanesced after Peter the Great.

CHAPTER SEVENTEEN

Vika rematerialized on the back of the statue's saddle. She yelped, for the speed at which the statue galloped almost threw her off the horse, and she looped an arm around Peter the Great's thick bronze waist.

He snarled, the sound all sharp knifepoints and poisoned arrowheads.

Vika cringed. *I can understand how he won so many wars,* she thought. Even if this version was only a replica of the near-mythic tsar. But she maintained her grip on the statue and cast an enchantment to secure herself more firmly on the saddle.

Peter the Great snarled again, but when he couldn't shake her from the horse, he turned his attention back to the streets before him. They were charging into the center of the city now, over bridges and along canals.

"Grand Prince Karimov is alive, and he is the true heir to the throne!" Peter the Great shouted, his voice full and commanding, echoing through the narrow alleys. "Shame on you, Tsesarevich, for the attempted murder of your brother!"

Candles began to light the insides of apartments, as Peter the Great shouted the same accusations over and over, and his horse's bronze hooves roused the city from its slumber.

Vika whipped the wind to try to drown out the sound of the statue's cries. But he only yelled louder.

He needs a muzzle, she thought.

As they tore around a corner onto Nevsky Prospect, Vika spotted a few flags outside one of the pastel buildings.

That will have to do. She ordered a blue-and-gold one to rip itself from its mast. It hurtled through the air toward the statue, its fabric flapping violently in the wind, and slapped itself across Peter the Great's mouth like a gag. Vika charmed its loose ends around the bronze tsar's head and tied it into a tight triple knot.

The statue bit clear through the flag and spat its shredded remains into the snow.

Oh, mercy.

Peter the Great yanked on the reins then. His horse bucked. It jerked the breath out of Vika's lungs, and she lost her grip around the statue's waist. If not for her charm that kept her in the saddle, she would have been hurled off the horse and smashed against one of Nevsky Prospect's buildings. Or impaled by a flagpole.

But the most frightening part of it: this ruthless statue was Nikolai's enchantment. Memories of the Game flashed before Vika as she was tossed to and fro on the bronze horse—recollections of the stone birds that had tried to kill her on this very boulevard, the invisible box in Palace Square that attempted to compress her to her death, and the Imagination Box, elegant and captivating on the outside but capable of murder on the inside.

Not unlike Nikolai. Perhaps he was not so different from his earlier self at all. Perhaps this malice had been inside him all along, and Vika had only chosen not to see. Her chest constricted at the thought.

Peter the Great craned his bronze neck and saw that Vika still sat on his saddle. He roared, then dug his heel into his horse, and they charged down Nevsky Prospect. Vika clasped onto his waist as he began to bellow again, "Grand Prince Karimov is alive, and he is the true heir to the throne! Shame on you, Tsesarevich, for the attempted murder of your brother!"

I cannot play nicely if Nikolai isn't going to.

Vika climbed up onto her feet, balancing on the saddle in her boots, struggling to get upright even with the charm to keep her from tumbling off.

Finally, she managed to stand all the way up. "This ends now," she yelled at the statue.

She looked to the night sky, cloudy but for the spot where the moon shone through. She took a deep inhale, breathing and sensing the particles of electricity in the air. It was mostly water in the clouds, eager to turn to more flurries, but there were enough sparks for her to work with.

"If I cannot stop you as you are," she said to Peter the Great, "then I will change *what* you are."

She swirled her hands above her, and the air grew prickly. It crackled at her command. Then the electricity coalesced and shot down at an angle, a lightning bolt headed directly for Peter the Great's head.

Vika undid the enchantment that attached her to the saddle, and she leaped off just as the lightning struck the statue.

Peter the Great's face melted instantaneously, and his proclamations about Nikolai and Pasha devolved into incoherent shouts, his mouth full of molten metal. And then his mouth liquefied completely, and the proclamations ceased.

Vika rolled on the ground from the momentum of her jump, but she continued to command lightning bolt after lightning bolt. They hit Peter the Great and melted the rest of him into a puddle of liquid bronze, streaming off the saddle.

The horse, no longer having a rider to direct it, came to a standstill in the middle of Nevsky Prospect. It whinnied, and then a moment later, it transformed—along with Peter the Great's melted remains dripping off its back—back into lifeless bronze.

Vika propped herself against the Bissette & Sons storefront, the glass etched with a list of their tailoring services. She panted as she caught her breath.

Disaster averted.

Or so she thought. But then she looked up, above the shops that were shuttered for the night, and saw that many of the windows in the apartments on the second and third stories were open, their occupants in their nightclothes, hanging over the ledges. Some stared at what was left of Peter the Great with their mouths agape. A few shrieked hysterically.

But the worst were the ones who whispered to those beside them, yet never took their eyes off Vika. She caught the shape of the word "witch" on their lips, and heard the word "devil" in the wind. They crossed themselves, and she knew from Father's warnings during her childhood that these same people would soon conspire to hunt her down.

Vika might have stopped Nikolai's rampaging statue before it shouted its message through all of Saint Petersburg, but she hadn't stopped it soon enough. A good part of the city had seen a bronze tsar come to life and an enchantress command lightning to liquefy it.

Vika hurried down Nevsky Prospect, turning onto a side street as soon as she could.

Nikolai isn't our only problem now, she thought, her pulse racing. For the existence of magic, so long kept a tidy secret, had been unveiled.

CHAPTER EIGHTEEN

Ilya had been on guard duty tonight, and when Pasha snuck out of the palace, Ilya had followed. He'd crouched against the side of a building at the edge of Peter's Square and watched the entire confrontation unfold, far enough away that he could not make out what had been said, but certainly near enough to see. He had managed to keep himself from crying out in surprise—and revealing himself—by clamping his hand over his mouth when he first saw Nikolai's shadow, and again when Peter the Great's statue came to life.

But as soon as Nikolai departed the square, Ilya coughed, each sputter like its own cloud in the night air.

"The girl appeared out of nothing. Then disappeared, like she did to the tsesarevich," he said to himself. "And that was Grand Prince Karimov."

Ilya gave up crouching and sat in the snow banked against the building. The grand prince could command magic. And come back from the dead.

Or he had never been dead.

Ilya leaned back against the building as he tried to make sense of what he'd seen. It was unbelievable, and yet it was real.

He stared at the empty Thunder Stone and the square where the tsesarevich and the two enchanters had just stood. Then he shook his head as it slowly sank in.

"This changes everything."

CHAPTER NINETEEN

By morning, the churches of Saint Petersburg over-flowed with those afraid of the devil's arrival, and the streets filled with men concealing knives in every sleeve and pocket, whispering of capturing the witch and burning her alive. Vika was safely ensconced at home on Ovchinin Island, but she didn't need to be in Saint Petersburg to know the city was on the brink of panicked hysteria. She'd seen it and heard it stirring already as she tamed Peter the Great's statue. And fear always flourished in the dark of night.

With the sun rising behind her, Vika stood at the edge of the island's forests, looking across the frozen bay at Saint Petersburg in the distance. She was supposed to report to the Winter Palace to meet with Pasha and Yuliana. And yet the string that tethered her to Nikolai pulled insistently.

Where are you, Nikolai? She closed her eyes and tried to feel his magic. But there was nothing, not even a hint of his silken warmth. Vika sighed as she opened her eyes. He must have a barrier shield around him.

She shouldn't be wanting him anyway. Sergei had raised her better than to turn her back on the tsardom so easily. Father had been Russian through and through, all balalaika music and borscht and rustic saunas full of birch branches and leaves. The same love for Russia infused Vika's soul, and she knew in her blood that what the country needed was not a vengeful shadow as tsar, but a boy who had grown up in the imperial family, learning the history of the people and the art of ruling the empire. Vika might have loved Nikolai and loathed Pasha, but that didn't mean Nikolai was right for the throne. Not at all.

I suppose I must go, she thought. *Even though I don't want to.* Duty called.

So Vika evanesced into the former tsar's study in the Winter Palace.

Her head spun as she rematerialized; stars actually flickered at the edges of her vision. She seemed to arrive more quickly than it ordinarily took to cover the distance from Ovchinin Island to the city, as if the magic she commanded was more potent this morning, like drinking five or six cups of tea instead of one. How bizarre, especially considering that Nikolai was now sharing in Bolshebnoie Duplo's power. It took a moment for Vika to shake the stars from her head.

The young guard at the door—Ilya, she thought his name was—gawked at the space Vika occupied, where there hadn't been a girl a few seconds before. But there was no point in hiding her comings and goings. With the secret of magic out, everyone knew what she was.

When her vision cleared, she took in the study. A painting of Saint Petersburg hung behind the desk, and a portrait of Catherine the Great graced the wall to Vika's right. The entire room was decorated in royal blue and gold, from the crown molding to the trim around the floor-to-ceiling windows to the Persian rug upon the floor.

Yuliana sat at the late tsar's desk, naturally, and Pasha paced in front of the windows. He'd clearly been doing so since before Vika arrived; he'd worn a groove into the carpet with his boots. But why did Vika even care? She might have intended to defend his right to the crown, but it didn't mean he shouldn't suffer. Pasha had brought this stress—arguably, this entire turn of events—upon himself.

Yuliana cast a withering look at Vika. "You couldn't have put down the statue more discreetly?"

Vika scowled right back at her. "Next time *you* try your hand at taming a bronze tsar-come-to-life. We'll see how discreetly you manage it. Besides, you're not the one the entire city wants to roast on a stake, so I think I'm the one with a right to complain if anyone can."

Pasha groaned. "Enough. Bickering won't solve anything. Some believe the statue was one of the four horsemen portending the apocalypse. People have already begun to flee the city. And the black market in Sennaya Square is overrun by those who can't afford to leave, seeking wards against evil spirits."

"Oh," Vika said, but only partially in response to what Pasha had just said.

"Oh, what?" Yuliana asked.

"I just understood something. Belief begets more magic." Vika recalled the stories Father used to tell her about when Russia and other countries believed more openly in magic. "That's why it was easier for me to evanesce. Before today, only a handful of us knew about magic. But after Nikolai's statue, tens of thousands of people suddenly believe—or fear—magic, and that, in turn, stokes Bolshebnoie Duplo's ability to generate more." She held up her hand, which sparked visibly at the fingertips. She jittered as she tried to stand still on the carpet. Vika had never been one who could be easily contained, but this surge in the power gave new definition to the word "irrepressible."

Yuliana scrunched her nose. "However, it also means that not only are *you* more powerful, but Nikolai will be as well."

The sparks at Vika's fingers snuffed out, the momentary thrill of all that power suffocated by Yuliana's insight. There would likely be enough magic now that there would be no more hitches, real or dreamed. But it also meant bigger and more dangerous enchantments.

Vika crossed the study and sank into one of the pair of blue-and-gold chairs in the center of the room, angled to face the tsar's desk.

Pasha dropped his head against the window frame with a resigned *thunk*. "*Quel désastre.*"

"Agreed, it *is* a disaster." Vika leaned into the backrest of her chair. "We have to save Nikolai."

Pasha came and sat in the chair next to her. He made a miserable attempt to smile, which said quite a lot, because Pasha could always smile. His inability to do so made something inside Vika twinge, even though she was still furious at him for both the end of the Game and the asinine command to conjure him a midnight snack.

"Save Nikolai from what?" Pasha asked.

Vika shook her head. "I don't know. But it's obvious the boy from last night was not the same one who sacrificed his life for me at the end of the Game. Whatever is influencing him—or whatever change has taken root because he's a shadow—must be undone."

Yuliana laughed caustically. "I don't care if it's the devil himself who's possessing Nikolai. He made an outright threat on the tsesarevich's life."

Of course Yuliana knew everything. Pasha had undoubtedly shared every detail as soon as Vika had evanesced him back to the palace last night.

"That's treason," the grand princess continued. "There is no option to save someone like that. Nikolai must be arrested and executed."

"But he's done nothing wrong!" Vika said.

"You call threatening to usurp the throne 'nothing wrong'?"

Vika squeezed the armrest of her chair and took a deep breath. "Those were words spoken out of hurt. Perhaps he can be convinced to change his mind. He hasn't actually tried to take the crown."

"She has a point," Pasha said. "So far, Nikolai has committed only civil disobedience."

Vika stared at him. Was he really supporting her argument, even though Nikolai had threatened to kill him?

"You are both far too forgiving." Yuliana crossed her arms.

"I don't mean we should let Nikolai roam around, free to cause more trouble." Pasha turned to Vika. "Can you find and detain him somehow? If only I could show him how sorry I am, if he could see reason . . ."

Vika blinked, still somewhat disbelieving that he'd taken her side. Then she shook her head. "I don't know where Nikolai is. He has a barrier around himself."

"But you'll still try to find him?" Pasha asked.

She sighed. "Yes, I'll still try." It was a compromise sloppily covering a half-truth—for now, they could pretend they would jail Nikolai and somehow find a resolution that satisfied all of them, and satisfied justice. But the other half of the truth was that compromise was impossible. Yuliana wanted to kill Nikolai. Vika wanted to save him. And Pasha didn't actually want the same thing Vika did. He wanted the past undone and this problem to go away.

She decided to shift the conversation, at least temporarily, away from what to do about Nikolai. "The city needs calm after the statue's rampage last night," she said. "Perhaps we could reassure them by demonstrating to the people that my magic is good."

Yuliana tapped a quill against one of the gold map weights on the desk. She nodded. "Not a bad idea. And we'll show them that you and your magic are under control, that you're Pasha's."

"I don't belong to anybody!"

"But you do." Yuliana used her quill to point at the bracelet.

Vika banged the cuff against the armrest. "I—"

Pasha exhaled loudly but said nothing, as if telling the two of them not to fight was a cause so lost, it wasn't even worth uttering the words.

For the sake of reaching a solution, Vika swallowed her protest. It tasted of bitter herbs.

Pasha cleared his throat. "I don't know how I feel about putting you in the line of danger, Vika. The city's mad. There's a bounty on your head."

She laughed. She didn't mean to, but it burst forth before she could stop it. *I've survived another enchanter trying to kill me,* she thought. *Ordinary people are no match.*

Yet Pasha's concern thawed a touch more of Vika's resentment toward him. Here he was, facing not only a threat to the throne from Nikolai, but also a potential riot in the capital, and Pasha still had enough humanity within him to worry over Vika's safety. Perhaps he had not changed as much as she'd thought at the end of the Game. Perhaps he'd merely gone astray and was now finding his way back to himself.

"Thank you for your concern," Vika said. "But I'll be fine."

It was only if Nikolai came after her that she would have something to worry about. No, not *if.* When. For if Nikolai meant to take the throne, the bracelet around Vika's wrist ensured that he'd have to fight his way through her, too. Vika's chest tightened, as though her heart were locking itself from hurt and throwing away the key.

"It will be harder, if not impossible, to convince the people that Peter the Great's statue was a feat of engineering or a show," Pasha said. "Unlike during the Game, there were too many witnesses this time. We can't undo the people seeing the magic, can we?"

"No," Vika said, her voice thin as she tried to recover from her own thoughts. "I can't erase memories." She'd tried many a time before when she was younger, in hopes that Sergei would forget she'd done this or that wrong. It never worked; it only botched things further when he realized what she'd attempted, and got her in more trouble.

Pasha balled up his hands and pressed them against his eyes. "Damn it."

The magic swelled inside Vika. Seeing Pasha vulnerable helped her pull herself together. He needed her, his Imperial Enchanter. "What I'm suggesting," she said, "is that if we can't hide magic, we ought to trumpet it."

"I don't know if the people can handle it," Yuliana said.

"History isn't on our side in terms of revealing magic to the masses." Pasha slowly peeled his hands away from his face. "And yet, it's not as if Saint Petersburg hasn't already been exposed. I say we give Vika's approach a try."

Yuliana chewed the inside of her cheek skeptically.

But Vika smiled.

"Fine, if this is what you want." Yuliana abandoned her quill and picked up the map weight instead, tapping it on the desk. "Here's my proposal: Pasha, the people need to see you. They trust in your goodness. You should ride through the city, give them comfort, tell them that magic is not to be feared, while Vika shows them."

Pasha nodded slowly. "That makes sense."

"I'll stay behind," she said. "They don't like me much."

"Yuliana—" Pasha began.

She shook her head. "It's all right. We each have our strengths and our weaknesses, remember? You are the one the people need right now."

Vika nodded. For once, she agreed. "What sort of enchantment do you think would calm them?" she asked Pasha.

He snapped his fingers as he thought. "The holidays are approaching. You could . . ." *Snap, snap, snap.* "How about conjuring a Christmas tree that gives gifts to the children?"

"And throws fire at Nikolai should he come near," Yuliana said casually.

The color drained from Pasha's face.

Vika clenched her fists, digging her fingernails into her palms. "I'll do this on my own terms."

"No, we've just been through this. You use magic on *our* terms," Yuliana said.

Vika dug her fingernails deeper into her skin. Only a few moments ago, she'd been glad to be Imperial Enchanter. But now, even if she hadn't had the cuff around her wrist, she would have been able to feel the shackles tighten and the chain pull taut.

The thing was, she was no longer helping Pasha solely because her vow compelled her to, but that didn't mean she was choosing him over Nikolai. Nikolai clearly needed help, too. He wasn't himself, and locked heart or not, Vika did not intend to allow his new ambition to swallow him, not without Vika putting up a fight to find the old Nikolai, *her* Nikolai, beneath the shadow.

Also, she did not like being told precisely what to do. *I am not a mere foot soldier*, she thought. *I'm a general.*

And yet, the bracelet. Her wrist weighed heavily against the chair.

Yuliana continued talking, as if she hadn't just insulted Vika. Then again, Yuliana probably hadn't noticed. She was the grand princess after all, accustomed to giving orders and having them followed without question. "How do we protect my brother if Nikolai appears during your tour of the city?"

Pasha remained pale and silent in his chair.

"I'll . . . cast a shield around him while we're together," Vika said, forcing herself to ignore Yuliana's slight. If Vika was going to be Imperial Enchanter, she'd have to learn to let insults from the grand princess go, for there would surely be a multitude of them.

"And what about when you're not with him?"

Vika shook her head. "I can't maintain a shield when I'm not near. The magic required for an enchantment like that would be immense, because the shield would need to be able to respond to whatever harm threatened His Imperial Highness. If I knew that it was going to be something specific, like swords or bullets, I could cast a shield. But I have no clue what . . ."

Her mouth dried up. She couldn't finish the sentence.

"What Nikolai has planned," Pasha said quietly, finishing the thought for her.

Vika bit her lip and nodded.

"Well, we cannot leave Pasha completely exposed," Yuliana said, her tone surprisingly soft. She'd stopped toying with the map weight and now looked at her brother, as if memorizing him just in case his chair was empty the next time.

Vika might not have liked the grand princess, but she understood that look. Yuliana's love for her family and her country was both her strength and her weakness. It had propelled her to suggest the quick ending to the Game. And it would drive her decisions about stopping Nikolai.

"I have an idea." Vika touched the basalt pendant she wore around her neck. It glowed for a second as she infused it with an enchantment. Then she unfastened it.

"Here," she said to Pasha.

"What is it?" He reached across the space between the chairs to take the necklace.

But Vika remained where she was and, instead, floated it to him.

Pasha's face fell.

Touching him seemed too much like taking sides, and although she was beginning to see signs of the old Pasha again, she had made it clear that she also wanted to save Nikolai. Not wanting to choose sides was also why she still called Pasha by his title, at least to his face.

"I've charmed it, Your Imperial Highness," Vika said. "As long as you're wearing the necklace, the enchantment allows you to communicate with me even when I'm elsewhere, in case you need me. All you need to do is wrap your hand around the pendant as you're doing now, and I'll be able to hear you."

Pasha looked at the stone in his hand. Then he fastened it around his own neck. "Thank you." He smiled at her, no trace of his disappointment remaining. His years of growing up in the imperial family and practice with putting on facades was evident. Or perhaps knowing that Vika would be there for him offered him some comfort?

In any case, he scooted to the edge of his chair and sat a bit taller. "Our plan, then, is twofold. We attempt to locate Nikolai, make amends, and stop this madness before any more damage is done. And in the meantime, we work on calming the people and convincing them that magic will be used for good."

"So you want me to enchant a Christmas tree on the city tour?" Vika asked.

"Yes," Pasha said. "Please."

"I still think you should include fire," Yuliana said. "If an enchanter is going to burn at the stake, it might as well be Nikolai."

"Yuliana, no," Pasha said, his hand tugging on a lock of

hair. "I've made my decision. This is our plan. Now, I need to change clothes. Or, um, write down what I'm going to say. Or tell the Guard to ready a carriage." He practically vaulted out of his chair and hurried from the study.

When he was well down the hall and out of earshot, Yuliana rose from behind the desk, as if none of what had transpired bothered her. It probably hadn't.

She looked down her nose at Vika. "My brother's life is in your hands," she said. "As is the future of all Russia. Think carefully as you choose your loyalties and make your decisions." She held Vika's gaze for a long moment before she turned on her heel and whisked out of the room.

Vika stared at the door after them, sinking deeper into her chair. The weight of life and death and an entire empire was no small thing to bear.

CHAPTER TWENTY

One of Nikolai's stone sparrows had seen Vika through the windows of the Winter Palace, and Nikolai's curiosity had sabotaged him, tempting him here. He hovered on the edge of Palace Square, eyes narrowed at the green, gold, and white splendor in which the imperial family lived.

Nikolai had thought there was an unbreakable connection between him and Vika. He'd thought that being two of a kind tied their fates together. He'd thought, at the end of the Game, that she loved him.

But last night, she'd stopped his statue of Peter the Great, and now she'd gone to Pasha again.

To him, not me.

Nikolai sighed and turned his back on the palace.

Two enormous boxes sat before him in the center of the square. In the red one was a life-size jack-in-the-box; in the purple, a music-box ballerina. Nikolai and Vika, in enchanted puppet form. He'd created them during the Game to perform a pas de deux in the sky every evening when the clock chimed six o'clock. And just like his Dream Benches that continued his legacy, the Jack and ballerina still danced with each other every night.

But now, Vika had chosen Pasha. After all Pasha had done to them! Why would she do such a thing?

The cold ambition that had fueled Nikolai last night had weakened after he enchanted the statue of Peter the Great. It seemed to ebb and flow, lessening after he performed some feat of magic, and strengthening when he grew upset. At least this was what he'd observed so far. And true to theory, it flared up again now as Nikolai remembered how Vika had turned her back on him so easily, the chill flying through his veins like cold blue flames.

He narrowed his eyes. "I never want to watch these puppets again."

No one could see him, for Nikolai had cast a shroud around himself. Of course, he could have frightened them with his shadow form if he'd wanted to, but there was something twisted and lovely about causing mayhem and having the people blame Vika and Pasha.

Nikolai steepled his fingers together, and the crank on the Jack's box began to turn slowly. Its tinny tune rang through the square, and those who'd merely been passing through stopped to watch and listen. *Do, re, mi, fa, sol, la, ti, do.* C-major. Nikolai's fists tightened. *Do, re, mi, fa, sol, la, ti, do.* G-major. *Do, re, mi, fa, sol, la, ti, do.* D-major. His nails dug through the tips of his gloves. *Do, re, mi, fa, sol, la, ti, do,* again and again, all twelve major scales, faster and faster and faster, until Nikolai's hands flew violently open and *pop!* the Jack jumped out of his box.

The Jack was not dressed in the red and black diamonds

of a harlequin, as he used to be. Now the Jack was entirely gray. Dark, dark gray, from wooden head to wooden toe.

Nikolai's breath sped up.

Music from the ballet *Zéphire et Flore* began to tinkle out of the purple box. The lid cracked open, and the ballerina slipped out, no longer just a pretty thing in periwinkle tulle but something with a glimmer of cunning in her painted eyes. She curtsied to the Jack.

Instead of bowing and inviting her to dance, though, as he'd always done before, the Jack leaped into the sky. Nikolai's anger seemed to concentrate his power, to amplify it. The Jack spun for a moment in the air in a slow-motion pirouette.

Then it exploded in a burst of wooden splinters and metal gears, which in turn transformed into thousands of tiny mechanical birds that flapped away. The collective beat of their wings thrummed through the air.

The people in Palace Square issued a collective gasp. One woman screamed. A man shouted for everyone to find cover in the nearest church.

Nikolai's pulse matched the frenetic rhythm of the flock of birds. But the ballerina stood still, watching.

What was her reaction supposed to be? How had Vika felt, watching Nikolai die at the end of the Game and vanish before her eyes?

Nikolai clenched his fists tightly again, wanting desperately for the ballerina to collapse into a heap and cry. Or to fly into the air after the Jack, to chase every last bird and convince them to come back, because she loved him.

But instead, the ballerina's mouth only turned down at

its painted corners. She watched the last of the mechanical birds as it disappeared into the clouds. Then she twirled on her toe and descended into her purple box. Just like Vika had done now—disregarded Nikolai and moved on. How could she be so callous?

"What happened?" someone shouted, as the crowd in the square fled.

It was the exact question raging through Nikolai's head.

He blasted the boxes apart, sending shards of red and purple wood across the square and shattering the cobblestones beneath them. The few people who'd dallied ran screaming.

When the dust settled, the ballerina lay unharmed but limp in the middle of the rubble.

Click, click, click. Not clapping—for Palace Square was nearly empty now—but the sound of talon-like nails clacking together.

"So melodramatic," a familiar raspy voice said.

Nikolai whirled around. A hooded figure lurked behind him.

"Please don't glower at me like that," she said. "Even though no one else can see the expression on your face, *I* can feel it. A son's disapproval is a special weapon, and it wounds me to my withered core."

Nikolai almost felt bad. Almost.

"You extracted yourself from the Dream Bench," Aizhana said quietly. As if she'd already known but was simply confirming the fact. But how could she have known? She hadn't been there when Nikolai escaped.

"Renata came to visit me; perhaps there's something

about her that gave me the mental strength to break free. But in any case, you see I didn't need you."

Aizhana sucked in air between her missing teeth.

He exhaled. A scrap of sympathy found its way to Nikolai. "I'm sorry. I'm not accustomed to having a . . . *maternal figure* in my life."

"Or someone like me who continues to show up unannounced."

Well, that part I'm used to, he thought. Galina used to appear for lessons all the time when Nikolai least expected it, so often that he actually began to expect the unexpected. If that made any sense.

Aizhana ventured a step closer.

Nikolai took a step away. "If you'll excuse me, I have somewhere else I need to be."

"Which is?"

"None of your business." The truth was, he was going to see Galina. Nikolai might have had his sights set on the Winter Palace, but until that was officially his home, he'd need a place to stay. A base from which to plan.

"You know I'll follow you if you don't tell me where you're going," Aizhana said.

Nikolai sighed. He *did* know that. "Fine. I'm going to see Galina."

Aizhana swiped away a lock of greasy hair from her face and grinned. "Your best idea yet. You'll reap a great deal of energy by killing a mentor. Her power was nothing compared to what yours used to be, but her ability to command magic would likely benefit you."

"I'm not going to kill her!" Nikolai's earlier sympathy for his mother disappeared, and he glared at her. "I spent all night wandering the city. I need a place to sleep."

She shrank under her hood again.

He didn't care. He began to stalk away.

"Nikolai, wait."

He kept walking.

Aizhana scurried after him, her limp more pronounced when she had to hurry. "I have rooms at a boardinghouse in Sennaya Square if you want a place to live."

He didn't turn around. "Sennaya Square is a pit of filth and disrepute." It was the home of gamblers and drunks, of lice and whores. Nikolai knew this, for Sennaya Square was where he'd spent his little free time during his youth—before he met Pasha, that is—playing cards with louts and enchanting decks so he would win. He always felt sullied afterward. He shuddered now, thinking of it.

Aizhana stopped trying to keep up with him. "Sennaya Square is also the sort of place where people know not to look each other in the eyes. The sort of place where a resurrected corpse and a living shadow might survive without too many questions. Because that, in truth, is what we are, my son."

Nikolai's stomach turned, and he halted mid-stride. Was that what he'd been reduced to? A shadow no better than the boors in those dark alleys?

But no. He was more than that. Even if his body wasn't. "I'm going to restore my corporeal self soon," he said.

Aizhana let out a wheezing whimper. Or a groan. It was difficult to tell. Then she took in a long, quivering breath. "I am your mother. I will be here for you whenever you need me. And when reality catches up to you, you'll be able to find me at the Black Moth."

The most squalid of the sordid boardinghouses in Sennaya Square. Of course.

But Nikolai did not belong there. He *would* not.

"Best of luck to you," he said with a slight nod. And then he strode away.

CHAPTER TWENTY-ONE

Vika had run to the window of the tsar's study as soon as the screaming had begun in Palace Square. She'd watched in horror as the Jack exploded, followed by the boxes, with only the ballerina left behind.

She shook as she surveyed the remains.

"Did you spare the doll, or is she supposed to be dead?" she asked, as if Nikolai could hear.

But what she really meant was, *Is this what you intend to do to me? To us?*

Vika pressed herself against the windowpane and scanned the square for him. But if Nikolai was still there, she couldn't feel his magic. Perhaps it was his barrier shield. Or perhaps he was already gone.

Again, her heart contracted, locking itself, just in case. But the fact that Vika had to protect herself like that, that she had to watch as Nikolai turned against not only her and Pasha, but also against himself, hurt just as much as loving him.

Vika shook her head grimly as she surveyed Nikolai's damage in the now-empty square.

She snapped her fingers, and the lifeless ballerina disappeared in a burst of tiny bubbles. Vika flourished her left hand, and the cobblestones assembled themselves back to their rightful places. But even as she swept magic across Palace Square, there were some things Vika could not do—clear away the people's lingering fear, and the looming fog of her own.

CHAPTER TWENTY-TWO

It took much longer than Nikolai anticipated to reach the Zakrevsky house. If he'd been able to walk the streets like an ordinary person, it would have been a relatively short trip. But because a shadow-without-a-person could not simply stroll out in the sunlight—not if he wanted to preserve the illusion that Vika was the only enchanter and therefore to blame for the havoc wreaked upon Saint Petersburg— Nikolai had to skulk under bridges and in the interstices of the canals.

He nearly cried out in joy as he emerged from the darkness onto the boulevard that ran along Ekaterinsky Canal. Never had he been so happy to see Galina's home, three stories of neo-Baroque excess, against which all the other houses on the street paled.

How would Galina react when she saw him? Probably as if everything were the same, for Galina's heart was made of lead and was therefore unsusceptible to any emotion, surprise or otherwise. But that would be a good thing. He needed a place from which he could plan his course of attack against Pasha, and unlike Aizhana, Galina wouldn't constantly meddle in his affairs. Galina wouldn't care enough to exert the effort.

Nikolai climbed the front steps and listened through the door. It did not seem as if anyone was inside, at least not in the entry. He charmed the lock open and slipped inside. Then he glanced quickly around him, and hearing the servants in the dining room, he tiptoed down the hall, up the curved staircase, and straight to his bedroom.

It had been redecorated as a library.

Nikolai stood immobile in the doorway. "Where are all my things?" He hadn't meant to say it so loudly, but, well . . . Where in the devil were his desk and his bed and the armoire full of clothes he'd painstakingly tailored? He'd only been gone for two weeks.

Galina glided down the hall behind him. "I thought you were dead." As Nikolai had expected, she was not rattled at all by his presence.

He turned to face her. She didn't draw back.

"I'm clearly not dead," he said.

"You look a little dead."

"That's actually impossible for you to judge, for you can't even see me."

"I amend my earlier statement. You don't look particularly *alive*."

Nikolai sighed and rested his forehead on the door frame. "Well, I am. And I have nowhere else to go, because it's not exactly easy for a shadow to walk into an inn and ask for a room. Can I stay here?"

"It's a library, Nikolai. And the Game is over. I am no

longer your mentor, nor am I required to house you."

He pressed his head into the doorway for another moment before he stood up straight. "Right. Of course you'd say that. I don't know what I was thinking." He turned back to the stairs. He would go down to the kitchen in the basement to Renata.

"I'm sorry," Galina said.

Nikolai paused.

"After my brother passed away," she said, "I couldn't bear to have your things right here, inside my house, reminding me that you were gone as well. So I got rid of them. I did not expect you to come back."

Nikolai tilted his head at her. "Galina, do I detect a sentimental spot—"

She cut him off with a scowl. "You still can't stay. Have you looked at yourself in the mirror? You'd frighten the servants to death."

Nikolai nearly laughed. He'd forgotten how stridently forthright Galina could be.

But then he walked past his former mentor to the mirror that hung between paintings of proud Zakrevskys from the past. The mirror in which he'd always made one last check of his appearance before he left the house.

Nikolai gasped at his reflection.

He touched his face. He was all blur, his edges not quite defined, and the rest of him, a haze of charcoal gray. Like a storm cloud in boy form, he was just there enough that his finger did not pass straight through his cheek, but not quite there enough to be solid.

Galina was reflected behind him, her lips curled in what might have been an amused grin, if her mouth had known what to do with such an expression. But smiles were foreign to it, so she merely looked like a wolf surveying her supper. "It's not as if you haven't been a shadow before," she said.

True. But before, his silhouette had only been a shroud, a deception created for the oath at Bolshebnoie Duplo so that his opponent in the Game—so that Vika—couldn't see him. But Nikolai had been himself beneath the shroud then. Now he was shadow through and through.

He dragged his finger along his jaw, as if that would make the line clear and sharp again, like it used to be. It didn't.

"I need to see Renata," he said, his voice as faint as his appearance. Renata would console and ground him.

Galina turned up her nose. "She's not here. I fired her."

"You what?"

"She disappeared in the middle of her work yesterday, leaving laundry unfolded and dishes to be cleaned. Intolerable."

Yesterday afternoon. She was with me, in the steppe dream. Nikolai grit his teeth as guilt pricked him.

"Where is she now?" he asked.

"I do not know and I do not care. Are we done here? I'm glad you survived the Game. It was . . . interesting to see you again." With that, Galina levitated, as was her wont—she never did like her feet to touch the floor for long—and floated past him, down the hall to her own rooms. She shut the door.

This, as Aizhana had predicted, was the moment when reality caught up to Nikolai.

He had no one else to go to, no one else who wanted him. He didn't know where Renata was, and he couldn't face

Vika, not after the way she'd looked at him when he'd animated Peter the Great, the horror and disappointment in her eyes. And an inn, as Aizhana had pointed out, would not rent a room to a shadow.

In the past, Nikolai could have spent a night or two at the Winter Palace. He temporarily warmed at the memory of the times he'd slept on the chaise longue in Pasha's antechamber.

But the potent indignation that had appeared inside Nikolai as he escaped the steppe dream now reared its head again.

No, he thought, as he stopped his reminiscing. The memories piled up against one another, like a caravan of carriages halted too suddenly. Nikolai clenched his jaw and ignored them. *I will not set foot in the palace again until it is mine.*

Soon enough.

But for now, there was nobody left. Only his mother.

Nikolai watched himself in the mirror for another minute, his once proud shoulders slumped.

Then he trudged down the stairs and out the front door. To the Black Moth, the only place, apparently, he belonged.

CHAPTER TWENTY-THREE

Aizhana couldn't read the expression on Nikolai's shadow face, but she knew he did not want to be here. She looked around at the dingy room—even at a boardinghouse as disreputable as this, a hooded woman who refused to show her face could rent only a room in the shack behind the decrepit inn's main building—and she saw the home she'd offered her son through his eyes. The straw mattress crawling with lice. The washbasin in the corner, cracked and stained brown and yellow-green by things better left unknown. The stench from the outhouse just outside their window.

"It is better than nothing," Aizhana said.

"I have my doubts," Nikolai said, turning for the door.

"Stay."

"Why?"

"Because I want you to."

Nikolai hesitated.

Did her love finally mean something to him? Or had he

simply been forsaken by everyone else? Either way, hope bubbled inside her, like a mud pit in a sulfur spring. It was an awful thing to hope that her son's former friends and mentor had abandoned him, leaving Aizhana as his last resort, but if that was the only way . . .

"It's not much," she said, "but at least you would have me. Which I realize also isn't much. And if you have nowhere else to go . . ."

Nikolai pointed to the mattress. "I won't sleep on that."

"This is the only place that will take me," Aizhana said. "I've tried." She hunched over herself. Nikolai's resistance shriveled her black heart even more than it already was. All she wanted was to be close to her boy. Through eighteen years of ante-death underground, that was all she'd wanted, and it held true even now.

She watched as he shook his head and took in the room again, his disgust palpable. Should she tell him that it was actually she who'd given him the energy he needed to escape from the Dream Bench? Would that win him over? Or would he hate her more, because of where her power came from? He'd mentioned time and time again that he didn't want anything to do with her energy.

But Aizhana didn't have a chance to say anything before Nikolai spoke again. His tone now softened. "I meant I won't abide this filth. I won't have you staying in quarters like this."

Nikolai snapped his fingers at the bed of lice, and it burst into an accelerated but contained fire, quickly burning itself to nothing. Then he snapped his fingers again, and two solid oak frames appeared. They were followed by a mattress and a heavy brocade blanket.

He narrowed his eyes. "*Two* mattresses, damn it," he muttered.

"What do you mean?" Aizhana asked.

"I meant to conjure two fine horsehair mattresses. Not a single lumpy one." He scowled at the bulge at the foot of the mattress.

But the muddy bubbles in Aizhana's soul simmered giddily. Her son had attempted to take care of her. And he'd conjured *two* bed frames. "Does this mean you'll stay?"

Nikolai nodded and sank onto the edge of the mattress-less bed frame, as if he were suddenly too tired to even be angry. "Thank you for taking me in, even though I've been less than grateful."

"You owe me no apologies, my son. I am overjoyed you are here with me. And your magic—you have your power again."

Nikolai sagged as his silhouette flickered. "Apparently not. Transforming the beds has taken much of the energy I have, and I didn't even do it right. I'm sorry, Mother. The second mattress will have to wait, and the washbasin . . . perhaps tomorrow."

Aizhana grinned with what remained of her teeth. She couldn't care less about the washbasin. Nikolai was here. With her. And he'd called her "Mother."

"I challenged Pasha," he said. "I intend to take the throne. But I'm a fool if I think I can beat him like this. He has Vika on his side." Nikolai's shadow was fading, as well as losing its shape at its borders.

"I would do anything in my power for you. I will help you overthrow Pasha—"

Nikolai shook his head. "I don't want your help."

There it was again. Aizhana sighed. But she pulled him to his feet and led him to the bed that had a mattress. "Rest," she said, as she draped the blanket over him. "And do not worry about your magic. You can always glean more energy."

Nikolai yawned and nodded. "Right. I can always borrow more." He sighed quietly and lowered himself onto his bed. Even with the fatigue, his movements were elegant, like the principal dancer in the Bolshoi Ballet, lying down to slumber onstage. Or so Aizhana imagined, for she'd never seen a ballet, but she had been a beautiful dancer, too, when she was young and her body was new. Her son had the same rare grace she'd once possessed. Probably more. Pride swelled in her putrefied chest.

Nikolai fell asleep within seconds. *Poor dear*, Aizhana thought.

He had made it clear he did not want what she could offer, but Nikolai needed this energy whether he wanted it or not, so she reached over and rested the pads of her fingers on the back of his neck, mindful to avoid grazing him with her claws.

This way was not optimal. Nikolai could wake and throw Aizhana across the room, or worse, cast her out into the street and never speak to her again. But this was her curse: condemned to trickery and sneaking in the night, even when it came to her own son.

But so be it, she thought. For mothers will do whatever needs to be done.

She poured energy into Nikolai until he shaded darker and his edges were less blurred again. He remained insubstantial—that was *his* curse, for now—but he was more here than not.

Here, with Aizhana.

"I love you, Nikolai," she whispered.

Then she released him and kissed him on his forehead. "Sleep well. I shall return soon. I am going to have a little chat with your former mentor. One does not reject my son without consequence."

CHAPTER TWENTY-FOUR

In winter, Lazarevskoe Cemetery was a crowded plot of gray tombstones and statues and memorials, all covered in a heavy mantle of snow. Bare branches hung over the cemetery like outstretched claws. The old Church of St. Lazarus loomed in the background, somber and severe and a bit foreboding. Aizhana snickered, her quiet laugh like twigs snapping; Lazarevskoe Cemetery was the kind of place in which she felt particularly at home.

Galina floated over the snowy pathways until she stopped at a grave marked by a marble cross cascading with roses. Aizhana hurried after her, her gait awkward in the uneven snow.

"Do you have me where you want me?" Galina asked without turning around.

Aizhana froze where she was.

"You followed me all the way from my house to my husband's grave," Galina said. "So I ask again, do you have me where you want me?" She slowly turned around.

Aizhana expected Galina to recoil, as everyone did upon seeing Aizhana's half-dead face. But Galina did not. Perhaps because Aizhana's hood still covered her, and the branches above filtered out the moonlight and made her features less conspicuous.

"You're hideous, you know," Galina said.

She can *see me*. Aizhana frowned. This was not the effect she'd been hoping for at all.

"Well, let's have it then," Galina said. "Who are you and what do you want?"

"I am here to kill you."

Galina laughed, but it was the sound a wolf would make if it laughed: delighted and entangled with a snarl. It echoed though the cemetery, giving the effect of an entire pack of laughing wolves. Even Aizhana shuddered. "And why," Galina asked, "would you want to kill me? It's not that I believe you unjustified; I've affronted many during my lifetime. But I am curious what *your* particular reason is for hating me."

There were multiple answers to her question. Galina had bought Nikolai for the mere price of four animals, as if he were an animal himself. Viewed him simply as a pawn in the Game. Failed to love him.

But most important right now, Nikolai needed more energy, and since Galina was a mentor, her energy would be particularly valuable—it would carry with it the ability to use magic. If Aizhana killed her, she could steal her energy and pass it on to Nikolai, and with the infusion of both Aizhana's power and Galina's magical ability, Nikolai would be unstoppable. He would no longer have to worry about fading. He could crush Pasha and take the crown. Aizhana bared her yellowed teeth in a smile.

"I am Nikolai's mother."

"Hmm. Well, he certainly didn't get his looks from you, did he?"

Aizhana bristled, but she wouldn't take the bait. Galina was trying to distract her from her purpose. "When Nikolai came to you today, asking for a place to stay, you tossed him onto the street without remorse."

Galina set her hands on her hips. "And that, you believe, is an offense that merits my death?"

"He had nowhere else to go."

"Nikolai is resourceful."

"You are heartless."

Galina sneered and looked pointedly at Aizhana's chest. "I would wager you are, too. Quite literally."

The black energy inside Aizhana bubbled to boiling. She lunged at Galina.

Galina jerked out of the way and flung out her arms, sending a wave of magic at Aizhana. It hurled Aizhana against a statue of a weeping angel and knocked the air out of her withered lungs.

But she scrambled quickly to her feet. She had not managed to kill the tsar by being weak. Galina might have a little magic on her side, but she was not skilled in combat. Aizhana, on the other hand, had managed to defeat the soldiers who guarded the tsar, as well as Alexander himself. And Alexander was no fool with a pistol or sword.

Aizhana charged, her bladelike fingernails flashing. Galina clapped her hands twice in rapid succession, and the tombstones in Aizhana's path fell like dominoes in a death trap. Aizhana darted out of the way of the first and second ones, but the third fell on the tail end of her cloak and tore it with a loud rip from her body, leaving her in only a threadbare *koilek* tunic. And the fourth tombstone was more towering pillar than grave marker. Aizhana barely escaped it crushing—and possibly severing—her bad foot.

Galina was more formidable an opponent than she'd anticipated. It was one thing to be able to foresee the tsar driving a sword through Aizhana's belly—which she'd casually removed and then healed herself, much to Alexander's chagrin—but another thing entirely to fight someone whose skills allowed her to move unpredictably. *I need to trap her. But how?* The cemetery was too open. And Aizhana would not be able to back Galina into a corner, not when Galina had the ability to levitate and move faster and in more directions than Aizhana could.

But what if Galina thought she had me *cornered? Instead of me chasing her, she can chase me.*

Aizhana gasped and fell to the snow, clutching her foot as if the falling pillar had, indeed, wounded her. She cradled it in her hand and, with a movement hidden from Galina's line of sight, snapped off one of the toes. It didn't matter; it was frostbitten and Aizhana couldn't feel it anyway. Besides, it was the foot that was already damaged. But she whimpered as if painfully injured. "You broke my foot!" She hissed as she held the severed toe up in the air.

She crawled up to standing, wincing and clutching the nearest cross for support. She hissed again at Galina. "You may have won tonight, but I will be back to repay you, tenfold." She began to limp away.

Galina's laugh was a wolf's snarl. "If you think you can attack me and then simply walk away, you are sorely mistaken." She stepped toward Aizhana.

Facing away from her, Aizhana smirked. *Yes, follow me.*
She limped as fast as she could toward a mausoleum, as if she
were wounded prey seeking a hiding place from her predator.

The doors were locked. But Aizhana didn't need the key
to get in. Her fingernails were as good for picking locks as
they were for slashing throats. Galina closed the distance
between them. Aizhana slid her nails into the lock, and a
few seconds later heard the satisfying click of the mechanism giving way. She shoved the heavy mausoleum doors
open and limped in.

Where it was completely dark. The faint moonlight outside did not penetrate the crypt. Aizhana stumbled into the
marble coffin at its center.

There was a faint wisp of wind as Galina glided in.

"I should lock you in here," Galina said, her voice echoing against the marble walls. "You're mostly dead already.
The tomb would finish the job."

"I survived being buried for nearly two decades. I doubt
locking me in here would be enough to kill me this time,
either," Aizhana said, partly because pride made her defend
herself, and partly to draw Galina farther into the mausoleum, toward the sound of her voice.

Galina was too cautious. She remained near the doors.

But no matter. Aizhana's eyes, being accustomed to living six feet underground, had already adjusted to the lack of
light in the crypt. Especially with the faint moonlight in the
background, she could see Galina's silhouette perfectly. And
Galina could not see her.

Aizhana pounced. She lanced a nail straight into the center of Galina's chest, the needle tip of it spearing through

pulsing, thick muscle. It turned out Galina did, in fact, have a heart, one bursting with energy like Aizhana had never felt before, because Galina's energy was threaded through with the ability to call upon magic. It would be nowhere near as powerful as Nikolai's, of course, for Galina was merely a mentor, but the surge of it was still enough to make Aizhana moan with pleasure, like absorbing fireworks along with Galina's life. This energy was what Nikolai needed.

Galina gaped at Aizhana. "You . . ."

"I . . . what?"

"You don't deserve Nikolai."

Aizhana thrust her fingernail harder through Galina's heart. Galina cried out. A moment later, she slumped as the last of her energy drained from her haughty body into Aizhana's blighted one.

Aizhana tried to extract her nail, as if she were withdrawing a sword, but the movement was too violent, and her nail snapped off, remaining firmly lodged in Galina's chest.

"Damn you," she said. "Even in death you do harm to me and my family." She spat on Galina's corpse. And then Aizhana spat again, for good measure. "*You* don't deserve Nikolai, either."

But there was someone who might deserve Nikolai, if she could prove her worth, her willingness to help him. It was that servant girl he'd mentioned. Aizhana smiled.

She would find Renata next.

CHAPTER TWENTY-FIVE

The next afternoon, Vika rode beside Pasha in the open carriage as they departed the Winter Palace. Pasha might have been a wreck on the inside—he purposely averted his eyes from where the Jack's and ballerina's boxes used to be in the square—but on the outside, he was nothing but regal serenity. He wore a crisp black military uniform with gold epaulets on his shoulders, red piping along the edges, and mirror-shined brass buttons down the front. His hair was neatly combed (this alone let Vika know that his appearance was but a facade), and a stately black feathered hat that marked his training in the cavalry.

I feel the same way, Vika thought. Composed on the outside, but a bundle of nerves on the inside. Yuliana had insisted that Vika could not appear by Pasha's side wearing her favorite green dress. It was, apparently, "an out-of-date eyesore" that was "an affront to the empire." So now Vika wore a tightly corseted blue gown, as pale as Pasha's uniform was dark. The contrast, Yuliana had insisted, was necessary.

Everything in how they presented themselves to the public had been calculated down to the last thread by the grand princess. Vika had actually suggested she conjure a dress like the blizzard she'd worn to Pasha's birthday masquerade, but Yuliana had quickly squashed the idea. Vika was to demonstrate magic to the people, but not too much, or they would be frightened rather than reassured. (However, Yuliana had approved the use of magic to keep the carriage unseasonably warm, which would negate the need for heavy overcoats and better show off the outfits she had meticulously chosen. Vika had rolled her eyes.)

Their carriage arrived at the beginning of Nevsky Prospect, the very same boulevard where Vika had tamed the statue of Peter the Great. People already spilled out from shop fronts and leaned over their apartment balconies and windows, for word of the tsesarevich's procession had come well in advance of Pasha's arrival. But a collective gasp echoed along Nevsky Prospect as the citizens realized who else rode in the carriage beside their prince. Some of the windows slammed shut. Shouts sliced through the frigid air: "Witch!" "God have mercy upon us!" "Burn her!"

"I suppose Yuliana didn't announce that I'd be in the procession," Vika muttered.

"Sorry," Pasha said.

Of course he'd known. But from the crowd's reaction, Yuliana had probably been right to omit that part. Even Vika had to concede that.

Pasha's Guard slowed their horses. Gavriil, the captain of the Guard, shouted, "His Imperial Highness, the Tsesarevich, Pavel Alexandrovich Romanov!"

The people, who would ordinarily fall to their knees and

cheer for Pasha, remained eerily silent.

Unfazed—at least outwardly—Pasha rose in the carriage, which now moved at a tortoise's pace. He offered his hand to Vika.

She tilted her head in question.

"Stand with me," he said quietly. A soft smile reached his eyes.

Vika hesitated. But the cuff tightened around her wrist.

This was what I wanted, she reminded herself. *To be Imperial Enchanter. To be free to use my magic without limit or having to hide.*

But was that what being Imperial Enchanter really was? Vika looked at the bracelet. It marked her accomplishment. It also shackled her to less freedom than she'd had before. She hadn't imagined that achieving her greatest desire would come true, but with the precise opposite of what she'd wanted: to fly without bounds.

"Vika?"

She slipped her gloved hand into Pasha's. Her breath caught at both the softness and steadiness of his fingers, and for a brief moment, she remembered the maple grove on Letniy Isle, where they'd almost shared a kiss. Of course, it wasn't that she wanted that now. Far from it. But the memory was a sudden reminder of Pasha before the tsar's death turned him and everything else horribly sideways. It was easier to take his hand when Vika remembered that he was just a boy—a golden-haired prince, but still, a real boy beneath the royal facade.

"My dearest citizens," Pasha said, his voice as bright and intoxicating as one of Saint Petersburg's sunlit summer nights, "I know some of you have recently witnessed magic, which may seem unreal and frightening. I understand your fear, for evil can come from such power. But you have nothing to worry about, because magic has always been with us. Enchanters have existed throughout all of Russia's history; they have been quiet advisers to the tsars and defenders of our empire.

"Today I have the honor and pleasure of introducing you to my Imperial Enchanter, Baroness Victoria Sergeyevna Andreyeva. Although I hope she doesn't mind if I simply introduce her as Vika."

"Vika . . ." Whispers of her name passed over hundreds of lips, like a haunted wind blowing through the boulevard. Vika shivered, despite the enchantment to keep the carriage warm.

"There is no reason to fear her, or magic itself," Pasha continued. "With Vika by my side, our empire is stronger against its enemies, and that will mean peace, prosperity, and happiness for all of you."

His grip on Vika's hand tightened.

Vika did not squeeze back. *Who am I that I succumb so easily to a lie?*

And yet it was what was necessary to restore calm. Being Imperial Enchanter—and being part of the machinery of the tsardom—compromised Vika's natural compulsion to speak the brash truth. Her skin crawled, as if allergic to what she had to do.

"I want to see the witch up close!" A little girl, around seven years old, broke free of her mother and ran toward the carriage. Pasha's Guard and their horses immediately closed ranks around the carriage.

Her audacity reminded Vika of herself at that age.

"Let the girl through," she said.

The Guard looked to Pasha, who thought for a second, then nodded. The Guard parted slowly, and Ilya slipped off his saddle to take the little girl by the hand. He led her to the carriage and motioned for the mother to follow.

The woman trembled, paralyzed over what had just happened and what to do.

After all, Vika thought wryly, *her child has just approached a very dangerous witch.*

"She'll be all right," Pasha said loudly so the woman could hear. Then he leaned over the side of the carriage to be closer to the girl.

The girl pointed at Vika. "What I want to know is, what if she does *bad* magic?"

Vika's fingers twitched, a reflex of defiance—or perhaps defensiveness—yearning to prove everyone here wrong. She clutched her hands into fists to still them.

The crowd listened intently, as if their fates were in the hands of this little girl's words. They held their breaths for Pasha's response.

He shook his head solemnly. "Vika won't do any bad magic. But you are a very brave and perceptive girl to ask. What's your name?"

"Lena." The girl peered at Vika like at an exotic animal in a circus cage, menacing but fascinating all the same. "How do you know for sure she won't be bad?" Lena asked Pasha. "Mama said Vika is a hag riding the devil's broom into Saint Petersburg."

Vika crossed her arms, hands still balled into fists. "I'm not a hag."

Lena took her in from head to toe. Then toe to head.

"No," she said, after she'd finished her assessment. "You're very pretty. But it could be a trick to make us like you better."

Pasha cleared his throat.

Vika bent down and stretched out her left arm toward Lena. "Well, even if it was a trick, I wouldn't be able to be bad, because of this." Her stomach curdled as she took off her glove and revealed the gold bracelet circling her wrist. "I am bound to serve the good of the Russian Empire. The cuff will burn me if I do anything against His Imperial Highness's commands."

Lena's mouth dropped open. She reached a pudgy hand toward the bracelet.

"Lena, no!" her mother shouted.

Lena didn't withdraw her hand but stopped short of the cuff.

"It's all right," Vika said. "You can touch it. It only gets hot if I'm naughty."

Lena glanced at her mother, who still stood trembling on the side of the boulevard. Then the girl giggled as if she'd just discovered how free she was to do whatever she wanted in the moment, and she ran her little fingers over the bracelet's gold vines. She petted the feathers of the double-headed eagle.

After a minute, she looked up at Vika again. "But what about the statue that went mad? And the exploding boxes near the Winter Palace?"

"Um . . . those were mistakes," Vika said as she tugged her glove back on.

Pasha raised his brows quizzically.

Trust me, she mouthed. Vika wanted to keep Nikolai's

current, tainted existence a secret. Then, when she figured out what was wrong with him, he could return as a beloved prince. It was better this way for Nikolai, and for Russia. And selfishly, for Vika, too. If the people feared and hated Nikolai, Yuliana would have a stronger argument for executing him. But if Vika could protect Nikolai until she was able to save him from himself . . .

She didn't want to explain all that to Pasha, though, and even if she did, now was not the time. *Trust me*, she mouthed again.

Pasha's brows stayed up, but he nodded slowly.

Lena huffed, reminding them she was there. "Prove it," she said.

Vika frowned. "Prove what?"

"That you're nice, not naughty."

Vika glanced at Pasha. He nodded. It was time for the Christmas tree.

She opened the door to the carriage to step out. Ilya was quickly there to offer his assistance.

"Thank you," she said.

His eyes lingered upon her a few moments longer than necessary. The way he looked at Vika was not the admiring gaze of a young man, however, but rather, an appraisal—an assessment of good and evil—similar to Lena's.

Interesting. Vika tucked away the observation to consider later.

She walked away from the carriage. Lena began to follow, but Vika looked back at her and shook her head. Pasha invited Lena into the carriage instead, and from the way Lena beamed as she sat beside him, it was obvious Pasha had won over another adoring admirer for life.

He doesn't need magic, Vika thought. *Pasha is his own quiet force to be reckoned with. He just doesn't entirely know it.*

Vika walked a few more blocks from where the initial crowd had gathered. Here, too, there were people along Nevsky Prospect, but they were fewer and farther between, and they shifted away to give her a wide berth when she stopped in the center of the boulevard.

Vika closed her eyes, and with Nevsky Prospect quiet, focus came rather easily, even though the stability of the city hinged upon her performance. She pictured the fir tree that grew outside her cottage, and the thought of home made her smile, despite the circumstances. She and Father used to decorate it every year, dressing its lopsided branches with golden beads and wooden ornaments and Vika's favorite, moths she enchanted to flutter around it with glowing wings. She'd heard, as a child, of lightning bugs in warmer climes, so she'd worked with what she had here in Russia to create her own sort of fireflies.

When Vika opened her eyes, what seemed like stars on a string appeared in the sky. They twinkled brightly, even though it wasn't night. As they drew near, their forms came into view. Moths, with lighted wings, carrying a twig from her fir tree.

They dropped the thin branch into Vika's waiting hand. "*Spasiba*," she thanked them.

They bobbed in the air for a second, then flew to the rooftop of the nearest building, landing to rest after their speedy flight from Ovchinin Island.

Vika examined the twig the moths had brought. The wood was healthy and strong; the leaves, full and dark green. She brought it to her nose and inhaled. There was possibly nothing better than the smell of Christmas. Hopefully, the people of Saint Petersburg would think so, too.

"Let's make you into a tree, shall we?"

She knelt and set the twig on the ground. She rubbed her gloves together and flung her hands apart.

The twig seemed to explode as it burst from one small branch into thousands of enormous ones. The crowd gasped, and the force of the twig's instantaneous growth pushed even Vika backward.

The tree trunk kept expanding and expanding until it was several feet across, and the treetop reached at least a hundred feet high.

Vika's smile broadened, amplified by the heady perfume of fir mingled with sap and snow.

"And now for decorations." Vika clapped her hands, and immediately, lacy garlands of pale-blue flowers—blue mist sage, one of Father's favorites—appeared and draped themselves around the tree. Chunks of ice creaked and leaped up from the Neva, then melted until they formed themselves into glistening crystalline orbs hanging like ornaments from the branches.

The moths resting on the palace rooftop flew back toward her and fluttered their wings impatiently. Vika nodded.

They zipped through the air to the tree. As they did so, even more glowing moths flew in from all around the city, lighting the sky. They wove in and out of the branches, swooping up and down—magic, glimmering tinsel.

Vika looked around at the people on the boulevard. The crowd was much closer now. Most of their eyes didn't glisten with fear anymore, either, but with the wide-eyed curiosity Lena had earlier displayed.

But Vika wasn't finished. She still needed to charm the tree to give gifts to children who approached it.

What could the tree give? If this were Nikolai's enchantment, he could conjure intricately wrapped presents, each with a different toy—a kit for building model bridges, a windup doll, a music box that played Christmas songs. But that wasn't the sort of magic Vika excelled at. She was better with the elements and nature, but a child like Lena wouldn't be happy with a box full of snow.

There was, however, food. It would be tricky, because food conjured from magic was never, as Father had claimed, as delicious as that cooked by hand.

But what child was ever picky about candy?

Vika snapped her fingers, and deep-violet sugarplums appeared all over the tree, hanging by black licorice stems. The lower boughs of the tree grew heavy with enormous candy pinecones, each a different color and flavor, from strawberry red to marmalade orange to honeysuckle-berry blue. And tufts of white cotton candy, like sweet snow, floated down onto the branches. Wherever a child could reach, a treat could be found.

Vika stepped back to survey her tree. It was impressive and lustrous and above all . . . innocent. She couldn't use something this pure as a weapon. And she wasn't going to kill Nikolai anyway.

I'll give it fire, Vika thought, *but not as Yuliana wanted.*

Vika conjured a small flame at her fingertips and blew on it. It flew to the base of the tree and wended its way to the center of the trunk. From there, it began to light the tree from within, fiery and hot. The flame burned in the trunk but remained contained inside the thick layers of bark, and it shot up, up, up through the middle. The fire destroyed the tree's soul and at the same time fueled it, imparting the wood itself with light and life from the inside out.

Finally, the flame reached the very top of the tree and exploded forth, flickering fiercely into the sky.

Lena cried out and clapped her little hands together.

But Vika didn't celebrate. She looked at her enchantment and saw herself. And Pasha and Nikolai. *It's only a question of whether our bark will hold . . . or whether the fire will eventually consume and kill us all.*

The rest of the people on Nevsky Prospect remained quiet and still. They no longer shouted about witches and devils, but they also didn't clap or cheer. It was as if they understood how precarious everything was, and that darkness could not be deterred by a single fiery Christmas tree.

Or a single fiery girl.

CHAPTER TWENTY-SIX

Yuliana's antechamber was littered with paper. Several boxes of her mother's correspondence were upended across the floor, the remnants of the late tsarina's floral perfume haunting the room like a ghost. Yuliana's own notes cluttered the small desk in the corner, displacing the stack of Imperial Council reports, which stood so tall on the floor that it was nearly impossible to see her sitting cross-legged on the rug behind them.

She was combing through her mother's letters—well, the ones that were sent to the tsarina, since Yuliana obviously didn't have the ones her mother had sent out—and looking for mentions of Alexis Okhotnikov, as well as anyone else who could have been the tsarina's lover nearly eighteen years ago. Her mother had often felt isolated in court life, and hence was an incessant letter writer, finding solace in news from her friends.

The problem, however, was that her mother's friends had also been incessant letter writers, which meant there were thousands of envelopes to go through.

But there must be something in here that either proves the tsar was Pasha's father, or that he wasn't. Already, Yuliana had found a few letters from noblewomen reporting to the tsarina on seeing Okhotnikov at this or that ball, in this or that parlor, and what he wore that night, with whom he danced, if he complimented anyone for their piano playing. There were mentions, too, in earlier letters of other men, possible lovers. Yuliana sighed. She didn't know if she wanted to grow up. Court life for women seemed so terribly predictable and dull.

At least if Pasha became tsar, he'd let Yuliana help. He understood that she was more Catherine the Great than Marie Antoinette. Although Yuliana did have an appreciation for petits fours and beautiful gowns.

She laughed, something she only allowed herself rarely, even when alone. Then she bent over a new pile of letters, even though her neck ached from the hours of reading before.

"I will solve this," she said, as she opened another envelope. "One way or another."

CHAPTER TWENTY-SEVEN

"Can you make room for my mother?" a boy asked that evening, as he pushed his way into the mass of people in the nave, the church's main room. He neared Pasha, who stood in the center of the crowd, disguised as a dockworker. Behind the boy trailed a woman with a gray shawl wrapped around her head, her posture stooped and her footsteps halting. She was probably no older than thirty, but life was hard on ordinary Russians, the ones who swept streets and labored in factories and raised a half-dozen children before they died of cholera or consumption or simply exhaustion. The rest of the worshippers wore similar expressions, weary and resigned, as they stood in the nave awaiting the liturgy.

"Make way," Pasha said, parting the crowd with his arms. The boy and his mother nodded gratefully.

The church was a simple one on the outside, nothing much to look at compared to the grand cathedrals in other parts of Saint Petersburg, but those were churches for the moneyed. This was a place of worship and shelter for everyone else.

And yet intricate, gilded icons of the Holy Trinity and saints throughout history adorned the iconostasis, a wall-like screen that divided the nave from the altar, and up above, the ceilings were painted with holy scenes. No expense was spared when it came to honoring the Lord.

Pasha settled back into the crowd. He wore a plain tunic and trousers, as well as a false beard to cover most of his face, but it didn't matter much, for everyone was too busy whispering their own prayers to look at those around them.

"Please save the tsesarevich from the devil's magic."

"Have mercy and spare us from the witch."

"Tell us what to do, O Lord, send a sign, and we will follow."

The nave seemed to grow smaller; the curdled smell of fear lay like a heavy blanket in the church, and it was harder and harder for Pasha to breathe. He wove through the masses, but everywhere he turned, they whispered the same entreaties. *Help us. Rid the city of the witch. Exorcise the demon from the tsesarevich.*

It seemed Vika's tree and Pasha's entreaties to the city to believe in him had not convinced everybody. Not even close.

He strode out of the nave and burst out through the doors of the church. The frigid air outside rushed into his lungs, and he gulped it down in ragged breaths. Had he made a mistake in endorsing magic? There was a reason the tsars and the church had hidden it in the past—most people could not handle that there were powers larger than they are. Now, however, they knew about magic again, and things were spinning out of control.

I don't know how to do this, Pasha thought, as he leaned back, head tilted against the chilly church walls. The wind bit into his cheeks, stinging him with sharp needles of sleet.

I don't know how to be tsar.

CHAPTER TWENTY-EIGHT

After Galina fired her, Renata had scrambled to find work. It was only through the connection of another girl who'd worked at Ludmila's temporary Saint Petersburg kiosk last fall that she secured a position at Madame Boulangère, the Parisian-style bakery on Nevsky Prospect.

It wasn't a glorious job, although no bakery job could ever be called such. The air was always sweltering from the constant heat of the ovens, the hours were grueling, and the owner of the shop, the so-called Madame Boulangère herself, had lost her taste buds in a childhood accident but refused to acknowledge it, and thus complained constantly of the lack of flavor in the store's pastries, when any lack thereof was the fault of her own tongue.

Still, it was employment. Besides, Renata had weathered much worse working under Galina all those years. A tasteless proprietor was nothing remarkable to bear.

Renata was often the last at the bakery, for she was also the newest employee, and thus had the dubious honor of cleaning the shop. She was about to light more lamps—it was only early evening, but the sun set by late afternoon in the winter in Saint Petersburg—when the front door opened and closed again.

"Uh, hello?" she called into the near dark. She thought she'd locked the door. Perhaps Inessa, the girl who'd helped her secure the job, had come in to help? Although Renata had no idea why anyone would volunteer to do so.

"Renata Galygina, I've wanted to meet you," a raspy voice said.

Definitely not Inessa. Renata backed up behind the bakery counter. "I—I'm sorry. We're closed for the evening." She looked around for a knife, a spatula, anything with which to defend herself, but either the girls had tidied up too well during the previous shift, or there wasn't enough light in the shop for Renata to see. Or both.

"Do not be afraid, my dear. I mean no harm. I am Nikolai's mother, Aizhana Karimova. I am here to ask for your assistance with my son." Aizhana did not advance, but rather remained near the entrance of the bakery.

"Nikolai's gone," Renata said. She had returned to the steppe bench after he'd wiped most of it away, but she hadn't found him there again. She hadn't worried, though. If he could survive the Game, he must've survived the bench. But she wouldn't tell this stranger of a woman any of it. Not until she knew for certain who she was.

Renata wrapped her fingers around a rolling pin. Finally, some measure of defense.

"On the contrary," Aizhana said, "he's come back."

He's come back . . . so she does *know that he's alive but was elsewhere for a while.*

"How do I know you're telling the truth?" Renata asked.

"It's your choice whether you believe me or not." Aizhana laughed. "After Nikolai escaped the bench, he went to his old home to seek shelter and to find you. His former mentor turned him out, and you had been relieved of your duties there. Since then, he has been, shall we say, preoccupied, but I know he would like to see you again." And then Aizhana proceeded to tell Renata about Nikolai's challenge to Pasha.

Renata dropped the rolling pin on the counter. It clattered and fell onto the floor.

Nikolai threatened to destroy Pasha and take away the throne? That didn't sound like the Nikolai she knew at all.

"You will assist him," Aizhana said.

"I beg your pardon?"

"I am not asking you. I am telling you." Aizhana began to limp toward the bakery counter. She crossed into a sliver of light cast from the streetlamp outside, and Renata saw her skeletal face and the patches of long, greasy hair.

"Wh-what are you?"

Aizhana paused. "I am a faith healer. A woman who clawed her way back from ante-death. A mother who cares for nothing else in the world but her son. Nikolai needs energy, Renata. He may have returned to reality, but his hold on this life is tenuous. If he is to have a chance of defeating the tsesarevich, Nikolai will need more energy soon."

"How am I the answer?"

"You are merely the means. I possess the energy he needs, but he refuses to take it from me. You, however . . . he thinks it was your presence that helped him escape the steppe dream, and you must mean a great deal to him if he sought you out at the countess's house. Therefore, I am going to transfer some of the energy I possess to you. You, in turn, will find a way to convince him to take it from you."

"I—"

"No more idle chatter. Will you assist my son willingly, or shall I force it upon you?" Aizhana brandished her hand in the air. Her fingernails extended like blades, all save the one on her index finger, which appeared to have broken off. She began her advance toward Renata again.

Renata's foot found the rolling pin on the floor next to a sack of flour. But it would be no use. There was no stopping a mother motivated by love, even if the love was awry. Or especially if it was awry.

There was also no reasoning with a girl who was in love. Even if the boy she loved wanted to do something with which she did not agree. It was Nikolai. Renata would give herself to whatever he needed.

She stepped over the rolling pin and around the counter. She put on her bravest face. "I'll help Nikolai willingly," Renata said. "Just tell me what to do."

CHAPTER TWENTY-NINE

Nikolai had slept nearly an entire day, and when he woke in the early evening, he felt brighter and more buoyant than before. Yet, paradoxically, he also appeared deeper gray. He rolled out of his bed at the Black Moth and tried to use his revitalized power to cast a shroud about himself, such that he would appear like an ordinary person, but his silhouette form seemed to fight back, and the shroud kept sputtering.

Nikolai furrowed his brow. It was both a relief that his edges were no longer blurred and a concern that his shadow form seemed to be growing more stubborn. And how? Was it simply rest that reenergized him? Yet he'd slept plenty in the steppe dream, and he had woken only once feeling more powerful, as he did today.

But did it matter? The more powerful the energy that coursed within him, the less Nikolai seemed to care. In fact, as he stretched himself fully awake, a cold swell rushed inside him, and he laughed as he remembered he had a throne to take. And a tsesarevich to kill.

Speaking of which, Nikolai needed to visit a toy shop on Nevsky Prospect. He had something fun in store for Pasha. Well, perhaps "fun" was not the right word for how Pasha was about to feel. But it would be fun for Nikolai.

The thought made him colder—and stronger—still.

He made his way from Sennaya Square to the nicer part of Saint Petersburg, to a shop with a window display that featured a dolls' holiday fete. "*C'est parfait*," Nikolai said as he slipped inside the store. He cast a quick enchantment to topple a stack of boxes in the back to draw away the shop-keeper's attention, and while alone, Nikolai pocketed the miniature tables, tiny platters, and Christmas garlands from the window display. He took the dolls in tulle gowns and frock coats and trousers, as well as a small orchestra.

He snuck out of the shop before the boxes in the back had even been gathered.

A little girl and her father approached, and Nikolai pressed himself into the narrow alley next to the store.

"The dolls' party is gone!" the girl said as she peered into the window.

But I'm going to give you something even better in its place, Nikolai thought.

"Someone probably bought the set," her father said.

The girl pouted but followed her father as they continued on their way.

Their shadows lingered.

Nikolai squinted at them. The shadows stretched out, thinner and thinner, like black taffy, one end connected to the girl and her father, the other end stuck to—or attracted to—Nikolai.

"Shoo!" he whispered, waving them off.

They stayed a second longer. Then the shadows suddenly

retracted and sprang back into normal shape behind the people they belonged to. Nikolai blinked. Had that really happened? Or was he losing his mind?

He shook his head. He must have imagined it; shadows didn't have wills of their own.

Or did they? He looked at his own shadow hands. But he quickly shoved them into the pockets of his greatcoat.

His fingers grazed his coin purse. *Oh. I didn't pay for the dolls, did I?*

But Nikolai paused before he went back inside the toy shop. Never before would it have occurred to him to steal from a store. And yet here he was, paying for the dolls as an afterthought.

What's gotten into me? he thought, as he retrieved a stack of rubles. He set the money in the window, where the display had been. He left and hurried down Nevsky Prospect.

"What do right and wrong mean, anyway?" Nikolai asked aloud. Could something seem wrong when isolated— such as helping oneself to a dollhouse set—but be right in the larger scheme? It was like fighting a duel. Gentlemen fought them to rectify insults and to defend their honor every day. Sometimes a duel resulted in death, but it was unquestionably the right thing to do. Which was precisely what Nikolai was doing now by challenging Pasha: protecting his honor and making Pasha pay for his betrayal.

Besides, I'd make a better tsar. Nikolai could offer a perspective to ruling the empire that Pasha couldn't, for Pasha had grown up in the opulent confines of the Winter Palace, whereas Nikolai had scraped his way up from nothing. He'd supported himself by doing odd jobs—delivering packages for Bissette & Sons, sharpening swords and knives for the officers in the Imperial Army, assisting with dance lessons from Madame Allard. Unlike Pasha, Nikolai knew what life was like for ordinary Russians. And they deserved to have a tsar who understood their lot.

That was what Nikolai told himself, anyway.

He reached the embankments of the Neva River, now a vast expanse of empty ice. A blank slate on which to host the most spectacular fete the city had ever seen. Nikolai snapped his fingers, and a heavy note card appeared:

PAVEL ALEXANDROVICH ROMANOV
Invites all of Saint Petersburg
To a holiday fete
ELEVEN O'CLOCK TONIGHT
19 DECEMBER 1825
UPON THE FROZEN NEVA RIVER.

Then Nikolai snapped his fingers, multiplying the fake invitation. When ready, he would send them flying away to every person in the city. The people were barely pacified by Vika's Christmas tree. It wouldn't take much to tilt them to the other side of the scales, to fear and hysteria, again. "Let's see what they think of 'Pasha's' party and his supposedly good use of magic. . . ."

But first, he had to create it.

Nikolai conjured blades onto the bottoms of his boots and skated onto the ice. No one could see him working here in the dark, which was what he wanted. Nothing would be unveiled until everything for the party was ready, to the last detail.

He stopped in the center of the river and knelt, taking all the dolls and other pieces from the pockets of his coat and setting them on the ice.

There had been only two long wooden tables in the window display, each covered with a blue satin cloth, and a handful of chairs with cream-colored cushions, but the paucity was not a problem for Nikolai. He passed his hands over the tiny furniture, and it multiplied, and multiplied again and again, until he had a hundred tables and more than a thousand chairs.

Then he flung out his arms, and the tables and chairs followed his arc, throwing themselves across the frozen river until they were spread out, evenly spaced, over nearly a mile. Nikolai squeezed his eyes shut and concentrated on each table, each chair, seeing them in miniature. In his mind, they began to grow. Just as he'd done for the Dream Benches on Letniy Isle, only by a hundredfold.

Wood creaked all around Nikolai as the tables and chairs stretched. Inch by inch, they expanded from doll-like proportions to human ones. By the time they were full size, Nikolai was drenched in sweat. He opened his eyes slowly.

He could not see all the tables and chairs in the dark, but they were there, lined up across the Neva River, ready to be made resplendent with a feast.

Compétent, he said to himself. Not a compliment, but an acknowledgment of sufficiency. So far. He wiped the sweat from his brow.

Next, the decorations. Nikolai looked down at the pile of gold garlands and bells and velvet bows. But he had no walls upon which to hang them.

I have birds.

Nikolai made a series of chirps. A minute later, the sky filled with the soft murmur of hundreds of wings flapping. "*Bonsoir*," he said to the stone sparrows he'd created during the Game to watch and attack Vika. He smiled at their quiet elegance.

As with the table and chairs, Nikolai enlarged the dolls' decorations until they were much, much larger. When he was finished, he gestured to his birds. "If you please," he said.

One by one, they descended, picking up gold garlands and bells and brightly colored bows. They flew along the Neva and artfully arranged themselves in the air—at Nikolai's direction, of course—over and around the tables. The evening sky chimed, and then it sparkled as Nikolai lit it with chandeliers of tiered candles.

"And now to populate the scene," he said.

Dozens of dolls—women in burgundy tulle gowns, men in charcoal frock coats and trousers, with burgundy cravats to match—bloomed to human size. Their faces were finely featured in porcelain, their painted smiles joyful and flawless. In the dollhouse scene, they'd been the ones dancing; at Nikolai's fete, they would be the ones welcoming guests, pouring wine, and serving food.

Next came the musicians. It was not a full orchestra, as Nikolai would have liked, more a large string section, but he would deal with what he had. The dolls set up their violins, violas, cellos, and double basses near an open expanse of ice, which would be the dancing—or, as the case might be, the *skating*—floor.

Nikolai smiled at what he'd created, even though he was light-headed from exhaustion. His stomach growled, too; he was hungry from all the exertion. Magic was as demanding (or even more so) as any physical activity.

"Only one more thing."

Nikolai conjured tureens full of borscht, platters of baked

sturgeon with mushrooms, and loaves of dense rye bread. There were baskets full of crackers to eat with sauerkraut, and plates full of cabbage piroshki, steaming hot. And of course wine, and ice-cold vodka with an assortment of pickles to go with it.

Later, there would be dessert, including cranberry *pastila* confections and deep-fried *syrniki*—fat cottage-cheese pancakes—served with honey, powdered sugar, and sour cream. This was a party for everyone in Saint Petersburg, including the merchants and sailors and maids, not just the aristocracy, so Nikolai wanted the food and drink to reflect the preferences of everyday Russians.

What a shame that many of the ingredients for tonight's feast had gone rancid, the flavor masked completely by magic. The people would blame the tsesarevich for their ills, their bodies and their minds sickened. And should Pasha show his face—surely he would, for how could he not if the invitation had come ostensibly from him—the food that touched his lips would be even more potent.

Possibly deadly.

As Nikolai had promised, he would rob Pasha of the people's love. And then he'd kill him.

Nikolai smirked. But it wasn't his usual smile, the kind with the single dimple in his cheek. It was sharper, darker, like Aizhana's.

He did not fully comprehend how much he'd changed.

CHAPTER THIRTY

The invitations arrived at the Winter Palace like a storm of paper seabirds, diving through doorways and down chimneys as if plummeting into the ocean for fish. They landed at the feet of every attendant, footman, and maid. And at the feet of Yuliana and Pasha, too. They were just winding down the evening with a game of chess (which Pasha was invariably going to lose).

A servant rushed to pick the envelopes up off the carpet and presented them to the grand princess and tsesarevich.

Pasha stared at the envelope on his plate.

"Are you going to open it?" Yuliana asked.

He shook his head slowly. "The last message I received via magical delivery did not go so well."

She reached over and touched her brother's arm to soothe him.

"I'll do it then," she said, and without waiting for his assent, Yuliana tore open the envelope and pulled out the heavy white card inside.

She scrunched her face as she read the invitation.

"I'm afraid to ask what it is," Pasha said.

Yuliana set the card on Pasha's plate. "Apparently you've invited all of Saint Petersburg to a fete tonight. It begins in an hour."

Pasha looked at it and sighed. "I suppose, then, we'd better get dressed. But I suggest we go in disguise."

CHAPTER THIRTY-ONE

At a quarter past eleven, Pasha stepped outside the Winter Palace. He stroked his blond mustache (not real, but convincing enough) and adjusted the fake spectacles on his nose. His uniform, too, was carefully planned, from a common soldier's hat down to his boots, all covered with a plain gray greatcoat.

Yuliana linked her arm through his. She grumbled as she looked down at the worn brown coat Pasha had "borrowed" for her from a servant girl.

"The wool itches," Yuliana said.

"It's better if we go to the fete like this," he said.

"I know. But it still itches."

Pasha laughed—blazes, it felt good to break the tension like that, if only for a second—and led the way toward the Neva, where Nikolai's party was already lively on the ice.

Every man and woman in Saint Petersburg appeared to be here. They skated to the music of a string orchestra. Laughed beneath chandeliers of candles, and gold garlands and bells and bows held aloft by stone birds in the night sky. Devoured a feast and talked with their mouths full, chairs packed with merchants next to sailors next to laundry girls.

And all around them, life-size dolls with porcelain faces bustled about, refilling wineglasses and refreshing empty platters with more food.

Pasha shivered. The dolls were beautiful, but they were also all wrong. Elegance tainted with haunting. "They're like the Jack and ballerina, gone spine-chillingly mad."

"I think Nikolai himself has gone mad," Yuliana said as she took in the scene. "Perhaps you should use your necklace to summon Vika. If the invitations went out only to the people of Saint Petersburg, she won't have received one out on her island."

Pasha frowned. "We've asked a great deal of her lately. Give her a night at home in peace. Besides, you and I have been to enough fetes in our lives that we can handle another one. We're merely gathering information."

Yuliana pursed her lips at him skeptically.

A group of fisherman walked past, and one said, "This party is extraordinary." He took a long swig from a bottle of vodka.

Another nodded, a bottle in his hand, too. "Let's hope the tsesarevich does this for us every year."

A third fisherman chimed in, "If he does, I think I could get used to magic."

"Hear, hear!" the first man said. He raised his bottle in the air, and the group guffawed and continued through the snow to the ice rink.

"Well, that's a good thing, that they're beginning to accept magic," Pasha whispered to Yuliana.

She clutched his arm a bit more tightly. "It would be if you and Vika had truly created this fete. But it's Nikolai's. Something is bound to go bad."

Pasha shivered again.

Someone cleared his throat behind them. Pasha nearly jumped out of his boots.

"My apologies, Your Imperial Highness," Ilya whispered as he leaned in. "But I only wanted to make my presence known in the event that you need me."

Pasha settled back into his boots. He'd made the decision to tell the Guard that he and Yuliana would arrive at the fete later, around midnight, which was partly true, for he'd only meant to steal through the party right now as reconnaissance before making an official appearance, as himself, later on. But of course, if anyone would discover that he'd snuck out of the palace early, it was Ilya. This was, after all, why Pasha had chosen him to spy on Volkonsky and the constitutionalists. Ilya was awfully good at knowing and seeing things he wasn't supposed to know and see.

Pasha's stomach growled.

"Perhaps you'd like something to eat while you investigate?" Ilya asked.

"Not a bad idea."

"It's a terrible idea," Yuliana said.

A life-size porcelain doll skated by carrying a fresh tureen of borscht. Pasha inhaled deeply, the warmth of the beet soup wrapping around and through him, just as another doll glided up to him with a plate of miniature tarts, filled with caramelized onions, gruyere cheese, and thyme.

"*Tarte à l'oignon?*" she asked in a dainty voice perfectly suited for a porcelain doll.

He smiled. *"Merci."* He popped one into his mouth as Yuliana cried out, "Pasha!"

He swallowed and shrugged. "I couldn't resist. It's been so long since supper, and *tarte à l'oignon* is one of my favorites."

Yuliana flung herself at him and shook him by the shoulders. "I know! And Nikolai knows! Why else would he serve a French country tart at a party where all the other food is Russian?"

"Sacré bleu," Pasha whispered.

The sweetness of the onion was already turning acrid on his tongue. No, not acrid. Metallic. Yuliana was right. Nikolai had done this on purpose. He must've seen through Pasha's disguise—of course he knew most of what Pasha had in his wardrobe, since they'd snuck out innumerable times together over the years—and sent a doll specifically with the tart.

"Yuliana—" Pasha clutched at his throat with one hand and his stomach with another. His knees gave way beneath him as something sharp lanced through his insides.

Ilya lunged and caught him.

"Quickly, we need to get him out of plain sight," Yuliana said to Ilya under her breath. She laughed—forcibly—and said loudly enough for those nearby to hear, "You really shouldn't drink so much before eating."

Ilya hoisted Pasha's arm around his shoulder, and the two staggered back toward the palace with Yuliana close behind.

But Pasha doubled over after a few yards. He convulsed and coughed into the snow.

"I think I'm bleeding," he whispered when the fit had passed.

Yuliana gasped as Pasha's hand came away from where he'd covered his mouth. It was slick and deep crimson.

"Here," Ilya said, steering them to the other side of a snowbank. It wasn't much, but it was some cover from the partygoers.

Pasha collapsed. He coughed some more, and red spattered the dirty snow. His consciousness rapidly bled out with it.

But just as everything was about to go black, Pasha grappled at the collar of his uniform and yanked the basalt necklace out. He clutched his fingers around it.

"Vika," he whispered. "Can you hear me? I need you."

His voice and his lungs gave out. And then everything went as dark as the basalt.

CHAPTER THIRTY-TWO

Vika jerked upright from the log upon which she sat. She was home on Ovchinin Island, next to Preobrazhensky Creek, but Pasha's voice was as clear as if he were sitting right beside her.

He sounded like the bewildered boy who'd stumbled upon her here in the woods, in the middle of lightning and flame. The one who'd asked her for her first dance at his masquerade. The boy who'd almost kissed her in the maple grove.

Unlike Nikolai, who had become increasingly, painfully unfamiliar, this sounded like the Pasha she knew. Vika's remaining resistance against him crumbled like a fortress made of sand.

"I hear you," she said. "And I'm coming."

Vika appeared at the snowbank along the Neva moments later.

"He ate a tart that Nikolai tainted," Yuliana said.

Vika took in the crimson snow. It was all she needed to know that whatever Pasha had consumed had been a tart only in appearance. *Nikolai, what have you done?* Her heart stopped beating.

It resumed several seconds later, but the rhythm was different. Their mazurka was forever done. Vika's entire body drooped.

"Can you evanesce him back to the palace?" Yuliana asked.

Vika stared, half here but half still lamenting the loss of Nikolai.

"Vika!"

"What? Oh." Vika shook her head, jostling away the heaviness that was Nikolai. She had before her a boy who was still here and who needed her attention, right now. "The tsesarevich is too fragile. I don't want to risk it. But I can cast a shroud so that if anyone comes upon us, they'll see only a mound of snow." She enchanted the air around them, then dropped to her knees.

"Pasha, it's Vika. I'm here." She was fully aware this was the first time in a long time that she'd called him by his name, in his presence. But that was because it finally felt necessary and right again. He wasn't just "Your Imperial Highness." He was Pasha.

He stirred, eyes closed and body limp. "Blood . . . Nikolai . . . fitting this is how it ends . . . ," he muttered.

"This is *not* how it ends," Vika said. "I'm going to strip you from the waist up."

"You'll do no such thing!" Yuliana said. "He's the heir to the throne."

"Well, he won't be heir if he dies, and I'll be much better

able to see whatever it is inside him if I strip off his clothes. So I'm going to do it whether it's proper or not."

"He'll freeze to death."

Vika scowled but snapped her fingers, and a fire roared to life at her side. There was no wood, just flame rising out of the snow.

Yuliana shut her mouth, another unprecedented move. But there was no time for Vika to gloat.

She began to unbutton Pasha's greatcoat. He moaned and gripped it closed.

"Shhh. I'm trying to see where you've been hurt. Then I'm going to heal you."

She finished removing his greatcoat and took off his uniform jacket and shirt.

"The rabbits are dancing in the clouds," Pasha murmured. "They're pretty."

"You're losing him," Yuliana said. "Hurry."

Vika rested her hands on Pasha's muscled chest and listened to his pulse. It fluttered, but it was there. His breathing was ragged but consistent. Then he shivered.

"Cold," he said. "Winter is so cold. Even the polar bears are gone."

The fire wasn't enough. He needed heat directly on his skin.

She could be that heat. . . .

Vika's temperature certainly rose a little at the thought.

It wasn't appropriate in the least. But if he was dying, that called for drastic measures, whether respectable or not.

Besides, this was about saving Pasha's life.

Of course it was.

She rested her cheek on Pasha's bare chest and curled her

body alongside his, laying her arm across him, her hand on his right shoulder blade. But despite lying on the snow, Vika flushed at her proximity to him. She felt all his muscles—from fencing, from archery, from the myriad other activities he did—and she tensed. But Pasha sighed and relaxed against her.

Yuliana, surprisingly, did not say a thing. And Ilya stood stoic, the consummate soldier.

Vika breathed Pasha in. He was sweat and blood, but he was also soap and a hint of clove.

Don't think about him like that. He's the tsesarevich.

He's also a brave, wounded boy. He's Pasha.

Vika's resentment over the end of the Game had already begun to thaw before this, but now the rest of it melted away.

She shut her eyes. With her cheek pressed against him, she could more easily see the fibers of his flesh. Not literally see them, but she could sense them, how they wove together and layered. And where they were torn apart and frayed.

Oh, heavens. What lay in his stomach might have looked like a tart when he ate it, but now it was a gear, like a component of one of Nikolai's machines. Except the spoke-like edges were razor sharp, a wheel of knives in miniature. And that wheel had rolled all the way down Pasha's insides and left a shredded, bloody mess in its wake.

Nikolai was probably pleased with himself for tricking Pasha, a boy who loved being in disguise, with a deadly weapon, also in disguise.

"What happened to him?" Yuliana asked.

Vika opened her eyes but didn't answer, only shook her

head. Then she closed her eyes once more and lay back down on Pasha's chest.

I can fix him, she told herself. She'd healed injuries in the animals on Ovchinin Island for years. She'd stitched herself back together after the knife slashed through her organs at the end of the Game. *Just like fixing a broken bone, I can do this, too. I have to.*

She cast an enchantment to pin him down. "Pasha, this is going to hurt, but trust me. I know what I'm doing."

It was an utter lie, but she wasn't going to tell Pasha—or Yuliana—that. She just had to hope that the increase in Bolshebnoie Duplo's magic would be enough to push her power farther than she'd accomplished before. And that she'd be able to keep the magic steady. It was already jittering and sparking inside her, like racehorses about to take off on a steeplechase.

With her head on his chest, Vika placed her hand above his stomach and focused on the spot where Nikolai's gear lay. She was going to evanesce it out, but it was imperative that she get it right, for she could not afford to evanesce away a crucial part of Pasha's body.

She concentrated until she saw every sharp ridge. Every protrusion. And every bit of muscle and organ and blood that touched the metal. Then Vika took a deep breath and imagined the gear transforming into bubbles.

It dissolved, but as it did so, Pasha shrieked and shuddered beneath the enchantment that kept him immobilized against the ground. Yuliana and Ilya jumped forward at his cries. Vika threw a wave of magic to keep them back. "There's a wheel of knives inside his body that is making its way out," she said, trying to maintain as even a voice as possible. "The evanescing particles still need a path on which to travel, so a wound has opened, and he's feeling it right now."

Vika pressed her cheek against Pasha's chest and shook along with him, her trembling coming from holding tightly to the magic to control it, and his from the pain. She blew what she hoped was warm, numbing air from her lips to the nearly undetectable opening on his abdomen from which the bubbles streamed.

As the gear's particles made their way out of Pasha's body, Vika could feel them scraping against the wet fibers of his flesh while they tore open an exit route. She cringed, feeling Pasha's screams as if they were her own. But still, she held the magic steady, even though it wanted to burst out like water freeing itself from a dam.

Finally, the last of the gear came out. It rematerialized in Vika's palm, and she dropped it onto the snow, red splattering on white. She shook nearly as wretchedly as Pasha did.

But she couldn't take too long, for Pasha's insides had been shredded, and he would die soon if she didn't save him.

Keeping her face pressed to his chest above his heart, Vika splayed her hands over Pasha's stomach and at the base of his throat. *Knit yourselves back together*, she commanded the sinews of his muscle. Now she could let the magic flow more freely, for she wasn't extracting knives anymore. The power gushed forth smoothly, like warm honey.

She guided Pasha's broken muscle fibers. The veins and nerves that crisscrossed his torso slowly wove themselves back into place. He cried out as she guided his organs back together again. His entire body convulsed.

"I've got you." Vika wrapped herself around him tighter. "Shh. I've got you."

And then, finally, the last of his muscles smoothed over. *Thank goodness.* Vika collapsed on top of him.

Her basalt pendant lay askew on his chest. She almost kissed it. Kissed him.

But Vika tore her gaze away. She had to get him somewhere that was actually warm and safe for him to recover. She had to stop thinking about him as more than . . . whatever he was. Her employer. Her ruler. Her . . . friend.

"Let's go," she said. Then, knowing he was slightly less fragile now, she evanesced Pasha back to the Winter Palace.

CHAPTER THIRTY-THREE

Nikolai had stayed for most of the fete, although he'd remained shrouded and hidden in the dark. It had been a pleasure, at first, to watch his plans fulfilled, to see people eating and laughing and toasting Pasha for the party. And then there had been the moment when he'd recognized Pasha in the crowd and sent the doll with the *tarte à l'oignon*. Nikolai had laughed, the thrill of power washing over him, cold rushing through his veins.

But his laughter had been cut off by Vika's appearance. He'd watched helplessly while she healed Pasha, both unable to get past her shield and horribly fascinated by the work she undertook. For Nikolai's poisoned gear should have shredded Pasha's insides beyond repair; it wasn't a clean slice like a knife. The growth of Bolshebnoie Duplo's magic was affecting Vika's strength, too.

As she evanesced them away, Nikolai threw his top hat into the snow. His knuckles cracked as he balled his hands into fists. Damn it! Pasha was still alive. And Vika . . . how quickly she'd appeared at Pasha's side, and how tenderly she'd nursed him.

Nikolai grumbled and glared at the revelers around him. Many were beginning to clutch at their stomachs, their complexions tinted slightly green now, rather than ruddy from the wind and snow.

"The fete is over," he said.

He snapped at his stone birds. They dropped their decorations from the sky and started to dive at the partygoers instead. People shrieked, fell to their hands and knees on the ice, and cowered under tables. The birds smashed around them, explosions of rock, leaving nothing but dust.

Nikolai nodded at the dolls, who until that second, had still been bustling about, serving dessert and wine. Now they began to fling whatever they had in their hands—food and platters and bottles—at the crowds beneath the tables.

The people screamed even louder. They crawled out of their hiding places and scrambled to their feet, standing, then falling, then trying to get up again on the icy Neva. Wine and vodka bottles shattered. Plates crashed. *Syrniki* pancakes splattered everywhere, making the ground even more perilous with cottage cheese and honey on top of the already slippery ice.

Everyone fled. Nikolai's dolls made sure of it. And then, when the last of the partygoers was gone, he slashed an arm through the air and decapitated all the dolls. Their lifeless bodies smacked into the ice, their porcelain heads shattering.

The Neva was a graveyard of revelry and regret.

Nikolai's edges were a blur. Standing suddenly seemed too much effort. He sank down onto the bank of snow.

He shivered, but not from the cold that had fueled his

rampage, for he'd expended so much energy, he could feel only a trace of that powerful chill inside. Instead, it was the actual weather that got to him. He pulled his greatcoat more tightly around himself.

The more Nikolai faded, the less single-mindedly angry he became. Or was it the other way around? Regardless, as he sat on the snow, taking in the disastrous remnants of his party, he began to remember another time when Pasha had fallen ill.

Nikolai had been fourteen then, and Pasha, thirteen. They'd spent an afternoon in the woods near Tsarskoe Selo, building elaborate traps to capture squirrels, However, they had used up all their lunch as bait, and after a few hours, Pasha complained of starving. Nikolai, in his youthful arrogance, picked mushrooms, charmed the poison out of them, and gave them to Pasha, assuring him they were safe to eat.

Pasha gobbled them up without hesitation, and fifteen minutes later, he was pale and sweating and then fell unconscious. Nikolai panicked, punched Pasha in the stomach to try to make him vomit, shook him to try to jostle him awake. Finally, Nikolai's senses returned, and he levitated Pasha and charged through the forest to their horses. He'd never ridden faster than that in his life to rush his best friend back to the palace at Tsarskoe Selo.

Now Nikolai looked at the spot near the fete where Pasha had lain only minutes before.

What have I done?

But immediately, a tiny chill roused itself and trickled in his veins.

No. This is what I wanted.

Well, not exactly this, for Nikolai had wanted Pasha

dead, and he was not. But this devastation was part of a plan that Nikolai had set in motion, and he would see it through. He was not a quitter. The coldness inside him, although running thin, persisted.

Nikolai stood. He needed to glean more energy. He tripped, though, and nearly toppled into the snow.

First, before finding another source of energy, he needed some rest, to get his head straight again, to refocus. He turned toward the Black Moth.

And this time, he looked forward to the sordid inn.

CHAPTER THIRTY-FOUR

The clock on Madame Boulangère's wall struck midnight as Renata kneaded dough for the bread the bakers would put in the ovens in a few hours. And yet, despite how late it was, Renata felt lighter on her feet. A second wind, perhaps, like the kind that comes after one has been awake so long, one bypasses sleep and starts over again?

But Renata frowned. This was more than that. It was as if her blood was twirling through her veins, when all it was supposed to do was flow from heart to limbs and back again.

Heavens. She knew this sensation. Like she'd drunk nectar offered by mischievous fairies. It had been the same when Aizhana had transferred energy to her earlier tonight, unforgettable not only for the feeling itself, but also for the surprise that embracing a corpse could have produced such impish joy.

Now that thrill whirled through her veins, except it was wilder and brighter than before. *I wonder if this is how magic feels to Nikolai?*

She laughed at the thought. Magic? In me? How silly.

But then . . . why not?

The floor was covered in a fresh dusting of flour from the dough she'd just kneaded. Renata scrunched her face and stared at a broom in the corner. "Sweep," she said, as she snapped twice like she'd seen Nikolai do.

The broom remained stubbornly in the corner.

Renata glanced over her shoulder. Not that there was anyone else inside the bakery. Still, she flushed, embarrassed for even half hoping she could use magic like an enchanter could. She was only a servant girl, after all.

She poured herself a cup of tea and leaned against the pastry display. The steam curled up like wispy acrobats, somersaulting into the air. She took a sip, but the tea scalded her tongue.

"Ugh. Hurry up and cool down." Renata set the cup on the counter and turned back to her bread dough, setting each round in a basket and covering it with a towel for its final rise. Then she picked up the broom that had refused to budge and swept the floor as ordinary people did.

But behind her, the steam acrobats had vanished, and the tea had already—much quicker than normal—cooled enough to drink.

CHAPTER THIRTY-FIVE

Vika sat in an armchair in Pasha's room and watched as the blue-and-gold blankets that warmed the tsesarevich's bare chest rose and fell with his breath. Yuliana had left at one o'clock to rest and had promised to come back well before sunrise, but for a little longer, Vika could be with Pasha alone. The crease between his brows was relaxed, and his blond lashes fluttered against his cheeks in what was hopefully a happy dream. In his sleep, he was just an unguarded boy.

She bit her lip, though, because when Pasha woke, that crease between his brows would reappear, carrying with it the weight of being attacked by his brother, on top of all the other responsibilities and worries that being the next tsar would hold.

But hadn't they all changed? Life happened without permission, and it swept everyone along in its violent wake. Pasha was no longer the innocent tsesarevich. Vika was no longer a carefree girl from the forest. And Nikolai . . . Vika wasn't sure *what* Nikolai was now, but he was no longer purely elegance and melancholy. He was still those things, but twisted and magnified.

Nikolai and Vika were no longer two sides of the same enchanting coin. How could she save him if she couldn't even understand him anymore? Her stomach turned.

Beneath the covers, Pasha stirred. Vika stood and hurried to his side.

He groaned as he found his way back to consciousness. As Vika had predicted, the crease on his forehead reappeared even before his eyes opened.

He squinted at the single lamp that lit the room. Then he turned to his bedside. "Vika?" Pasha's voice rasped. But he moved to sit up as soon as he saw her.

"Don't strain yourself!" She held out her hand as if to stop him.

Pasha sat up anyway. Of course he did. He was the tsesarevich, and that meant he did whatever he wanted. That is, unless Yuliana said otherwise.

"You saved my life."

Vika shrugged.

"You're terribly nonchalant," Pasha said. "It's as if you do this every day." He laughed, but it was flatter than usual, weighed down, most likely, by why it had been necessary to save him in the first place. Then he stopped laughing altogether and held on to his stomach. Magic might have put his pieces back together, but that didn't mean he wouldn't feel the aftereffects, like a patient after surgery. Pasha managed to shoot Vika a smile, though, through the pain.

Vika smiled, too. It was nearly impossible not to in reaction to his charm. Plus, without the blankets covering him, she could see the ripples of muscle on his chest and abdomen. She tried not to stare. "I'd rather not have to stitch you back together every day. It's not exactly easy, and I can't guarantee it'll work every time. So if you don't mind, try not to get yourself almost killed again, all right?"

"I'll try," he said. "But I must warn you that tsars are often high on assassination target lists."

"Good thing you're not tsar yet, then."

As soon as she said it, Vika wanted to take it back. *Really?* she chastised herself. *You said that in the midst of everything that's happening?*

Pasha let out a curt laugh. "Right. Good thing I'm not yet tsar."

I am an idiot, Vika thought.

Pasha brushed his fingers over the place where Vika had extracted Nikolai's gear. Once. Twice. Three times.

"I'm sorry about what I just said." Vika couldn't take her eyes off Pasha's fingers, still tracing and retracing where his brother had wounded him. "But I've been thinking. I ought to protect you better."

Pasha shook his head. "You saved me. There's not much better than that."

"No, I meant a permanent shield, which I'd thought before was impossible, because that sort of magic requires a great deal of power and, therefore, proximity. But now that Bolshebnoie Duplo is generating more magic than ever before . . ."

"You might be able to do it." His fingers ceased their obsessive tracing.

"*Might*. I'll try, but that doesn't mean you can toss caution to the wind. It's possible it won't work, and we won't know until Nikolai tries to harm you again."

Pasha cringed. Vika did, too, for she had said it as if another attack by Nikolai was inevitable. She and Pasha both knew it to be true, even if they didn't want it to be.

"Do I need to, um, do anything?" he asked.

"No, just sit still."

Vika stood from her chair but took a second to breathe and feel the magic sparking inside her. It brightened even more as she called to it, so much so that she almost felt there was a torch within. She welcomed its eager flames— she was, in this moment, pleased that magic was no longer secret, that the people's belief had stoked more power for her to use—and then she focused on Pasha, outlined the space around him with her eyes, and conjured an invisible shield around him.

She imagined it as a soft, flexible material, one that would not repel bullets or enchantments but rather, would absorb them until she could dispel them safely. It seemed a better approach than conjuring a rigid barrier like a more traditional shield, for something like that could potentially shatter.

Then again, all this was theory. Vika didn't even know if this enchantment would hold.

She stumbled a bit when she finished. Conjuring a shield that strong, and to last indefinitely, had taken more out of her than she expected.

"Sit and rest," Pasha said, as he patted the edge of the mattress. "And thank you."

Vika eyed the spot where Pasha's hand lay. Heat flashed through her again, but not from magic this time. It would be incredibly improper to sit on *any* boy's bed, but especially the future tsar's. Not that Vika hadn't already been ridiculously close when she'd healed him. Nor had she ever been constrained by propriety before. But still. This seemed different. Perhaps she was growing up and becoming more responsible. Perhaps she was learning to play by the rules.

Oh, please. Vika scowled at herself. *As if I ever want to be the sort who plays by the rules.*

She sank onto the edge of Pasha's bed. She did, however, sit closer to his feet than his hand, and she kept both her own feet firmly planted on the ground. She was an Imperial Enchanter and a baroness, after all.

Pasha retracted his hand and frowned. "I wasn't going to do anything untoward."

"I know," Vika said, even though she didn't. Or maybe she was worried that *she* would be the one to do something untoward, so great was her relief that Pasha was all right, and that her attempt to heal him had actually worked. Even though she was no longer angry at him, and even though she could no longer love Nikolai—not as Nikolai was—Vika would not allow herself to fall into someone else's arms, simply because they were open. She didn't say all that, though. Instead, she asked, "What if Yuliana came in and thought there was something inappropriate going on?"

"I didn't know you cared what others thought."

"I don't." Vika crossed her arms. But then she dropped them to her sides, onto the blankets. "Well, sometimes I do."

Pasha smiled. "All right, sit far away if it makes you feel better." He had the grace not to rub it in that Vika had been acting, well, self-important. *Just because he wanted to kiss me once, on Letniy Isle, doesn't mean he always wants to kiss me when we're alone*, she thought. *Or that he even wants to kiss me at all, after the nasty things I've said.*

But then Pasha's hand crept toward hers on the bedspread, although he stopped before he actually touched Vika. His fingers were long and impeccably manicured, evidence of his life in the Winter Palace. Hers were smaller, of course, with nails smooth but permanently stained from dirt beneath them, a fond reminder of her life in the unkempt woods of Ovchinin Island.

When she glanced up, she found he was looking at their hands, too.

"There's a story that Plato told," he said softly. "That people were once happy and whole. They were so powerful, they seemed a threat to Olympus. So Zeus split each person in two, such that they were then halves, each imperfect and damned to wander the earth, flawed and no longer competition for the gods. But if a half happened upon his or her other side, they could be united, happy and whole and perfect again."

Vika looked at their hands as she contemplated the anecdote.

"So I'm a half?" she asked.

"Everyone is a half."

"Then you're saying I'm imperfect."

Pasha laughed. "Of course *that's* what you'd gather from my story. *Everyone* is imperfect. That's the point. You can't keep looking for perfection, because it doesn't exist on its own."

"Only when you're united as a whole."

"Exactly. Then somehow, two imperfect halves come together and form a perfect whole." He leaned a little bit forward so his fingertips could just graze hers. Vika's entire body tingled.

Pasha retracted his hand and smiled to himself.

"What?" Vika asked.

Pasha shook his head, still smiling. "Nothing. Just . . . that was nice. I'd like to keep that moment. I'm going to tuck it away somewhere safe."

Vika blushed at his sweetness. This was why she'd liked him in the past. This pure Pasha, who could appreciate a single moment of life even in the midst of attempted murder and an unknown future.

He closed his eyes and leaned back against the headboard. She listened to him breathe, and once again thanked the heavens (and magic) that he was still alive to do so.

Then Pasha opened his eyes, and the crease between his brows reappeared, heralding the end of their respite. "I suppose we should discuss how to deal with Nikolai. He's clearly gone beyond civil disobedience now."

Pasha's eyes were rimmed red, and his hand went to his stomach again. "I can't believe he actually tried to kill me."

Vika's breath caught, as she felt again those memories of Nikolai pulling and piercing her at the same time.

"Yuliana wants him dead," Pasha said softly.

Vika clutched the bedspread in her fist, even though she'd known this was coming. "And what do you want?"

"Too many things . . . including not making the same mistakes again." Pasha bit his knuckles as he thought. "But what can be done? He tried to kill me, Vika. My own brother. And part of me has already died, just by Nikolai making the attempt." Pasha pounded his chest, as if trying to revive his heart.

"You have to catch him, Vika. And I hate to ask this of you, but then you'll also have to help to execute him. An enchanter won't die by simple hanging."

For a moment, Vika lost control of the powerful magic in her fingertips, and she singed the bedspread. Smoke spiraled up in menacing swirls.

Pasha jerked back.

She doused the smoke but didn't apologize. Vika was sorry for burning the blanket, but she was not sorry for having and showing her emotions.

She had been tasked with killing Nikolai five times during the Game. She would not do it again, not if there was any possibility of saving him.

But Vika turned to Pasha and said, "I'm at your command." She might be a dragon on a leash, but she was still a dragon. She would stall. She'd find a way to fix this, bracelet or not.

Or, like witches, she and Nikolai would both burn.

CHAPTER THIRTY-SIX

Ilya returned to the barracks after seeing the tsesarevich back to the Winter Palace. He preferred staying in the Guards' quarters even though his family's mansion was only a few streets away; as the fourth son, no one paid him much attention, for there was hardly enough attention to go around for three boys, let alone for number four. But Major General Volkonsky had noticed Ilya when he was a cadet training for the Guard, and ever since then, the army felt more like home to Ilya than his parents and brothers at Koshkin Place.

Tonight, however, he was not greeted by smacks on the back from his fellow soldiers, but instead by their retching into buckets and moaning through cold sweats in their beds. The sole medic darted from cot to cot, also sweating, but from exertion rather than whatever ailed the rest of the men.

"What happened, Boris?" Ilya asked, throwing his greatcoat onto a hook and rolling up his sleeves to help in whatever manner he could.

Boris made the sign of the cross across his body. "They all went to the fete on the Neva and ate the magical food and wine. It's made everyone violently ill. No good can come of gifts from the devil, and the tsesarevich and his witch are proof."

Ilya lowered his voice. "You could be arrested for speaking against the tsesarevich like that."

"After tonight, see if there aren't more men who agree with me." Boris threw his arms in the air and gestured at the soldiers around them. "Besides, I doubt anyone can hear me above this noise." More retching and groaning echoed through the barracks.

"What can I do to help?"

"You can start by emptying buckets. We're going to need more soon."

Ilya made the error of looking into one and gagged. But he was a soldier and had spent his share of time on latrine duty in school, so he pulled a handkerchief out of his pocket, tied it around his nose and mouth, and picked up the bucket.

Come tomorrow, the underground movement for a constitutional monarchy would have plenty of men to recruit. They could use as many soldiers as possible for their cause, as they were planning a revolt in the summer. And Volkonsky would count on Ilya to convince these men to turn on the tsardom.

Ilya's stomach twisted again, although this time, it was because the reality of the revolt drew closer. And it wasn't against Tsar Alexander now, as originally planned. Since the tsar was dead, it would be a revolt against Pasha, whom Ilya actually liked.

These were the reasons Ilya hadn't reported anything

to Pasha about Volkonsky. Ilya's loyalties were conflicted in too many ways.

But he believed in the constitutionalists' cause. Nobles and serfs and everyone in between should be equal. Even as the fourth son of an aristocratic family, he'd felt the sting of being cast aside as unimportant. He could hardly even conceive what indignities serfs had to suffer.

Most of all, Ilya believed in Volkonsky. So he would do it. He would clean vomit tonight and recruit men tomorrow. And when the revolt came, he would stand behind Volkonsky. Even if it meant no longer serving by Pasha's side.

CHAPTER THIRTY-SEVEN

As soon as Vika left Pasha and stepped out of the Winter Palace, she whistled into the dark sky, a long, melodic summons.

A few minutes later, an albino rat appeared on the cobblestones at Vika's feet. She knelt and scooped Poslannik up onto her shoulder. They didn't have to wait long for the hum of moths' wings and the hiss of all the city's stray cats to fill the air. Vika circled her pinkie over them and made the enchantment permanent this time, so that they would be able to understand each other without the need for additional magic every time.

"I need you to find Nikolai," Vika told them. "He's cast a barrier over himself, so I can't trace his magic. You might be able to find him, though. It's not as if he's invisible, just . . . stealthy. But so are all of you. You'll be much faster than I am, traipsing through the streets and alleys and bridges on my own."

Poslannik, who acted as general of this army, squeaked his assent to her command.

"Oh, one more thing," Vika said. "Nikolai is a shadow now, so don't look for an intact person."

The moths batted their wings and the cats hissed in understanding.

But Vika shuddered as what she'd said resonated fully, for it was true in a horrible sense, wasn't it? Nikolai was not intact. He'd been broken, and it was as if a jagged shard of his soul was leading the remainder of him.

And now, just as the tea leaves had predicted, Vika was fighting against him. Trying to trap him. Ushering in death once again.

But it had to be done. Nikolai's threats were not abstract anymore, and Russia's future teetered on what Vika did. She would find him, put him somewhere safe only she could access, and then save him. Somehow.

Well, perhaps I can just focus on the first and second steps now and deal with the third later.

Vika waved her arm in the air, and thousands of moths flew off all at once, the noise of their wings like a forest shedding its leaves all at once. The moths filled the sky, first as a white cloud blocking out the moon, and then they spread out, a net cast over Saint Petersburg in a hunt for a shadow boy.

The hair on the backs of the cats stood on end, and they scratched at the icy cobblestones at their feet. Vika nodded at Poslannik. He squeaked a series of commands. And then the cats screeched and bolted out of Palace Square in every direction, a beautiful pandemonium of determination.

I hope Nikolai surrenders easily, Vika thought as she watched the last of Poslannik's army go.

But what were the odds of that? Absolutely none.

When the sound of her army dissipated, though, it was

not quiet that fell upon the night, but pandemonium of a different kind.

Shouts. Deep, rhythmic, and unified.

They were not far away, possibly on the Neva, where the disastrous fête had been. Vika evanesced herself to the frozen river.

She gaped at the detritus of Nikolai's party, not only tables covered with leftover food dripping off their dishes and overturned chairs, but also decapitated dolls with their heads smashed in. It was like the state of Nikolai's soul, laid bare on the ice.

There was also a crowd gathered on the embankment. They formed a circle, surrounding something Vika couldn't quite see. But their chanting was unmistakable.

"Burn the witch! Burn the witch! Burn the witch!"

Vika gasped and ducked behind a nearby tree. This was what Sergei had warned her about when she was young, that normal people would not be able to understand magic, that their fear would propel them against her.

And it was Vika they wanted to burn, not Nikolai, for she'd convinced Pasha and Yuliana that it was better not to reveal the existence of another enchanter, because the city was frightened enough of one. Hence, Vika shouldered the blame (again) for what Nikolai had done. But it was to protect him, and to keep some semblance of sanity in the empire.

Vika was not sure if the latter was working.

A girl's scream pierced through the mob's shouts. "Let me go! I'm not the witch! Someone help!"

"Tie her tighter," a man yelled. "Don't believe her lies!"

Oh, mercy, they're trying to burn someone else in my place! Vika spun away from the tree and hurtled toward the mob.

She probably should have cast a shroud around herself, a disguise or at least less identifiable hair, but all she could think about at the moment was getting to the girl.

The crowd was larger than she'd initially thought. They formed a tight-knit ring, six to seven people deep. Vika tried to shove them aside but was met with snarls and elbows.

One of the men she attempted to push away glared at her. But when he looked at her—or, more likely, recognized the black stripe in her red hair—he grabbed her arm. "You!"

Vika jerked back, but his grip tightened. "You're the witch! You're the one who has my Misha vomiting blood tonight!"

"It's not my fault," Vika said, not that he would believe her. "But it's not that girl's either, and I have to stop them from burning her before it's too late. Release me."

The man spit in Vika's face. "You're not going anywhere. And for all we know, that's your sister at the stake. Better to burn her just in case than to be sorry."

Vika charmed the spit off her cheek and flung it back at the man's face. He yelped.

"I respectfully disagree on both counts," Vika said. "It is not better to kill someone 'just in case.' And I am absolutely going somewhere."

With that, she commanded the wind to rush at her assailant, and it lifted him off his feet, hurling him onto a snowbank several yards away. The string of profanities he shouted at Vika were equally blown away.

And then she evanesced into the center of the mob.

They cried out as she rematerialized. "It's another witch! The girl has called her kin!"

Vika stepped between the red-haired girl, who was

tied to one of Nikolai's upended tables, surrounded by broken chair legs, and the hysterical crowd. "You poor thing,"
she said to the girl, "to be born looking like me. But don't
worry. I'll get you out of here safely." Vika conjured an
iridescent bubble around herself and the pyre, and she
charmed the ropes that lashed the girl to the firewood to
come undone.

The girl fell to her knees. Silent tears and snot streamed
down her face, and her entire body shook.

The mob pounded on the outside of Vika's bubble shield.

Vika wrapped her arms around the girl. "You're safe
now."

The girl shook her head.

"I put up an enchantment to protect us."

"But what about after you're gone?" The girl's voice was
so hoarse, it was more like scratches on dry air than proper
words.

"You can't hide from us forever!" a woman punching at
the shield yelled.

A man opposite her shouted, "The Lord will bring justice! Beware, daughters of the devil!"

Vika looked from them back to the girl. "Where do you
need to go? Do you have family? I'll take you where you feel
secure."

The girl shook her head again. "They won't stop at me.
Everyone who looks like this . . ." She tore at her hair. It was
plastered against her head by tears and sweat, the dampness
making it all the redder. "We're doomed."

Vika touched her own hair. What was she to do? She
couldn't change the color of every red-haired girl in Russia. Besides the impossibility of so large an enchantment,

it would also be held as evidence against the girls of their witchcraft.

Vika had to capture Nikolai soon. His dark magic had to be stopped. It was the only way to end this.

"Come on," Vika said, gathering the girl closer to her chest. "We're leaving."

"But what about them?"

The crowd had begun to stab at the bubble shield with knives, sticks, anything sharp they could find.

Vika looked at the mob. If only she could distract them. But what could possibly steal the attention of a crowd intent on killing witches?

More witches.

Vika chewed on her lip. She'd never conjured illusions before. Yet she had just cast a permanent shield around Pasha (or hoped she had), and she'd never done that before either. Ironically, it was the people's new belief in magic that was fueling Bolshebnoie Duplo to generate more power, which in turn allowed Vika to cast stronger enchantments to use against the very people who feared them.

"I don't know if this will work, but it's worth a try," she said.

She plucked a hair out of her own head and waved her arm at the smoke billowing off the base of the pyre. Vika tossed the hair into it, and the smoke swirled into the shape of a girl with a head full of wavy red hair.

Vika commanded the wind to blow through the smoke girl, breaking it into tiny puffs and carrying it to the outside of the mob's circle. There, each puff expanded into a full-size illusion of a girl made of flesh and blood, not smoke. The crowd was suddenly surrounded by dozens of witches.

The people screamed. "It's an entire coven!"

"The devil has brought his army!"

"Everyone, fight back!"

In their panic, they turned away from the pyre and lunged at the new witches who had appeared.

Vika leaned toward the girl. "They'll be occupied for a few minutes. Tell me where we should go."

The girl trembled. "Lake Ladoga," she whispered. "My aunt has a dacha in the woods."

"All right then. Don't be alarmed, I'm going to dissolve us into tiny bubbles in order to transport us there."

The girl didn't even flinch. Vika doubted much else could compare to the horror of being nearly burned alive on a pyre.

Vika took one more look at the red-faced crowd around her, battling an imaginary enemy. Then she evanesced herself and the girl away.

CHAPTER THIRTY-EIGHT

In other parts of the empire, the growth of Bolshebnoie Duplo's magic manifested itself in wilder ways. . . .

In the middle of the Siberian woods, a dilapidated hut shook as if it were a bird ruffling its feathers. Its two front windows blinked, shaking off the dirt and moss that had accumulated on its sills during the centuries the house had slept. Beneath the foundation, stilt-like chicken legs stretched and lifted the entire hut twenty feet off the snow-covered floor. The joints of the chicken legs—and of the hut itself—creaked as they began to stomp through the forest.

Baba Yaga's house was awake. Now it needed to find its owner. Then they could begin tricking—and eating—unsuspecting travelers again.

On the Kamchatka Peninsula in the far east, volcano nymphs grinned with needlelike teeth and danced, their lithe, naked red bodies like flames in a bonfire. The frosty ground around them quaked, and their volcanoes spewed smoke and ash. The craters had been dormant for hundreds of years, since their caretakers—the nymphs—had not had enough magic to stoke the fires in the volcanoes' bellies.

But now, by some miracle, they did. And as the air above them clouded red-gray, the nymphs laughed and drank blue honeysuckle wine and felt giddy with the knowledge that one day—hopefully soon—they would be strong enough to make the volcanoes erupt, to chase away the humans who dared to build villages and encroach on what was the nymphs' land.

In the southern part of the empire, along the Volga River, a peasant boy trudged out of his family's cottage to fetch water. He shivered in the winter chill, and it was difficult to see, because the moon barely shone through the cloud cover. But the boy pushed onward. His mother had been ill for days, and she desperately needed more to drink. The pitchers in the cottage were empty. This task could not wait until daylight.

The boy set down his bucket on the riverbank and began to chip at the ice with a pickax.

It should have taken him a long while to get through the river's surface. And yet, three swings in, the ice cracked and parted. Water gushed upward, as if it had been waiting for the boy to free it. He hurriedly pressed the lip of his bucket into the water before it froze over again.

When the bucket was full, the boy hauled it out of the river. He turned away. He lifted a snowy boot in the direction of his home.

There was a sudden loud crack behind him. But there had been no one else out on the river. As the boy spun around to see what had happened, a giant catfish burst out of the Volga. Its head alone was larger than the boy. Bedraggled strands of what appeared to be algae hung and glistened from the monster's head. It glared at the boy's bucket.

The boy dropped the bucket and ran as fast as he could through the snow. He didn't stop until he'd reached home and barricaded the door.

Because he remembered the fables his grandfather had told him—when the moon is in the sky, the river belongs to Vodyanoy, the catfish king. And Vodyanoy did not look kindly upon those who tried to steal from his kingdom.

CHAPTER THIRTY-NINE

At two in the morning, there was a quiet knock at the door of the shack behind the Black Moth.

"Nikolai? It's me."

He rolled over slowly in bed, where he'd been half-asleep, nursing a splitting headache.

"Renata?"

"Yes. Can I come in?"

He glanced over at the other bed (he'd eventually managed to conjure the second mattress he needed). It would be uncomfortable to have Renata here with Aizhana in the room.

But his mother wasn't there. Nikolai wasn't surprised. She was a creature of the night, and she often roamed the streets when it was dark.

Nikolai climbed out of bed and started to comb his hair into place, but he stopped abruptly when he caught a glimpse of himself in the mirror above the washbasin. It didn't matter if his hair was neat or messy, because the shape of it was the same anyway—a splotchy blur.

And his face . . . he could practically see through it, for

it was light gray now rather than charcoal black. *Mon dieu!* How had he faded so much? He was even weaker than last night after the fete.

Nikolai slumped. He took a hat off the nearby rack and set it atop his head. The hat, too, was gray, but at least it had a defined shape.

He flicked his wrist and the lock on the door unlatched with a click.

Renata rushed in, all braids and smiles. She threw her arms around him. He held her, and she melted into his chest. Or rather, Nikolai melted into hers, damn it, because his edges weren't solid.

But as soon as she touched him, he felt a bit better. And he warmed as he realized it was rather intimate, being so close. Nikolai flushed, which probably showed as the tips of his ears shading a touch darker, and pulled away.

"I went looking for you," he said. "But Galina—the harpy—had fired you. Where did you go? Are you all right?"

Renata nodded, still smiling and holding lightly on to Nikolai's arms. "I'm fine. I have a job at Madame Boulangère. I just finished up for the night. And I'm sleeping on the floor in one of the girls' quarters."

"You're sleeping on the floor?" Nikolai flung his hands in the air, inadvertently tossing Renata's off.

"It's all right. I have plenty of blankets, and a place next to the fire to keep me warm. Really, it's better than I could have hoped. But you . . ." She reached out to touch his arm again. "Nikolai, you're still a shadow."

He sighed.

"You need more energy."

He shook his head and scrubbed at the back of his neck. Did she know he was behind the party and all the illness that followed? That that was why he was so weak?

But Renata didn't say anything, and Nikolai decided not to, either. She was the only person he cared about that he had left. As destructive as he'd felt of late, he needed someone right now (besides Aizhana) to still be on his side.

"It's not just that I'm a shadow," Nikolai said. "I'm fading. Literally. I don't know what to do."

"You can take energy from me." Renata nodded to encourage him.

"What? No."

"I'll give you all you need."

Nikolai retreated to the other side of the room. "I can't. I won't. . . . Vika's mentor died because he channeled all his energy to her. And I nearly died at the end of the Game, trying to save Vika, even though I thought I knew what I was doing. I won't accidentally kill you; I wouldn't be able to live with myself afterward."

Renata marched over to him, cornering Nikolai by the washbasin. She grabbed his hand and placed his fingers on her neck. She leaned into him. "Please. I want to do this for you." Then she met his gaze and held it steady, steadier than he'd ever seen her dare to hold it before. "And I want to do this for *me*."

Nikolai flushed again as his body blurred into hers where they touched. He was a conundrum—ethereal enough that their edges blended, yet corporeal enough that she did not pass straight through him.

"Renata . . ."

She placed a finger over his lips. "Nikolai. I love you. Let me do this."

He held his breath. He should say no again, but he wanted to say yes, too. He could already sense her energy beneath her skin, pulsing and yearning. And he was so empty.

Instead of saying yes or no, Nikolai said nothing at all.

Renata lifted her chin and brought his head down to meet hers. Nikolai's heartbeat quickened.

I do need more energy, he thought. *I can't generate enough on my own if I want another chance at Pasha and the throne.*

Renata brushed her lips, just barely, over his.

And then Nikolai's mouth was on hers, gentle but full of wanting. He shouldn't be doing this, not when he knew his love belonged to another girl, with whom his heart ached even now to dance another mazurka. But that girl had chosen Pasha. And here, in his arms, was Renata, insistent yet yielding, and offering something Nikolai needed to feel strong again. Something to destroy his enemy with.

Renata moved herself closer and twined her hands through Nikolai's hair. He sighed at the feeling of her fingers, both for the comfort of them and for the fact that even though he was fading, he was still real enough for her to hold on to.

Renata's lips parted. He could taste a hint of something sweet, the memory of black tea swirled with lemon and two lumps of sugar, what Renata drank every day.

Nikolai pressed his mouth harder against Renata's, and she let out a gasp as his tongue found hers. As he kissed her, he drew energy from her, and it, too, tasted of sugar and lemon and tea.

Black tea, strong and hot.

Renata slid her hands from his hair, down the nape of his neck. Her fingers trailed down the back of his shirt and under the hem. They slipped inside, her palms against Nikolai's back.

He quivered, now connected to her not only at their lips,

but also through her hands on his bare skin, his shadow blurring into her touch. Her energy poured into him as if from a samovar, and Nikolai drank as if inconsolably parched. He wanted, needed, more. He wrapped an arm around Renata's waist to draw her closer, as if his shadow could merge completely into her.

And then, in the next room, a woman yelled at a man and threw what sounded like a pot at him, as it clanged against the wall.

Nikolai jerked away from Renata and released her waist.

"What are you doing?" she asked, eyes still half-closed.

There was a part of Nikolai that wanted to keep kissing her. It was not only the physical wanting, but also the knowledge that he needed more energy if he was ever to be whole again, and Renata was willing to give.

But he was still a gentleman. At least in the moments like right now, when he wasn't overcome by the cold in his veins. And that gentlemanly part of him knew he shouldn't kiss Renata any longer. Nikolai rubbed at his temples. *Think. No, don't think. Just . . . Argh.*

Renata's eyes were fully opened now.

"I'm sorry," Nikolai said. "I shouldn't have done that. I took advantage of you."

"No, you didn't. I offered myself. I knew what it meant, and also what it didn't mean. You don't have to worry about that."

Nikolai reached over and stroked her face. "I always worry about you."

Renata rested her cheek on his hand. "I may never have you entirely, but now I've kissed you, and that was worth it. Don't worry about me. I'm stronger than most people think."

"I know you are."

For a moment, they stayed like that. Then Nikolai pulled his hand away. It was too tempting to draw her back to him if he remained.

"I heard that the countess is gone again," Renata blurted out to break their awkward pause.

"Oh?" Nikolai cocked his head. "Where has Galina disappeared to this time?"

"No one knows. She went for a walk two days ago and never returned."

"She's probably in London or Paris again. It must be nice to be wealthy enough to do that. Simply go and buy what you need when you arrive."

Renata twisted the folds of her skirt. "Yes, but she didn't tell anyone."

"Who would she tell? Cook? The footman?" Nikolai asked wryly. The countess wouldn't think her servants important enough to inform of her whereabouts. The only people she'd bothered to tell in the past when she'd gone on a trip on a whim were her husband and Nikolai, the latter only because she'd task him with some impossible challenge to master while she was away. But Count Zakrevsky was long dead, and Nikolai no longer resided there.

"I'm sure Galina is fine," he said. "She's likely scowling at street urchins in London as we speak. And then one day she'll return, and we'll wish she'd stayed abroad to torture the British orphans instead."

Renata bit back a smile. She'd worked for the countess for so long, the obedience literally beaten into her, that it was hard for her to accept that she was actually allowed to laugh at Galina's expense now. It was like when Renata had been afraid to eat an apple tart during the Game even though Galina was exiled, because servants were never permitted such treats.

"Do it," Nikolai said.

Renata looked up from her skirt. "Do what?"

"Laugh. It's allowed. Besides, if you don't, I'll be offended. I thought what I said was rather funny."

The laughter Renata had restrained came spilling forth.

"It's nice to see your smile again," Nikolai said.

"If only I could see yours, too."

For once, Nikolai did not bristle at being reminded he was a shadow. "Smile or not, right now I feel like I could rule the empire."

Renata's smile faltered. "The empire?"

"It's a long story."

"I have time."

So Nikolai nodded and told her. But as he relayed the details, Renata never once pulled on her braids as she normally did when she was anxious. Only when he finished telling her he'd tried to kill Pasha did it dawn on Nikolai— Renata already knew.

The taste of sugar and lemon and black tea hit him again. She'd known, and she'd come anyway. Not only that, but she'd helped him.

Nikolai should have been happy, and yet his heart felt as if it had been wrapped in chains. It was too bad he didn't love Renata.

But he couldn't. For there was only one who could unravel him, and she wasn't here.

CHAPTER FORTY

Vika nearly collapsed as she stumbled into Cinderella Bakery. She had just returned from safely depositing the hunted girl at her aunt's dacha near Lake Ladoga, and now the entire night—Nikolai's fete, the attempt on Pasha's life, the pyre intended for Vika—had begun to catch up to her.

It was only half past four in the morning, but Ludmila's was where Vika needed to be. Her cottage was too empty without Sergei, and the bakery was the closest place to comfort she knew. The door to Cinderella was ajar, and as Vika stepped inside, the scent of yeast and sugar wrapped around her like a favorite blanket, warm and smelling of home.

The entire surface of the counter was already covered with the morning's loaves. There was a glass bowl filled with apple jelly, and another with sour cherry jam. The *pech*—an enormous stone oven that took up the center of the bakery—was full with trays of *piroshki* and an iron pot of kasha simmered in its hearth.

"Vee-kahhh!" Ludmila sang as she bounced around the

kitchen, waving a wooden spoon. "How wonderful to see you. I'm just about to have a snack."

"Actually, I—"

"Oh, my sunshine!" Ludmila stopped with her spoon in midair. "You look like you've flown through a hurricane of hail. Sit down and I'll . . . I'll get you something to eat. Cookies. You need cookies." She pulled out a chair from the small table in the corner and practically shoved Vika onto the seat. Before Vika could say a thing, she'd already pushed a plate of *sushki*—ring-shaped cookies—in front of her.

"Please, eat," Ludmila said. "No, first tell me you're all right, and then eat."

"I'm not going to lie and say I'm all right when I'm not." Vika poked at one of the *sushki*. "But I'm alive, which I suppose is something."

Ludmila's forehead creased, and she shook her head. "They ask too much of you."

Vika sighed. "It's my job to do what needs to be done."

"But fighting Nikolai again? That was not part of the bargain."

The last time Vika had seen Ludmila was right after Nikolai had threatened to take the crown from Pasha. She had been too busy to visit the baker since. Ludmila would worry even more if she knew all that had transpired in the days that had passed.

Ludmila used a long, fork-like stick to pull the pot of kasha from the hearth but nearly upended the kasha in the process. Vika startled but managed to cast a quick spell to form a gentle barrier, protecting Ludmila from the pot, and the pot from Ludmila. The baker didn't even notice anything had been unsteady. She set the pot on the counter and began to ladle kasha into bowls instead.

A white moth flitted in through a crack in the window and landed in Vika's hair, near her ear.

Vika listened to it intently.

"That was quick," she said, once the moth had finished. "Well done. Thank you."

The moth fluttered its wings and took off through the opening in the window again.

"Do I want to know what that was about?" Ludmila asked.

Vika began to push her chair back from the table. "Poslannik's army found Nikolai."

"They did?" Ludmila set down the bowls of kasha so abruptly, some of the porridge spilled onto the tablecloth.

This time, Vika didn't bother with a charm to clean it up. She was too preoccupied with the moth's news. "He's staying in Sennaya Square."

"Sennaya Square . . . it doesn't seem the sort of place a boy like Nikolai would live."

"Not the Nikolai I used to know. But this one . . . perhaps he fits into Sennaya Square just right." Vika frowned at the kasha. Not because the porridge had done anything wrong, but because it was the most immediate thing in her sight.

"So what will you do?" Ludmila asked.

"I have to arrest and imprison him."

"Nikolai will hate being confined. He only just escaped from the steppe bench."

"I know." Vika buried her face in her hands. "But he tried to kill Pasha last night—"

"He did what?" Ludmila flung her hands in the air and knocked a basket of *raspisnye paskhalnie yaitsa*—intricately painted Easter eggs—off the edge of the table.

"My eggs!" Ludmila flew out of her chair.

Vika conjured a cushion onto the wooden floor. The *raspisnye paskhalnie yaitsa* tumbled onto it, a split second before they would have shattered on the ground.

Ludmila crawled on her hands and knees. "You rescued them. Bless you."

There were several dozen, one for each year since Ludmila had been old enough to take part in the painstaking process each Easter of drawing on the eggshells with beeswax, dying them to color the unwaxed parts, and repeating the process many times with more wax and different layers of dye, until the eggs were multicolored and delicately patterned.

Vika crouched to help her and picked up a blue egg decorated with white spirals and a gold serpent in the middle.

"The symbols all have meanings, you know," Ludmila said. "That one is a talisman against evil and disaster. Maybe you should carry one with you when you go after Nikolai."

"I doubt a talisman will help against him," Vika said. "He was powerful before, but now there's something awful driving him, and with the increase in Bolshebnoie Duplo's magic, I'm the only one who can stop him." She looked at the egg. "It *is* beautiful, though."

"Yes, it is." Ludmila's eyes brightened. "Nikolai appreciates beautiful things, doesn't he?"

"Yes . . ." Vika cocked her head, not following Ludmila's train of thought.

"What if you confined him not in an ordinary prison, but in a gilded cage, so to speak?" She tapped the egg in Vika's hand, a little more firmly than necessary. "He was a gentleman through and through, even till the last of the

Game, and I find it hard to believe some of the old Nikolai isn't still inside that shadow. Perhaps a little kindness will coax him out."

"I don't under— Oh." A smile spread across Vika's face. The egg could be enlarged, and Nikolai could be evanesced and trapped inside. Vika could make it comfortable, and as handsome within as the eggshell was without. It would still be a prison, but it would be as pleasing as a prison could be.

"Would you be willing to part with this egg?" she asked Ludmila.

She nodded. "That egg has been waiting all its life to be called to a higher purpose. Much grander than sitting at the bottom of a pile in my old basket."

Vika pulled her coat off the back of her chair and put it on. She tucked the painted egg into her pocket and headed to the door.

Behind her, Ludmila rose from the bakery floor. "You're not going to eat?"

Vika turned around. "Oh! I . . ."

Ludmila smiled kindly. "I'm only teasing. I think I can make a dent in this food on my own. You have an empire— and an enchanter—to rescue. Go, go!"

"Thank you, Ludmila," Vika said. "I really don't know what I'd do without you."

Vika made her way through Sennaya Square, toward the Black Moth. Before coming here, she'd stopped at Letniy Isle, where she'd set Ludmila's painted egg on its side on the ground at Candlestick Point and enlarged it to the size of a small house. There was no door, and there were no windows, for she couldn't allow Nikolai a way out. It still looked exactly like a *raspisnoye yaitso*, but much bigger. Inside, though, Vika furnished it as luxuriously as she could. Hopefully, it would be livable, as far as jail cells went.

As for location, Candlestick Point would not have been Vika's first choice, but it was both a big enough space and out of the way, the latter being important, considering she was using the egg to trap Nikolai and needed to isolate him.

Now, however, Vika slunk through the poorly lit streets of Sennaya Square. There was nothing fantastical about *this* place, only the grim reality of poverty and all the struggles and cunning it took to survive it. Prostitutes on the street corners sneered at Vika, as if she were competition they had to frighten away. Performers offered to show her magic tricks in exchange for a ruble, when the only magic was how quickly they could make that ruble (and the rest in the audience's purse) disappear. And everywhere, it was dank, and buildings were falling apart, and streetlamps went unlit, making the square even more wretched.

Vika heaved a sigh of relief when she found the Black Moth, although it was in worse repair than most of Sennaya Square, if that were possible. But this was where Poslannik's messenger had said Nikolai was. She still couldn't feel his magic; his barrier shield was strong. Vika had to hope Poslannik and his army were right.

She walked along the side of the inn and charmed open each set of drapes as she passed the rooms, peering in to see if she could find Nikolai. She scanned the entire building. Twice. No Nikolai.

But what if this was not the entire inn? Sometimes there was a courtyard where the washing was done. . . .

Vika evanesced to the other side of the building and

rematerialized in a small square of dirty snow, including a wooden tub, a scrub brush, and soap. *Molodets,* she praised herself for guessing correctly.

Here, too, was a squat shack so dilapidated, its walls seemed propped together only by the mounds of snow at the base of the rotted boards. There were three rooms, two with the curtains open and one with drapes drawn, with no candlelight inside.

She pressed herself against that filthy window. This close, she could feel Nikolai's protections, like thick walls of metal encasing the room.

Vika heated the air to sweltering. Perhaps she could attack his barrier by melting it, as she'd done to Peter the Great's statue.

His magic didn't budge. Only the snow all around the shack puddled and trickled away.

But there ought to be seams where the door opens. Possibly also at the windowpanes.

Vika directed her magic to prod where glass met wooden frame.

Solid, solid, solid . . . Seam.

All right, let's try this again. She held her breath as she focused her magic as intensely as a soldering iron. It might not have worked in the past, but now she channeled the amplified flow of power from Bolshebnoie Duplo into this one tiny point in Nikolai's barrier.

A corner of his enchantment melted open, and that was all Vika needed. She released her breath and charmed the curtains slightly apart. The moonlight slivered in, and there was Nikolai on the bed, his sharp, graceful silhouette dignified even in sleep.

The invisible string in her chest tugged fiercely, and she thought of the myth Pasha had told, about Zeus splitting a whole into two halves, who were damned unless they found their other piece again.

It was hard to imagine a pair more damned than her and Nikolai.

Which made it both inevitable and more difficult to do what she'd set out to do. "I'm sorry," she said through the window. "But this is for your own good."

Vika focused and dissolved him into bubbles. She cracked the windowpane open and watched as his components streamed out into the frigid air.

"To the painted egg," she directed his essence. The wind picked up and blew him in that direction.

Another shape stirred inside the room. Vika startled. Had Nikolai had a girl in there with him? Vika thought of Renata, and her stomach twisted and betrayed how much she still cared about him, how much she hoped that he could still be saved, despite trying to convince herself she couldn't love him anymore.

The figure in the room hissed and jumped from the bed. A patch of moonlight illuminated her face, and it was not, it turned out, much of a face at all. Nor was it a girl.

Vika gasped and evanesced herself away.

The last thing she saw was the thing's golden eyes, narrowed with drops of black at the corners, oozing like viscous ink.

CHAPTER FORTY-ONE

Nikolai woke with a shock, his head disconcertingly fizzy. Was it from kissing Renata? Perhaps taking energy from her was less like drinking tea with lemon and sugar, and more like wine spiked with stars. He rubbed his eyes and propped himself up on the bed to get his bearings. He couldn't have been asleep long.

His fingers gripped for the sheets but found themselves in a pile of loose feathers. But not loose, exactly, for although there was no mattress holding them together, they stayed in place in the shape of a bed. As if by magic.

"What is this?" Nikolai scrambled off the feathers and onto a rug of purple flowers, as soft as the finest Persian rug in the Winter Palace. "And *where* is this?"

He spun in a circle. He was inside a room, that was for sure, for there were walls painted blue with a pattern of small white spirals. But the wall was strangely arched, as was the ceiling. Nikolai ran out of the bedroom into the hall.

It connected him to a parlor and a small kitchen (no stove

or oven, he noted), both decorated with furniture as if the craftsman had never heard of nails or upholstery. Rather, there were enormous abalone shells with smooth, iridescent indentations suited for lounging, and lamps powered by glowing moths. And a desk made not of wooden boards, but of a single, polished boulder, with volumes about architecture and clock making, as well as memoirs of travelers from abroad, lined up on the stone.

"Am I in another dream?"

"I'm afraid we're both completely awake," Vika said.

Nikolai spun again.

There was no one else in the room.

"Vika?"

"I'm on the outside. I've sealed you in, which also means I can't enter, or I'd risk a breach in the enchantment and you could escape. You are under arrest for attempting to kill the tsesarevich."

Oh. How foolish to think this was merely a dream.

Nikolai let out a long breath. Then he cast a charm that allowed him to see through the walls.

The sun was not yet up—it did not rise till rather late in the morning in winter—but there was enough moonlight. . . .

And there she was, her hand and forehead pressed against the other side of the curved wall, her eyes closed. Vika didn't look angry, though, as her words had suggested. Was she tired? Frustrated? Resigned? Nikolai couldn't tell.

He crossed the room. He stood only inches from the wall and placed his hand against it, so that it lined up with Vika's, palm to palm, his shadow fingers longer and slightly curled as if they could cup over the tips of hers. She wouldn't know; seeing through obstacles was Nikolai's forte, not hers.

He wasn't happy that she had trapped him. But then again, she'd captured his heart long ago, so he'd already been her prisoner anyway.

"Where am I?" he asked.

"In an egg."

"In an egg?" Nikolai laughed despite himself.

Vika laughed a little, too. A sad laugh, but it was something. "A *raspisnoye yaitso*. A giant one."

"I can see that." He glanced up. The fact that this was an egg certainly explained the arch of the walls and the ceiling. As well as the blue and white paint. There was also a long streak of gold that began in the parlor and probably ran along the entire side of the egg. He'd have to look later. And if Vika's enchantment was strong—which Nikolai did not doubt—he'd have plenty of time. "A painted egg . . . It's an interesting choice for a jail cell."

Outside, Vika bit her lip but didn't respond. Behind her, a gray stone pillar rose into the sky, and beyond that, the ice of the Neva. Nikolai's mouth set in a thin line as he recognized where they stood. Enchanter against enchantress again, at Candlestick Point.

"An interesting choice of location, too," he said.

Vika opened her eyes. "You can see through the shell."

"Yes."

"How silly of me, of course you can. I'm sorry. . . . There was nowhere else to put you."

"Fitting, I suppose." Nikolai wanted to pound his fist against the wall, but then he'd scare her away. Why couldn't they be together? Why was there always something between them? And why was that something always the tsar's game or the tsesarevich's actions? *Clearly, the tsardom is the problem.*

Or, more precisely, the ones who have been wearing the crown. It would be different when Nikolai was on the throne.

"Nikolai?"

He blinked.

"Nikolai."

He blinked again. "Pardon?"

Vika pressed even closer against the outside of the eggshell. The corners of her mouth turned slightly down. "Why are you doing all this? What's happened to you?"

He sighed, the adrenaline of a moment ago now gone as Vika pulled him back to the present. What had happened to him? There was no adequate answer.

"You tried to kill Pasha. Please, stop. Find a way to make amends, however you can. Don't you care about us at all anymore?"

Nikolai crossed his arms. "How could you be with Pasha after what he did?"

"What do you mean, 'with Pasha'?"

"The end of the Game . . . I—I just don't understand. You should be with me, trying to destroy him."

Vika shook her head vehemently. "No, I shouldn't. Besides, you don't know the whole story."

"Then tell me."

Vika yanked off her glove, pulled up the sleeve of her coat, and held her arm up against the outside of the egg. An intricate cuff of gold vines encircled her wrist. The double-headed Romanov eagle was affixed to it, its ruby eyes on her like a guard. Not a guard to protect her, though. A guard to watch her. It did not seem like a gift for a beloved, as Renata had thought.

"What is that?" Nikolai whispered.

215

"Ownership," Vika said. "I'm bound to serve the tsar-dom."

"So you're not together."

Vika snorted. "You thought I was betrothed to Pasha? I hated him after the Game, Nikolai. I suffered from it, too, you know. But since then, I've come to understand Pasha and his actions a little more. Like me, he made horrible decisions in reaction to grief. But he regrets it, and because of that, I've forgiven him. But promised in marriage? No. The only way I belong to him is through the vow I made at Bolsheb-noie Duplo. As Imperial Enchanter, if I disobey the ruler of the empire, the bracelet burns me."

Nikolai's hand went to his left collarbone. He could still remember how it would scorch him. The phantom pain would likely haunt him his entire life. But Vika had a new mark that was anything but a ghost.

"If I became tsar," Nikolai said, "you wouldn't have to do Pasha and Yuliana's bidding." His voice grew louder as adrenaline began to rush through him again. "If I became tsar, it could be you and me together. Imagine how powerful we would be."

Vika shook her head.

All right, then. Power did not appeal to her. "We could do so much for the Russian people, you and I. With more and more magic from Bolshebnoie Duplo, we could increase the harvests by tenfold, and no one would ever be hungry again. We could give everyone the finest coats so they wouldn't die in winter anymore. And someday, our magic might be so great that we could cure all the disease in the empire."

"You don't have to be tsar to do that, Nikolai. We're enchanters. If Bolshebnoie Duplo's magic is strong enough, we could do those things anyway."

"It would be more fun, though, if we were tsar and tsarina."

"Fun?" Vika threw her arms up. "You've attempted murder of the tsesarevich and poisoned thousands of others. I may be bound to Pasha, but it's as if you're bound by something else, too."

Nikolai laughed. Perhaps she was right. Perhaps being a shadow was changing him.

Vika bit her lip again. "Nikolai . . . Tell me how to help you. *Is* there something else controlling you? Who—or what—was that at the Black Moth with you?"

Merde. Vika had seen Aizhana? The thrill of imagining himself as tsar vanished, and Nikolai rested his forehead against the eggshell wall. He and Vika were both positioned that way now, as if they were sharing an intimate secret rather than pitted against each other.

"That . . . *person* is my mother," he said. "She saw you when you evanesced me?"

"'Saw' might be too tame a description."

"Aizhana is passionate, to put it kindly."

"And to put it unkindly?"

"She takes wrongs to me very personally and very violently. She killed my father for making me play the Game."

Vika pushed away from the eggshell. "Your mother killed the tsar?"

"I had no part in it," Nikolai said. He pressed his fingertips harder into the wall, as if that would somehow draw Vika back.

But she stayed where she was, boots planted in the gravel, there being no snow here in Letniy Isle's eternal summer.

"If you want to help me," Nikolai said, "fight with me. We're two enchanters; we'll figure out a way to circumvent the bracelet."

She moved farther away, shaking her head. "It's not right."

"Vika—"

"No. Your mother killed the tsar. I have to tell Pasha. I have to go." And just like that, she disappeared and left Nikolai standing there, alone.

Always, always Pasha. Pasha better than Nikolai when they were kids. Pasha demanding the end of the Game. Pasha taking Vika for his enchantress by his side. It was only a small consolation that Pasha hadn't also convinced her to marry him.

Nikolai slammed his fist into the wall, since there was no one on the other side to scare away anymore. The eggshell didn't even dent, let alone crack or indicate a means of escape. He grabbed a book off the stone desk and hurled it across the parlor. Then he enchanted all the books, and they flung themselves miserably and futilely at the walls, breaking their spines and tearing their pages until the carpet of flowers was littered with paper and words.

Nikolai shuddered. He took in the mess of the room. The beautiful room Vika had created for him.

The beautiful prison to which he'd been condemned.

But Pasha wasn't the only prince who was good at escaping. Nikolai had found his way out of the steppe bench.

And I'll find my way out again, he thought. *But this time when I get free, Pasha will die.*

CHAPTER FORTY-TWO

I'm actually glad I don't know who my real parents were, Vika thought as she rematerialized inside the Winter Palace halls. A tsar and a monster had given birth to an enchanter. What horrors might have combined to create an enchantress? Vika bit her lip and tried to shake the thought away. *Sergei,* she reminded herself. He might not have been her biological father, but he was all she'd needed. She clung to his memory and regained her focus.

Then Vika strode toward Yuliana's apartment. The halls along the way were decorated with holiday garlands made of hand-blown glass—too expensive for anyone other than the imperial family—but Vika didn't have time to stop to admire their delicate beauty. She whisked right past them.

"I have something important to tell the grand princess," Vika said to the guards as soon as she turned the last corner to arrive at Yuliana's doors.

The bearded, older one on the right lurched toward her. "How did you get in here? These are the imperial family's private residences."

Vika evaded his attempt to grab her. "The tsesarevich let me in," she lied.

The guard froze. "Uh . . ."

Was he thinking that she'd just emerged from Pasha's bed? But if so, what did it matter? Let them imagine what they would. This was important.

"I need to see the grand princess," Vika said.

The other guard, also bearded but much younger, said, "It's half past six, *mademoiselle*. The grand princess will have our heads if we wake her for some trifle."

Vika glared at him. She had half a mind to magically toss these guards in the air and cast open Yuliana's doors herself. But in a moment of extraordinary restraint (which she made note of to congratulate herself for later), Vika kept her magic and her temper tamped down and said, "This is not a trifle. And I guarantee the grand princess will have your heads if you do *not* wake her for it."

The young guard looked to the older one. Perhaps it was the early hour, or perhaps it was the ferocity of Vika's glare, but they nodded to each other.

The older guard knocked and slipped inside. She heard him apologize for the intrusion and announce her name to an attendant. A few seconds later, he reemerged and said, "The grand princess will see you now."

He held open the door, and Vika strode inside. She paused for a moment, though, wondering if she'd come to the right place. The room was far from the tidy sanctuary she'd imagined Yuliana's antechamber would be. Instead, piles of letters were strewn all over the floor, the mess evident even in dim candlelight.

Yuliana came in through another door that connected to

her bedroom. She wore an elegant silk robe wrapped around her nightgown, and even in the early morning, every ringlet was in its place. Now that was more what Vika expected. In fact, it was likely that Yuliana hadn't been asleep at all, but wide awake and hard at work on something.

There was a reason Vika had chosen to come see Yuliana, rather than Pasha, when she learned that Aizhana had killed the tsar. (Besides the fact that Pasha was still recovering from Nikolai's attack.)

"Is something wrong with Pasha? I checked on him an hour ago, and he was sleeping peacefully." Yuliana sat in the only seat not covered in stacks of paper, the chair at her desk.

"No, no. He's fine."

"Oh. Then what is it?" Yuliana said, even more blunt than usual. Which was almost forgivable, given the time.

Vika stood in the middle of the antechamber, because she hadn't been invited to sit. Not that there was any open place to sit. She did, however, charm several more lamps to light. Her news was too grim to be delivered in the dark.

"Your father didn't die of typhus," she said. "He was murdered."

Yuliana didn't flinch. Growing up in the imperial family probably involved frequent assassination plots against her father. "By whom?" she asked.

There was a twist in Vika's chest, like the plunging of a phantom dagger. Was she betraying Nikolai by revealing this? But she could not be sure whether he'd been complicit. Besides, Yuliana already hated Nikolai. One more thing would not make much difference.

"Aizhana Karimova. She's apparently Nikolai's mother."

"Hmm." Yuliana straightened the ribbon on her robe. "And how do you know this?"

"Nikolai told me. But he had no knowledge of or part in it," she added hastily. "And I've taken care of him."

Yuliana rose. "How?"

"I confined him," Vika said as unfeelingly as possible, even though leaving Nikolai imprisoned had felt like harpooning her own heart—it hurt terribly, especially since she was still tethered to him, the rope jerking at the harpoon's barbs embedded inside her. "I trapped him in an egg."

Of course, Yuliana didn't flinch. Again. She wasn't human; she was iron in the shape of a girl.

"Fine," she said. "Leave him for now. Arrest his mother. We'll hang her later this morning."

Vika's mouth fell open. "I beg your pardon?"

"Has the work of being Imperial Enchanter taken a toll on your hearing?"

"No, I just . . . isn't she supposed to have a trial?"

Yuliana crossed her arms. "The tsar is dead. The murderer is mother to the enchanter trying to destroy my brother. There is talk of treason and revolt underfoot. So no, I think we shall bypass a 'fair trial' and simply execute her. There are times when justice takes the form of swift action. That time is now."

"But—"

"If you wanted mercy, you would have gone to Pasha with this information. But you came to me, so don't grow cowardly now, Vika. Tell my guards outside to have the gallows prepared. Arrest Aizhana and keep watch on her until the hanging in the morning."

Vika stood in the middle of the anteroom. *Imperial*

Enchanter . . . I ought to be dubbed Imperial Jailer.

Or Jailer of Karimovs.

For a second, she thought of what Nikolai had offered: if he were tsar, she wouldn't have to do what Yuliana or Pasha said. *I could be tsarina, and Nikolai and I could rule Russia together, with magic in the open and no one to challenge or defy us.*

Vika inhaled sharply. She could be a jinni, unleashed, no longer confined to the walls of a bottle. Magic sparked inside her, exploding like miniature fireworks, and without meaning to, she started to levitate.

But then Yuliana tapped her slipper on the floor, and the bracelet heated around Vika's wrist.

Vika snapped out of it and landed back on the ground.

"What are you waiting for?" Yuliana asked, although it was clear she did not want an answer.

Vika answered anyway. "For the day I can create my own destiny."

"I beg your pardon?"

"Don't worry. Today is not yet that day." Vika shook her head to rid herself of the tainted thoughts of ruling the empire. For what Nikolai offered was not what she wanted, not the way she wanted to forge her fate. She wasn't convinced it was what *he* truly wanted, either. The magic inside her actually sparked again, as if in agreement.

So Vika gritted her teeth, because there was a more immediate task at hand. Nikolai had been captured. Now his mother needed to be arrested as well. And then perhaps they could resolve this and bring the city some peace.

At least, that was the plan.

CHAPTER FORTY-THREE

Vika returned to the Black Moth, but as expected, Aizhana had fled. There was, however, a lopsided set of footprints in the snow, as if one of her feet was heavier or slower than the other.

Vika followed the trail. She was well trained in tracking injured animals, healing them often involved finding them first. Then again, the way Aizhana had sprung at the window of the Black Moth when Vika had come for Nikolai indicated that Aizhana was no wounded creature. But at least her uneven steps made her easier to trace.

The tracks ended in a particularly ill-lit corner of Sennaya Square, in an alleyway littered with broken crates and smashed bottles, echoes of lost fights and drowned sorrows half-buried in dirty snow.

The magic inside Vika thrummed, eager to be let out. But her heart had also risen to her throat, for she was about to arrest Nikolai's mother, who was a monster, but his mother nonetheless.

Vika tried to swallow her heart back into its place. It budged just enough to allow her to make an official proclamation.

"Aizhana Karimova, you have been sentenced to death by hanging for the murder of the tsar," Vika said, even though Aizhana wasn't visible. She was here somewhere, hiding behind stacks of debris or inside one of the ramshackle buildings. "It's inevitable that I'll catch you, so you'd save us both some trouble by surrendering without a fight."

There was a small shift in a trash bin to Vika's left, and she spun to face it.

A white rat scurried out and to her side.

"Ah, Poslannik, of course it's you."

Poslannik climbed up Vika's leg, onto her arm, and to her shoulder. He squeaked in her ear what he knew: Aizhana was behind the door of the second building on the right, which was guarded by a barricade of bottle shards jutting out of the snow, like teeth in the mouth of the legendary Arctic yeti.

Vika petted Poslannik's head. He squeaked once more, then leaped back down to the snow, getting out of her way for the scuffle that was likely to ensue.

She could evanesce to surprise Aizhana, but evanescing was risky when Vika didn't know where she was going. There were always a few moments of disorientation as her essence came back together, and in this situation, that meant she'd lose the element of surprise.

There was also the small part of her that *didn't* want to surprise Aizhana, that wanted to give Aizhana a chance to prove herself harmless and worth sparing.

So Vika tiptoed slowly toward the door. There was a

lone, grimy window along the building, and she charmed an extra layer of dirt to spread across it, much like crystals of frost, only made of frozen mud, blooming like flowers of filth to obstruct the view.

She glided over the barricade of broken glass and pressed herself against the door. Then she pushed it open a sliver while simultaneously casting a ball of fire inside to light the room or hall into which she was entering. She held her breath, her magic and her pulse both pounding anxiously through her veins.

It was a storeroom of some sort, piled high with more crates—these intact—a few of which had lids pried open to reveal the bottles of vodka and beer within. Vika's fire flitted around the room, leaving small flames in each of the corners to illuminate every recess.

"Aizhana? I'm here to arrest you, but I don't want to hurt you—"

A crate came hurtling at Vika. And another and another and another. Vika flung out her hands and smashed each one in the air, the splinters of wood and glass blasting in all directions. Had she not been an enchantress with a shield around her, she would have been impaled at least a dozen times.

So much for hoping Nikolai's mother was a harmless woman incapable of killing the tsar.

When the crates stopped flying, Vika shook wood and glass slivers from her coat. She exhaled loudly. "Well, there goes your chance at me taking it easy on you."

Aizhana hissed and climbed up from behind a stack of crates. She crouched on a box, baring her yellowed teeth and wickedly long nails, a huntress ready to pounce.

"You killed the tsar," Vika said.

"I did it for my son. Whom you've taken."

"Nikolai is safe."

"I do not believe you."

Vika quirked her brow. "That's not my problem."

Aizhana shrieked, a high-pitched keening worse than a thousand nails screeching against an endless pane of glass. Vika cringed, and her hands flew to cover her ears.

Aizhana leaped over the crates, golden eyes glowing, talons extended. She slammed into Vika's shield, but because Vika had her hands over her ears, she lost her balance, and they both tumbled backward to the storeroom ground, rolling apart in a tangle of arms and legs, knocking into crates and shattering more bottles.

Vika scrambled to her feet, levitating to avoid the hazardous floor. Aizhana rose just as quickly. A wedge of wood protruded from her shoulder, and she ripped it out as if it didn't affect her and threw the stake aside. The blood on her tunic seeped out of the fabric and seemingly back into her skin.

"You can heal yourself," Vika said as she caught her breath.

"Never seen it done before?" Aizhana sneered.

"On the contrary. I, too, can heal wounds and mend broken bones. You're not as special as you may think."

"Arrogant child! You have not begun to see what I am capable of."

"I could say the same to you."

Aizhana lunged at Vika again.

But this time, Vika was prepared. She conjured a wall of ice in front of her. Aizhana crashed straight into it. Then, in the moment that Aizhana lay dazed on the wood and glass on the floor, Vika melted the wall and reformed it as shackles around Aizhana's wrists and ankles, the ice thicker and stronger than any iron forged by ordinary man.

Aizhana snarled as she came to. She struggled against the restraints, attempting futilely to smash them against each other, and rattled at the icy chains.

"I told you it would be better if you came without a fight," Vika said as she took in the mess of the storeroom. "Now look at what you've left for me to tidy up."

Aizhana hissed at her. Vika threw a gust of wind at her head and knocked her unconscious.

"I am not even sorry about that," Vika said.

Then she walked around the storeroom and charmed the broken crates back together, stacking them neatly in a corner. She commanded a broom to sweep up glass shards and a mop to clean away the alcohol (it would take too much time to sort the mud out of the liquid, and to separate the beer from the vodka and direct them back to the correct bottles).

When the storeroom was in some semblance of order, Vika returned to where Aizhana lay slumped on the floor. "I suppose the most efficient way to get you to the fortress is to evanesce you." But Vika wrinkled her nose at the thought of her magic touching each of Aizhana's putrescent particles. And who knew if the decaying body could survive being taken apart and put back together again? She could arrive as a pile of bones and strips of leathery skin.

Yuliana would be furious if she didn't get the hanging she'd demanded.

"All right, no evanescing," Vika said with no small

measure of relief. "I'll have to transport you another way, in a manner deserving of a woman of your stature."

She snapped her fingers and a wheelbarrow appeared. She levitated Aizhana and dumped her inside in a heap. She snapped her fingers again and a tarp—made of extra-rough hemp, for minimal comfort—secured itself over the lump of Aizhana's unconscious body.

"There we go, a prison carriage suitable for a monster."

Vika paused, though, as a wave of remorse roiled through her. This was Nikolai's mother, monster or not.

But a moment later, she remembered that Aizhana had murdered the tsar and tried to kill *her*, too, and any leniency Vika felt quickly evaporated. She opened the storeroom door and charmed the wheelbarrow to float over the glass yeti teeth, then land in the snow and roll itself. She also cast a shroud over them so passersby would not see.

And then Vika escorted the wheelbarrow onto the dark early morning streets, all the way to the Peter and Paul Fortress, where Aizhana would finally meet Death, once and for all.

CHAPTER FORTY-FOUR

Nikolai needed to escape the painted egg, but he also needed to conserve energy. He frowned as he looked at the curved walls surrounding him.

I suppose I could try reabsorbing Vika's magic. . . . It would be like repurposing his own magic when he'd attempted to escape the steppe dream. Of course, that hadn't worked, but hopefully this was different.

He snapped his fingers at the abalone chaise longues, and both disappeared, the magic seeping into Nikolai. It was liquid and sweet, like cinnamon sprinkled atop honeysuckle nectar. But something inside him recoiled at it, as if it could not mix with magic Vika had touched, even though the magic itself had originally come from Bolshebnoie Duplo.

Nikolai furrowed his brow, but as he took the desk made of polished rock, Vika's energy warmed him, and he dismissed his initial worry that there was something wrong with either him or her. The difference in his and Vika's magic was simply like oil and water; his had always been mechanical, whereas hers was natural. It made sense that his energy didn't quite know what to do with magic accustomed to commanding lilacs and eggs and wind and snow.

After he took the carpet of flowers, though, Nikolai noticed he could still feel the softness of petals beneath his feet. He looked around the interior of the egg, and phantom outlines of the chaise longues and the desk remained, neither there nor *not* there.

"What in the name of . . . ?"

It was as if they were placeholders for the furniture. Nikolai could take away the specific chairs Vika had conjured, but he couldn't take away the essence of "chair" itself.

Likely if he tried to vanish the walls of the egg, they would go translucent yet stay intact, just like everything else. "So this is how you keep me imprisoned, is it? Clever."

To test his theory, Nikolai vanished the entire kitchen—cabinets, counter, plates, and food. As he suspected, faint outlines of each item remained.

"But can I replace what you've created, as long as its concept is the same?" he asked, as if Vika were there and they were merely discussing a magical hypothesis. "Let's see."

Nikolai turned to the ghost of the desk, but instead of polished granite, he wanted a metal one. He focused on the outline and imagined it filling in. A bar of iron appeared, and then another and another, and within minutes, Nikolai indeed had a desk designed like a small truss bridge.

"*Voilà*," he said.

He tapped his fingers, and two armchairs molded of silver filled the space where the abalone chaise longues had been. Beneath his feet, a violet Persian rug replaced the carpet of live flowers. And the kitchen he redesigned like the exposed interior of a clock, with visible screws and pendulums and gears. One need only pull a lever, and an orange or a slice of bread would slide down a chute onto a plate made of a shiny brass cog.

Nikolai turned to the curved walls of the egg then and smiled. He had to concentrate harder on them, since they encapsulated the rooms of his prison completely and were therefore much larger than a few pieces of furniture, but after a while, the colors of the walls began to fade.

Vika's magic trickled into Nikolai, and it was both comforting in its spiced warmth and unsettling in how it warred inside him, like drinking a pitcher too many of mulled wine.

I'll have to dispose of Vika's magic as soon as I get out of here, he thought. He shifted uncomfortably in his skin.

The walls, however, had faded as he'd hoped, and while still solid and intact, were now an empty, pale gray. Now he could transform them into a material he could better control.

Nikolai turned the phantom walls into bronze. He lacquered the outside to mimic the intricate paint of the traditional *raspisnoye yaitso*, decorating it in blue with white enameled spirals swirling on the surface and a serpent made of pure gold wriggling across its center. He thought of Swiss cuckoo clocks and how they often had mechanized surprises inside, and thus created a hinge that would open to reveal the inside of the egg and its redone rooms and furniture. If Nikolai worked hard enough he could actually make the hinge work and . . .

Crack the egg open.

He tumbled out of the egg and landed on the gravel of Candlestick Point. The enormous egg behind him opened straight through the middle, like a jeweled music box, to reveal the contents inside.

If the people of Saint Petersburg weren't so frightened of magic now, they would have had a lovely new site on Letniy Isle to enjoy, Nikolai thought. Then he laughed sardonically, for the trouble with magic was, of course, his doing.

As soon as he got back onto his feet, he purged himself of Vika's magic. Beds of lilacs, blue hyacinths, and a rainbow of roses sprung up around Nikolai's egg. He took several steps back and stared at the garden for a moment. He'd never created something so vivid and alive before.

But then he shook it off. It had been Vika's magic, not his.

He returned to the Black Moth. But his mother was not there.

Damn it.

It did not take long to hear in the streets the announcement that the tsar's murderer had been apprehended, and Aizhana was to be hanged.

CHAPTER FORTY-FIVE

Nikolai located Aizhana easily. Her hanging was to take place in the courtyard of the Peter and Paul Fortress, and a crowd had already begun gathering around the gallows as the sun rose. She wasn't on the platform yet, but she would be led there soon. She had to be somewhere nearby.

Click, click, click.

That sound. Nikolai listened harder. Aizhana's fingernails.

Click, click, click.

Nikolai skirted the edge of the crowd, sticking to the shadows between the buildings that comprised the sprawling fortress. He homed in on the clicking and followed it to the red brick of the Kronverkskaya Curtain Wall.

She's here.

Nikolai could not simply free her, though. Aizhana wouldn't be under the watch of ordinary police. It would be Vika there, for who else could restrain a woman who'd slaughtered dozens of the Tsar's Guard and then the tsar himself? Nikolai hesitated for a moment. Every time he had to face Vika was harder than the last. He felt her slipping away from him, when all he wanted was to have her by his side.

Nikolai took a deep breath, though, and stepped inside one of the doors that led to the part of the building that housed barracks. Again, he kept to the shadows and darted through the halls past soldiers as they departed the mess hall and prepared for the execution.

Click, click, click.

I'm nearly there.

Two police stood guard at the entrance to where Aizhana was being held. Nikolai waved his hand in the air, and the men's pistols unholstered themselves and hit the guards in the backs of their heads. They slumped unceremoniously to the ground.

This was why ordinary men were insufficient for watching an enchanter's mother.

Nikolai opened the door and slipped inside another hall, this one darker than the ones in the barracks. A few lamps hung from sconces in the wall, their flames flickering and taunting. Which room was Aizhana in?

Vika leaned against a wooden door in the middle of the hall. "You liberated yourself from my painted egg."

"You made it difficult."

"Not difficult enough, apparently."

Nikolai advanced a few steps. "Is my mother in there?"

"Yes, but I can't let her escape, too."

"I don't want to have to hurt you."

"She killed the tsar, Nikolai. That's not excusable, and she's going to die today. That said . . . I'm not heartless. I didn't have the chance to say good-bye to Father before he passed." Vika looked directly at Nikolai, her eyes covered in a sheen of tears. "I'm going to walk over here, to the other end of the hall—which, mind you, is not very far—but I'm going to study this sconce on the wall, and if you should happen to find your way into the cell for a minute to say farewell to your mother, well, I might not notice."

Nikolai just stood there for a moment. He'd been seething on the way here, but Vika's kindness suddenly doused the anger.

"If you attempt more than a simple good-bye, though," she said, "*that* I will notice. And when you're done, you and I have some unfinished business."

"I . . . thank you."

Vika nodded and turned to look at the sconce as she'd promised.

Nikolai began to charm open the locks on the door. As the final one clinked open, Vika said, "And tread carefully in there. I have a couple of alligators inside, and they haven't been fed."

Nikolai laughed unintentionally. "Of course you do. Thank you for the warning." He eased open the heavy wooden door and stepped inside. It was even darker in here than in the hall. He conjured a candle in his hand and shut the door. "Mother?"

Shackles clinked in the far corner, on a platform raised just out of the alligators' reach. "My son. You have not been lost."

"It is not so easy to be rid of me," Nikolai said. "I believe it runs in the family." He snapped his fingers and two short lengths of rope appeared. They wrapped themselves around

236

the alligators' snouts and secured tidy knots, and Nikolai stepped over them as if they were merely logs. He crossed the cell and examined the icy chains on Aizhana's wrists, ankles, and around her entire body. She was shivering. "I'll get you out of here."

"No," she said. "They mean for me to die today, and I will. I only wanted to see you once more."

Nikolai still focused on the chains. He could undo the charms. They were much less complicated than the painted egg. "What are you talking about?"

"I was selfish in the past," Aizhana said. "I pretended I was selfless in giving a part of myself to you, but in truth, I was the opposite, for I did not give you *everything*, Nikolai. I wanted to live, too, so I could see you grow. I was selfish, because I wanted to be able to be your mother.

"But that isn't what you need from me, is it? You don't need a mother; you've survived on your own. I've only made things more complicated. So I'll give to you what I should have given you long ago, and the only thing I have to give. . . ." A black tear trickled from her golden eyes, down her skeletal cheeks.

Nikolai frowned at the tear. There was something familiar about it. . . .

"I'll give you my entire life," Aizhana said.

He shook away the half-formed thought about her tears. "Mother. No." He could not ask her to die for him.

"I am as good as dead already, Nikolai. I won't run from here with you. I would only bring you more trouble. So either I die now, on my terms and gifting my son all that I have to give, or I die on their terms, alone on a snowy platform with a noose around my neck. Have mercy on me and say yes."

"I—"

"Say yes."

She was horrible. She'd killed villagers on the steppe, soldiers, his father. . . . But she'd done it out of love. Misguided love. But love. How could Nikolai deny her one last act of love and mercy as her dying wish? Especially when this harmed no one. Not anymore.

Nikolai dropped to his knees before her. "All right, Mother."

Her tears flowed now, a slow and painstaking trickle like tar. Aizhana circled her bony fingers around Nikolai's shadow wrists, where they were exposed between shirtsleeve and glove.

"I love you, Nikolai," she said, her throat dry, her voice strained. "Know that everything I have ever done has been for you, and that I am proud of you. Not because you are an enchanter, but because you are intelligent and passionate and strong. And because . . . because even though you may never truly love me, you showed me tenderness. You let me into your life."

Aizhana closed her eyes. She nestled her head against Nikolai, and then she began to send her energy into him. It started as a thin stream, cold and sharp, and Nikolai gasped as he received the energy she'd gleaned from parasites that fed on rot and death, and from the bodies of all the people she'd killed.

Deuces . . . It was thick and sticky black. Like her tears.

Like the shadowed feeling that had been roiling inside him ever since he broke free of the steppe dream.

"It was you," he said as Aizhana's grip on his wrist grew tighter. "You transferred energy to me when I was unaware.

That's how I had enough power to escape the Dream Bench, and to enchant the Neva fete, and to free myself from the painted egg."

"For the first and second, yes, I gave you my energy while you were asleep. For the egg? I don't know about an egg. That was your friend Renata."

"Renata? But how could she make me so strong?"

"I passed Galina's energy on to her."

"What?" He ripped his hands away from Aizhana. She cried out as if the loss of the connection caused her physical pain.

Nikolai staggered away, shaking his head. "You forced Renata into your service! And Galina isn't abroad, is she? Oh, devil take me, you killed her, too."

Aizhana swayed and buckled to the splintered platform. Her skin was so dry now from gifting him her energy, it crumbled in flakes off her face. The sinews in her neck strained, and the golden light in her eyes was like a candle flame about to expire. "You expected less from me?" she rasped, every word now taking enormous effort. "It had to be done. She deserved it."

"No, she didn't." A complicated cocktail swirled through Nikolai, a mix of gentlemanly horror with the desire to heap misery and trauma upon Aizhana. Galina had not been particularly kind to Nikolai, but she *had* taken him into her own home and spent years training him. She deserved a better end than what she had been given.

Aizhana stretched her hand out to him. Her arm trembled from the effort. "My son. Please. Let me give you what remains."

He looked down on her. She recoiled. His disgust must

have been palpable, even on his shadow face.

Nikolai turned and started toward the door.

"Wait! Have mercy." Aizhana's chains rattled against the platform. "Don't leave me!"

Nikolai stopped in front of one of the alligators. "I left you a long time ago," he said without turning. "But because I'm a gentleman, I'll grant you a measure of mercy and not force you to face your death publicly on the gallows." He stepped over the beasts to the door.

He uncast the charm on the ropes, and the alligators' mouths snapped at their freedom. He clapped his hands, and the platform on which Aizhana lay disappeared, hurling her onto the stone floor. He exited the cell and shut the door, reengaging all the locks behind him.

It was gentlemanly mercy to spare her from the gallows, but the darkness from her energy, now raging inside Nikolai, qualified how that mercy was delivered. A *measure* of mercy, he'd said.

Aizhana's shrieks echoed out of the room above the snapping of alligators' jaws. Or perhaps it was the snapping of her brittle bones.

Vika whirled from the sconce, eyes wide.

He averted his gaze. "I'm finished. I've said my final good-bye."

"Nikolai . . ."

He shook his head. He stalked away.

Vika just gaped and let him.

CHAPTER FORTY-SIX

Vika sat immobile against the wall, staring at the door at the end of the hall from which Nikolai had departed. She hugged her knees to her chest as she replayed what had just happened, against the backdrop of silence in the fortress, for there were no more moans issuing from Aizhana's cell.

Vika could understand how Nikolai had felt when he'd left the cell. Aizhana might have been a monster, but she was still his mother. Sergei's death was recent enough that Vika curled into herself at the memory of the painful emptiness she'd felt at his loss.

The tsar and tsarina were gone, too. So much death, and Vika, Nikolai, and Pasha had all been forced to plow forward without mourning or grieving properly. The Game had demanded it of them. The empire had required it.

Look how well that had turned out.

But Vika could try, at least, to give Nikolai a chance to grieve. That was part of why she'd let him go. And she could also show him in another way that she cared. Perhaps she could reach the old Nikolai that was buried deep beneath his blinding anger. Perhaps that Nikolai could still understand that he was not alone.

Because she'd overheard, through the walls, his conversation with Aizhana. Now Vika understood what was wrong with Nikolai, why he was different. He had been absorbing energy from his mother, who was made of darkness.

But the way he had looked when he'd left, the regret mixed in his misery . . . there must still be some good inside him. Even if only a wisp. Vika wanted to believe it was not lost yet.

She closed her eyes and thought of the morning sky outside. She could feel the weight of the clouds, full of droplets of water, ready to blanket the city with more snow.

But not today.

Within the clouds, the droplets evaporated. In their place, yellow petals appeared in all shapes and sizes—long and thin, round and short, heart-shaped and oval and ruffled and more. The clouds grew even heavier.

Now.

At Vika's command, the clouds burst open. Yellow petals tumbled out, swirling around one another in the wind and coming together in a flurry of flowers, each as unique as the snowflakes they had replaced. There were dahlias that looked spun of honey, and roses with daisy centers, and marigolds on twin stems like yellow cherries. The sky over Saint Petersburg was an endless cascade of floating flowers, a memorial to all those who had been lost but not forgotten.

"This is for Sergei," Vika said quietly from where she

still sat inside the fortress walls. "And for the tsar and the tsarina, and even for Aizhana."

She hoped Nikolai would see the flowers and understand they were for him, too.

CHAPTER FORTY-SEVEN

Nikolai stood on the side of the road that led from the Winter Palace to the Peter and Paul Fortress. The sky snowed yellow funeral flowers about him, but he was too numb to be moved.

Instead, he'd cast an invisibility shroud around himself, so that no one would see him while he waited here. But he was full of Aizhana's energy now, and once he pounced, there would be no doubt who had attacked.

Soon enough, the sound of wheels spinning over icy snow filled the air, and a golden carriage approached. There was a painting of the Summer Palace on its door, and the handle was a graceful stretch of a swan's neck. The double-headed Romanov eagle ornamented the side of the carriage, and more eagles decorated the gold-trimmed roof.

"*Bonjour, mon frère,*" Nikolai said under his breath.

He waited for the Guard leading the way to pass. Then, as the carriage neared Nikolai, he jabbed at the air with his finger.

The bolts securing the wheels came undone. The carriage rocked violently, for it was going too fast for the momentum not to carry it. The wheels teetered and flew off the coach.

Shouts came from within—a boy and a girl, Pasha and Yuliana—as the carriage careened off the road. Nikolai slashed his hands in front of him, and in that second, the beautiful components of the coach morphed into sharp pieces. The painted panels became knife blades, and their edges pivoted inward like a life-size grater, but one made to shred a tsesarevich rather than carrots. The swan's neck that had served as a door handle turned into a beaked spear. The Romanov eagles melted, threatening to drop molten metal onto the occupants within.

The carriage began to topple onto its side. In moments, Pasha and Yuliana would be impaled against the blades. The guards in front and behind the coach yelled in alarm, but there was nothing they could do.

Nikolai laughed, and the energy he'd taken from his mother seemed to laugh with him.

The coach crashed.

Everything went eerily silent.

Gavriil, the captain of the Guard, leaped off his horse and rushed to the carriage. The rest of his men quickly followed, some on foot and some surrounding the fallen coach with their horses.

"Your Imperial Highnesses!" Gavriil called. "Quickly, help me pull apart the carriage," he ordered the nearest guards.

They tried to pry away the walls, but it was like gripping sword blades, and they cried out as they came away with bloodied hands. Gavriil attempted the door, but the swan spear stabbed at him. Nikolai smirked by the side of the road.

But then, from within the carriage, Pasha said, "Stand back."

Gavriil and the others startled.

What in the devil's name? Nikolai craned his neck to get a better look.

"You heard His Imperial Highness," Gavriil said as he gestured for his men to step away from the carriage.

The door burst up and open, kicked out from within. "Take the Grand Princess," Pasha said, still from inside the coach.

"No . . . ," Nikolai whispered. How could they have survived?

A white glove, stained by a bit of blood, emerged from the carriage and through the now-upward facing door. Gavriil hurried over and grasped it. Yuliana climbed carefully up and out over the sharp walls.

Pasha followed right behind her. He grabbed Yuliana as soon as he was out and embraced her.

Gavriil looked from them to the overturned coach to them again. "Your Imperial Highnesses, how did you—?"

"The Imperial Enchanter cast a shield around me," Pasha said. "It protected me from the blades."

Vika conjured a permanent shield? Nikolai gaped. As far as he knew, she was still at the fortress. He hadn't known it was possible to cast an enchantment as powerful as a shield that could last indefinitely and react to new threats, even while the enchanter herself was not near enough to see, precisely, what threats she needed to protect Pasha from. This was a clear evolution of their magic.

"Does the Grand Princess also have a . . . shield?" Gavriil asked. He said "shield" like he was reluctant to accept the concept and glanced about the rest of the Guard, as if realizing that his men were possibly obsolete.

"No," Yuliana said. "Pasha wrapped himself around me, the fool." But she huddled into her brother's chest and stayed there, stiller than Nikolai had ever seen her before. Her usually pristine ringlets were in disarray. Blood streaked her face where several cuts slashed across her cheek.

"I would do anything to protect you," Pasha said, as he tightened his arms around her.

Aizhana's energy was still so fresh within Nikolai, he didn't feel even a twinge of remorse as he watched Pasha and Yuliana. Instead, it occurred to him that he could put an end, at least, to Yuliana and the Guard right now. They stood on the side of the road, completely exposed, and Pasha would not be able to shield them all.

Nikolai looked up at the sky. Yellow petals continued to flurry down. The entire landscape was covered with the mournfully beautiful snow that smelled of honeysuckle.

Not just any honeysuckle, though. This was overwhelming, perfuming the entire atmosphere. Nikolai's head began to swim, and he swayed on his feet.

But Pasha, Yuliana, and their Guard seemed unaffected by the flowers. They continued to stand without problem next to the knife-edged carriage.

These flowers are for me, Nikolai realized. Vika must have done something to them, homed in on her botanical knowledge from Sergei and her understanding of Nikolai, and created blossoms to weaken him. Like catnip for a murderous enchanter.

Nikolai could hardly keep his eyes open, let alone cast anything competent to kill Yuliana and Gavriil. Plus, if he stayed here much longer, he might lose hold of his invisibility shroud. And given the chance to capture him again, Vika would not let him escape this time.

I have to go.

The yellow flowers continued to fall. They were intoxicating. A spark of warmth flared inside Nikolai.

Just a single spark, though, and Aizhana's darkness quickly smothered it.

Nikolai sent a drowsy glare in Pasha's direction. And then he retreated to sleep off the effects of Vika's enchantment.

But before he left for good, he snapped his fingers twice. It wasn't much, but it was all he could manage for now.

The falling flowers transformed to newspaper confetti, and every strip proclaimed the same words: *The tsesarevich is a bastard. His father was the tsarina's lover, Staff Captain Alexis Okhotnikov.*

CHAPTER FORTY-EIGHT

Footsteps echoed in the fortress hallway. Vika was still sitting on the ground, head bobbing as she dangled on the cusp of falling asleep. She hadn't been able to rest since . . . since when? So much had happened, she couldn't keep track of the last time she'd laid her head down in bed.

But Vika wouldn't get a chance to sleep yet, for a girl's voice echoed from down the hall. *"J'en ai eu assez!"* I have had enough!

That must be Yuliana, likely having come upon the guards Nikolai rendered unconscious—or killed?—on his way to Aizhana. And any second, she'd burst through that final door to find not only that her father's murderer was already dead and hence she'd be deprived of watching Aizhana hang, but also that Nikolai had escaped from imprisonment, and Vika had let him go. Vika dropped her head to the tops of her knees.

A minute later, the door did open, but it was not the angry stomping she'd expected. Vika looked up slowly.

Gavriil, captain of Pasha's Guard, entered with his pistol drawn. Ilya followed.

Pasha was right behind them, a gun in his hand, too. He scanned the hall, from Aizhana's locked cell to the flickering sconces on the wall and finally, to Vika curled up on the floor.

"Vika!" He stashed his pistol away and rushed across the hall. Gavriil and Ilya spread out to cover him.

"What happened?" Pasha asked as he reached her. "Are you all right?"

She couldn't respond.

Pasha gathered her in his arms, and for once, she let someone console her. She released her knees and allowed her body to go slack against him.

Yuliana stomped in through the door despite the protests of the last guard, who trailed after her.

"I assume it's all clear." She huffed as she crossed the hall to where Vika huddled against Pasha. "I'm not sure I even want to know the explanation for what happened here."

Pasha sighed. "Give her a minute, *s'il vous plaît*."

Vika stared at Yuliana. Her hair was a mess, and dried blood was smeared across her face. Vika looked to Pasha. His hair was also a mess, but that was normal, which was why she hadn't noticed before that something was awry.

Vika pulled herself together. "What happened? Are you all right?"

"The good news," Pasha said, "is your shield works. The bad news is, Nikolai tried to kill us."

Vika clambered to her feet. She'd feared something like this would happen, that Nikolai's grief would drive him to extremes again. "Are you all right?"

"Yes," Pasha said.

"No, we're not." Yuliana said, as she marched over to the door of Aizhana's cell. "Unlock this," she said to Vika. "I've had enough of the Karimovs. I'm going to strangle Nikolai's mother with my own hands."

"She's . . . already dead," Vika said.

"I beg your pardon?" Yuliana whirled to face her.

"Nikolai let the alligators loose."

"Alligators? Nikolai? You had better start explaining, enchantress."

Pasha squeezed Vika's shoulder. And she told them what had transpired.

When she was finished, Yuliana flew at her, grabbing Vika by both arms and shaking her. "Nikolai tried to kill my brother. And what did you do? An atrocious job at trapping him, and then you allow him to waltz in here to see our father's murderer and steal justice from us . . . and then . . . argh! You shower him with flowers as if in a parade, while he tries to kill us again!" Yuliana slapped Vika across the face.

"Yuliana!" Pasha grabbed her and yanked her away.

Vika rubbed her cheek and looked at the grand princess. "I deserved that."

"No, you didn't," Pasha said.

Vika stared at him. *How can he still be so good?*

"You deserve worse," Yuliana said.

Vika could not deny that.

Yuliana seethed. "You found a loophole in my orders and undermined them on purpose, didn't you, because you still have the absurd notion that you're going to save Nikolai. Well, there will be more specificity in my orders going forward to ensure that you comply." She looked pointedly at Vika's wrist.

Vika closed her eyes. She could already feel the cuff tightening, a precursor to the confines of her world narrowing.

"And furthermore," Yuliana said, "you won't use any magic at all unless explicitly commanded by Pasha or myself."

Vika's eyes flew open. "What? No! Why?"

Yuliana smirked.

But it was Pasha who answered. "I'm sorry, Vika. It's for the empire, though."

"Do you know what reports came into the Imperial Council this morning?" Yuliana asked, or, more accurately, accused.

But of course Vika didn't know. She'd been a touch busy here at the fortress.

Yuliana didn't wait for a response. "Farther south, peasants are beginning to refuse to go near the Volga River. There are tales of a monster—half catfish, half man—who will snatch and drown anyone who dares draw water after dark. The peasants are mad with fear, and the region grows more unstable by the day."

Vika gasped. It couldn't be . . . but it sounded exactly like Vodyanoy, the fish king from the old Russian fables Ludmila used to tell when Vika was little. Vika wondered what other wild magic was waking up in Russia that they didn't yet know about. Her stomach turned.

Pasha tried to put his hand on her arm, but she pulled away. He looked at the floor as he spoke. "The more magic the people see, the more they believe, and the greater the power that flows from Bolshebnoie Duplo. That's good when *you're* the one using magic for Russia. But it's beginning to manifest itself in ways we can't anticipate—whether that fish monster is real or not, the people believe it, and that's what matters, at least for now.

"And then there's Nikolai. The magic is terrifying when Nikolai is the one wielding its growing power. After the harm he's caused our people and the attempts on my and Yuliana's lives, it's clear we need to stop him. If we can tell the people that magic is no more, Bolshebnoie Duplo's power will decrease, and Nikolai will become more limited. And perhaps we can quell the irrational fear in the countryside."

Vika shook her head. Her mouth curled into something that looked like a deranged smile, but it was panic, not happiness, that gave her the expression. It was as if her mouth didn't quite know what to do. "You need me and my magic. You need *me* to be able to trap and stop Nikolai."

"Yet it appears you cannot actually manage that," Yuliana said. "This morning is further evidence that we need a different tactic. All this magic is causing more trouble than it solves."

"And I'll be safe," Pasha said. "Your shield protects me."

"Yes, but . . . but you told the people magic was good," Vika said, grasping for arguments. "If you change your mind now, it will undermine you—"

"Vika." Pasha planted his hands in his hair and pulled at the locks. "I truly am sorry. Yuliana and I have enough to deal with, though, with the food poisoning from Nikolai's fete and the people's now-hysterical distrust of magic. Besides the rumors of the fish monster, witch burnings are cropping up all over the countryside, and here in Saint Petersburg, there are rumors of revolt underfoot.

"The tsardom can't be seen siding with your power except as a last resort. We'll say we made a mistake. I'm young; the people will forgive me a misstep. But I have to do this, because I need to reestablish stability. You know I wouldn't do this to you if I had a choice, right? It's for the empire."

Vika could only look from the double-eagled cuff to Pasha again.

"It's not forever," he said gently. "Just until we regain a semblance of calm and control. What we've been doing—allowing the existence of magic to be public knowledge—isn't working, so I have to try something else. But if we really need your magic, if this strategy proves wrong, we'll reinstate you right away." He relinquished the tugging of his hair and reached a hand toward her.

But unlike earlier, when she'd allowed Pasha's fingertips to nearly graze hers, this time Vika pulled away.

He couldn't take away her magic, only enforce the prohibition; the bracelet would scorch her if she tried to disobey. But even though Pasha hadn't taken her actual power away, Vika felt as if the constant sparks that had danced through her body ever since she was born had faded to the faint glow of dying embers. Her blood, which had always run hot, seemed to shift several degrees cooler. And the brash energy that ordinarily allowed Vika to command a room now dwindled, leaving her just another girl.

If she was a jinni, Pasha and Yuliana were her masters. And they had just stuffed her back inside a bottle that was markedly too small.

CHAPTER FORTY-NINE

Back in the Winter Palace later that afternoon, Pasha handed the signed edict to Gavriil. "Here it is. Make sure it's announced and heard throughout the city."

"Right away, Your Imperial Highness." Gavriil saluted.

"And you'll oversee the safe evacuation of any citizen with red hair, correct?"

"My men have made all the preparations you requested. We will offer to help anyone who wants your protection."

"Be careful, Gavriil. Evacuate them under cover of night, and remember, head east. A number of witch burnings have already been reported in the south, and the traders coming through the outposts there are not helping. They're passing off their ordinary trinkets now as wards against demons and black magic."

"East, then, Your Imperial Highness."

Pasha nodded wearily. "Thank you. Shut the door on your way out, please."

Gavriil saluted again and left to carry out his orders,

closing the door to the tsar's study behind him.

Pasha sank back into the chair. His own brother had tried to kill him again, while he was still trying to recover from the first attempt. And having to take magic away from Vika had only compounded what was already an unimaginably horrifying day. He wanted to lie on the floor and throw up, like he'd done at the end of the Game when he'd been filled with a similar whirlpool of conflicting emotions—anger at the betrayal by Nikolai and sadness that it all had to end, that someone would have to die. But this time, there was also anger at himself, along with remorse, for Pasha knew that none of this would have started but for his decisions.

Uneasy lies the head that wears a crown. Shakespeare had it right. And Pasha didn't even have a crown yet.

Of course, if he didn't find a way to stop Nikolai, Pasha might never even have the chance to be tsar. And if he did, there would still be trouble, for the city had now been reminded again that his mother had had a lover around the time he was conceived. Even Pasha wasn't sure of his own legitimacy.

His nausea grew keener, but only in part due to fear of death. It was also due to the possibility of never achieving what he'd been groomed for his entire life. Pasha clutched the edge of the desk as the realization hit him: he actually wanted to be tsar. He'd traveled abroad with his father and visited courts in England and khanates on the steppe. He had studied foreign policy, economics, and war, and although they weren't his favorites, they were in his blood as much as hunting or reading Greek tragedies or sneaking out of the palace were. Pasha loved Russia with the entirety of his being.

And he wanted to throw up because of the immensity of it.

He retired soon afterward to his rooms and did not leave the rest of the afternoon. Meanwhile, Gavriil and Ilya crisscrossed Saint Petersburg, announcing for everyone to hear:

"By order of Pavel Alexandrovich Romanov, Tsesarevich of all Russia: The use of magic is hereby forbidden and the position of Imperial Enchanter eliminated."

CHAPTER FIFTY

"Come in, it's freezing out there," Renata said as she ushered Nikolai into Madame Boulangère. There was no one else in the bakery—shopgirl or customer—for most were still too ill from the Neva fete. Renata shut the door behind Nikolai, flipped the sign to indicate the bakery was closed, and fastened the lock.

Nikolai looked around at the floral French wallpaper and the small café tables surrounded by brocaded chairs. "Not much different from Galina's."

Renata laughed. "In some regards, not much at all. Tea?" She darted behind the counter and began to fill a porcelain cup. She placed it on a tray, along with sugar and lemon and cream, and a *pain aux raisins*, since she knew it was one of Nikolai's favorites. In less than a minute, Renata came back around the counter and set everything down on one of the café tables.

"You don't need to serve me, you know," he said as he hung the greatcoat and top hat on a brass hook near the door. "Please sit."

Renata blushed and stood for a few seconds, unsure whether to keep her apron on or take it off. But given that the last time she saw Nikolai, they'd kissed, perhaps taking off her apron in front of him now would seem too suggestive? Or was she making too much of nothing? Heavens, she was probably making much too much.

Why are you here? she wanted to ask. Perhaps it was only a friendly visit. She and Nikolai used to chat every day when they lived at the Zakrevsky house. Or perhaps he wanted more energy from her. Which would mean he might kiss her again . . . Renata felt her cheeks grow redder.

"Are you going to sit?" Nikolai asked.

"What? Oh. Yes. Thank you." She sat on the chair, apron still on, hands balled up in the ties because she didn't know what to do with them. Either the ties *or* her hands.

Nikolai exhaled audibly as he lowered himself into one of the chairs opposite her. He closed his eyes and rubbed the back of his neck. His mouth turned downward in a frown.

Renata gasped in surprise as she realized what she was seeing. His mouth. His actual mouth. Nikolai wasn't a shadow anymore.

Nikolai opened his eyes again and raised his brows. "Why are you staring?"

Renata blinked. "Because I can see you!"

"Ah, right. My mother's dead. I took most of her energy before she passed, which finally gave me enough power that I'm able to cast a facade that looks like a facsimile of myself."

"I . . ." There was too much in those few sentences to know which to respond to first. Renata shook her head to sort them out. "Your mother died?" she decided to ask.

"Yes. She was arrested for murdering the tsar and

sentenced to death, but I took care of it before she was hanged."

Renata's mouth hung open.

Nikolai took a sip of his tea. "No need to be alarmed. She asked me to kill her out of mercy."

"Er . . . um, I see," Renata said, although she didn't see at all. Why was he so casual about this? Her brain scrambled to keep up with Nikolai's reasoning, but it couldn't seem to do it. She defaulted to her most common sentiment instead. "Are you all right?"

He let out a short bark of a laugh. "She wasn't much of a mother, and I'm not sure she was entirely human, either. It's no great loss that she's dead."

Renata recoiled from the table. This boy before her looked like Nikolai, but he wasn't the one she knew and loved. That Nikolai was so vulnerable to emotion, it actually tortured him. But this Nikolai . . .

"You said you've cast a facade," Renata said carefully. "Does that mean you're still a shadow underneath it?"

Nikolai smiled, but in a way Renata didn't recognize. It was too cunning, and it didn't invoke the dimple in his cheek like Nikolai's real smile would.

He released his facade and immediately turned to shadow again, although his edges were clearly defined, not blurred, now.

Renata's hands stilled in her lap, even more knotted in the apron strings than before.

"You said before that my being a shadow didn't scare you. Have you changed your mind?"

"N-no."

"Good." He recast his facade and smiled again.

Yes, there was definitely something very wrong with this Nikolai, for the one who had been Renata's dearest friend would have known she was lying.

"Galina's dead, too," he said without any hint of mourning. "It turns out she left the house to me, probably because there was no one else to leave it to. So I came tonight to offer you a job, if you'll take it."

"At the house?"

"Yes, your old job," Nikolai said. "Say you'll come."

The apron strings were wrapped so tightly around Renata's hands that they cut vicious white lines into her skin.

"Please," he said, but he was not smiling anymore.

Renata nodded. "Y-yes, of course."

"I knew I could count on you." He drained the rest of the tea from his cup and rose, leaving the *pain aux raisins* untouched. Before Renata could even get to her feet, he had his greatcoat and hat on—they were both pitch black; in fact everything he wore was black, she noticed. There was no splash of colorful lining inside his coat or even a fanciful handkerchief, unique touches Nikolai used to pride himself on.

"I'll see you at the house then." He didn't even say goodbye as he unlocked the bakery door and let himself out onto the snowy street.

Renata stared after him. But once he was out of sight, she turned back to the table to clear the plate on which she'd brought the *pain aux raisins* and the cup and saucer for Nikolai's tea.

His cup was nearly—but not quite—drained. He never drank the last drops around her, even though she'd long ago promised she wouldn't read his leaves without explicit permission. As Nikolai had left them, the leaves suggested death was once again near.

But as she stood over his cup, something inside her sparked. She wasn't touching the tray or the table, yet his tea leaves shifted.

What? Did that really happen?

Renata squinted at the pointed black leaves. One of them had turned a little in the cup.

"I did that . . . ," she whispered. The remnants of the energy Aizhana had given her danced a jig in Renata's veins.

If it had been a true prophecy—if Nikolai's cup had been entirely drained—these leaves would've meant that death was a little delayed.

And perhaps even more important, if Renata could influence how the tea leaves fell inside their cups . . .

Did that mean that fates could be changed?

CHAPTER FIFTY-ONE

Nikolai looked over his room at the Black Moth one more time.

I'm certainly not leaving this cesspool with the improvements I conjured. He whipped his hand in front of him as if swiping away the furniture, and indeed, the beds and horsehair mattresses and porcelain washbasin he'd created vanished. He snapped, and the old louse-ridden, chipped, and stained furniture reappeared.

He wrinkled his nose at the once again filthy space. There was nothing at the Black Moth that he needed to take with him, not even memories. He'd had a mother, briefly, and that had turned out to be quite enough. Besides, she'd left her legacy with him, in the form of the unforgiving darkness coursing through his veins.

"*Au revoir,*" Nikolai said as he spun and left the room. "*Et bon débarras.*"

And good riddance.

He strode through the streets of the city to Ekaterinsky Canal. It was much faster crossing Saint Petersburg, now that Nikolai could cast a shroud to look like a normal person and didn't have to slink in the shadows. *Finally, something's going right.* He smirked to himself as he passed by one of the many granite posts along the canal's embankment.

The post smirked back.

Deuces! Nikolai staggered a step and looked at the post again.

It was indeed smirking. And it was no longer a post, but instead a gargoyle, and a grotesque one at that, with a wart-ridden, troll-like face, seven gnarled horns curling out of its head, and blank eyeballs that rattled and rolled in their sockets.

"Did I just . . . ?" But surely not. Nikolai hadn't even thought to create the gargoyle, let alone cast an actual charm. And yet, it was not the sort of thing Vika would conjure.

It was as if the gargoyle were a tangible manifestation of how Nikolai actually felt inside. Just like his shroud was a physical version of how he—still a shadow, really—felt he ought to look.

I don't know if it's a good thing I can now use magic without having to think about it, or if it's bad that it's not entirely under my control.

But then Nikolai thought of what this meant in terms of power—the magic prickling at his fingertips was colder and stronger than ever—and his eyes twinkled, although not brightly like stars. Rather, like black holes, swallowing light into their depths.

At the mere hint of Nikolai's delight, all the posts along

the rivers and canals in the city transformed themselves into gargoyles, with vacant eyes that watched and followed every movement of passersby. And the renewed energy inside Nikolai roiled gleefully at the mayhem this new enchantment would cause.

He marched up to the Zakrevsky house with a dark spring in his step and charmed open the door. He walked into the foyer and had only a few seconds to take in the familiar setting—the Persian rugs, the heirloom grandfather clock, the crystal chandelier and the staircase that curved up behind it—before Vadim, the footman, ran out to greet him.

Or perhaps not to greet him, seeing as Vadim wasn't dressed in uniform but wore a plain tunic and trousers and had dry spittle crusted on his face. He must have been recovering from the food at the Neva fete, like most everyone else. His eyes bulged, and he came to an abrupt halt when he saw it was Nikolai in the foyer.

"M-Master Karimov," he said, falling immediately into a bow. "I mean, Grand Prince, Your Imperial Highness, w-we were not expecting you."

Nikolai motioned with his hand for Vadim to rise.

"Is it really you?" Vadim asked.

"Yes. Surprised?"

"There was a rumor that you were alive, but no one had seen you, so most dismissed it."

"And what did you believe?" Nikolai narrowed his eyes.

"I, er, always supported you, Your Imperial Highness. All the staff in your house did."

My house. Nikolai smirked.

"Speaking of the staff," he said, "where are they?" He'd

been friends with Renata while he lived here, but not with the rest of the servants, for his status had lain awkwardly in between the staff and the count and countess. Besides, the servants had steered well clear of Nikolai, who was often holed up in his room working on mysterious projects that involved a great deal of banging and cursing and the occasional explosion (they were Galina's lessons to train Nikolai for the Game, but the servants knew none of that and only thought him eccentric and a bit intimidating).

Vadim looked off in the direction of the back stairs, which led down to the basement, where the kitchen and laundry and the guts of the house lay. "We were informed by officials of the countess's death and were thus dismissed from employment, as there would be no one to pay us. Besides, most of the staff have taken ill from the party the other night. Only Cook, Kostya the messenger boy, and I remain to take care of the unfinished business."

"Well, I'm here now," Nikolai said, choosing not to acknowledge that Vadim was looking wan and wobbling on his feet. "I'd like a proper household. I want you and Kostya to fetch the others. They will have employment under me."

"Thank you, Your Imperial Highness. It will be a great honor to serve you." Vadim bowed, a bit unsteadily, then hurried away.

Nikolai went up the staircase to the second level and walked along the hallway of portraits of past Zakrevskys. He stopped in front of the mirror at the center of it. It was the first reflection of himself he'd seen since he cast his shroud.

"Not too bad," he said. His hair appeared as he liked it,

kept neat and short with minimal sideburns. His jaw was sharp as a knife blade, with cheekbones to match. And his eyes were dark half-moons. . . .

Nikolai scowled. The color of his irises was too black, a glimpse of his shadow self piercing through his careful shroud.

He glared at the mirror, and the glass disappeared. A second later, a portrait of Galina in an opulent silver gown—formerly hanging in her room so she could admire herself anytime she wanted—took the mirror's space. It was a better fit, anyway. This was a hall of Zakrevskys. A reflection of Nikolai had no place there.

Nor do I want one.

He continued into his room, which was still a library as it was the last time he'd been here. But that would not take too long to rectify. *It's my house now. I have free rein to redecorate as I choose.* He nearly smiled, but the darkness within him didn't quite let him. Interior decorating was the sort of thing that would have made the old Nikolai happy, but not the new one. Still, it needed to be done.

The first thing that had to go were the draperies. While Nikolai appreciated the quality of the pale rose silk and had nothing against pink itself—he owned several cravats in varying shades of pink, or he *had*, before Galina had tossed out all his belongings—he just wasn't in the mood for curtains in that color. He snapped his fingers, and black began to bleed down from the tops of the drapes, consuming the more delicate rose until the pink was no more.

Next, the shelves. They were full of books on fashion—French, British, Italian—so Nikolai was loath to be rid of them, but the shelves couldn't stay, for there wouldn't be enough space once he had a bed and an armoire in here.

But they could go in Galina's room. The corner of his mouth turned up smugly. *She made my bedroom into a library as soon as she thought me dead. It would be more than acceptable for me to do the same to hers.*

With Vadim and Kostya out running errands and the cook downstairs in the basement kitchen, Nikolai could use magic without hiding it. He flicked his wrist, and the furniture in Galina's room cleared. With a flick of his other wrist, the shelves and books in his own room migrated down the hall past the Zakrevsky portraits, marching like awkward soldiers, and settled where Galina's canopy bed used to sit.

Nikolai turned back to his own room and exhaled. It was nearly empty now, other than the desk, and that had originally been his, so it could stay. He shifted it a few feet over to where it belonged near the farthest window, but that was the only change.

Soon thereafter, he conjured a wooden bed frame stained in black, its posts intricately carved with curlicues and feathers. Atop it lay a fine mattress and fluffy pillows and a black blanket stitched at the edges in gold. Gold, after all, was the color of the tsar.

Next came an armoire, in carved black wood to match the bed, and gold feather detailing on the handles and hinges. The feet he conjured in gold with talons, like garuda claws.

If only it weren't empty, Nikolai thought as he opened the armoire doors. He could conjure clothes, but conjured clothing was always inferior to what he tailored himself, for nothing could compare to meticulous measuring and remeasuring, and cutting the cloth by hand. Well, perhaps not "by hand," but his scissors under the direction of his magic were as good as extensions of Nikolai's dexterous fingers.

No one had cared what a shadow wore, especially since he'd tried not to be seen. But his new facade required decent clothing, and in all honesty, "decent" wouldn't suffice for Nikolai's pride.

I'll need to acquire several bolts of wool, and needles and bobbins of thread, and pretty much everything else required to tailor a new wardrobe. Nikolai frowned at the vast black emptiness of the armoire. He'd send Renata to Bissette & Sons as soon as she arrived back here to work; he could trust her to pick fabrics and buttons that he'd like.

Nikolai conjured a pad of paper and pencils and began to sketch furiously a design for a frock coat he had in mind. It had notched lapels. . . . No, no, that wouldn't do, he was the grand prince, and formality dictated that his lapels be decidedly *un*notched. He laughed to himself. Galina would have liked to witness this; she'd always disdained his penchant for notched lapels.

He tore out the sheet of paper, crumpled it, and started anew.

An hour later, he had a design he was satisfied with. But as Nikolai looked at it, he saw the futility in it. What was the point of a new coat if he had nowhere to wear it to? It was like being a debutante in a gown without an invitation to a ball.

I need to secure the crown once and for all, Nikolai thought. Then he'd have plenty of places to be in his fine clothes. Not that that was the reason he wanted to depose Pasha. But it was an amusing one. He laughed under his breath.

His head ached, though, and he didn't have any ideas for

how to attack Pasha next. What Nikolai wanted was an evening to regroup. And something to eat. He suddenly craved bread and smoked fish, and the dark corners of a tavern.

The Magpie and the Fox, *then*, he thought, pushing back from his desk. *That's exactly what I need.*

CHAPTER FIFTY-TWO

An evening storm blasted Ovchinin Island with snow, and Vika huddled inside her cottage by the *pech*. She wore her thickest sweater, a scarf, and a hat Ludmila had knit for her years ago. On top of that, she'd wrapped herself in Father's favorite blanket, a fraying thing he'd brought back from one of his scientific expeditions to the Kamchatka Peninsula, and it seemed that the memory of Sergei was one of the only things that kept Vika from shivering to death.

The storm grew angrier and shook her house. Its bitter wind suddenly found every exposed crevice in the walls and howled its way in. Without thinking, Vika snapped her fingers to seal the cracks near the windows.

The bracelet immediately seared her skin.

"Agh!" Vika crumpled on the floor, clutching her arm while also calling off the enchantment on the house. The cuff stopped burning.

But because she could not use magic to heal herself, Vika didn't stop hurting. Tears streamed down her face as pain continued like hot irons on her skin. She curled on the rug, teeth clenched as she tried to bear the lingering heat.

I'm just an ordinary girl now. Vika nearly choked on the thought, and she curled more tightly on the rug, attempting to hold herself together.

And the pain wouldn't go away. She hugged her singed arm against her chest and sucked in short breaths through her teeth.

"Vee-kahhh!" Ludmila's singsong call cut through the storm outside. "I brought you supper, my sunshine." Her ruddy face, wrapped in a fur-lined hood, peered in through the window. "Oh my goodness—!"

The baker shoved open the front door and rushed to Vika on the floor. She tossed aside the parcel she carried and gathered Vika into her bosom. "What happened?"

"Burnt . . ." Vika forced herself to release her arm from her chest and show Ludmila her wrist. It was covered by the bracelet, but Ludmila would know what she meant.

Ludmila cradled her arm. "Did you cool it with water?"

Vika shook her head. Cool it with water? Was that what normal people did?

The horror of being ordinary slammed into her again, as viciously as the storm pummeled everything outside. She slumped.

"Wait here." Ludmila gently laid Vika on the rug, grabbed a large mixing bowl off the counter, and hurried out the front door. A minute later, she returned with a bowl full of snow, which she set on the floor at Vika's side. She added some water from the pitcher on the kitchen table. "Now give me your wrist."

Ludmila plunged her arm into the bowl. The icy water rushed all around Vika's singed skin. She gasped at the cold.

But slowly, the pain gave way to a chilly numbness, and

she could breathe more fully again.

"Better?" Ludmila asked, as she dabbed at Vika's wrist with a towel.

"Yes, thank you. It still hurts, but it's better."

"It will probably scar."

Vika's unharmed hand went to her collarbone.

Ludmila's eyes widened. "Oh, my sunshine, I'm sorry, I didn't mean to——"

"It's all right," Vika said, even though it wasn't. The crossed wands of the Game had been when everything *not* all right had begun. "I'm just glad you came when you did."

"Me too. I'm also glad I brought you food." Ludmila got to her feet and picked up the brown paper parcel she'd tossed aside when she first came in. She offered her hand and helped Vika up and to the table.

"I thought a fresh Borodinsky loaf and sausages might cheer you up. And it's a good thing I brought *oreshki* cookies with me, too. You could certainly use some of those." Ludmila unwrapped the package and laid supper out before them.

Just listening to the warm, musical lilt of Ludmila's voice felt like a breakthrough of sunbeams, however weak. A hint of a smile touched Vika's mouth as she settled in at the table, tenderly resting her burnt wrist on the tablecloth. She picked up one of the walnut-shaped confections, its two halves stuck together with rich caramel, and nibbled at it. The sugar touched her tongue and then went straight through her veins to her wrist. Or so it seemed. Cookies really were the best medicine.

"I can't believe you trekked all the way up here," Vika said.

Ludmila kissed her on the head.

Vika melted.

"Will you be all right if I leave you? One of my customers' nieces is getting married tomorrow, and I still have to bake all the sweets for the wedding. If you need me, though—"

"I'll be fine, thank you. Now that the worst of the pain is past, I can make a poultice for the burn using one of Father's herbal compounds. But really, truly, thank you. You're so busy, yet you still traipsed through a storm to bring supper."

Ludmila shrugged. "I love you, my sunshine. And that's what happens when you love someone. Sacrifices stop being sacrifices simply because they make you happy. Caring for you makes me happy. So it's not a sacrifice. It's what I want to do."

Vika set the rest of her cookie on the table and threw her arms around Ludmila. The melting snow on Ludmila's cloak pressed cold and wet against her, but Vika didn't care. All she wanted was to hug this incredible woman, who was not her mother but was, Vika realized, *better*. Ludmila had been here Vika's entire childhood, as had Sergei. Perhaps this was why, even after the revelation that Sergei was not her biological father, Vika hadn't felt the need to know or search for her supposedly "real" parents. Ludmila and Sergei were more real than anyone else could ever be.

Vika buried her face against Ludmila's soft chest. "I don't know who I am without magic."

Ludmila stroked the black streak in her hair. "We are not defined by what we *can* do, but by what we *actually* do. You're a fierce, smart girl, Vika, and you will find a way to make your mark even without magic in your veins. I know who you are. And I think whatever happens next will help you see who you are, too."

Vika lingered in Ludmila's embrace, comforted by her caramel-scented warmth. Vika still felt hollow inside, but at least she knew this was home.

A moment later, she released Ludmila. "I suppose I ought to let you return to the bakery. *Bolshoie spasiba* for helping with the burn, and for supper."

Ludmila flicked a finger under Vika's chin. "Hold your head high, my sunshine. Remember, it's not magic that defines you. It's *you* that defines you. That's all the truth that there is."

Vika watched as Ludmila left and hiked back down the snowy hill. Thankfully, the storm had slowed to a flurry. When she was gone, Vika returned to the kitchen.

Her wrist hurt, but not as much anymore. She made a poultice with herbs from various glass jars Father had kept in the cabinet, and wrapped the cool bandage around her forearm and bracelet. Then she sliced the Borodinsky bread Ludmila had brought, heated a sausage, and made tea.

Vika sat down near the *pech*, warmed by the fire, and took a bite of her bread, chewing thoughtfully.

She might not have been able to use magic, but Ludmila was right—she wasn't powerless, either. *I am who I make myself to be.* She finished her bread and sausage and sipped at her tea.

Then Vika smiled, picked up an *oreshki* cookie, and popped the entire thing in her mouth.

It was time to figure out what, exactly, she was going to do, and who she was going to be.

CHAPTER FIFTY-THREE

As Nikolai stepped inside the rowdy tavern, he was hit by memories. The Magpie and the Fox used to be his and Pasha's, where they came when Pasha wanted to sneak out of the palace and be anyone other than tsesarevich, and where Nikolai could put aside the strains of his enchanter training and feel like a normal boy. Nikolai's stomach soured. He almost turned back around to head for the door.

But then what had begun as a queasiness in his stomach quickly shifted to a hard knot of anger. Why should Nikolai have to abandon the tavern simply because Pasha had once frequented it? Not everything should default to Pasha for the mere reason that he was heir to the throne. Besides, Nikolai would take the crown from him, somehow—perhaps even more easily now that Vika was forbidden from using magic—and then everything that was once Pasha's could and would become Nikolai's.

He just needed to figure out how. He needed a new plan.

He also needed something to eat.

Nikolai snuck into a dark corner of the tavern—he hadn't cast his facade, for he wanted to move about unseen, a shadow among shadows—and swiped a few slices of rye bread and smoked fish off a wooden platter at a table where the conversation had grown too animated for the patrons to pay attention to their food.

He moved deeper into the tavern and lurked around a group of rowdy gamblers, who already had five empty vodka bottles on their table next to their piles of coins and bills.

"You should have seen the look on the girl's face when I cornered her," one of the men said, his mouth full of half-chewed pickle.

"Did she scream with horror when you unbuckled your belt and she saw how tiny your member was?" another man said, as he drew a card from the deck.

"I think you're confusing your own experience with mine." The first louse of a man spit on the floor. "The only screams were from the girl and her sister begging me for more." His fellow gamblers guffawed, and he sneered in victory.

A serving girl walked by at that unfortunate moment, and the man smacked her rear end. He was met with more hoots of approval from his drinking mates.

Swine, Nikolai thought. As a silhouette, his sense of propriety might have waned, but it had not yet disappeared entirely.

But the dark energy within him bubbled for another reason—it wanted more of its own kind, even though Nikolai didn't necessarily need it, since Aizhana's strength was more than enough. But the energy was greedy, and it craved more darkness. That made these men perfect targets.

Nikolai reached out of the shadows to touch the first gambler's back.

The energy shuddered through to him, and with it, he felt the magic in his fingertips hum ever stronger, pulsing with shadow. Nikolai almost sighed out loud, for energy was like water—no, vodka—after being parched for too long. He took and took until the man's head bobbed, drowsy from what Nikolai stole.

His friends only pointed and laughed. "The Great Stanislav of Sennaya Square can't hold his drink anymore!"

Nikolai let go. *The Great Stanislav of Sennaya Square?* He edged around to get a better look at the man's face. No, not a man, but a boy Nikolai's age. The face was rougher than he remembered, skin leathered from long days in the sun, but it was the same reprobate with whom Nikolai used to play cards. Stanislav was a liar and a swindler and a brute, and that was only a list of his best qualities.

Stanislav mumbled something, then slumped onto the table, face in a platter of herring, and began to snore. His friends laughed harder, then emptied his pockets of the rest of his rubles.

Each is worse than the next, Nikolai thought as he watched them. *All the better for me.* He decided to take energy from every single one of them.

When he was finished, they were all asleep with their faces smashed in the herring. Nikolai scooped up the bills and coins and poured them into the serving girl's apron pocket as she walked by. "For you," he whispered. It was that tiny bit of propriety, that sliver of sunlight that still existed within him, that made him do it.

The servant girl looked all around her but couldn't find

her benefactor. When she dipped her hand into her apron pocket, though, she smiled and said, "Thank you."

Nikolai felt both wonderfully vile and horribly saintly in the moment, and that strange oil-and-water roiling churned within him again, like it had when he'd absorbed some of Vika's magic in the egg. He frowned and spat on the floor, as if that would rid him of the discomfort of being good.

He began to walk away, but then he paused. Stanislav's and the others' shadows were following him. Well, not exactly following, for they weren't alive by any means, but they stretched thin, as the shadows of the girl and her father at the toy shop had done, one end stuck to their owners, the other attracted to Nikolai.

He took another step, and then another and another, and the shadows from other patrons began to cling to him, too. Nikolai watched as more shadows joined, stretching thinner and then thinner still, until he was on the far side of the tavern. The Magpie and the Fox was striped with eerie, willowy silhouettes from one end to the other.

Nikolai grinned. And then, when the shadows were on the brink of nearly snapping, he waved his hand to release them from his pull. They sprang away.

He'd let them go back to whom they belonged. For now.

The shadows closest to him returned to a table near the wall, where a boy his age and three men in their midthirties huddled. Nikolai furrowed his brow as he studied them, for he could tell they weren't the sort who normally met in the Magpie and the Fox. They had attempted to dress below their station, but unbeknownst to them, their mannerisms gave them away—they ignored everyone around them, customers and servers alike, in the manner of the highborn, who were accustomed to not seeing those beneath them. Nikolai simultaneously hated them and wanted to be them.

"I have no problem with the tsesarevich," one of the men said. "The tsesarevich has a reputation for generosity. It's the grand princess I take issue with."

Blazes, that's Major General Sergei Volkonsky. Nikolai recognized him, of course. Everyone in Saint Petersburg knew him. But what was a man like Volkonsky doing in a hole like the Magpie and the Fox?

"It is substantiated fact," said a man with a pinched face, as he gesticulated with a pickle in his hand, "that the grand princess was always at the tsar's right hand. She attended every meeting of the Imperial Council, whereas the tsesarevich did not."

A third man, this one long-faced, cleared his throat. It was Colonel Sergei Trubetskoy, another prominent member of the nobility whom Nikolai recognized. "The grand princess would see a continuation of their father's policies," Trubetskoy said. "But Russia cannot continue like this. We need a constitution. We need accountability."

Nikolai listened intently from his dark corner. Perhaps he had misjudged these men earlier. Perhaps they ignored all those around them not because they thought themselves superior, but because they were so engrossed in their patriotism that they saw nothing else.

And he was empathetic to their ideals. If anyone understood the inequality of Russian society, it was Nikolai.

"We should kill the grand princess when we revolt," the pinched-face man said.

"Pavel Ivanovich Pestel," Trubetskoy whispered urgently. "Keep your voice down. We will not condone murder."

But I would. The wheels in Nikolai's head began to turn. What were these men up to? And could they be of use to him?

Pestel leaned back in his chair. "What we discuss is all treason. It is just the degree of severity that matters."

"There must be another way," Trubetskoy said.

"There is," Volkonsky said. "That's why Ilya is here tonight. He has an interesting proposal."

Nikolai squinted in the dim light. Yes, it was Ilya Koshkin, whom he knew because Ilya was the only member of the Guard who ever had a clue where to find Pasha when he snuck out. Ilya was also, in a way, like Nikolai. Both were ignored at home—Ilya, because he was the fourth son, and Nikolai, because he'd never really had parents to begin with—but both boys were still ambitious enough to make something of themselves outside of that.

Nikolai shifted a little closer to the table, at the same time the other men turned their attention to Ilya.

Ilya fidgeted in his seat, but then cleared his throat and said, "I suggest that, instead of waiting until next summer to revolt, as we'd originally planned when the tsar was still alive, we ought to act sooner. The tsesarevich is scrambling to fix the mess that's been made with magic, and I've been working to recruit more soldiers to our side as a result of it. They're afraid of his witch, edict or not."

Trubetskoy sipped on his beer. "This is interesting."

"The timing is perfect for a coup," Ilya said. "The tsesarevich has not been officially crowned. And there are rumors that the tsar wasn't his father. Politically speaking, this is optimal for us. We wouldn't be usurping a tsar; we'd be taking the throne from an illegitimate son."

Volkonsky nodded, a smile on his face like a proud father watching his child come into his own.

"But who would we install in the tsesarevich's place?" Trubetskoy asked.

"No one," Pestel said. "We create a democracy."

Trubetskoy frowned. "We've been over this before. Russia isn't ready for that. Look at the disaster that ensued in France when they demolished the monarchy too swiftly."

"But the United States—" Pestel began.

"Is much different from Russia," Volkonsky said. "They are a very young country. We are much more like France than America."

Trubetskoy nodded. "We must take the long view and shift first to something in between, hence my preference for a constitutional monarchy. I know you disagree, Pestel; you always have. But the majority of us believe this is the right course for the country."

"Fine then." Pestel crossed his arms. "Who would you propose to lead your so-called constitutional monarchy?"

I could do it, Nikolai thought, and he began to smile. In fact, this was precisely what he needed—a path to the crown with political legitimacy. It would also be easier for the Russian people to accept him as tsar if he didn't murder Pasha outright. Better if he let a bunch of revolutionaries do it for him. As a bonus, they would be making a better Russia. Yes! A better empire for those like Nikolai, who were not born privileged or free. He was so gleeful at having a new plan, he almost laughed out loud.

Nikolai cast a shroud to make himself appear more

himself, then pulled up a chair and inserted himself at the table between Pestel and Trubetskoy. The men startled and jerked away.

"I suggest you install me on the throne," Nikolai said.

"Grand Prince Karimov," Ilya whispered, gawking. He pushed back from his seat and began to rise so he could bow.

Nikolai smiled but put his index finger to his mouth. "Let's keep my identity among the five of us for tonight, shall we? Otherwise, how will we surprise the tsesarevich if it's public knowledge that I've joined you?"

Ilya nodded furiously and sat back down.

But as a precaution, Nikolai conjured a shield around them to muffle their conversation.

"How do we know it's you and not some magical trickery ordered by the tsesarevich?" Trubetskoy asked, carefully treading the sword-thin line between skepticism and respect in case Nikolai really was Nikolai.

"You don't, but believe Ilya when he tells you who I am. In fact, you and I were acquainted in society before my paternity was known. I was Countess Zakrevskaya's ward. You may ask me anything you like to verify my identity. Once you have been satisfied, I should like to speak with you about helping with your plans, and you with mine."

"Plans?" Trubetskoy cast his gaze about the tavern. "We have no plans."

"Very well then, you have no plans." Let Trubetskoy be cautious. Nikolai would have done the same were he in the other man's shoes, for the previous conversation alone was enough grounds for a conviction of treason.

Ilya grinned at Nikolai. Pestel appraised him. Volkonsky watched him a bit more cautiously, but hopefully.

Trubetskoy, however, narrowed his eyes and shifted in his seat subtly. He hadn't become a celebrated war hero by being foolish. Nikolai would have to volunteer information to gain his trust.

"The first time we met face-to-face, Colonel, was at a ball two years ago at Count Rostov's home. You gave a toast that night, to commemorate the new ballroom in which we danced."

"Anyone could know these facts."

"All right. Then how about this? You know I used to sharpen swords for a lieutenant in your regiment in exchange for lessons. In May of last year, you declared that the very knife you're fingering in your belt now was destroyed, but your lieutenant told you I could fix it. He brought it to me at our next lesson, the blade snapped an inch from the hilt. I don't know what you did to the knife for it to buckle like that—what remained attached to the hilt had been bent forty-some degrees—but I did fix it."

Trubetskoy didn't put his hand on the table where Nikolai could see it. He kept it right where it was, on his belt, close and yet no nearer to his knife. "How do you know this?"

"I told you; I'm the one who fixed it. My initials are stamped onto the base of the blade. You can check it. In fact, I insist you do."

Now Trubetskoy unsheathed the dagger and turned it in the light of the single lamp on the table. He focused on the metal near the hilt. Nikolai knew what he'd see—the letters *NK* engraved in Nikolai's own handwriting, for he hadn't needed a blacksmith's stamp. He'd used his magic to etch his mark into the blade.

Trubetskoy examined the knife for several more seconds before he tucked it away. Then he dipped his head in respect.

A smile of relief broke across Ilya's face.

Pestel leaned closer to Nikolai. "If I may ask, what happened to you? Is it true your brother tried to kill you, but you survived?"

"Well, more accurately, the grand princess," Nikolai said. "Yuliana, as you know, can be rather ruthless. But Pasha was complicit."

"Her influence over him is even worse than we feared," Pestel said to the other men.

At this, the energy inside Nikolai began to burble again. "We can rectify the situation," he said. "I like the ideas you and the others put forth."

"You would support us in the reforms? You would abolish serfdom and be willing to entertain a constitutional monarchy?"

Nikolai's smile was laced with the ugliness of retribution. "If you would support me on the throne, I would support your reforms."

All four men dropped their heads, bowing without standing or making a show of it.

Finally, Trubetskoy spoke. "This is more than we could have hoped for. My men and I are behind you."

"Whatever you need is yours," Volkonsky added.

"Excellent," Nikolai said. "Then let's discuss how we achieve our goals. Ilya mentioned staging a coup soon. I suggest we do it by blocking Pasha's coronation."

"That's only a few weeks away," Ilya said.

"Can you have your soldiers ready?"

Trubetskoy cleared his throat. "We are one of the

greatest armies in all of Europe. It won't be a problem to mobilize."

"The coronation will take place in Moscow," Nikolai said. "Ilya, you're privy to the tsesarevich's conversations. Has he discussed the route they intend to take?"

Ilya shook his head. "Not when I've been there. But perhaps they'd been counting on the Imperial Enchanter to evanesce them and whatever they needed to Moscow."

"Evasens?" Trubetskoy stumbled on the unfamiliar word.

"That's how she magically appears and disappears, isn't it?" Ilya asked.

Nikolai cocked a brow.

"I—I was there at Peter's Square when you argued with the tsesarevich," Ilya said. "I saw her appear out of thin air, then and another time."

Huh. Nikolai had thought that he, Pasha, and Vika were alone that night he animated the statue of Peter the Great. Apparently, Ilya was even better at sneaking around and tracking Pasha than he was given credit for.

But Nikolai didn't want the others to know he was an enchanter. He didn't know how they'd react, especially since Trubetskoy had been wary of "magical trickery" when Nikolai first pulled up to their table.

Nikolai pursed his lips and subtly shook his head as he looked at Ilya.

Ilya blinked, then nodded, once. He bit back the smile forming on his lips.

Nikolai would have to take that as a sign of comprehension. "The Imperial Enchanter is forbidden to use magic now," he said to Trubetskoy, Volkonsky, and Pestel. "That means Pasha will be forced to travel by carriage. He'll be exposed."

Pestel scooted closer to the table. "They'll use the main road. The alternate routes are nearly impassable in winter."

"It's good that we know where they'll be," Volkonsky said. "Easier to know where to ambush them."

"But bad that the weather will be punishing, even on the main road," Trubetskoy said, tapping his vodka glass. "It will make things difficult for us, too."

"Still," Nikolai said, "I like this idea." He didn't say that they wouldn't be entirely on their own, that he had magic to assist them. "Can you work on the details of the battle plan and present it to me soon?"

The four men bowed their heads again. "Of course, Your Imperial Highness."

"Excellent." Nikolai poured five shots of vodka.

Ilya raised a glass. "To Karimov and a constitution," he said quietly.

"To Karimov and a constitution," Trubetskoy, Volkonsky, and Pestel said.

Nikolai smiled as Aizhana's black energy simmered inside him. "I like that." He raised his own glass. "To me. And a constitution."

CHAPTER FIFTY-FOUR

Vika looked over the granite embankment into Ekaterinsky Canal in the morning light. During the Game, she
had enchanted all of Saint Petersburg's waterways to shift
in color—from ruby red to fire-opal orange, then golden
citrine, emerald green, sapphire blue, amethyst, then back
to red to start the rainbow again—and as winter had set
in, the canals and rivers had frozen in whatever color they'd
happened to be in. Ekaterinsky Canal, in particular, had
iced over in an unflattering hue between yellow and green.

But that wasn't the only thing Vika noticed. A while ago,
Nikolai had changed all the posts into gargoyles, each more
monstrous than the next, and their vacant stone eyeballs
seemed to shift in their sockets as people passed. Nowa-
days, the citizens crowded into the center of the streets and
alleys to get away from the embankments; some took longer
routes in an attempt to avoid walking along the waterways
in general. And instead of festive Christmas tinsel tied to
the posts, some braver souls had fastened small bundles of

sticks, leaves, and sprigs of winter berries. *Poisonous* berries. Wards against witchcraft.

Vika's resolve to do something, rather than wallow in self-pity at home, strengthened. Declaring that magic would no longer be used clearly hadn't improved much, other than some people had begun to come out from hiding in their houses. A different tactic was needed. Vika just didn't quite know *what*.

When she reached the Zakrevsky house—or was it the Karimov house now?—she hesitated in front of the steps. The last time she was here, she'd sent in Poslannik's army to destroy all of Galina's and Nikolai's belongings. She'd left their home in ruins: broken chandeliers, shredded Persian rugs, and most of Nikolai's wardrobe, eaten through by the moths. Then Vika had run away in cowardly remorse.

She winced. There were so many things wrong with that move. It had been an enormous, multifaceted mistake.

But I'm not that girl anymore, Vika thought as she forced herself up the steps. She still didn't know who exactly she intended to be, but it wasn't *that* version of herself. She also knew without a doubt that how she defined herself would involve how she dealt with Nikolai. Even without access to magic, even with her heart wary, she could still feel the string that connected them.

The question was whether she was supposed to destroy him, save him, or rule the empire by his side. This was what Vika hoped to answer if she could see him.

Regardless of the outcome, though, she wouldn't be subordinate to anyone. Not Nikolai, not Pasha. It didn't matter that she didn't have use of magic right now, or that she was bound by a bracelet. *I am Vika Andreyeva, and I am as important as anybody else.*

Vika rang the bell and studied the carvings of roses on the door while she waited for an answer. A minute later, a footman opened the door.

"*Bonjour, mademoiselle,*" he said.

"*Bonjour.* I'm here to see Nikolai."

The footman clucked his tongue at her. "*His Imperial Highness* is not accepting visitors."

"Oh, are we doing that now, using formal titles?" Vika bristled. "Then tell *His Imperial Highness* that the *Baroness* Victoria Sergeyevna Andreyeva is here to see him."

The footman blanched. "You're the witch. You're the one who made us all sick from the fete."

"I did no such—"

The footman shut the door in her face.

Vika tried to charm the door to unlock. But her bracelet singed her immediately, and she cried out and crumpled on the front steps.

She clutched her wrist and pressed it onto the ice on the step in an attempt to cool it faster. The pain would subside soon, for it was only a brief burn like touching a hot pan, but she sucked air through her teeth while the hurt faded.

Damn you, Yuliana. And Pasha, too. Vika was chained to the tsardom, but they'd forbidden her from using the very magic that provided the basis for why she was chained in the first place. Like this, Vika wasn't a dragon on a leash; they'd rendered her a mere lizard.

And yet, she knew she had been the one who'd taken the vow to the crown. She had been the one who wanted to be Imperial Enchanter. Under no circumstances would she have given up her ability to use magic, even knowing that the power came at a steep price.

Vika would just have to create her own destiny with what she had. She knocked on the door again.

It opened and the footman reappeared. "You're still here."

"Yes, and I'm not going away until I can see His Imperial Highness."

The footman frowned but said, "At least I don't have to chase you down to deliver this. His Imperial Highness, in all his magnanimity, has a message for you." He clearly disapproved of Nikolai's supposed "magnanimity," though, for the footman hurled a note card at Vika. It ricocheted off her coat and into the snow. Then he slammed the door again.

Unbelievable.

Still, Vika fumbled for the note in the snow.

I cannot be seen associating with you. I am sure you understand why.

But it doesn't mean we cannot meet where circumstances are not quite so real.

Close your eyes. Feel the magic.

And find me there.

—N

CHAPTER FIFTY-FIVE

Vika tried to shut off her brain and *feel* the magic, as Nikolai had instructed. She used to do that more often when she was younger, but ever since the Game began, she'd found herself thinking more and feeling less.

She closed her eyes. She didn't need to enchant anything to sense the presence of magic that already existed. Even normal people, if they were aware enough, would be able to identify what was ordinary and what was extraordinary. They just hadn't had the practice to know the difference.

The invisible string that connected Vika to Nikolai twitched. She let her feet follow, and she tripped a little down the steps, along the canal, through the streets toward the bay.

Toward Letniy Isle.

Of course. Nikolai's benches were there, and where else were circumstances less real than there, where dreams constituted a reality in which a shadow boy had lived?

Despite everything that had happened, Letniy Isle was

the place that still tethered them together.

Or it could be a trap.

Vika stood on the banks of the Neva a moment more. It would be wiser not to go.

But sometimes, destiny pulls so taut, one follows no matter what the consequences might be. Besides, caution was not part of Vika's vocabulary.

Well, perhaps a tiny bit of caution would be smart, given that she didn't have use of magic right now. She rang the bell again.

The footman opened the door and didn't even bother to speak this time. He simply arched a brow.

"Could I borrow a quill and ink?" Vika asked.

"If you have a response for His Imperial Highness, I can simply relay it to him."

"No, I'd rather write it down."

The footman sighed, closed the door in her face (again), and returned a minute later with a quill and an ink pot. Vika flipped over the note card Nikolai had sent her and, holding it on her lap, composed a quick message on its blank side:

Pasha,
I've gone to Letniy Isle to meet Nikolai. It's possible it's a trap, although I hope not.
However, if you do not hear from me by sunset, please reinstate my ability to use magic so that I can free myself.
—V

The footman tapped his boot. Vika rose and pushed the quill and ink pot back into his hands. "Thank you." She turned and descended the front steps.

"What about the note for His Imperial Highness?" the footman asked.

Vika turned back and winked. "Oh, it's for a different Imperial Highness."

The footman puffed out his chest and grumbled.

Vika smirked as she hurried off, stopping at the Winter Palace to leave the note for Pasha with a guard (the palace was on the way to the ferry), then made her way toward the singular place that existed only because of her and Nikolai.

She closed her eyes when she arrived; she didn't need to see what they'd created. Vika knew the layout of the island because she'd invented every tree and rock, every path and every dead end. She knew the lanterns Nikolai had charmed to drift above the leaves and branches, and she knew his Dream Benches. But what she didn't know was where their magic truly intersected, and how.

The tugging in her chest guided her. It was still faint, so she lost the pull as she wandered through the maple grove, overwhelmed by the remnants of her own magic and the sugar-sweet scent of syrup in the air. Vika almost opened her eyes, but she stopped herself. She concentrated harder instead.

Remember Nikolai, she thought. *Remember his warmth and elegance, not the cruel magic from the dolls' fete and the carriage of swords, but when his magic was like silk dancing in the wind.*

The breeze quickened around Vika—her breath did, too—and with it came what felt like a wisp of silk that curled around her body before it spun away again.

But it was enough. She chased its wake, and, although

she lost the feel of the silk, she heard something. The wistful melody of an oboe. She followed it and found the thread
again. The music accompanied Nikolai's magic! Not like the
orchestra at his party on the Neva. This was as quiet as the
lullaby a bird murmurs to its unhatched eggs.

Had music always been there?

Vika knew that the answer had to be yes. Only she
hadn't noticed, because she'd been too busy trying to kill
Nikolai during the Game, or at least not be killed herself,
and she'd only seen what his power could do on the surface.
She'd never listened, never delved deeper.

What else is there, Nikolai?

With her eyes still firmly shut, Vika walked past the
pink and red flowers she'd planted along the gravel path and
turned onto the main promenade. The oaks rustled above,
and the birds warbled a folk tune, but these were all Vika's
creations, so she ignored them. She held fast to that single
wisp of silk, though, with its melancholy oboe, and as soon
as she moved near the first Dream Bench, she was hit by
the fragrance of sun-drenched grass mixed with mandarin
and . . . was that thyme?

"Nikolai." It was not as if he smelled of all those things,
or any of them, for that matter. Not when Vika had been
in his physical presence. And yet, the combination was the
steppe and Saint Petersburg, French and Russian, all at once.
It was the perfumed footprint of his magic, another dimen-
sion Vika had never noticed before. How had she missed so
much of him? And was it lost completely now, to the darkness that consumed him? Vika worried her bottom lip.

The fragrance and the music led her past the Moscow bench, past the ones for Kostroma, Kizhi Island, and

Yekaterinburg, until she arrived at the bench for Lake Bai-kal in Siberia.

She lowered herself onto the bench, slowly enveloped by the pale purple mist that surrounded it. She inhaled, and then she dozed off.

Vika woke on the other side of the bench in the dream-world of Lake Baikal. Before her spread a sapphire pool of fathomless blue, pure glacial water in a crater created by a volcano. Violet-gray mountains surrounded the lake on all sides, and a cool breeze blew across the water, even though it was summer here.

Vika gasped as she stood and looked around.

But she'd hiked these mountains before, in the dream, and they had been just as beautiful. What was it that was drawing her here now? What was special about this place?

"Nikolai," she said aloud, "I'm here. I'm looking for you. Where are you?"

A trail appeared before her, as if the mountains had opened and created a new ridge for her to follow, although when she inspected it more closely, the mountains hadn't moved at all. But wasn't that the beauty of Nikolai? He could be so contradictory. He could appear to be one thing and be something else entirely, brooding and ambitious yet joyful and self-sacrificing. Of course his magic could be opposites at once as well.

Vika hiked along the path that was and wasn't there, leading her between two of the violet mountains. The sky here was so blue, it seemed counterfeit. *But of course it is,* Vika thought. *This is Nikolai's creation. He can make the sky any color he pleases.*

On distant peaks, animals moved, perhaps deer hopping

from ledge to ledge, or wolves out for a hunt. Vika's trail was quiet save for her boots crunching on the rock, the path behind her disappearing as she walked, the way before her unfurling with each step forward.

As she pushed onward, the music grew louder, almost audible to a normal ear now. What a strange sensation to be hiking alone though the mountains of Siberia with an oboe accompanying her. At one point, she looked back over her shoulder, and Lake Baikal was nowhere to be seen. It was impossible to judge the distance she'd traversed. For all she knew, Nikolai could be leading her to the Arctic Circle now. But she continued walking, not only because there was no trail back, but also because the tugging in her chest grew stronger. This was a path solely for her, and no one else. She had to follow it to its end.

And then the season changed abruptly. Vika's eyelashes froze at the tips, and she shivered, even though she wore her coat from the real Saint Petersburg winter. A gust of snow blasted at her and nearly knocked her off the path, which had now become a tightrope of sorts, a thin line of pebbles floating over a vast abyss, with nothing but sharp crags and the gaping mouth of a valley below.

I can't die in a dream, I can't die in a dream, Vika told herself, but she couldn't stop her heart from pounding when it seemed as if she really could slip and fall to her death at any moment. Why had the terrain suddenly changed? It was as if Nikolai had wanted her to find him, but now that she had come, he had changed his mind. Was she supposed to turn back? But how? Even the tightrope disappeared behind her, leaving the tiny stepping-stones ahead of her as her only option.

Or perhaps it was a test of her own will, and whether she really wanted to find him or not.

The magic of Nikolai's dream swirled around her, the silkiness and the perfume sliding against her skin, the oboe crescendoing. *He's not just a shadow boy with darkness in his veins.* The thought came to Vika like a recollection. Like she'd forgotten he was an actual person and only now remembered—*truly* remembered—that Nikolai was complex and real. She had made a similar error earlier with Pasha, forgetting he was more than the black-and-white caricature she'd painted of him in her head. She would not make the same mistake with Nikolai.

I do want to find you, she thought, as if he could hear her.

The sky turned dark, like midnight, and the tightrope vanished. Vika shrieked at the sudden changes and grasped at the air, as if she could hold on to the nothingness to break her fall. She began to plummet like Icarus from the sky.

A golden eagle, larger than any in real life, soared down from the moon. It dove straight at her, but then caught Vika on its back.

"Oh, thank heavens." She nestled into its warm brown feathers and lay herself flat across its back, not wanting to ride it like a horse and be blown off by the wind, for the eagle careened through the sky at near-reckless speed. Her ears popped as the eagle darted in and out of the clouds, and Vika's hair trailed behind her like a flame, so bright that if anyone were watching, she and the eagle would appear to be a shooting star, streaking across the night.

Vika's heart skittered like a frightened rabbit, but against her ear, she could hear the eagle's pulse beating steady and strong. She tried to calm her own heartbeat.

Then it occurred to her that this was the type of magic she would have thrilled at before the Game. Before Nikolai tried to kill Pasha. Before she was suspicious of everything Nikolai did.

Vika half smiled. She sat up on the eagle's back now, opened her eyes, and tried to enjoy this respite from reality, the cold night air blowing across her face. She looked at the stars above them, and it was as if they were sailing through the immense sea of midnight, explorers charting oceans where no one else had ever been. Nikolai's oboe was now joined by an entire symphony, and the woodwinds crooned along with the gentle melody of the strings, the chimes ringing softly like a sprinkle of starlight.

The eagle soared faster, and Vika whooped, smiling broadly now, feeling alive even though she was asleep, feeling whole even though half of her lay on the other side of the bench. Magic, how she had missed it!

The eagle landed softly at the top of another mountain. But it had taken only two steps when the ground trembled beneath them. Steam and heat and the stench of sulfur rose nearby.

Vika froze.

A volcano. Like the one on which Sergei had found her, an exact replica, it seemed, of the volcano etching he'd carved into her wardrobe at home. Vika touched her scarf; her mother's basalt pendant lay beneath it. Only the necklace wasn't there, for she'd given it to Pasha. Her throat suddenly seemed too exposed despite being covered with a thick layer of wool.

"Why did you bring me here?"

The eagle shrieked. She couldn't understand it, because

she couldn't use magic to translate what it said.

The eagle growled and shook her off its back. Without waiting for her to move out of the way, it flapped its great wings and took off into the air, leaving her stranded on the mountainside.

Vika clung to a small shrub to avoid being blown away. She shivered in the snow, but when the eagle was gone, she rose and brushed the ice off her coat. "I am fierce," she said, repeating what Ludmila had said of her. "This is only a dream. I refuse to allow something as silly as an imaginary eagle and a made-up volcano to rattle me." She walked quickly, proudly, to the edge of the crater, as if this would further prove her point.

But it was not a cauldron of lava, as Vika had expected. Rather, it was a long, narrow tunnel that went straight down, like a cylinder bored into the volcano.

Vika bit her lip. There was nowhere else for her to go but down. The only other option was to wake herself from this dream, and that was not an option, for Vika did not simply back away because something was perilous. Like caution, quitting on account of danger was not a part of her lexicon.

She looked at the hole again. It was a perfect circle, something created not from nature but by something—or someone—else. She latched onto a nearby tree and leaned over the edge of the opening. "Hello?" she called down.

Pure, untainted silk swirled up to meet her.

And then . . . *"Bonsoir,* Vika."

She'd found Nikolai.

CHAPTER FIFTY-SIX

Nikolai could see her silhouette framed by the imaginary moonlight coming through the circular opening above him. He hadn't known if she would come, or if she would be able to without the use of magic, but he thought that if they were still connected as they'd been before the end of the Game, then . . . perhaps there was hope for them yet. After all, she'd come to his house. It was possible, now that Pasha had taken away her magic, that Nikolai could convince her to join him.

"I'm coming down," Vika yelled.

Before Nikolai could answer, Vika simply dropped straight from the hole in the ceiling, plummeting quickly at first, but then floating down like a feather to the ground. In fact, she *was* riding on a feather. From the golden eagle he'd conjured to bring her here.

"You do know how to make an entrance," Nikolai said.

She curtsied.

"What are we doing in this volcano?" he asked, still

hanging back in the shadow, out of the moonlight.

Vika stuck her hands on her hips. "Funny, I thought *you* would be able to tell *me*. You didn't create this?"

Nikolai shook his head as he took in the porous black rock that constituted the walls of the cylindrical room around him, and sulfur nipped at his nose. He had no connection with volcanoes. Vika was the one whose mother was a volcano nymph. "I just reconnected myself to the magic that created the Dream Bench," he said, "but I didn't dare enter it fully. I thought I might get stuck again."

"So you're not sitting on the bench with me right now?"

"No. I'm nearby, though."

"This is neutral ground for us to meet, then." Vika gestured to the dark room, which was incredibly detailed— being, uniquely, a cell carved in the depths of a seething volcano—and at the same time, blandly black and nondescript.

"I still don't quite know how we created it," Nikolai said. "It's as if you've tapped into my magic to combine something of yours with mine."

"Except I'm not casting any enchantments right now."

Nikolai frowned. He'd forgotten for a second that she couldn't use magic. But if not, then how was it that his thoughts were blending with something of Vika's? Was it because he'd taken apart her egg and touched her energy then? Or did it go farther back, to the end of the Game, when he'd given her nearly all of his?

"I'm not allowed to use magic," Vika said, as if Nikolai didn't know about Pasha's edict. "I've been declared illegal by the tsardom."

"I—I'm sorry about that," he said, which was not at all

a sufficient answer, but it was the only one Nikolai could come up with, as he was still wading through his own questions.

"Not as sorry as I am." Vika frowned.

This brought him away from his thoughts, and he smiled. She was so pretty, even when she was piqued—even more so, actually, because it made her wildness glint in her eyes.

Nikolai wanted to kiss her.

The old version of him would have held back. But this one, with ambition and audacity in his veins, didn't. He took one long stride and wrapped his arm around Vika's waist.

She froze.

Nikolai bent his head and crushed his mouth against hers. His shadow had substance enough that although he blurred slightly into her, he could still feel the warmth and softness of her lips.

Vika gasped and pulled back. She gaped at him.

But then she reached her hand to the back of his head and drew him down and smashed her mouth against his. She kissed ferociously, just like her enchantments. Her lips parted, and their tongues found each other and danced like their mazurka at the masquerade, frenzied and hot. Their bodies pressed closer. Nikolai's edges blurred into hers.

Kissing Vika was like consuming fire and being consumed by fire, all at once. It heated away some of the chill that coursed through him. And this was a kiss that wasn't even real; it was happening between figments of themselves in a dream. How would it feel to kiss Vika on the other side of the bench?

She ripped her mouth away.

Nikolai let out a small breath. Still wanting.

"I don't know what to do with you," Vika said, her face only inches from his. She seemed torn between wanting to lean in again and wanting to run away.

Nikolai looked at her but didn't say anything. He couldn't.

"We're tied together, you and I," she said. "But I don't know if I'm drawn to you because I'm supposed to love you, or if it's because we're destined always to fight."

"Perhaps it's both," he managed to say.

"I don't want it to be both."

He cast his facade so he would look like the boy she'd once trusted. He held out his hand to her. "Then reconsider my offer. Join me."

CHAPTER FIFTY-SEVEN

He looked precisely how Vika remembered him before he'd become a shadow—like a poisonous autumn crocus, deadly beautiful with no antidote. Her breath caught and her entire body went weak for a moment, just like at the masquerade ball during the Game. It took a great deal of restraint not to take his hand or to reach up and caress the elegantly sharp lines of his face.

But, hard as it was, Vika resisted.

Nikolai held her gaze, though, and she couldn't look away.

"Why did you come to my house?" he finally asked.

She blinked and broke from the trance induced by his eyes. Had he done that to her on purpose? Or was it merely a side effect of being near Nikolai?

Both, most likely.

"I wanted to see you," she managed to say.

"Is that the only reason?"

There were many reasons, but right now, *wanting* to see

him seemed to overshadow them all.

"It's the only reason that matters," she said.

The walls in the black room suddenly glowed with specks of orange, as if lava had been resting deep inside and now came closer to the surface through the basalt's pores. Vika's heart slammed against the bodice of her dress.

Nikolai's new brand of magic, cold and smooth, wrapped like black silk around them. Vika shivered as he looked down at her, and she, up at him.

"I'm sorry about your mother," she said.

"I'm not." His eyes, despite his shroud, were still shadow, but they shaded even darker after he said that.

The lava behind Vika began to seep out of the walls, viscous and too slow to be a threat yet, but definitely hotter.

Nikolai grasped her arms, whether to keep her with him or out of instinct, to protect her from the lava, she didn't know. She also didn't know if she wanted to break free from his hold. A different sort of heat ran through her at his touch. Fire through her core.

And to think, they weren't actually even touching each other. This was a fantasy. Their real selves were elsewhere.

"May I have the honor of dancing with you?" Nikolai asked.

Vika looked all around. The lava had flowed down the walls and to the floor now, pooling and flaring in a circle around them. "Here?"

"Why not?"

She didn't move. "Why now?"

"Because you didn't take my hand earlier when I offered it. You came to my house, but you haven't decided yet what to do with me. So I must convince you. Perhaps a dance will do it. And if not, well, it's possible you or I may die soon—truly die—with you on Pasha's side and me on mine, and if that's the case, then I would like to have danced with you once more."

She hesitated. *But perhaps, if he still loves me as he did during the Game, a dance will remind him of what he used to be like. Perhaps I can still help him.*

"What shall we dance?" she asked. "I must warn you I don't know the waltz or the polonaise or anything fancy."

He laughed, and in that laugh, she heard a small measure of the former Nikolai. Her breath hitched with hope.

"You know the mazurka," he said. Music began to play in the volcano, a very lively tune.

But she didn't, not anymore. Nikolai had changed too much, and her heart had forgotten their rhythm.

Yet when he offered his hand again, there was no possibility of her saying no, even if he'd wanted her to dance with him off the edge of the earth.

Because the mazurka was the essence of their beings.

Nikolai held one of Vika's hands in his and placed her other hand on his shoulder before wrapping his free arm around the middle of her back.

Suddenly, she remembered how it had felt to dance with him at Pasha's masquerade.

"Will you trust me?" he had asked.

"To do what?"

"To dance for you?"

"No," Vika had said.

Nikolai had shrugged. "No matter. I'm not giving you a choice."

Then magic had rushed around her and levitated her off

the floor. Without needing to think, Vika and Nikolai had glided and spun, swiveled and sidestepped, a blur of movement together, as if lifted by the music and the wind.

Vika wanted to feel that again. Here. Now. In this volcano dream.

"Charm my feet," she breathed into Nikolai's ear. "Like at the masquerade."

He squeezed her hand and pulled her closer.

Smooth black silk unfurled around Vika, chilling and beguiling her at the same time. But she would not let go of Nikolai. The lava swirled ever closer around them.

The music flared. Their feet glided over the black rock, their bodies turning and stepping and twirling in perfect unison. It turned out that her heart had not forgotten the mazurka after all, merely locked its memory deep inside to protect her. But now the lava glowed brighter, and everywhere there was black silk and orange flame, and Vika was a wild girl with fiery hair, dancing with the Prince of Darkness and not caring that they spun together through this imagined hell.

They danced at a furious pace, blowing up all the dust from the volcano floor and surrounding themselves in a whirlwind of it. Vika's boots lifted off the ground, and Nikolai levitated, too, and soon enough they were dancing above the lava, weaving in and out of the plumes of smoke. Vika let out an insouciant laugh.

Eventually, though, the song ended, and Vika and Nikolai floated back down to the ground. Their breath still came and went with the rhythm, inhales and exhales in triple time.

They held on to each other longer than they needed to.

"I love you, Vika," he said softly. "Nothing about that has changed."

"But everything else has."

He tightened his grip on her arms, and a surge of his magic, a black part of it that he'd kept cleverly hidden from her until now, swept through her, skittering like a thousand centipedes that nipped at her with their venomous beaks.

She gasped at their touch.

Vika shivered, despite the lava creeping nearly to where they stood in the center of the room. Nikolai's magic couldn't keep her warm. It could only take from her, and from everyone else.

She tried to break away. But she couldn't. This was his Dream Bench, his creation, and she was just an ordinary girl.

"If you joined me against Pasha, we could dance like this together forever," he said. "Tsar and tsarina. Magic on the throne."

She shuddered at the ambitious lust in his tone. *What would a Nikolai like this do once he had power? There would be no one to counter him.*

No one, unless Vika stood her ground against him. The sense of duty—and of what was right—that Sergei had instilled in her burned in her core.

"I don't want to rule Russia with you," she said.

"We would be magnificent."

"No. We would be terrible."

Nikolai exhaled slowly, in that haunting, painful way only a shadow could. It was impossible to know whether he was angry or disappointed, or if he could see at all the truth of that particular future.

"But . . ." Vika looked up him. She remembered his laugh from not too long ago, the glimmer of the old Nikolai still buried inside this one. "I do love you."

He pulled back a little in surprise. "You don't act like it."

"I do. The Nikolai I once knew would see it."

He shook his head, as if doing so would obliterate the truth that there was a difference between him and whom he'd once been.

"Please, stop whatever you're planning. Your mother's energy taints you. But together, I'm sure we could still make things right."

He furrowed his brow. "I doubt that." He turned as if to go.

"Nikolai, wait."

He didn't look at her again, but he hesitated, his hand still in hers.

It was something. More than something. She would hold on to it as long as she could.

"No matter what happens," Vika said, "don't forget."

"Forget what?"

"That I love you."

His fingers tightened around hers for a brief moment. "I love you, too," he whispered.

He shook himself and disappeared from the dream.

Vika stayed, looking at the spot where Nikolai had stood. Only minutes later, however, the walls of the volcano began to tremble. No, not just tremble, but quake. Chunks of basalt rained down on her, and lava began to roar into the room. Vika shrieked and backed into a corner.

"Don't be afraid, my dear," a voice that sounded eerily similar to Vika's said, echoing throughout the cylindrical chamber. "You were born of this. It won't hurt you."

Vika pressed herself against the wall anyway. She stretched and yawned and shook herself awake, just as the lava began to lick at the soles of her boots.

She gasped as she jolted upright on the Dream Bench. She gulped in the fresh air, no fire and ash here.

Then she hurried back to the dock for a ferry. *I'm really beginning to hate dreams.*

CHAPTER FIFTY-EIGHT

A guard knocked on Yuliana's antechamber door and announced Pasha. She looked up from where she'd been working at her desk.

Pasha frowned as he walked in. He took in the room, still full of letters and envelopes, then looked pointedly at Yuliana. "Who are you?"

"What?" She scrunched her nose.

"This room is a disaster. My sister would never tolerate something like this. Therefore, you are clearly an imposter."

Yuliana could see the grin itching to break at the edge of his mouth. "Very funny."

"I thought so." He allowed himself to grin now and cleared a small space on the chaise longue. He picked up an envelope as he sat down. "So tell me, why *is* it such a mess in here?"

Yuliana rose and grabbed her notes from the desk, then wove through a thin break between the stacks of papers. Pasha shifted on the chaise to make space for her.

"These are Mother's things," she said as she sat down beside him.

Pasha nodded. "I recognize her perfume on the pages. But that doesn't answer my question of why it appears a storm has blown through your quarters."

"I went through her letters to figure out who your father was." Yuliana shoved her notes at Pasha. There were pages and pages of neat columns, listing dates and descriptions of the contents of each letter.

His grin disappeared. "I'm afraid to ask what you've discovered."

Yuliana scooted closer to him and took back her notes, shuffling through them until she found what she was looking for. "Well, to be honest, I haven't found anything definitive yet. The rumors are that Mother and Okhotnikov were involved early in 1808, right? Which would mean he could be your father, since you were born in October that year. And yet, look." She pointed to several entries, dated 1807. "These are the letters in which Mother's friends console her over the loss of 'the candle that lit her nights.' From what I can gather from her other correspondence, that's code for her lover."

Pasha leaned in for a better look. Yuliana could hear that he was holding his breath.

"He died in 1807?" Pasha said.

She nodded. "I think so."

"But you're not sure."

"I'm going to keep reading."

Pasha rose and kissed his sister on the top of her head. "I'll check the Imperial Army's historical rosters. That ought to give us an answer for good."

313

She looked up at him. "All right. But be careful."

He tilted his head quizzically.

"It's been too quiet since Nikolai tried to kill us with the carriage made of swords. He's up to something."

Pasha sighed. But then he nodded. "I'll figure out what he is doing."

CHAPTER FIFTY-NINE

The soldier on duty at the Imperial Army's office was asleep at his desk. Pasha frowned. He had gone to all the trouble of disguising himself as an infantryman from a regiment out of town—complete with a story about why he needed to access his uncle's records for an honor his fabricated city was bestowing upon said uncle—but it seemed all his preparations were unnecessary. It was also a bit disappointing that this was what a soldier in Pasha's army did when no one was looking. Then again, this was a records office, not an outpost at the edges of the Ottoman Empire. Even Pasha had to admit that if his job were sitting at this desk, he'd nap to pass the time too.

He slipped into the back of the office, past the snoring soldier, and availed himself of the files in the drawers.

The records were tidy, and this was certainly something of which Pasha could be proud. The Imperial Army was one of the finest in Europe, from their fighting against Napoleon down to their polished boots, from the wisdom of their commanders to the documentation for every soldier, so precise it was as if Yuliana herself had made the notations for each one.

Pasha riffled through the yellowed papers, working backward in time until he found 1807.

Please, let there be a record here of Okhotnikov's death.

He peeked through the door to the soldier out front, and upon hearing him still snoring, pulled a fat stack of papers from the drawer. Pasha sat with them on the floor, out of the soldier's line of sight, in case he woke.

Records of new recruits. Of retirements. Of promotions and approvals for sick leave.

And then, a notice of death.

Alexis Okhotnikov, staff captain of the Guard.

Cause of death: stabbing, assailant unknown.

Pasha's breath came fast and shallow. He clutched the paper to his chest, squeezed his eyes shut, and leaned back against the wall.

Before he'd left Yuliana's chambers, she'd shown him the rest of her notes. After the loss of "the candle that lit her nights," there were no more mentions of other lovers, and the tsarina began to write her friends more of the tsar's renewed attention to her. And then of her pregnancy.

With Okhotnikov's death record still in his hand, Pasha covered his face and processed the information.

"I really am a Romanov," he whispered. "I am the tsesarevich. The crown belongs to me." His voice shook as he uttered the words.

No, not just words. The truth.

But then he suddenly pulled his hands from his face and sat upright. Just because he was the legitimate heir didn't mean his ascension was guaranteed. Plenty of kingdoms had been wrenched from their rightful rulers. Nikolai had been relentless in pursuing the crown. He wouldn't stop simply because Pasha had evidence that he was first in line.

Pasha pounded the floor with a fist and got to his feet. His job was not done. For now he knew for certain he was supposed to be tsar.

"And I'm going to prove it."

Outside one of the larger barracks, a crowd several men deep was ringed around a pair of wrestlers, who circled each other, shirtless. The snow had been cleared half an hour ago, when the soldiers had grown listless and had too much to drink—they'd managed to "procure" three crates of vodka from an unattended cart on Sadovaya Street—and now they pummeled out their boredom with fists and wagers and, of course, more vodka.

Pasha, still in disguise as a soldier from another regiment, threw himself into their midst. If he was going to rule the empire, he had to do so in a way that worked for him— diving into the reality of his people.

Pasha *had* attended a recent Imperial Council meeting, though (much to the council members' surprise), and he'd learned that the constitutionalists were leveraging Nikolai's fete and the evils of magic to bring the army to their side. Until now, only a minority faction of the nobility had supported the idea of a constitutional monarchy, and even then, it had been an academic, almost theoretical discussion. But recruiting common soldiers was alarming, because it took a philosophical idea from fancy parlors and turned it into a real potential threat.

Ilya had turned out to be a lousy spy—he hadn't overheard anything worthy to report—so now Pasha had to see for himself if it was true.

"Hey, you gonna make a wager? Bogdan or Grigory?" A

soldier lurched toward the group of men beside Pasha.

"Nah," one of them said. "Not stupid enough to bet on the bear with such pathetic odds, and not drunk enough to put money on the scrawny one."

The soldier laughed and slapped him on the back. "Hear, hear."

Bogdan was indeed a bear of a man, not only in size but also in the sheer amount of fur on his chest, and he'd beaten five straight soldiers in the last fifteen minutes. He took a swig from a bottle offered him from one of his friends and paced the snowless ground some more.

Grigory was smaller. He was slower, too, both in wit and actual speed. But he was far less drunk than Bogdan, which made him a contender. He bounced on the soles of his boots as Bogdan cracked his knuckles.

"I'll wager Grigory wins this match," Pasha said.

The soldier lifted a brow. Then he grinned. "Well, well, a patron for David in his battle against Goliath. How much?"

Pasha was tempted to toss in twice whatever the highest gamble had been. But right then, Bogdan slammed an elbow into Grigory's nose and left his face a fountain of blood. Pasha heard Yuliana's voice in his head, reprimanding him for being too impetuous, and so he reluctantly said, "The minimum."

The soldier snorted. "Not actually much of a patron, are you?"

"Just not comfortable with too much risk," Pasha said. Which wasn't true at all. Yuliana was the rule follower. Pasha was the one always getting scolded for taking risks. But he passed a rumpled bill and a few coins to the soldier anyway.

As soon as the money exchanged hands, Bogdan smashed

his fist into Grigory's chest, and Grigory collapsed onto the cold ground. Bogdan hovered. The ring of soldiers went silent as they waited. Grigory didn't move.

Bogdan dropped his defensive stance and stepped closer to Grigory. Someone shouted from the crowd, "You better not have killed him!"

Grigory groaned and rolled onto his back. The soldier who was acting as judge shouted, "Bogdan wins again!" Bogdan flexed his biceps and grunted.

The man next to Pasha slapped him on the back. He reeked of vodka, and he slurred as he asked, "Who are you, stranger? Anyone here would know that wagering against Bogdan is always a losing bet."

Pasha gave the man beside him a practiced look of dismay. "I'm on leave from my company outside Saint Petersburg, just here visiting family. I ought to refrain from betting at all, for I enjoy it when the dark horse wins, and I bet on them more often than not. But they're 'dark horses' for a reason."

The soldier offered Pasha a half-drunk bottle of vodka. "Drown the loss?"

Pasha grabbed the bottle by its neck and took a long swig, wiping his mouth afterward with his sleeve (and being careful not to disturb his temporary mustache). He handed the bottle back to the soldier. "Thank you, er . . . ?"

"Name's Yuri."

"Just Yuri? No patronymic?" It was odd to introduce oneself without the middle name that honored one's father. Then again, Yuri wasn't exactly steady on his feet at the moment. It was perhaps a feat for him to remember any part of his name at all.

Yuri took another drink. "My mother was rather, shall

we say, *popular* in her youth. You know, like the late tsarina."
Yuri laughed, spitting sloppily as he did so.

Pasha drew back a fist. "How dare you insult Her Imperial Majesty!"

"My apologies. Were you one of her lovers?" Yuri grinned.

Pasha was about to swing at Yuri when someone behind him caught his arm.

"Hey," Bogdan growled, spinning Pasha around to face him. "No punching the drunkards. It's not fair. I'll fight you instead, Pretty Boy."

Pasha looked up at Bogdan. The fur on his chest was matted with sweat. His muscles flexed. He was a real-life Goliath.

But Pasha seethed with indignation, and he wasn't about to back down. Besides, it would be embarrassing and dishonorable to back down. "Fine," he said. "If you want to pay for Yuri's insult, I'll fight you. But since you talk of fairness, let's account for the obvious—size. I propose we use swords rather than fists to make it an even fight." Pasha was the best fencer in Saint Petersburg. He stood a chance with swords.

"Whatever you want. Doesn't matter, 'cause I don't lose." Bogdan cracked his knuckles.

The drunk soldiers around them looked from Bogdan to Pasha for a moment. Then a cheer swept the crowd. "Fight! Fight! Fight! Fight!"

The soldier who'd been serving as judge of the wrestling matches appeared with two swords. He gave Pasha first choice.

Pasha picked up both blades and weighed them in his hands. He chose the lighter one. Not as strong, but easier to maneuver. Agility was often underestimated in the face of strength.

Bogdan grabbed his sword with one hand, and his crotch with the other. The gesture that followed was the opposite of polite.

All right. This wouldn't be anything like the gentlemanly fencing matches to which Pasha was accustomed. But he'd adjust. It couldn't be *that* different, could it?

Bogdan swung his sword in a broad arc, viciously enough to sever Pasha's head. Pasha yelped and leaped backward.

Never mind. It was very different.

"Pretty Boy is quick on his feet," Bogdan said. The crowd jeered.

Pasha advanced and attacked.

Bogdan parried and lunged at Pasha.

Pasha deflected and attacked again. Their swords moved quickly, like flashes of violently choreographed silver. Once in the rhythm of the fight, it was not so different from the beat of fencing. *Parry-riposte, parry-riposte, parry-riposte.* Deflect-attack, deflect-attack, deflect-attack.

Bogdan lunged again, but Pasha suspected it was a feint. He didn't parry. Bogdan quickly recovered and changed tactics.

Pasha dodged. But then he stumbled as a muscle in his abdomen cramped, exactly where Vika had extracted Nikolai's poisoned gear.

Luckily, Bogdan was slow, at least in comparison to Pasha. Pasha inhaled sharply, forcing himself to ignore the cramp, and advanced to execute his own feint.

Bogdan moved to parry. Not fast enough, though. Pasha circled his sword under Bogdan's and pressed the point of his blade against Bogdan's hairy chest, right in the center above his heart.

Bogdan's nostrils flared like those of an incensed bull. He scowled down at Pasha.

Pasha's muscles ached, but his hand was steady. A bit more pressure from his sword, and Bogdan's blood would spill.

Bogdan glared at Pasha for another long moment. Then he dropped his sword on the ground and raised both hands in defeat. Suddenly, he began to laugh, a deep, rumbling belly laugh. "Not bad, Pretty Boy. Not bad."

Pasha held the cramp at his stomach. "I beg your pardon?"

"You're the best fighter here. Other than me, of course."

Pasha didn't point out that he had actually just defeated Bogdan.

"How long are you in town, Pretty Boy? And how strong is your allegiance to the imperial family? Do you really care about that bastard tsesarevich, or were you just defending the late tsarina's honor out of respect, as any good man should?" Bogdan shot a glare at Yuri. Yuri shrugged and giggled.

Pasha carefully set his sword on the ground. As carefully as he could he answered, "I don't think it's fair to insult the dead. They cannot defend themselves."

"And what about the living?" Bogdan asked.

"The living can fight."

Bogdan grunted in agreement. "We could use more men like you. Especially since your company is stationed outside the city."

Pasha borrowed a bottle from a nearby soldier and took a couple of drinks before he spoke again. "What do you mean, you could use more men like me?"

"Do you believe in Russia?"

Pasha nodded.

"And do you believe all men are worth the same in God's eyes?"

The soldiers around them began to chuckle under their breaths.

"Watch out!" Yuri shouted, seeming to have forgotten that Pasha had been about to punch him not too long ago. "Bogdan will try to recruit you to fight the tsesarevich and kill his witch."

Bogdan glared at him.

"It's all right," Pasha lied. "I already know. Word has reached my company, too."

A crooked smile spread across Bogdan's face then, revealing a bear's worth of yellowed teeth. "Better than we'd hoped. We'll see you then, when we march against the tsesarevich and block his path to Moscow?"

Pasha hesitated. The constitutionalists already had concrete plans? They were going to ambush him on the road next month so he couldn't go to his coronation ceremony?

"Don't look so worried," Yuri said, pointing his near-empty bottle in their direction. "If you and your men don't show, Bogdan will single-handedly block the road. He'll just sit in the middle of it. And he'll sit on the witch, too!"

The soldiers broke into rowdy guffaws and clinked bottles. Pasha pulled himself together and faked a hearty laugh along with them.

But Bogdan didn't laugh. And inside, Pasha didn't either.

CHAPTER SIXTY

The creeping of Nikolai's energy, like those centipedes within her veins, still haunted Vika, even a couple of days later. It was powerful, of course, for Bolshebnoie Duplo's magic had only grown with the people's increasing fear, but there was something else to it that worried Vika more: it was restless, its hundreds of thousands of feet in nonstop motion, impatient to get wherever it was intending to go. And the fact that even before Aizhana's death, before Nikolai had grown even colder and angrier, he'd tried to kill Pasha . . .

This was why Vika had tasked herself with following Nikolai. Something was afoot. Another plan. Another attempt at the throne. And having fought against him in the Game, she knew his next move would only escalate.

The one benefit to not being permitted to use her powers was that she could trail him undetected. She didn't need to cast a barrier shroud around herself. She could simply wear a large-brimmed hat and pull her scarf over her nose, and she blended in with the rest of the people hurrying through Saint Petersburg, going from here to there or generally trying to get out of the streets as soon as possible in case of another magical debacle.

Nikolai left his house in the early evening. Vika, with Poslannik riding in a pocket in her coat, kept some distance between them, but she never let him get too far. He walked briskly along Ekaterinsky Canal, then turned onto Nevsky Prospect. She hurried so she wouldn't lose him in the bustle of shoppers, which at this point consisted mostly of servants picking up crates of crackers, cured meats, pickles, and other provisions for their masters, who seemed (from the servants' hurried conversations) to think they might need to barricade themselves indoors in the event of magical apocalypse. It was the sort of scenario that ordinarily would have made Vika laugh for its ludicrousness. But given the violence of Nikolai's enchantments, she could not find even a splinter of humor in the people's reactions now.

For a moment, she lost Nikolai in a sea of top hats that had emerged from Bissette & Sons. The shop was closing for the night, its customers released back into the world in a stream of bespoke suits and fine wool coats. The men began as a cluster, but then parted and all began to go their separate directions, weaving this way and that through the crowds.

"No, no, no," Vika said, as her eyes tried to follow first this hat, then that one, then another. "I can't lose him," she muttered. "I won't."

But in addition to that was the worry that this diversion was no mere coincidence. *Does Nikolai know I'm following him? Did he make those men spill out of Bissette & Sons all at once on purpose?*

Not that that would deter Vika; it would just make trailing him more complicated.

She focused on the hats again, their owners now spreading farther apart and away on their disparate paths. Black hat, narrow brim. Black hat, narrow brim. Another black hat with . . . ugh, a narrow brim.

Nikolai's hat would be different, though, Vika thought. He wouldn't have purchased a hat like everyone else's. He would have crafted his own, for fashion was what Nikolai loved best in his rare moments of free time. *So what I need to find is a hat that* isn't *black, or that doesn't have a narrow brim.*

She was too short to see over the heads and shoulders around her, and meanwhile, her target was getting away. If only Vika could levitate.

Or climb a streetlamp. She'd climbed many a tree growing up in the woods. A streetlamp was not too different, except it was utterly inappropriate to scale a light in the middle of a city street.

Vika grinned.

She jumped up the base of the nearest streetlamp and latched onto the pole, hoisting herself up as nimbly as a tree squirrel (with a bit of help from the Christmas garlands twined around the lamp). The people closest to her gasped. One servant dropped her bag into the snow. A little girl whined, "Papa, I want to do that, too."

You should, Vika thought. She winked at the girl. *Don't ever let the rules stop you.*

Vika scanned the boulevard again. Black hat, narrow brim. Black hat, narrow brim. Black hat . . . shinier and darker than others. Fabric that caught the lamplight and at the right angles, rippled and shimmered like ink reflecting a candle flame. The hat also had a decidedly wider brim.

"Aha," Vika said. "Got you." She hopped down from the streetlamp and threaded through the crowd.

Nikolai turned along the embankments of the Fontanka River. Vika veered after him and followed.

CHAPTER SIXTY-ONE

There were innumerable bridges along the waterways of Saint Petersburg, but the Chernyshev Bridge over the Fontanka River had always been Nikolai's favorite, especially in the evening. It had four Doric pavilions carved from stone that housed the drawbridge mechanism—being the mechanical sort, Nikolai particularly liked this fact—and the pavilions themselves looked like miniature palaces against the deep blue twilight sky.

He leaned against the railing, staring out over the river frozen in jeweled green. The color was the same shade as Vika's eyes, almost too deep and too mesmerizing to be real.

But of course, the ice wasn't real, or at least its greenness wasn't, for it was the wintered result of one of Vika's earlier enchantments. Yet even though the water was frozen, Nikolai could still sense her magic floating off it, wild and powerful and scented with cinnamon, incongruent yet perfectly right. He inhaled deeply, closed his eyes, and thought of their kiss in the volcano dream.

It only made him more morose. She'd turned him down again.

People bustled behind him across the bridge. Nikolai kept himself well concealed, and the blue-purple darkness of the gloaming made short work of any lingering curiosity about the gentleman at the edge of the bridge.

Eventually, footsteps approached Nikolai that were, in fact, meant for him.

"Your Imperial Highness," Ilya said into his own coat, so that no passersby would hear.

Nikolai nodded in greeting but continued to look out over the river.

Ilya came close enough that they could talk, but he, too, looked straight out over the river, such that it appeared the two boys were not conversing at all, but rather, lost in thought over the sight of emerald ice.

"Our forces are shaping up beautifully," Ilya said. "Trubetskoy has been officially appointed the leader of our movement, with Volkonsky and some of the others reporting directly to him. The soldiers are already predisposed to join us because so many of them are afraid of magic; thus, our proposal for a constitution appeals to them, for it prevents sole power from resting in the tsar and by association, his witch. I think it's looking good. The Decembrists are twenty thousand strong."

Nikolai cocked his head. "The Decembrists?"

Ilya grinned. "It has a daring sound to it, don't you think? I came up with it. It will unite us, make the soldiers feel a part of something important and grand."

"The Decembrists," Nikolai said, letting the name tarry on his tongue. "I do like it. But I thought our plan was to move against Pasha in January? Why name us after *this* month?"

"The timetable has moved up," Ilya said. "The tsesarevich and grand princess learned of our original plans to block the coronation."

Nikolai looked away from the river at Ilya. "Yuliana?"

He shook his head. "It was actually the tsesarevich this time. I overheard him telling his sister."

"Right. You're one of his Guard." Nikolai tapped his fingers on the bridge's railing. "So then . . . ?"

"We'll continue to use the plan to block the coronation as a decoy," Ilya said.

"Don't tell the soldiers it's a ruse, though," Nikolai said. "The crown has its ears everywhere." He gestured at Ilya, case in point.

Ilya laughed under his breath. "Of course. We will continue to tell the soldiers that the plan is to target the coronation. But we have another, different opportunity the day after tomorrow. That's when the army is supposed to swear an oath of allegiance to the tsesarevich. But we'll refuse it."

Nikolai drummed his fingers on the railing of the bridge as he contemplated this. He knew what Ilya was talking about—before the ascension of every new tsar, the Imperial Army held a symbolic ceremony during which they swore their allegiance to the crown. There would be multiple ceremonies throughout Saint Petersburg, held at each garrison.

This was a better idea, actually. The problem with trying to block Pasha's coronation was the distance. The road to Moscow was long, and it would be difficult to coordinate the actions of the men from afar. But if the coup could happen right here in Saint Petersburg . . .

Then Nikolai wouldn't have to wait weeks. He could secure the crown two days from now.

"I like the new plan," Nikolai said, pushing off from the railing. "But what do you mean to do after refusing the oath?"

"Demand a constitution, and that you be put on the throne."

Nikolai shook his head. "Talk won't be enough. We need to march against Pasha to show our physical force, just as in our original plan to block his coronation."

Ilya looked over his shoulder to make sure no one was listening, then back out onto the river. "What do you suggest?"

"The ceremonies will be spread out all over the city. We need to assemble our forces together in one place after they reject the oath."

"Palace Square?" Ilya suggested.

Nikolai pictured where his Jack and ballerina had been. "No . . . if we have twenty thousand men, the space is too small. We'd be trapped if a fight ensued." He thumbed the brim of his hat as he thought. "What about Peter's Square?"

Ilya nodded eagerly. "It's bigger."

Vika had returned the statue of Peter the Great to its place after its rampage on Nevsky Prospect. "Peter the Great came to life once to tell the people of the tsesarevich's wrongs," Nikola said. "The statue is the protector of our city. I like the symbolism of Peter the Great watching over us and our cause."

Also, Nikolai thought, *Peter's Square is personal.* Because that was where he had first told Pasha he would take the throne. It would be perfect to actually make good on his threat on the same site.

If Nikolai weren't wearing a facade, his silhouette would have shaded a bit darker.

"All right," Ilya said. "I'll inform the major general and colonel of your wishes to march on Peter's Square."

"Twenty thousand men, you say?"

"Yes. And the remainder of the Imperial Army is far-flung on the Kazakh steppe and near Missolonghi and elsewhere. Therefore, we ought to meet little resistance. The tsesarevich and grand princess will have only their guards. Minus me, of course."

And they'll have Vika, Nikolai thought. Surely Pasha would renounce his edict when Nikolai's coup arose. Vika would be allowed use her magic again. But Nikolai didn't bring that up. Let the Decembrists worry about ordinary men, and he would worry about enchanters.

"Tell the troops to prepare for a snowstorm," Nikolai said.

Ilya looked at him, with a question in his eyes.

Nikolai shrugged and looked back over the ice-jeweled water. "I have a feeling the weather may be especially fierce that day."

CHAPTER SIXTY-TWO

Vika couldn't hear Nikolai and Ilya's conversation, so Poslannik had scuttled back and forth on the bridge, between the boys and where Vika hid, in order to tell her what was happening. She'd had to cover her mouth with both hands to avoid exclaiming during the entirety of their conversation. Even after Nikolai and Ilya left the bridge, she pressed herself into the interior corner of the pavilion where she'd stashed herself.

If I tell Pasha what I overheard, he and Yuliana will find a way to crush Nikolai.

But if I don't report this, Nikolai will ruin them.

Everything around her seemed to move in half time, including Vika's ability to process what to do.

Her bracelet didn't burn because there was no direct order that she disobeyed. This would have to be Vika's decision, and her decision alone.

It was the freedom to determine her own fate that she'd yearned for.

Vika lingered in the pavilion a few minutes more. Then she hurried off the bridge, hugging her coat closer against her to fight off the cold, and turned away from the river toward the Winter Palace.

CHAPTER SIXTY-THREE

The sun was long gone, but Pasha liked the challenge of shooting in the dark. Well, nearly dark, for Gavriil would not allow the tsesarevich to practice at the archery yard—or anywhere, for that matter—without any light, both because it was a danger to Pasha (it made it impossible for the Guard to protect him if they couldn't see) and because it was a danger to any poor soul who wandered into Pasha's line of fire.

Not that anyone would do that. And not that Pasha would miss his targets, even if he couldn't see them. Archery might not have been a necessary skill for war anymore, but it didn't stop Pasha from being one of the best archers in all of Europe. He knew this for a fact. He'd triumphed in many a challenge—for sport, of course—by princes and military officers across the continent and in England whenever he'd gone abroad or hosted them here in Russia's court. And Pasha did not mean to ever give up his place in those elite ranks.

He nocked an arrow against the bowstring in the swift motion of someone for whom the weapon had become a natural extension of his own body, and he released the arrow just as quickly, listening to it streak through the air and hit an icicle on a nearby tree in a satisfying shatter of crystal. Pasha didn't need the torchlight to let him know his arrow had landed on its intended icicle, even though the branch was lined with them. He already knew by feel what the arrow's trajectory had been, and by sound the precise distance it had flown.

He also knew by feel and by sound when Vika approached the archery range, not only because all the guards shifted slightly, standing a bit taller at the presence of a woman, but also because the wind seemed to blow a little more fervently.

Pasha's hand, steady a moment ago, now shook. He hadn't seen her since he and Yuliana had taken away her ability to use her powers.

The torchlight illuminated her. Vika's features were pinched, and she glared at the guards, almost like Yuliana would. Pasha handed his bow and quiver to Gavriil and walked slowly (he wasn't eager to be yelled at) to meet Vika in the middle of the range. His boots crunched on the fresh snow.

"Send them away," she said, eyeing the guards.

Pasha frowned. He hadn't expected to jump straight into whatever business was at hand.

Vika kept looking at the guards.

"Gavriil," Pasha said, turning to his captain. "A moment, please. All of you."

Gavriil hesitated but then bowed, and the guards moved

to the outer perimeter of the archery yard. Still watchful, but out of earshot.

Pasha turned back to Vika. "What happened? Are you all right?"

She scowled at him for a moment.

Of course she wasn't all right. He'd taken enchanting away from an enchanter. "I'm sorry," Pasha said. "I know it's difficult—"

"I'm not here to discuss that. Well, not yet." Vika inched closer to Pasha and angled her chin to speak into his ear.

"Oh. Then what is it?" He bent slightly to get closer to her. He exhaled at the same time, relieved that she wasn't here to protest the edict.

"Nikolai is planning a coup, to take place in two days."

All the tension that target practice had released now came rushing back into Pasha's body. "What? How?" From what Pasha had learned in the barracks, the talk had been about blocking his coronation next month. Not an imminent revolt.

"I overheard him and your guard Ilya Koshkin talking about a group called the Decembrists. They supposedly have twenty thousand men already committed. They'll refuse to take the oath of allegiance to you and instead install Nikolai on the throne."

That familiar spiral in Pasha's stomach began again, caused by Nikolai, making Pasha pay for what he did. And now Ilya, one of his best guards, betraying him as well. Had Ilya been one of the constitutionalists all along? Was there no one upon whom Pasha could rely?

Vika looked up at him. "So what are we going to do?"

He blinked. "We?"

"Yes, *we*," she said. "This has gone on too long. It needs to end. And I am here—not at your service, but by your side as an equal—if you'll have me."

Pasha furrowed his brow, but he nodded. Because while everything else was wrong, this was right. Vika was the sun, and she could not be eclipsed. She'd never deserved to be labeled as "lesser."

Neither had Pasha. All his life, he'd doubted himself, second-guessed his ability to wear the crown. He wasn't lesser, either. Lesser than his father, than Yuliana, than Vika or Nikolai. The furious eddying in his stomach slowed, then came to a stop.

Pasha was also a sun in his own right.

He strode through the snow to the nearest weapons rack and retrieved a bow and two quivers of arrows. Gavriil and some of the guards began to move back into the yard, but Pasha shook his head, and they halted.

Across the yard, there was a large, blank sheet of canvas. No bull's-eye, just plain cream. Pasha plucked an arrow from the first quiver, took aim, and let it fly. It hit square in the center of the empty space.

He took three arrows in his hand now and fired them rapidly, one after another, and before the third had landed, he had another three in his hand. *Thwack, thwack, thwack*, over and over, the first quiver empty and onto the next, arrow after arrow after arrow in the same sharp rhythm until the second quiver, too, was spent.

The entire yard was silent. Vika stared at the canvas with her mouth slightly open.

The arrows formed the shape of the Great Imperial Crown.

"I intend to be tsar," Pasha said. "I denied it all my life when it seemed inevitable and forced upon me. But now that the throne could be taken away, it's as clear as the icicles on the trees that I want it. And I am willing to fight, to risk my life, to prove it."

Vika stared at him, much like she'd stared at the canvas full of arrows. "I might need to start calling you 'Your Imperial Highness' again, because that was the most kingly thing you've ever said."

Pasha clutched the bow in his hand. "Is that good?"

"I like this version of you," Vika said. "And I think the people will, too, even more than they already love you. That is, if we defeat Nikolai and survive. Can I use magic again?"

"Would it be possible to be . . ."

"Discreet?"

Pasha grimaced at the reference to Yuliana's complaint at how Vika had handled the statue of Peter the Great. "I wouldn't have put it that way," he said. "But yes, something like that."

"I'll try not to do anything that would further frighten the city. I just need to have magic at my disposal again to help you."

"I know. Yes, you're free to use your power again. It seems the damage of Nikolai's aggressions has already been done anyway, if he's amassed twenty thousand troops. I will prepare my men for your presence."

"Do you need to renounce your earlier edict? Or . . . get Yuliana's approval?"

Pasha barely stifled a wince at the allusion to his past inability to make decisions without his sister. But it was the truth, and it would take a while for him to establish a new presumption that he could, in fact, act like a tsar on his own.

"No. Yuliana has helped me in the past, but your oath as Imperial Enchanter binds you to the tsar. I'm the closest to that at the moment. And the edict was just a declaration for the benefit of the people."

Vika nodded, her lips pressed together in a way that was neither smile nor frown, but something in between. Which was precisely how Pasha felt, too. What they were about to embark upon would not be easy.

"If this is really going to happen, we should both get some rest," he told her. "Be careful in the meantime."

"I don't believe in careful," Vika said. The moonlight glinted in her eyes.

As she walked away, Pasha knew one thing for certain: he'd never love another girl quite the same.

CHAPTER SIXTY-FOUR

Pasha had briefed Yuliana on everything Vika reported regarding Nikolai and the Decembrists' planned coup, and by the next afternoon, Yuliana had set her own plans in motion.

"Colonel Trubetskoy, I'm so glad you could join me for tea," she said, as a guard showed the long-faced nobleman into the room. He wore a dapper gray frock coat and a cream-colored cravat. His dark hair was neatly combed and kept short, other than the sideburns along his entire jaw.

As secretive as the constitutionalists thought they were, the Imperial Council had known for a while that Trubetskoy was one of the original founders of the movement. They also knew his previous groups had disbanded and failed. Internally, Yuliana smirked.

Trubetskoy bowed. "Your Imperial Highness, it is an honor to be asked to join you."

Yuliana dipped her head. She was already seated, the three-tiered displays of sandwiches and desserts set before her. "Please, do sit."

Trubetskoy obeyed.

A servant girl brought porcelain cups painted in a cobalt lattice pattern and rimmed in pure gold. It was Catherine the Great's favorite design, and therefore Yuliana's favorite tea set. The servant filled both Yuliana's and Trubetskoy's cups with fragrant black tea scented with dried orange.

Yuliana picked a vegetable tartine from the savory display of sandwiches and offered it to Trubetskoy.

"No, thank you, Your Imperial Highness."

"Perhaps you'd prefer sweets?" She swept her hand to the three tiers of jam tarts and chocolate and candied nuts. "The palace kitchen works miracles."

Trubetskoy gave her a strained smile. "Well, then, I cannot refuse Your Imperial Highness's generous offer." He took a chocolate and a handful of candied nuts and placed them on his plate.

"Good. Now that we're through with the pleasantries, let me get to why I asked you here. You've been one of the voices for the constitutionalists for quite some time, have you not?"

"Well, Your Imperial Highness, I wouldn't say I was a 'voice,' per se. I am interested in the philosophical discussions."

Yuliana rolled her eyes.

Trubetskoy faltered but then pressed on. "I promise, the conversations have been nothing more than private chatter, and I'm not sure who spoke of them to you, but—"

"I'll take that as confirmation," Yuliana said. "I honestly don't know how all you noblemen think you're getting away with this talk, as if the tsar were unaware. My father knew everything you were up to. But he let you continue on, as long as you were merely spouting high principles and hot air among the aristocracy.

"But now my sources tell me you've moved on to agitating the common soldiers. You mean to take the idea of a constitutional monarchy out of your dinner parties and into the barracks, and eventually, this palace and the empire. You intend to block my brother from traveling to Moscow for his coronation next month." She purposely did not mention that she knew of their actual plans to stage a coup tomorrow. It was like chess. One did not reveal all of one's moves.

Trubetskoy nearly choked on the walnut in his mouth. He whipped a handkerchief out of his pocket and coughed into it, then swallowed and hastily drank some tea.

"You do realize, Colonel, that that would be treason? It would be such a shame if a man such as yourself—descended from a noble line with a proud history of defending the empire—were to lose his head."

"I—I . . . The death penalty was abolished in Russia."

"Oh, was it?" Yuliana said, even though she knew perfectly well that it had been. "Well, new leadership, new rules. There was supposed to be a hanging the other day, did you hear? That's what happens to those who act against the tsardom."

Trubetskoy braced himself on the edge of the table. "Your Imperial Highness, I promise you, whatever you've heard about me, it isn't true."

Yuliana took a dainty bite of her tartine. She sipped on her tea. She dabbed her mouth with a cloth napkin, folded it, and set it precisely back in its place. "What would your lovely wife, Ekaterina Laval, do if you were to be executed? Or even if the tsesarevich were lenient and merely sentenced you to *katorga* in the Siberian labor camps for the rest of your life? Would she be able to live without the riches to which she is accustomed? Would she accompany you to the penal colonies and watch you toil in shackles in the mines?"

Trubetskoy cleared his throat. "Again, I insist that whatever you imagine you've heard, it is not true. And if it were, my words and actions would be mine alone. Ekaterina is a complete innocent."

Yuliana folded her hands before her. "Well, if you've done nothing wrong, there is nothing to fear. But, Colonel, if you leave here today understanding only one thing, let it be this: my brother will be tsar. If you attempt to rise against him, you will fail, and those involved—including all associated with them, through marriage or otherwise—will be found guilty of high treason. Do I make myself clear?"

He remained steady. "As clear as Russia is great, Your Imperial Highness."

"Excellent. I'm so glad we could have this little chat. You may go now."

Trubetskoy rose from his chair, bowed, and retreated from the room.

When he was gone, Yuliana stabbed at a jam tart. Trubetskoy's insistence on his innocence hadn't faltered when she'd mentioned his wife. He hadn't even shuddered or given a hint that Yuliana had intimidated him. The afternoon hadn't gone quite as she wanted.

Yuliana twisted her fork. The tart crumbled beneath it.

She could only hope that beneath his calm exterior, Trubetskoy had been frightened. And that his fear would impact the Decembrists' plans against the throne.

CHAPTER SIXTY-FIVE

Vika sat at the kitchen table in her cottage, absentmindedly stirring a bowl of borscht as she contemplated the revolt to come.

Someone tapped at her door.

She frowned and pushed back from the table. Who would visit her here? The knock sounded too timid to be Ludmila.

Vika opened the front door, and snow blew in from the darkness, along with a windswept Renata.

"I'm sorry to come unannounced," Renata said. She looked around at the entry and began to step backward into the snow again. "And I didn't mean to barge in. It was the wind—"

"It's all right." Vika pulled Renata into the entry and locked the winter out. "Let me take your coat."

Renata stood as if still frozen from the snow.

"Shall I charm it off you?" Vika asked. Sparks rushed to her fingertips. She'd been deprived for what had felt like an eternity—although it had actually been less than a week—such that the promise of even such a simple enchantment made her entire body hum.

"I thought the tsesarevich forbade you to use magic?"

Vika smothered the smile that had crept to her lips. She'd always liked Renata, but then again, if forced to choose, she knew Renata would pick Nikolai. "Pasha and I have an understanding," Vika said carefully.

Renata hesitated but then didn't answer. She shrugged off her coat and let Vika hang it on a hook by the door.

"I—I came to ask you for tea."

Vika narrowed her eyes. "Oh, really? They don't have tea in Saint Petersburg?"

"I mean, I came to show you something. It's about Nikolai, in a way. And tea leaves."

Vika scrutinized her again. But it was just Renata, with her wide, innocent eyes and even more innocent braids. There was not a whisper of guile within her.

"All right. This way." Vika led Renata into her kitchen. She cleared away the uneaten bowl of borscht and grabbed two cups from the cabinet. Her teapot was already heating on top of the samovar, as Vika had intended to brew tea for herself earlier (except that she had forgotten, she'd been so lost in stirring her soup).

She fetched her strainer and was just about to pour *zavarka*—the dark tea concentrate in the pot—into the cups when Renata stepped forward and said, "Wait."

"You don't want tea?" Vika asked.

"I do. But please don't strain out the leaves."

Vika nodded and set her strainer down. She poured some *zavarka* (with the leaves) into each cup and diluted it with hot water from the samovar. "Please have a seat."

The girls settled themselves at the kitchen table—it

didn't escape Vika that Renata waited until Vika was seated before she herself sat down—and cradled their cups in their hands. Steam spiraled off the surface.

"So . . . what is it you wanted to show me?"

Renata took several sips. "I—I can move the tea."

"What do you mean?"

Renata drank until there was only a quarter of the tea left. "Let me show you."

She stared at her cup. Nothing happened at first. But then ripples fanned out from the center of the liquid, and the leaves inside it began to quiver, subtly floating toward the edges, as if there were a current in the tea.

"Heavens," Vika whispered.

Renata blinked. The tea stopped moving.

"I interrupted your concentration," Vika said. "Forgive me. Continue, please."

Renata gritted her teeth and stared again at her cup. The leaves quivered, then continued to drift. They stopped close to their original place, but in an entirely different pattern.

"You can control the leaves." Vika shook her head, still astonished by what she'd just witnessed. "But how?"

Renata smoothed a wrinkle in the table runner. It was one Ludmila had knit for Vika and Sergei ages ago. She kept going over the same spot, even though it was already smoothed down.

"Renata?"

"Aizhana gave me some energy," she blurted out. "But it wasn't for me. It was for Nikolai. Some must still be inside me, though, and now I can do this." She waved her hands at the cup.

Aizhana had given Renata energy? *But why, then, isn't Renata doing horrible things like Nikolai?* Vika thought back to the conversation she'd overheard between Nikolai and his mother, right before her death.

Aizhana had explained her love for him, her desire to help him at all costs, which explained why she'd stooped to passing her energy to him through trickery. And . . . oh.

Aizhana had also confessed to killing Galina. Which meant it was Galina's energy, not her own, that had been passed on to Renata. Could that explain the difference? Could it be that the mentor's magical energy heightened Renata's talent for fortune-telling?

But how would Aizhana have managed to transfer only Galina's energy, without tainting it with any of her own? Vika frowned. She didn't know the mechanics of energy transfer. That was a Karimov specialty.

"Please say something," Renata said. "Am I a monster now, too, because of Nikolai's mother?"

Vika shook her head. "I don't know what exactly Aizhana did, but I doubt you could ever be a monster. You're too good and pure."

Perhaps that was it. When Aizhana gave Nikolai energy, he was already weak, a shadow in the Dream Bench, driven by anguish. But Renata had been strong, and driven by love.

"Think of the cup half full, right?" Vika said. "You can now change fate."

"I . . . I don't know."

"Well, on the chance that it's true . . . I have an idea." Vika rotated her hand so her palm opened upward. She smiled as a small woven pouch appeared in it. Even the simplest feats of magic provided such joy now.

Renata craned her neck to get a better look. "What's inside?"

Vika loosened the drawstring and poured several threads of bright red saffron into her hand.

"It looks like your hair," Renata said.

"Exactly." Vika plucked the thread on top and dropped it into her tea. "That will represent me. Should I drink until there's only a little bit left?"

Renata nodded slowly, beginning to catch on.

Vika did so and set the cup back on its saucer. Black leaves settled on the bottom in a V. The thread of saffron hovered over the point at the base of it, where the leaves diverged into two lines. "What does that mean?" she asked.

Renata fingered her braids. "It means there are two people whose paths have split. And you—the saffron—are doomed to be caught between them."

"That's painfully accurate," Vika said. "Now let's change it. How would it look if I helped bring them back together, rather than simply standing where they pull apart?"

Renata chewed her lip as she thought. "I suppose if the saffron is not at the split but at the top of the V, arching like a bridge reconnecting the paths."

"Can you do that?"

Renata took a deep breath. "I'll try." She gripped a braid in each hand and focused on the cup.

The tea inside quivered. Then, slowly, it began to ripple, but only near the red thread. The black leaves remained in their V shape, but the saffron floated away.

Five minutes of intense concentration later, the saffron bridged the top of the black paths.

"You did it!" Vika said.

Renata slouched in her chair. "Not quite. There's still tea left in the cup. It's not a prophecy until the liquid is gone. But I don't know how you're going to manage to drink it without moving the leaves some more."

Vika smirked. "You forget I'm an enchantress." She eyed the cup, and a second later, the last of the tea rose up as if through an invisible straw, only there was no straw at all, only air. Vika winked as she slurped the final drops of tea.

The leaves stayed exactly where Renata had placed them.

Both girls simply looked at the prophecy for a while.

"Do you think it will work?" Renata finally asked.

Vika sighed. "Nikolai thinks our fates are already determined. I refuse to believe that. Otherwise, I wouldn't be trying to change them. It would be even better if you could shift not only *my* leaves, but also Nikolai's. It would be more direct that way. Do you think you can?"

"I don't know. I promised him I'd never read his leaves unless he wanted me to."

"I think this, if any, is an acceptable time to break a promise."

Renata nodded, although she also frowned. "But how would I get him to drink the tea only partially like I asked you to do?"

Vika looked at her own leaves, then pushed the cup away. "You'll have to manipulate the leaves when his cup is dry."

"I'm not sure I can."

Vika reached across the table and squeezed her hand. "It's worth a try."

CHAPTER SIXTY-SIX

That night, Evgeny Obolensky bowed as he entered the armory to greet Nikolai. "Your Imperial Highness, it is a great honor to finally meet you." Obolensky had a soft, round face that made him appear younger than his twenty-nine years, but Nikolai knew better than to judge by appearances. Obolensky was aide-de-camp to the most elite of the Imperial Army's regiments, and his family could trace their noble roots all the way back to the age of Rurik, the dynasty that ruled Russia centuries ago.

Major General Volkonsky and Ilya were with him, and they bowed as well.

"I'm glad you could come." Nikolai pushed off from the wall against which he'd been leaning, between two racks of muskets. He wore his facade again, so he looked like a person, but the habit of hiding in the shadows was hard to shake.

"Where is Trubetskoy?" Nikolai asked. If Trubetskoy was supposed to be the leader of the entire movement, his absence the night before the coup was mildly disturbing.

Volkonsky shrugged. "Don't worry about him, Your Imperial Highness. If there is anyone whose blood runs thicker with the ideals of our cause than Trubetskoy, I haven't met him."

"I saw him earlier," Obolensky said. "He had something urgent to take care of for his wife."

"More likely for Lebzeltern," Volkonsky said. "His brother-in-law."

"That's the Austrian Empire's minister here in our capital," Obolensky added.

Nikolai crossed his arms. "I know who Lebzeltern is." He'd made it his business long ago to know everyone who was important in Saint Petersburg, even if they did not know him.

"Of course. My apologies, Your Imperial Highness." Obolensky dipped his head.

"Tell me all your men are ready," Nikolai said. Obolensky and Volkonsky had better make Nikolai comfortable that tomorrow would go as planned.

"As ready as the swords and pistols in this room," Ilya said, his first words since entering the armory.

Nikolai looked at the weapons, hanging on racks and tucked away in cases and shelves. As if asleep. "That is not particularly encouraging."

Ilya reddened and looked at his boots.

Volkonsky stepped forward. "Your Imperial Highness, you may rest assured that the soldiers in all the regiments stationed in Saint Petersburg shall support you. We have fought with these men in battles across Europe. We have eaten with them in the camps, lay wounded with them in infirmaries, charged into enemy lines with them by our sides. The men are loyal to the commanders with whom they've sweated and bled, not to a figurehead they hardly know. They will follow us tomorrow morning in rejecting the oath to your brother. I have no doubt."

"And how many soldiers do we have?"

"Twenty thousand," Obolensky said, confirming the number Ilya had provided.

Nikolai picked up a pistol and weighed it in his hand. The military portion of the coup was meant to establish Nikolai's legitimacy among not only the soldiers, but also the people of Saint Petersburg. They wouldn't understand or rally behind him if he simply deposed Pasha secretly by magic. But if some military might was shown, and the large numbers of the Decembrists overwhelmed Pasha's smaller forces—which they ought to, given the element of surprise—then Nikolai could securely ascend the throne.

Securely, but not simply. For there was also the complication of magic.

"We must be ready for a blizzard," Nikolai said, pistol still in hand. "I have no doubt Pasha will allow his Imperial Enchanter use of her powers again once we march against him. She'll command the elements against us."

"We'll see to it that our men are prepared," Obolensky said.

"All right," Nikolai said. "Unless there is anything else, I will see you in Peter's Square in the morning."

Obolensky, Volkonsky, and Ilya bowed. "Until morning, Your Imperial Highness," Volkonsky said. They left the armory.

When the door shut, Nikolai set the pistol down in its

place. He surveyed again the walls lined with muskets, and the swords hanging, points down, blades gleaming.

Yes, he would have twenty thousand men marching for him tomorrow. But he could not leave his future solely in the hands of those men.

Nikolai threw a commanding look at the muskets. They leaped off the walls and floated in the air, barrels pointed forward, all in a neat row, as disciplined as the soldiers who would carry them in the morning. He nodded to the pistols, who sprang from their shelves and lined up beneath the muskets, like another regiment ready for battle. And then Nikolai looked to the swords, and they sliced through the air in a satisfying metallic swish, ready to come to the artillery's aid.

"Another marvelous thing about being an enchanter," Nikolai said aloud to himself, "is that I don't even need guns in order to use their bullets." He charmed open the drawers in the armory, revealing all the ammunition inside. He'd be able to command them as easily as he gave orders to the weaponry. Vika might be able to create a storm of snow, but Nikolai could direct a blizzard of bullets.

"Well done," Nikolai said to the guns, swords, and ammunition. "I shall see you, too, in the morning." They relaxed and returned to their racks and shelves and drawers, like soldiers at ease, going back to their barracks for a good night's sleep.

As for Nikolai, there would be no rest. Adrenaline swirled through his veins and stirred the energy within. And although he didn't think Vika would try to find him again in his dreams, he didn't want to risk sleeping. Dancing with her once, hearing her utter the three words he'd longed to hear, had been enough to make him falter in his resolve. But she had not agreed to join him, and she was still on Pasha's side, so Nikolai could not return to his dreams.

There was entirely too much at stake.

CHAPTER SIXTY-SEVEN

Renata carried a breakfast tray up to Nikolai's room quite early. She knew he was already awake; in fact, she was sure he'd never gone to sleep. He'd been pacing since before she woke at four, his footsteps on the floorboards keeping her company as she dusted downstairs and tidied the house to be worthy of a grand prince.

His pacing stopped when he heard her knock.

"Nikolai, it's me."

Immediately, the five locks unlatched and his door swung open. Not terribly wide, for he was not the type to fling open doors, but enough that Renata knew he was glad it was her.

"I'm happy you're back in this house," he said.

"So I can bring you breakfast?"

"Because you shouldn't be sleeping on the floor in a stranger's apartment. You belong here."

With you, Renata thought. But she shook the notion out of her head. *The tea. I'm here to get him to drink the tea.*

"I'm happy to be back," she said, as she busied herself with unfolding a length of cloth to cover his desktop and placing upon it the teapot, cup and saucer, a bowl of kasha, and apple jam. She poured him some tea with a single squeeze of lemon and slipped a thread of saffron into the cup.

"Here," she said, walking over to where he stood by the windows and pressing the cup into his hands. "You must be thirsty. You've been up for hours."

"You always know what I need." Nikolai sipped at it. "Interesting flavor. Is that . . . saffron?"

"A new blend the countess acquired just before she passed away," Renata lied. "Imported from the Greeks. Or was it the Spaniards? One of those."

I shouldn't have said those last bits, Renata thought. It was so obvious that she had no idea what she was saying. She held her breath, waiting to see if Nikolai would drink more.

He took another small sip, then floated the cup back to the desk.

Don't panic, Renata thought. *He'll drink more with breakfast.* "Kasha?" she asked, offering Nikolai the bowl.

"Not right now, thank you. I'm not hungry."

"Uh . . . all right."

Nikolai quirked his mouth and came over to the desk. "You really want me to eat, don't you?"

"It's just . . . I've missed looking after you, is all. I was excited to bring you breakfast and forced myself to wait until a reasonable hour before I knocked, and even then, most would not call half past five in the morning reasonable." It was mostly the truth, just bent to fit what Renata needed done. She shifted in place. Lying to her superiors was not commonplace for her. She actually couldn't think of the

357

last time—if ever—that she'd done it.

"You're too good to me." Nikolai sat down at his desk and spooned some jam into his kasha.

She smiled and went over to the other side of the room, so that she wouldn't crowd him. Once there, though, she didn't know what to do. Ordinarily, she would take out her duster and start tidying, but Nikolai's room was spotless, not a smudge or mote in sight.

Renata decided to look at his new furniture instead. It was more regal than the simple walnut pieces he'd had in the room before. A bit more menacing, too, with the black wood and gold feathers at the handles and hinges, and the talons on the armoire's feet. It gave the effect, Renata thought, of garudas, which had also featured on the yurts in the steppe dream. It seemed as if a claw inched toward her. She backed away from the armoire and hurried over to Nikolai's desk again.

"Why are you up so early?" she asked. She looked into his teacup. The level of liquid had gone down just a sip or two.

"We're staging a coup today." He said it nonchalantly, as if it were nothing at all. Was this what the dark energy in his veins had done, made Nikolai so callous he couldn't feel or see what he was doing? It was what he'd hated about Pasha at the end of the Game. First one brother had lost his humanity, and now the other.

Renata's hands fluttered to her braids, but she'd pinned them up this morning, so there was a frustrating lack of anything to twist or pull on. "I thought I'd have more time."

Nikolai set his spoon in the bowl. He'd only eaten a few bites of the kasha. "More time?" He scooted his chair away from the desk. "Time for what?"

"N-nothing."

"Renata." He gave her the look that she'd seen so many times, the one that meant he knew she wanted to say something but wouldn't without a little coaxing. She sighed to herself. She loved him so much, it felt like physical pain.

"I'm just . . . scared for you," Renata said. *And everyone else.* She embraced him and buried her face into his chest, nuzzling against his perfectly knotted cravat. This could be their last hug.

"Please drink your tea," Renata said into his vest. If she didn't ask, Nikolai wouldn't do it. His mind was already elsewhere, concentrating on the coup. "Let me read your leaves."

Nikolai let out a single breath of a laugh and pulled away from her. "Is that why you wanted to bring me breakfast?"

"I wanted to see you. I was happy we were both back in this house."

"And you wanted to read my leaves."

Renata reached over to the desk and picked up the cup. "And I wanted to read your leaves."

Nikolai took the teacup but didn't drink. "I don't want to know what they say, Renata."

"Then I won't tell you. But I can't bear not knowing if you're ever coming back. I almost lost you at the end of the Game, and now it's happening all over again. Just drink the tea and let me read the leaves and I'll keep the prophecy to myself."

"It tastes terrible, you know. Whoever created this blend ought to lose his job."

Renata half laughed, half cried. "So you'll do it?"

"If it means you'll stop slinking around and trying to

trick me, then I will. I like you better when you're forth-right." He put the teacup to his lips—those beautiful lips that had once touched hers—and drained the cup of its strange saffron brew. His mouth puckered as he placed the cup back in Renata's hands.

His touch lingered for a moment. As if Nikolai was considering whether to stay.

And then he inhaled sharply and pulled his fingers away. "I should go."

"No, wait." She glanced down at the leaves.

"You promised."

"I won't—"

"If I stay longer, I'll know whether they're good or bad based on how you react." He kissed her on the top of her head, and she threw herself into his arms once more.

"Good-bye," she murmured into his chest. *And do the right thing*, she thought. *I know you can.*

"*À la prochaine*," he said as he broke away. He crossed the room in three long strides and took his coat and top hat off their hooks. He didn't look back as he slipped out the door.

Renata ran to the window. A white rat sat perched outside on the ledge, watching her with unblinking red eyes.

"Shoo," Renata said, banging on the glass, but the rat did not move.

A minute later, though, Nikolai descended the front steps and onto the icy street below, and Renata forgot about the rat. The morning was still an infant, swaddled in night-time black. Nikolai disappeared quickly into its dark folds.

Only then did Renata sink onto his bed with the teacup cradled in her hands.

She stared. And stared some more. She imagined the

leaves moving, willed them to.

They wouldn't budge. Fate was not so easily manipulated.

Renata whimpered, both frustrated and disappointed, as she fell back all the way onto Nikolai's bed, the cup—with its stubborn leaves—still in her hands.

"*À la prochaine*," he had said. *Until next time.*

But it was impossible to tell if she would ever see Nikolai again. For the leaves were a tangled pile of pitch black in the inner circle of the cup, and the saffron thread hung separate, away from the rest.

What did it mean? Had Vika's leaves not mattered? Or did they somehow make sense together?

The only thing Renata knew for sure about today was this: there would be death, lots of it, and it was going to be a tragic mess.

CHAPTER SIXTY-EIGHT

The sun had barely risen when Vika stood outside the Winter Palace, its grand green walls and white columns muted, washed out in the early light. Soon, the troops would be asked to pledge their allegiance to Pasha. Soon, many of them would refuse.

Vika adjusted her gloves.

At that moment, Poslannik skittered across the icy cobblestones, up the side of Vika's gown, and onto her shoulder. He panted, having run across half of Saint Petersburg to reach her.

Her tiny messenger reported everything he'd seen at Nikolai's house, ending with Renata falling backward onto the bed in despair.

No . . . She must've failed in changing Nikolai's leaves. Vika squeezed her eyes shut.

"I wish there were a way I could save both Pasha and Nikolai," she said to Poslannik. "I would give anything for that to be true."

Poslannik nuzzled against the woolly scarf around her neck.

Be careful what you wish for, Vika had once warned Pasha. But she didn't heed her own advice.

CHAPTER SIXTY-NINE

Volkonsky inspected his soldiers. The regiment had gathered in their garrison, ostensibly to swear their allegiance to the tsesarevich. The men stood before him in fastidious lines, their navy blue jackets immaculate—down to the red trim along the edges and the polished silver buttons—and their white pants contrasted gloriously with their shiny black boots.

The officers approached Volkonsky. Their uniforms were even more impressive than the common soldiers', with gold epaulets upon their shoulders and gold braids and medals draped across their chests. They saluted.

"Are we ready?" Volkonsky asked.

"Yes, Major General," the officers said. "The men have been instructed what to do."

"Very well. Let's begin."

One of the officers strode over to the official who had been sent by the tsesarevich and informed him that the ceremony could begin. The man climbed up to a short dais before the troops.

Volkonsky hardly heard the oath, for the official was possessed of one of those unattractive, droning voices with which bureaucrats were often afflicted. Besides, Volkonsky was watching his soldiers, standing at attention. He caught only an odd word or phrase here or there. "Duty." "Imperial Army." "Mother Russia."

The official launched into a long-winded speech about honor and the greatness of the Russian Empire. He lauded the men for their past service and for all they would do in the future. The troops began to cast sideways glances at one another. Volkonsky frowned. This was not the behavior he expected from his men.

After too many minutes, the official paused, then said in his most affected, grandiose voice, "Do you, the soldiers of the Imperial Army, swear your allegiance to His Imperial Highness Pavel Alexandrovich Romanov, future tsar of all of Russia, and promise to give your lives to protect the empire?"

Volkonsky pressed his lips together. *The silence of the garrison will be resounding. And then we shall march onto Peter's Square, joined by all the other troops in the city who are, at this very moment, also rejecting the tsesarevich's oath.* All these years of hoping for change, and the moment was finally here. Volkonsky was a man of rigid decorum and restraint, but even his heart skipped a beat in anticipation.

But instead of silence, the soldiers before him shouted, "We swear our allegiance to His Imperial Highness and the great Russian Empire!"

"What?" Volkonsky spun to look for his officers. They were caught off guard, too, looking at their men with mouths agape. Why hadn't the soldiers followed his orders to reject the oath?

The official at the front of the room looked down his nose at Volkonsky. "Is there a problem, Major General?"

Volkonsky was without words. These were his men. He'd won their loyalty on the battlefield. They'd been frightened by the emergence of magic. Why hadn't they followed his orders?

Then one of them, who was the size of a bear and just as furry, broke the lines of the soldiers. "I renounce the oath! To Karimov and a constitution!"

Volkonsky's heart dared to beat again.

"I will march," Bogdan shouted. "My loyalty lies with my commanding officers, and if they say march, I march." He glared at the men around him. He didn't spare the bureaucrat on the dais, who quickly busied himself with gathering his papers.

Volkonsky pulled himself together and ascended the dais. *These are my men. They will listen if I stand before them.*

"I march on Peter's Square now," he said, "and I demand a witch's trial, a constitution, and Grand Prince Karimov on the throne. Who is with me?"

Bogdan threw a meaty fist into the air. "I am with you, Major General!"

The rest of the troops shifted in their places.

Volkonsky stared sternly at them. He was a war hero. He was *their* war hero. He would will them to follow him. "Who is with me?" he asked again, more forcefully.

A soldier in the front row said, "I am also with you, Major General."

"You will need my flags," one of the color guard in the back of the room declared. Others nodded and stepped forward with their regiment's banner.

"As well as drums." Several more soldiers saluted Volkonsky.

Confused conversation broke out across the room.

"Are we supposed to go with the major general right now? I thought we were blocking the coronation next month."

"No, there was a change of plans, remember?"

"But we already gave our oath to the tsesarevich. I don't want to be punished for disobedience."

Volkonsky looked to one of his officers and said quietly, "Detain the bureaucrat. We'll deal with him after the coup."

The officer nodded and "kindly" escorted the paper-pusher to an adjoining room, where he would be tied to a post or otherwise secured so he could not run ahead to warn the tsesarevich.

Most of the other officers joined Volkonsky in the front of the room.

"Our brothers await us in Peter's Square," Volkonsky said so all could hear. "And we march now to protect our loved ones and to change the course of Russia's fate. Come with me, or face punishment for disobeying your commander."

He would have to see who, and how many, would follow. But it was now or never.

CHAPTER SEVENTY

Yuliana let herself into Pasha's antechamber. He turned from where he stood before the mirror, tugging on the sleeves of his uniform. It was the jacket originally commissioned for his coronation, the blue one he'd hated with the high black collar, gold epaulets, and red sash across the chest.

"I'm surprised to see you wearing that," she said.

He turned back to the mirror and twisted his mouth at his reflection. "It looks all right, doesn't it? I figured if there were a time to look like the next tsar, today might be it."

Yuliana came up next to him and adjusted the way the sash fell over the gold buttons. "It looks grand, Pasha. And you don't just *look* like the next tsar. You *are* the next tsar."

He laughed, though a tremble accompanied it. "Right."

"Believe it, and it will come true." Yuliana kept her smiles in reserve, for the rarer something was, the higher its value. But she gave one to Pasha now.

He smiled back as best he could.

Yuliana straightened Pasha's collar. It was terribly stiff and went all the way up to his chin. "No wonder you complained about it before."

"It's actually all right. You know, Father once had a jacket like this."

"I know. That's why I asked the tailor to design this one."

Pasha really did smile now. "Of course you thought of that. Every last detail."

She fussed with his collar a little more, then stepped back. Yes, now it looked right.

Yuliana took a deep breath. "I came to tell you that the Decembrists are marching," she said.

Pasha froze. "Already?"

"Don't worry. They'll be surprised that we're ready for them. And you have me and Vika by your side. That helps, doesn't it?"

"Yes, it does." Pasha stood taller.

Yuliana looked at her brother in the mirror. And hoped the confidence she inspired was deserved.

CHAPTER SEVENTY-ONE

Nikolai made his way to the edge of Peter's Square, where the majestic statue of Peter the Great presided again. Flags flapped in the breeze. Soldiers' drums beat in rhythm. And the grand Neva River provided the backdrop on the far edge of the square. How fitting that it would all end here, in this square where Nikolai's challenge to Pasha had begun.

However, the square, according to the Decembrists' plan, was supposed to overflow with soldiers who had refused to swear their oaths of allegiance to Pasha. But "overflow" was not at all the right word. Nikolai scanned the square and did a rough count. By his estimate, there were only three thousand or so soldiers standing before the statue of Peter the Great. Nowhere close to the twenty thousand that the Decembrists had claimed.

Please say more are coming. He'd staked everything on this revolt. They had to win, and quickly, or he'd end up in a prolonged battle with Vika, which was the last thing Nikolai wanted.

He needed to find Trubetskoy, Obolensky, or Volkonsky. Someone who was in charge. Nikolai wove through the loosely formed regiments. The first of the three men he found was Volkonsky.

"What's happening?" Nikolai asked. "Where are all your men?"

Volkonsky startled but quickly composed himself. "Your Imperial Highness," he said, quietly enough that his men nearby did not hear, but loudly enough to pay his respects.

"I thought you claimed you could carry twenty thousand soldiers." Nikolai tried to mask his anxiety by making his tone disappointed. Imperious. Like an heir to the throne. "This is but a fraction of that number."

Volkonsky stood tall. "There was some confusion at the garrison when the oath of allegiance was given. Not everyone refused to swear loyalty. But we are still strong. This is enough to force a coup d'état."

"Where are Trubetskoy and Obolensky and their men?"

"Obolensky is over there." Volkonsky pointed to the soldiers in formation to the right. "Trubetskoy . . ."

"Trubetskoy what?"

"He, er, cannot be found. But Ilya is looking for him, and he's the best at tracking people."

"Your fearless leader is still doing something 'important' for his wife or Lebzeltern?" Nikolai did not hide the sarcasm.

Volkonsky checked over his shoulders, as if afraid the soldiers were listening. They were not. They milled about and chatted casually among themselves, surreptitiously passing flasks to warm themselves against the morning chill. "I know this doesn't look promising, Your Imperial Highness, but I swear, even without Trubetskoy, this will work. We shall prevail."

Nikolai clenched and unclenched his fists. All his life, he'd had to rely on himself. Had he erred now in counting on the Decembrists?

"Get your men in order," he snapped at Volkonsky.

"Yes, Your Imperial Highness." He saluted Nikolai.

Nikolai nodded to dismiss him, and Volkonsky gave a quick bow and marched off.

Not long after, he saw Ilya speaking with Obolensky. Trubetskoy had not returned. *Damn it.*

But then a shout resounded across Peter's Square. "Attention!" A collective stomp answered the call. What had seemed to be only a mass of men a moment ago now filed in unison into straight lines and proud regiments.

Nikolai couldn't help that his mouth dropped open. The precision of the troops was glorious. What had been a milling mess was suddenly neat rows of uniforms and weapons. All chatter among the men ceased. The drums beating in the background gained a magnificent ferocity. They certainly were impressive, and Nikolai could see now how men like these had defeated Napoleon. *Perhaps we have a chance after all.*

Obolensky stood below the statue of Peter the Great, at the Thunder Stone. With Trubetskoy absent, he must have assumed the lead. "Loyal soldiers of the Imperial Russian Empire," he called out. "Today is a momentous day. Today is the day we give Russia back to the people to whom it belongs. Today is the day we fight for our liberty and human dignity.

"Many of you fought bravely against Napoleon. On the battlefield, it mattered not whether you hailed from noble or peasant blood. We were all Russians together, and we brought glory to our empire.

"Now, however, without war to unite us, the monarchy has returned to its old ways, enslaving farmers to their lords. The imperial family has forgotten how serfs and nobles alike laid down their lives for our country. And we aim to remind them. To Karimov and a constitution!"

The soldiers pounded their boots and flagpoles on the ground and roared, "To Karimov and a constitution! To Karimov and a constitution!"

A smile spread across Nikolai's face. These were his people. Royal blood or not, Nikolai had come from a tiny nomadic village on the steppe and spent his entire life fighting for respect. He'd been an errand boy for a tailor, and he'd polished shoes for a cobbler. He'd bartered for dance and sword-fighting lessons by trading his time and his services. So these men who stood before him, these ordinary soldiers, were his brethren.

But then the thundering of hooves drowned out the shouts of the Decembrists. The men in the square all turned away from Obolensky toward the sound.

"No," Nikolai said.

It was not, as the Decembrists had hoped, reinforcements from other garrisons. It was Pasha's cavalry and infantry. They were close to ten thousand strong.

They were still some distance away, but Nikolai felt as if their horses were already stampeding him.

Because the Decembrists were now outnumbered by more than three to one.

CHAPTER SEVENTY-TWO

Vika rode to Pasha's left as he led the cavalry into Peter's Square. Yuliana rode to his right, unwilling to accede to his requests to stay behind or at least ride behind the front line. Their horses had to tread carefully on the icy cobblestones.

The Decembrists were lined up in formation in front of the statue of Peter the Great.

The forces Pasha commanded were much more daunting.

"Infantry," Pasha shouted, "surround the square, but maintain distance from the rebels, and do not fire unless ordered to."

His commanders snapped to action, and their regiments marched to take strategic places around Peter's Square.

"I want light artillery there"—Pasha pointed to a spot in front of one of the infantry units, facing Peter the Great—"and here," he said, indicating a line to shield where he and his horse currently stood. They would be able to see the Decembrists from this vantage point but remain protected by several regiments of infantry, along with the light artillery.

"Cavalry will ride to flank the rebels," Pasha said. "I want the Decembrists to have to look *up* at us."

The officers and their soldiers marched off to their places. Vika looked from Pasha to the square and back to Pasha again. "Very impressive, Your Imperial Highness."

Pasha gave her a curt nod, a serious commander of troops. But a smile curved at the corner of his mouth.

"Count Miloradovich, where are you?" Pasha asked.

The count, a war hero who, like Obolensky and Volkonsky, was admired by the troops, hurried to Pasha and saluted.

"Speak with Obolensky," Pasha said. "And if possible, address the men. They can still change their minds. I will let them walk away."

On his right, Yuliana snorted in disapproval. Pasha ignored her.

"Yes, sir," Miloradovich said. He saluted again, then marched toward the rebels' formations in the center of the square.

Pasha turned to Vika. "Is Nikolai here?"

She could feel the tug at her chest as she scanned the square. "I don't see him, but I feel him. Even if I couldn't, I know he'd be here. The Decembrists mean to put him on the throne. That means they are Nikolai's men. And Nikolai is not the sort to stand aside and leave the unhappy work to others. So yes. Nikolai is here." Her heart beat faster, remembering the mazurka in the volcano dream. If only this scene were a dream, too.

Pasha began to run his hand through his hair but stopped, as if he'd suddenly remembered he was being watched by thousands of his men.

"Kill Nikolai," Yuliana said to Vika.

Vika took in a sharp breath of air, and everything inside her flipped upside down. Of course she knew it was more than a possibility that she would have to hurt Nikolai, perhaps even kill him, but a possibility was far different from a direct order spoken aloud. Especially since the cuff would enforce it.

Pasha steadied his horse beside her. He was a shade paler than usual. "Don't—"

"Pasha." Yuliana whipped her head around to glare at him. "You tried to show leniency last time by having Vika capture him. But Nikolai escaped the egg and tried to kill you again. We cannot count on being able to capture and contain him this time."

Pasha swallowed hard but nodded. "Vika, find Nikolai and . . ." His voice cracked. "Well, you heard Yuliana."

Everything inside Vika remained upside down. Her pulse throbbed inside her.

In the middle of the square, Miloradovich spoke to Obolensky. The men puffed out their chests and stood with legs anchored wide. Hot clouds billowed where their breaths met the winter air. The discussion did not appear at all friendly.

Vika's horse shifted beneath her.

"Have you located Nikolai?" Yuliana asked.

Vika had to do it. She had chosen Pasha's side, and not just because a bracelet burned her. But she would try her best to do this *her* way. She could at least have that much integrity.

"I'm narrowing it down." Vika concentrated on the far right of the Decembrists' formation, where the air seemed to be disturbed not by weather, but by magic.

Miloradovich spun away from Obolensky and climbed up onto the Thunder Stone. "Listen, my fellow soldiers—"

A shot rang out before he had a chance to finish the sentence. Soldiers yelled. Miloradovich toppled to the ground.

Obolensky reacted immediately, unsheathing his sword and holding it above him so it glinted in the early morning light. Then he ran it through Miloradovich's body.

"Oh, mercy," Vika said.

"Murder!" "Treason!" Pasha's troops shouted in shock.

The Decembrists began to yell too and drew their weapons.

The sudden outburst surprised the horses in Pasha's cavalry, and they jostled against one another while shrieking. Their riders tried to calm them.

But a few of the horses slipped on the ice, casting off Pasha's soldiers as they fell. It sent the rest of the cavalry into even more disarray.

The Decembrists aimed their muskets.

Forget finding Nikolai right now, Vika thought. *We need a distraction to give our men time to regroup.*

"I'll be back!" she said to Pasha, and she abandoned her horse and evanesced into the air, rematerializing on a cloud. From up here, she could see all the troops clearly. The Decembrists stood in two formations, a square and a rectangle, in front of the statue of Peter the Great and the Neva. They were surrounded on all sides by Pasha's cavalry and infantry (other than a small gap along the river). And Pasha and Yuliana sat on their horses on the far side of the square behind a line of light artillery.

Vika hid herself in the folds of the cloud and threw up her arms. "I need a storm. A ferocious one."

The wind howled in answer to her command and shot into the clouds around her, stirring them into a gray frenzy. The clouds spread across the sky like a blanket of gray fleece and grumbled with thunder in their bellies.

Ice like liquid silver swirled around Vika's torso, stronger than she'd ever felt the weather before. A blizzard whipped around her skirt. Snowflakes drifted from her fingertips.

She'd become what she'd once worn only as a costume: she was Lady Snow.

She whipped sashes of snow from her blizzard skirt and hurled them, one after another, and they grew as they traveled, changing from small arcs to a full storm. She inhaled deeply and blew with all her might at the Decembrists below, and her breath transformed into bitter, blistering wind that screamed as it tore through the sky. The clouds around her, too, burst open, unleashing lightning and sleet, needles of fire and ice pelting down from above.

Pasha wanted the Decembrists to look up at us, after all. And so they did, eyes wide at the surprise storm—or perhaps afraid of magic—their muskets lowered in a frantic attempt to hide from the blizzard that seemed to attack only their section of Peter's Square.

In the meantime, Pasha's cavalry calmed their horses and re-formed their lines.

The liquid silver of Vika's bodice chilled the air until it dropped to near-Arctic temperature. She continued to stoke the storm by adding more from her skirt. Each time she took a sash, more snowflakes flurried to take its place. She was eternal winter. *Ironic,* Vika thought, *for a girl born of a volcano.* Within seconds, the Decembrists were buried knee-deep in snow.

And then the blizzard halted. Or rather, it continued to rage around Vika but somehow failed to reach its targets on the ground.

"What? No."

A shield, cast not of Vika's magic, pushed up against her storm. It was invisible to the ordinary eye, but from her vantage point so close to it, she could see its components, a thousand clear umbrellas blocking the onslaught. Snow piled on top of the umbrellas, accumulating like icy white clouds in contrast to the gray ones that had created them.

Vika tried to throw more of her blizzard. But Nikolai's shield stubbornly persisted.

When a mountain's worth of snow had piled on each umbrella, they began to tilt, all away from the Decembrists in the center of the square and toward Pasha's forces around the edges.

Oh no.

"Watch out!" Vika yelled, even though there was no way they could hear her from so far away.

The umbrellas fell sideways all at once, and an avalanche plummeted from the sky. Pasha's troops looked up and shouted. Some tried to dive out of the way, but gravity was unforgiving, and the torrents of snow smashed down on the soldiers.

Suddenly, it was quiet. Pasha's men had been buried alive.

CHAPTER SEVENTY-THREE

Nikolai looked up at Vika as his umbrellas caused an avalanche to crash down on Pasha's soldiers. Wind and snow whipped around her, stirring her hair into a frosty fire of fury.

A warm flame inside Nikolai flared to match it.

Her strength intimidated the Decembrists. Yet it made Nikolai want her more.

But then the chill of ambition washed over the flame, the wanting. Nikolai turned away from the sky.

He had buried Pasha's soldiers, but his own men needed something more to encourage them. Reinforcements. But where to find them?

Nikolai closed his eyes. And smiled.

Dolls, like at his fete. He could supplement the Decembrists' forces with toy soldiers.

With eyes still shut, Nikolai recalled every toy shop he knew of within Saint Petersburg. There was the one from which he'd acquired the servers for the Neva fete, and another closer to Ekaterinsky Canal, where he'd purchased the marionettes during the Game, when he was working on what would become the Jack and ballerina. There were dozens of other stores, too.

Nikolai clapped his hands twice.

Across the city, wooden soldiers bolted awake. They creaked upright and oiled their metal joints. They gathered their muskets and their ammunition, straightened their felt hats, and marched, their boots upon the shelves like the staccato of gunfire, in response to Nikolai's summons.

When the toy regiments were all assembled, their tinny bugles sounded. Their generals barked commands. The soldiers burst through shopfronts, leaving shattered glass in their wake. They sped through the air, and within minutes, an army in miniature had assembled alongside the Decembrists in Peter's Square.

Nikolai's soldiers shifted their focus from Pasha's men, many of whom were beginning to dig themselves out of the snow, to the toy soldiers, who had begun to grow, rapidly, to full human size.

"What in heaven's name—!"

But then, some of the men began to look from the statue of Peter the Great to the Neva, to the toy soldiers. Nikolai could almost see the cogs and gears turning in their minds as they put it all together. The enchanted statue. His fete. And now this.

"They're like the dolls from the tsesarevich's party on the river," someone said.

Nikolai stepped out then from where he'd been hidden among the troops. He looked enough like himself—that is to say, he wore his facade so he did not appear as shadow—that some of the Decembrists recognized him. Not all of them, for Nikolai had not been famous before he became, well, infamous for surviving death, but a few soldiers here and there recognized him, perhaps from the occasional moments he waved from the window of his house.

"Your Imperial Highness," those men said, and saluted.

Nikolai stood before them. "It's true, I am Nikolai Alexandrovich Karimov-Romanov"—he had decided to take the Romanov name, since the late tsar had, in fact, been his father—"and I am the prince for whom you are fighting."

Murmurs spread through their ranks, and soon all the Decembrists had their hands to their hats in salute.

"But I am not only the grand prince," Nikolai said. "I am also an enchanter."

The Decembrists gaped. Some drew back, their shaking visible.

Damn it. The aftermath of the fête's food poisoning was how Ilya had convinced many of the men to join the Decembrists. These ranks before Nikolai included many who feared magic.

"Don't be afraid of my powers," he said to them. "Remember, the tsesarevich already has an Imperial Enchanter, and they've wreaked havoc on our city. But with my magic on your side, we will defeat them and take back our empire and our lives."

With a wave of his hand, Nikolai jolted the toy soldiers to life, bringing their wooden muskets away from their shoulders and into position to aim and shoot.

And then Nikolai held his arms out to either side, palms up. Cold swirled in his core. Vika was Lady Snow on the outside, but Nikolai was Lord Frost on the inside. The chill from Aizhana's energy surged and Bolshebnoie Duplo's magic leaped to his fingertips. His entire body shuddered, almost unable to contain its force.

The shadows of every soldier—man and toy—came apart from their owners and stood as separate entities. They had muskets, too, silhouette ones, with silhouette bullets inside. But those bullets could kill a real man.

Nikolai breathed heavily. It was the greatest enchantment he had ever cast.

But other than a lingering shudder from the power of the magic, he wasn't tired at all. Bolshebnoie Duplo's strength now was extraordinary. Or perhaps it was Nikolai's own power, fueled by vengeance and fury.

The Decembrists stared, not responding, for a few seconds. And then Ilya shouted, "To Karimov and a constitution!"

A bear of a soldier in a nearby regiment grunted and yelled, "To Karimov and a constitution!"

All around them, men began to stand taller. Some even cracked smiles as they echoed the rallying cry, for the vision of an army of additional soldiers—even if they had been toys and shadows only moments ago—roused the battle lust in the Decembrists' souls. They were fighters, after all, not ordinary citizens, and the lure of victory pounded in their chests like snare drums.

"Now, gentlemen," Nikolai said, both to the real men and the magical ones. "About-face! Look our opponents in the eye."

The men spun in unison. They all turned outward, so that their formations pointed at the infantry and cavalry surrounding them.

"Muskets at the ready," Nikolai commanded. Thousands of muskets snapped into position in their soldiers' hands, again demonstrating the beauty of military precision. These men had been drilled to the exacting standards of the late tsar. On their own, they could load and fire close to four shots every minute. But with Nikolai's magic assisting them, they'd find their ability remarkably heightened to nearly double that.

Add to the equation the new soldiers, as well as the fact that I will be conjuring and firing additional bullets without any muskets. Pasha might still have more men, but Nikolai had more than enough weaponry and ammunition for a fight.

Nikolai looked at his soldiers. Their jaws were set and eyes focused. He nodded his approval.

Above, all but one of Vika's storm clouds vanished. The sun blazed down like midsummer, and the snow trapping Pasha's men began to melt and trickle away, leaving only damp cobblestones in its wake. They shook the water droplets off their boots and returned their attention back to Nikolai and his soldiers.

And all the Decembrists' muskets pointed straight at them.

CHAPTER SEVENTY-FOUR

One of the officers in charge of the artillery line hurried to Pasha. Fear shone in his eyes, but he adhered to his duty. "Your Imperial Highness, you should retreat to safety."

Pasha shook his head. "I'm staying. This is my fight." His knees trembled a little, but he pressed his legs tightly against his horse so no one would see his uncertainty.

"Your Imperial Highness—"

Pasha gave him a look so stern, even Yuliana would approve. "I'm staying."

His sister waved the officer over. She bent from her horse to whisper something in his ear.

"Yes, Your Imperial Highness." He darted a glance at Pasha, saluted to Yuliana, and ran back to his troops.

"What was that about?" Pasha asked.

"You'll see," she said. "Trust me."

He considered pressing further. But Yuliana arched a brow, and he knew she would not relent. He looked up into the sky and touched the basalt pendant at his throat instead. "Vika? What can you see up there?"

Her voice came through as crisply as if she were still on a horse beside him. "I'm sure you noticed the soldiers who've doubled the Decembrists' forces." She said it matter-of-factly, possibly because magic was, actually, a regular fact of life for her, but also possibly for Pasha's benefit, to keep him calm. "They're preparing for attack, which under normal circumstances, your men could take. But Nikolai will be able to fire those muskets faster than an ordinary soldier can reload."

Pasha again wanted to cram his hands into his hair. But he was the commander of an army at the front lines, no longer a boy who stayed home at the palace while others fought his wars. He had to think clearly, despite facing a threat stranger than any his father must have faced. He took a deep breath. "So even though we're nearly ten thousand and they are only . . . five or six, we have to consider this an even fight."

"Right," Vika said.

Pasha swallowed the sour stomach acid that had crept up his throat. "All right. We'll try to hold our own down here on the ground. And you . . ." Pasha glanced at Yuliana and remembered her order to kill Nikolai. "Do what you need to do, Vika. However you can."

CHAPTER SEVENTY-FIVE

Vika looked down at the square and focused on Nikolai. He glanced up at the same time, as if the string that connected them tugged on him at that moment, too. His gaze locked with hers.

Don't forget, she mouthed.

His shroud flickered for a second, only long enough for her to glimpse the shadow beneath. She didn't know if he'd done it on purpose, or if her message had pushed its way through to him for that brief moment.

Irrational hope fluttered inside her.

She collected herself a second later. Nikolai had had plenty of chances to back down. He hadn't. And now they were here, in the thick of a battle.

Vika bent her head in one last gesture of mourning for the boy she'd known.

Then she threw her arms out in front of her, and the winter wind rushed in their wake, whipping through the air, through the Decembrists, and knocking Nikolai to the ground. She struck her hands together and hurled ice crystals in his direction. The frost clung to him, and more and more layers piled on. Within seconds, Nikolai was frozen, completely suspended in a translucent block of ice.

The bracelet tightened around her wrist, but it didn't burn. Because Vika wasn't necessarily defying orders. In the rush of giving the command, Yuliana had forgotten she ought to specify *when* Vika was to kill Nikolai. And Pasha had only told Vika to do what she needed to do.

Her entire body quivered.

For an infinitesimal moment, Peter's Square was quiet.

But then Pasha's own artillery began to fire. Vika watched as Pasha whirled around to Yuliana. "What's happening?" he shouted, his voice coming through since he still clasped the necklace in his hand.

"I commanded them to fire on the rebels," Yuliana said. She was within range of the necklace so Vika could hear. "It's time to finish this nonsense."

Vika gasped.

"Those weren't my orders!" Pasha said.

"Your orders weren't aggressive enough."

The soldiers loyal to the throne continued shooting at the Decembrists. But the Decembrists were not ill-prepared mercenaries. They were men from the same army who fired upon them. Their commanders shouted, and the rebels loaded and fired back. Bodies began to fall on either side.

At the same time, some of the shadow soldiers turned and aimed at Nikolai. Or rather, at the mass of ice. He must have been commanding them from within, for they opened fire and blasted off ragged chunks. They shot at him again and more ice fell away.

Vika flung more frost at him, but she couldn't replace quickly enough the pieces that were exploding away.

Nikolai burst free from the inside, sending spears of ice through the air. They harpooned through some of Pasha's soldiers. Then he began snapping his fingers, conjuring bullets, hundreds at a time. He shot them at Pasha's forces, and as Vika had warned, it was as if there were ten thousand Decembrists facing them.

Despite heavy fire, Pasha held his horse steady. "Vika," he shouted over the whiz of bullets and the battle cries of the men, "we need to do something to break their formations!"

"I know . . . but what?"

"Shake them somehow!"

"All right." Vika nodded to herself. *I'll literally shake them off their feet.*

She stared down at the center of the square.

Focus. Focus. Focus.

The ground near the Decembrists' boots began to ripple, like soft waves on a peaceful day along the Neva. Some of the men lost their balance. Others continued to fire, though, including Nikolai with every snap of his fingers.

But then the cobblestones cracked like bolts of thunder, and Vika's rocky waves grew, the crests higher and the lengths longer. The ground reared and hurled the Decembrists ten feet in the air and every which way. When they landed, the men's bodies snapped. The shadow soldiers burst in puffs like smoke.

Mercy. Nausea wracked Vika's body with every broken bone and limp soldier. They lay one on top of another, a chaotic jumble of limbs and muskets and drums and flags.

Vika had thought she would need this power if it came to war with foreign enemies. She'd never imagined she'd use it against Russia's own men. Her heart rose to her throat. She wanted to look away, but she couldn't.

Pasha's army continued to fire.

The Decembrists shrieked as their front lines collapsed. Some shoved their dead comrades out of the way and fumbled for their muskets again. But too many had fallen.

"Retreat! Retreat! Retreat!" the Decembrists yelled.

They stumbled over the dead bodies. More soldiers crumpled under fire. The ones still capable of running clambered over the piles of men, tripping over them onto the icy, blood-stained cobblestones, and fled past the statue of Peter the Great. They retreated onto the frozen Neva.

Pasha's infantry was quick to respond. They were already loading cannons and aiming at the river.

"No!" Vika cried.

Too late. The cannons fired and blasted through the Decembrists and the ice, flinging hundreds of men into the Neva's frosty depths. They would freeze and drown in a matter of seconds.

Even though they were Nikolai's men, Vika threw magic at the river, like fishing lines to haul the soldiers out. There was already too much death. The tea leaves had been right, and it seemed that she and Renata had failed at changing the prophecy. All Vika could do now was try to minimize the lives that were lost. From the sky, she attempted to keep the Neva from freezing over while she also dragged body after body out of the water, hundreds of invisible lines cast at once.

But there were too many. She had so much power, and

yet she could not save them all. Tears streamed down her face as winter prevailed and the Neva froze over, hundreds of men trapped in the icy graveyard below.

"Cease fire!" Pasha yelled.

The relentless firing of cannons was deafening, and his officers didn't hear. More cannons fired. More ice collapsed, taking with it several hundred soldiers more. The toll would be at least a thousand, and Vika was nearly spent. Yet she renewed her attempts to save these men from drowning, too.

Nikolai still stood at the Thunder Stone. He flung his arm out in front of him and pointed at the cannons.

A regiment of toy soldiers spun on their heels and charged. The creaking of their wooden legs squealed even over all the explosions and gunfire, a disturbing cacophony of magic and war whipped together.

A cannonball ripped through the toy soldiers' advance, blasting off painted heads and splintering limbs. But the rest of the toys continued undeterred. They had no feelings, no fear, only Nikolai's orders, whatever those were.

And then the toy soldiers were upon Pasha's men. The two sides grappled with each other, fighting flesh to wooden hand. A few of Nikolai's troops seized cannons and began to shift where they were aimed.

Pasha's soldiers—or were they Yuliana's?—raised the butts of their muskets and smashed the toy faces. They took back the cannons and pushed down on the barrels to realign them.

Nikolai pushed farther out with his arm, and the cannons flung the men off them and swiveled their aim straight upward, so that any cannon fire would shoot up and fall directly back down on Pasha's men, rather than on the broken Neva that was drowning and freezing the Decembrists.

Except one cannon did not pivot completely. It was angled upward but still slightly toward the river, and the fuse was burnt to its end.

In the midst of the chaos and the noise and her attempts to save the drowning, freezing men, Vika didn't see the cannonball until it was already careening toward her.

She gasped, paralyzed for a moment.

Then her instincts kicked in, and she commanded the wind to shift the cannonball's path.

It was going too fast, though, and its heat carried it straight through the blizzard undeterred. Vika tried to throw herself out of its way, but she was a split second too late, and the cannonball smashed into her left hand.

It ripped it off completely.

Vika screamed. It was as if a lightning bolt had shot through her arm and lit it on fire from within. She hurtled through the air. The sky went dizzyingly round and round. Everywhere there was shouting and smoke and cannon fire.

And then all of it snuffed out to black.

CHAPTER SEVENTY-SIX

N o!" Pasha shouted as Vika began to tumble from the sky, blood following her like crimson streamers. He kicked his horse into action, and as they charged into the center of the square to try to catch her, he yelled at his infantry, "Cease fire! Cease fire! Cease fire!"

They finally heard him and stopped their attack.

Pasha spurred his horse to jump the last distance and caught Vika just as she was about to hit the ground.

"Stop everything!" Nikolai yelled at the Decembrists, although not many of them actually remained. At least a thousand had perished into the icy Neva. Hundreds lay dead on the cobblestones. Volkonsky had fled with most of his men in retreat. But the few hundred who remained fighting halted. The toy soldiers went rigid without Nikolai's magic to move them, and the last of the shadow regiments dissolved in smoke.

"Is she all right?" Nikolai ran to where Pasha held Vika on his horse.

As if this wasn't his fault. As if he could simply ask Pasha something like that, after all of this.

But right now, Pasha didn't care. All he cared about was Vika.

He slid off his saddle as his horse came to a halt. He laid Vika on the frozen ground and cradled her head in his lap. Blood continued to gush from her wrist where her hand had been severed, red mingling with the snow and filling the crevices between the cobblestones. He tore off his uniform jacket, sending buttons flying, and grabbed a handful of his shirt to tear a strip from it. He wrapped her wound tightly with the fabric. "Vika, can you hear me?"

She didn't respond.

Nikolai knelt beside her. "I'm sorry, Vika. I didn't mean for this to happen—"

"What did you think would happen?" Pasha snapped, suddenly coming back to the reality of what had transpired.

Nikolai narrowed his eyes. "I could've asked the same of you about the end of the Game."

"And yet you didn't learn from my mistakes."

"You forced her into this." Nikolai pointed at Vika's bandaged wrist.

Except the bracelet he was looking for was no longer there.

Pasha's stomach lurched. The gold cuff had been torn off with her hand.

Vika was nearly as pale as the snow now, as her life drained out red onto the tourniquet he'd made. Pasha held her closer. "This can't be our final fate."

CHAPTER SEVENTY-SEVEN

Nikolai glared at Pasha. It was his fault that this had happened! If Pasha hadn't turned on Nikolai at the end of the Game, then Nikolai wouldn't have had to exact revenge. . . .

He could end it now, though. Pasha was right in front of him. Vika, too. She was unconscious, on the brink of death. Nikolai could finish her and eliminate Pasha's fiercest weapon protecting the crown.

But at the thought of killing Vika, Nikolai's silhouette flickered. It was already faint after the fatigue of battle, and now when he looked at Vika, his anger sputtered.

He had stopped his soldiers' attack for a reason. For Vika. The battle had taken a toll on his strength, as well as on the cold darkness that fueled his obsession with vengeance, and in the moment she fell from the sky, a flash of warmth had flared inside him, a sliver of his past.

She was dying, and if she was gone, his hope of one day being tsar with Vika as his tsarina could never exist. Nikolai sagged in the snow.

What was left of Aizhana's energy rumbled inside him. *Don't give up. You're so close to the throne*, it seemed to say.

Nikolai hadn't been able to fight the chill before, but the stark reality of a future without Vika sparked the truth of what he wanted. He had spent his entire life feeling alone, and she was his chance of finally having someone else who understood him. Someone else who was different. Someone with whom to explore and push the bounds of what they could do.

I don't want what Aizhana wanted for me. I don't want to be tsar at the cost of those I love. He had known this before his mother infected him with her energy. Now he had enough clarity to know it again.

He pushed back on the chill that tried to spread inside him. It was all he had left of his mother, but Nikolai could remember her love while still understanding that it was deeply flawed.

Au revoir, Aizhana.

Yuliana ran up to where he and Pasha sat with Vika in the snow. "Save her!" Yuliana said to Nikolai. "Do whatever it is you did at the end of the Game. Give Vika your energy."

Nikolai shook his head. "I . . . I can't."

"What do you mean, you can't?" Pasha said.

"My energy is tainted. It came from my mother; there's too much death and darkness in it." Even as he said it, he fought internally with the cold that still lived in his veins. But he looked around him to strengthen his resolve. He looked at the soldiers—those who were still alive—standing tense, staring at their two princes and princess on the bloodied snow. At the dead men who littered the cobblestones. And at the ones beyond his line of sight, who had drowned in the icy river. "Devil take me, look at what that energy has done to me, what *I've* done with it. I won't transfer that to Vika."

"You'd rather have her die?" Pasha asked, head shaking, the space between his brows creased.

Nikolai closed his eyes for a brief moment. When he opened them again, he said, "If it means choosing between that and making her live as I have, then yes, she'd be better off dead."

Yuliana lowered herself to the small space of ground between the boys. "Can you transfer someone else's energy to her instead?" she said quietly. She slipped off her glove and offered her hand.

Pasha blinked at his sister. Nikolai was surprised, too. Yuliana had never shown this sort of tenderness to anyone outside their family before.

Yuliana smiled sadly at Pasha. "You love her. So I love her, too."

Her unexpected warmth thawed some more of Nikolai's chill.

"If it's going to be anyone's energy," Pasha said to Nikolai, "give her mine." He released Yuliana's hand and pulled back his jacket cuff to offer his wrist.

Nikolai grimaced at Pasha's bared skin, the blue of his blood visible at his wrist. "I'm not a vampire. Besides, I can't do that. If I try to transfer your energy, mine will get commingled with it as well."

Pasha glared at him for the vampire comment. But he withdrew his arm and wrapped it around Vika instead.

Nikolai looked down at her in Pasha's lap. Their clothes

and the makeshift tourniquet were soaked with melted snow and blood.

"We need to stanch the bleeding," Nikolai said. "But I can't heal wounds like she can. Even if I had her hand . . ."

His eyes shifted to the statue of Peter the Great.

"What about her hand?" Yuliana said.

"I wouldn't be able to mend flesh," Nikolai said, gaze still on the statue. "But perhaps I could manage metal."

"What in blazes are you talking about?" Pasha said.

"Peter the Great," Nikolai said. "It's not made of just any metal. It's full of old magic."

Yuliana turned to Nikolai. "Can you use it?"

He took a deep breath. "I hope so."

Pasha looked down at Vika, the bandage bloodred. He swallowed the growing lump in his throat. "I hope so, too."

Nikolai knelt on the frozen cobblestones by Vika's side. There was every chance this would not work. There was every chance that it would. He fought the instinct to hold his breath until he knew which way it would turn out.

"What are you doing?" Yuliana asked.

"Shh," Pasha said. "Let him work."

Nikolai nodded to him briefly in thanks. All the soldiers (both his and Pasha's) seemed also to follow Pasha's command, for the whole square fell silent.

Nikolai hardly noticed, though. All he saw and heard was Vika, unconscious, breathing unsteadily.

Hold on, he thought. *Please.*

Nikolai rose to his feet and focused on the statue a few yards away. Peter the Great seemed to watch Nikolai in return.

"I've never thought that sash across your chest added

much to your outfit," Nikolai said, as if the statue could hear (or care about) his opinions on fashion. "But I believe we can use it for a better purpose." He reached out and pinched his fingers together, then pulled back, as if he was drawing something in.

The sash, indeed, followed his motion. It slipped off Peter the Great and floated through the air like metallic silk. When it reached Nikolai, it melted. The bronze shimmered in the cup of his palms.

He turned back to Vika and knelt beside her.

"Tools," he whispered.

An entire toolbox's worth of gears, cogs, nuts, screws, and springs appeared on a mound of snow next to him.

Nikolai looked at Vika's right hand—her *only* hand—and nodded at it. The liquid bronze trickled upward, into the air, from his palms and began to replicate the shape of Vika's other hand, but mirror opposite, a metal left to her flesh-and-bone right.

With his own hands now free again, Nikolai plucked a series of tiny, delicate springs from the snow and inserted them into the bronze. The springs sank into the metal hand and found their way to its fingertips.

Next, he added levers and gears to the fingers, mechanisms that would allow them to bend. He conjured some oil and squirted it into the metal, willing it to find its way to grease the new joints.

Then he crafted a flexible network of lightweight rods, connected by filament-thin wire and tiny screws. It could bend and curl, open and close. He merged this into the shiny metal palm.

When finished, the hand appeared cast of smooth bronze

but moved as if both molten and entirely human at the same time.

"*Et voilà,*" Nikolai whispered.

"An artificial hand," Pasha said, not bothering to hide his wonder. "You're going to attach it?"

"I'm going to try," Nikolai said. "That's where the old magic comes in, I hope. I wouldn't be able to do this on my own." He gestured at Vika in Pasha's lap. "Transfer her to me, please."

Pasha hesitated.

"You must, *mon frère,*" Yuliana said.

Pasha stroked Vika's hair. He closed his eyes. But when he opened them, he shifted Vika gingerly over to Nikolai's lap.

Nikolai's pulse raced, not like the mazurka his and Vika's hearts had twice danced to, but more akin to the frenzied height of a Kazakh folk dance.

He took the bronze hand from the air. "Please let this work."

He charmed the tourniquet to unwind itself from her wrist—it was soaked so thoroughly, the red was nearly black—and Nikolai put everything he had in concentrating on Vika's wrist. He pressed the bronze hand to meet her bloodied stump.

As soon as metal touched flesh, the old magic from the statue seeped into her, and the bronze began to meld to her skin. Metallic streaks streamed up her forearm, like glimmering watercolor bleeding into flesh-colored paint.

She went from limp to stiff. She inhaled sharply.

Vika woke with a start. She looked up at Nikolai. Then down as she flexed the bronze fingers of her left hand.

"What have you done?" Her brow furrowed.

"I . . . I'm sorry," he said.

She turned her bronze hand from side to side.

"I'm sorry," he said again, for it was the only thing Nikolai *could* say.

Vika glanced around them, past Nikolai and Pasha and Yuliana, to the soldiers standing watch, no longer fighting, around the square.

"Is it over?" she asked Pasha.

Pasha nodded slowly. "I think so."

She looked at Nikolai. *Through* Nikolai. He was so weak now, he was hardly even a shadow anymore. But he nodded, too.

She frowned at her metal fingers some more. Then she said to Nikolai, "Quite honestly, it's ugly. And heavy. But it will be more satisfying now to punch you."

He didn't know if he was supposed to laugh.

"Why did you do it?" Vika asked. "You could have won and taken the throne with me incapacitated."

Nikolai sighed. "Because when you were hit—when it was like the end of the Game and you were going to die again—what I truly wanted broke free of the darkness, and everything became clear."

"I don't understand."

He looked into her eyes. Her fiercely beautiful, defiant eyes.

His single dimple crinkled his shadowed cheek, as he smiled fully for the first time in a very long time. "It's because you said you loved me. And I didn't forget."

CHAPTER SEVENTY-EIGHT

"I see you," Vika said.

Nikolai shook his head and looked down at his fading silhouette. "I'm hardly here."

But he was. He was faint, but her Nikolai was still there, as she'd hoped all along. He had found a piece of himself and fought Aizhana's energy.

And yet, his mother's darkness still lived within him. Would it come back after Nikolai had rested? Would it take over his body and his will again? If only there were more of the old Nikolai to fight it.

Vika looked at her new bronze hand. It was a shame she couldn't simply punch Aizhana's energy out of him. She flexed her fingers, still adjusting to the feel of the metal. She was made of so many different parts now: the statue's old magic, Nikolai's energy at the end of the Game, Sergei's energy through his bracelet.

Wait. Nikolai's energy! Vika's mouth dropped as the realization hit her. All this time, energy had been transferred to her. But what if Nikolai could reclaim some of his own energy he'd given her during the Game? The pure, self-sacrificing Nikolai she'd been searching for might still exist in her own veins.

"Give me your hand," she said as she reached with her human fingers for his shadow ones, so faint they were like dissipating wisps of smoke.

But as soon as she touched him, a jolt of heat shot through her. It knocked all the air out of her lungs.

"What's happening?" Pasha demanded.

Neither she nor Nikolai could answer. He was swallowed by light, first a dull glow where she held his hand, but then expanding, brighter and brighter until they were engulfed by a halo so blinding, she had to squint.

It was like touching him for the first time at the masquerade, and wanting him to kiss her in his bed, and dancing with him in the volcano dream, all bound in a ribbon of mandarin and thyme and fire.

Vika gasped for air. It was working. *But why now? Why hasn't this happened before?* There had been plenty of interaction between the two of them recently.

But there had always been something between her and Nikolai. An egg. A dream. Misguided ambition.

Now, though, there was nothing separating them.

Their connection was both torment and rapture. It was bewildering yet simple, wretched yet joyous, but in a way that Vika could not, and *did* not, wish to escape.

It was life, compacted to its essence.

As his old energy—and some of her own—flowed back to him, Vika could also feel the dark, chilly edges of Aizhana's energy. Vika squeezed Nikolai's hand.

His shadow began to recede where they touched, like spilled ink dripping away from his fingertips back into an unseen well. The coldness of Aizhana's energy also drew back, chased away by the warmth that tumbled from Vika's body.

"I know this energy," Nikolai whispered.

Vika imagined pushing harder on his shadow, and more of it fell away. Nikolai's human form slowly returned—traveling first from his fingertips and up his arm, then across his torso, into his other arm, his legs, his feet. It spread over his collarbone, where the wand scar had once been. Up his neck, along the line of his jaw, and over the sharp planes of his cheeks.

The shadow had receded. Vika gasped, hand over mouth, hardly believing who was before her.

But it was him again. Finally. Her Nikolai.

He looked down at himself, held his arms out and turned them from side to side, touched his face and his chest, all as if not quite believing. Finally, though, he looked at Vika. "You saved me."

"*You* saved *me*," she said.

"Perhaps we saved each other. It seems we have a habit of doing that."

Vika looked from her own hand to Nikolai's, now also flesh and blood. Then she laughed, not so much from happiness, but from extraordinary, overwhelming relief. "Yes. It seems we do."

CHAPTER SEVENTY-NINE

Pasha helplessly watched the halo surrounding Vika and Nikolai.

"It's how they defied the Game, isn't it?" Yuliana said, linking her arm through his and gesturing at the same time at the halo. "They're part of each other. And stronger when united."

There was a pain in Pasha's chest, the dying of hope that Vika would choose him, but he gritted his teeth and nodded. *It was never a choice*, he realized. *It was always Nikolai, whether any of us knew it or not.*

He stood, pulling his sister up with him. "This is what Plato meant," he said, although mostly to himself, "when he wrote of two broken halves finding each other."

Nikolai looked at him and shook his head. "I don't believe that. Or, more accurately, it's only part of what we're all looking for."

Pasha stepped back. He wasn't surprised that Nikolai knew which allegory he spoke of—they'd always had a shared love of books—but he was surprised at Nikolai's tone. It was almost as if they were in the library in the Winter Palace, debating philosophy. Friends again.

"What do you mean?" he asked, mindful of the fragility of this conversation. Was it possible to recapture the past, to mend what they'd broken? Pasha ran his hands through his hair.

"I mean, your interpretation contemplates only romantic love," Nikolai said quietly, as if he, too, understood the significance of their conversation. "But what about family? And friendship? I think we've all been blind to the importance of those. Me, most of all." He rose and helped Vika up. When he released her hand, their halo of light vanished.

Pasha exhaled. It had been almost too intimate, seeing them glow together like that. "So you're saying . . ."

Yuliana linked her arm through his. "The four of us here are the broken halves we've been looking for all along."

Pasha held tightly to her. He was beginning to understand what Nikolai meant. Vika and Nikolai together made a whole. But so did Pasha and Yuliana, as family. And Pasha and Nikolai, not only as brothers, but also as friends.

Vika stood between him and Nikolai. She looked back and forth at them, pausing also to look at herself as if she were a fragile bridge that connected them. Perhaps she was.

She turned slowly to Nikolai. "The darkness is gone from your veins. You're you again, right?"

He nodded.

"Then forgive Pasha for what he did to us at the end of the Game." Her voice took on a sterner quality or perhaps more accurately, a fiery one. She was very much the passionate, resolute girl from the woods Pasha and Nikolai had encountered before the Game. "Grief and fear can twist even the best of us to do what we shouldn't," Vika said to Nikolai. "Give up the fight for the crown."

"I—"

"It's not you, Nikolai." She shook her head, but her expression softened. "It was never what you wanted. Not really, anyway."

He looked at the death surrounding them. At the soldiers who stood silently, obediently, waiting for their commands. "Blazes, what have I done?"

Nikolai closed his eyes and scrubbed at the back of his neck. But then he nodded again. "You're right. All I ever truly wanted was to belong—to Saint Petersburg. To a family. To you."

Pasha's heart leaped into his throat. For more than one reason.

Vika turned to face him next. "Pasha, forgive and pardon Nikolai. He wasn't himself, and the Decembrists had already plotted against you and your family ages ago. Nikolai was merely a convenient means to an end for them."

Out of the corner of his eye, Pasha saw Nikolai flinch at Vika's description of his role, belittled. He may have been humbled, but he still had plenty of pride.

It was that very pride that had blown up and propelled Nikolai to pursue the throne. To try to kill Pasha, twice. Could he forgive so easily?

And yet, look what *not* forgiving had led them to. Pasha had essentially sentenced Nikolai to death at the end of the Game. Then Nikolai had returned the favor.

It was not the most natural thing in the world to forgive your brother for attempting to murder you. But Nikolai was willing to swallow a great deal of pride to forgive Pasha. Pasha could do the same.

"We've both made mistakes," he said. "Enormous ones."

Nikolai scrubbed the back of his neck. "Yes, we have. I am eternally sorry. Words do not suffice."

Pasha had to lean on Yuliana, so great was his relief. "I am sorry, too. For the end of the Game. For everything."

"*Mon frère*," Nikolai said.

Pasha smiled. "*Mon frère.*"

Yuliana touched Vika's shoulder, and Vika stepped back, leaving space between Pasha and Nikolai.

Pasha crossed the short distance and pulled Nikolai into an embrace.

Nikolai tensed for a moment. Then he threw his arms around Pasha, too.

Together, they were whole.

Around them, the soldiers began to murmur their confusion over what the princes' reconciliation meant.

Nikolai released Pasha from their embrace and said, "I fear I've slashed open a wound in Russia's side with this coup."

Pasha shook his head. "Yes, but at the same time, it would have happened, one way or another, as Vika pointed out. If our father hadn't died, the Decembrists had been planning to rise against him next summer anyhow. They only moved sooner because they thought we wouldn't be organized enough to counter them. But they didn't account for Vika and Yuliana."

"Or you," Nikolai said. "I underestimated you, as well."

Vika smiled at them and took Nikolai's hand. They glowed again as if the sun shone down on them with particular favor.

But this time, Pasha didn't wince. He would get used to it.

"Now that you have all made up," Yuliana said, "what shall we do with the Decembrists?"

Pasha looked at the square. Bodies lay splayed on the cobblestones, eyes wide but empty. His men had begun rounding up the rebels who were still alive.

He thought he recognized Ilya in the distance, near the Neva, arms up in surrender. Perhaps Pasha was wrong. But he was quite certain he wasn't.

His stomach turned. Yet he didn't let the nausea take over. As tsar, there would be many more difficult moments like these. He forced himself to look away.

"Pasha?" Yuliana asked.

He took several breaths. "Bury the dead with all the proper rites. Send the police to arrest those who've fled."

"And then?"

And then what? Pasha looked at Ilya once more. He'd been a good guard. A friend, almost. A veil of sadness descended upon everything Pasha could see.

But Ilya must have had his reasons, just as Pasha and Nikolai had for what they'd done. And if Pasha could forgive himself and Nikolai, if he could understand that they were real people who'd made mistakes, then he could understand the Decembrists.

Pasha would allow himself to be sad, and angry, and everything in between. But he would also learn from his mistakes, and he would rule the empire his way, with compassion and love, even for his enemies.

"We'll find a way to punish them," he said, turning away from Ilya for the last time. "But no executions. And while I will not abolish the tsardom, I *will* consider some of their proposals to better the lives of the common man. It will take time, perhaps years, even decades, but we will set things in motion and do right by our people in the end." He braced himself for Yuliana to scowl.

Yet she only took his arm and leaned her head against his shoulder. "It would be easier if we simply maintained Father's course. But I admire you for making the harder decision. It's not what Father or I would have done, but yours is the right one."

"You think?" Pasha said.

She lifted her head and smiled, a warm, clear smile, the kind reserved only for her brother. "You'll be a great tsar, Pasha."

He smiled, too.

"Yes," Pasha said. "I do believe I will."

CHAPTER EIGHTY

With Pasha and Nikolai reunited again and Saint Petersburg on the mend, Renata and Ludmila relaxed next to each other that evening, leaning against the warm stone of Ludmila's *pech*. Renata drank the last drop of tea in her cup. She hadn't tried to manipulate it, even though the magic danced in her fingertips, growing more powerful with each passing day.

Ludmila crowded her to peer inside. "What does it say?" she asked.

Renata studied the cup for only a second before she grinned. The short black leaves were arranged in perfect concentric spirals, each bigger than the next, like a chrysanthemum with hundreds of petals.

"It says that the possibilities are endless."

"Our fates are not set in stone," Ludmila said.

"Or, more accurately," Renata said, "our fates are not set in our leaves."

Ludmila laughed and refilled their plates with more

cookies. Renata poured them both some more tea. Then Ludmila regaled Renata with tales of her circus youth, and they fell asleep by the *pech*, warm and hopeful and dreaming of acrobats and dancing bears, and fortune-tellers who could change the courses of fate.

And ordinary people who could change the courses of fate, as well.

EPILOGUE

Three weeks later, Vika looked around the Cathedral of the Dormition in Moscow. The hall was resplendent in red and gold, from the intricately patterned canopy above the throne, to the rugs that lined the steps and the church floor. The Guard wore red on their breasts. The head of the Church—the patriarch—and the other clergy wore robes of gold. And all the other men and women lucky enough to witness the coronation looked on in their smartest uniforms and gowns.

Pasha stood in uniform in the center of it all. A heavy gold mantle was draped over his shoulders, trimmed from collar to hem in lush, black-spotted white fur. His posture was tall and proud, and his blond waves were neatly tamed for once.

Of course, after Pasha, Nikolai was the best dressed in the cathedral, not only because he was part of the imperial family, but also because he was Nikolai. His uniform was somehow cut more precisely than anyone else's, the epaulets on his shoulders woven of brighter, nearly luminescent thread, and his boots polished to such a shine, his sword was reflected in the leather, just as the leather reflected off the blade. Vika smiled at him from her side of the dais. Nikolai attempted not to smile in return—to look proper—but his dimple gave him away. She almost laughed, and she clapped her normal hand over her mouth just in time.

Yuliana, seated on the dais, shot Vika a glare.

It only made Vika want to laugh more.

But she corralled her attention back to the ceremony, just as the patriarch finished a prayer.

The cathedral hushed. Pasha stood regally in the silence. This was the moment he'd been groomed for his entire life. The moment Russia wanted. That *Pasha* wanted.

He nodded to the patriarch, who handed him the Great Imperial Crown.

Its four-hundred-carat red spinel jewel and nearly five thousand diamonds sparkled as Pasha placed it on his own head. The patriarch said another short prayer, then bestowed upon Pasha his scepter and the orb.

"Pavel Alexandrovich Romanov, Tsar of all the Russias."

Pasha allowed everyone in the cathedral to look upon him for a moment. Then he lowered himself onto his red throne, with the Great Imperial Crown on his head, his scepter in his right hand, the orb in his left.

And Vika Sergeyevna Andreyeva, Imperial Enchanter, to his right. Nikolai Alexandrovich Karimov-Romanov, Grand Prince of all the Russias and also Imperial Enchanter, to his left. They had beaten the rules of the Crown's Game. They had freed themselves from the bonds of ancient fate and now lived—and served the empire—of their own free will.

They were more powerful and more valuable than any scepter or orb.

Now the coronation ceremony was near an end. It was time. Nikolai nodded at Vika.

Her bronze hand had taken some getting used to, but with Nikolai's help, she'd learned to harness the new magic to do more than she'd been able to before. Now Vika wasn't a master only of nature; she was also skilled at enchantments of the man-made, which had not been her forte before at all. And since her hand had come from metal, she found that medium particularly responsive to her command.

Vika flicked her bronze wrist, and the interior of the cathedral began to glimmer as thousands of tiny, double-headed gold eagles appeared from seemingly nowhere and fluttered beneath the tall ceilings. The audience gasped, but in awe, not fright, for this crowd had been carefully selected—and prepared—for the spectacle of magic today. It would take time to convince everyone else in Russia that Vika and Nikolai were united for the good of the empire, but they would prove it, day by day.

It had been explained to the people that the previous problems had stemmed from Vika and Nikolai fighting, but now that they had made peace, they would work together for the well-being of the empire. Of course, certain problems, like the catfish king, would be a bit trickier to resolve. There were other suspicious happenings around the empire, too, like rumor of Baba Yaga's house stampeding through Siberia, and the volcanoes on the Kamchatka Peninsula stirring simultaneously awake.

Vika and Nikolai had already been hard at work,

though—including conjuring shields over entire villages along the portions of the Volga where Vodyanoy had allegedly appeared—while they figured out more permanent solutions.

The acceptance of Vika's and Nikolai's powers by both the tsardom and the church at the coronation—the most significant ceremony for both institutions—was also an auspicious start.

The choir began to sing a prayer for many years of health for Pasha, and a prosperous reign. Nikolai burst open the cathedral windows, and a hundred stone birds, modeled after different species from all over the empire, flew in and joined in the song.

Pasha looked upon his Imperial Enchanters and smiled so brightly, the crown and the Romanov eagles and all the gold in the cathedral could not compare.

Vika looked to her boys and smiled, too.

Even Nikolai cast aside propriety and gave in to a grin.

They had been through much together. They had resented one another, failed one another, scarred one another. But in the face of everything, there had been courage. And love.

Vika cued the church bells to ring. Nikolai commanded a 101-gun salute outside the cathedral. The double-headed eagles sparkled above Pasha and the throne.

Right before the ceremony, Nikolai had sent Pasha off with an embrace and an old Kazakh proverb:

Nothing is more remote than yesterday;
nothing is closer than tomorrow.

Vika smiled at the wisdom of the words. For although the past would always be a part of them, it was, in truth, the past. What they had to look forward to was the future, where anything was possible.

Anything.

And there was no greater magic than that.

AUTHOR'S NOTE

Like *The Crown's Game*, *The Crown's Fate* is a work of historical fantasy set in an alternate Imperial Russia, although much of its foundation is based on true events and places. After Tsar Alexander I's death, there was, indeed, confusion as to which of two brothers ought to ascend the throne, and the Decembrist revolt was a real attempted coup that arose out of the Russian people's unrest and unhappiness. The revolt was led by prominent and respected men, including Trubetskoy, Obolensky, Volkonsky, and Pestel, who were subsequently hanged or sentenced to exile for their treason.

The Crown's Fate diverges from actual history, of course, in the story of *which* brothers could claim the throne, and the complications of their lineage. In reality, Alexander I did not have any sons to fight over the tsardom, but here we have Pasha and Nikolai fighting over the crown. I also took liberties with the tsarina's correspondence with her friends about her lovers and, in particular, Alexis Okhotnikov;

those letters do not actually exist, but they do here, for the sake of this story.

On an unrelated note: I had a bit of fun with historical Easter eggs in both *The Crown's Game* and *The Crown's Fate*. Did any of my readers notice? For example, there's a reference hidden in this book to *War and Peace*. Also, some of Nikolai's enchantments pay homage to Russian artists—the Jack and ballerina (the *Nutcracker* ballet), the statue of Peter the Great (Pushkin's "Bronze Horseman"), and the jeweled egg (Fabergé). However, since these books take place in 1825, Nikolai actually predates the famed artists. So if Nikolai existed before they did, he couldn't have copied them. Rather, I like to think those artists copied *Nikolai*.

Because why not?

As Nikolai himself says: *Imagine, and it shall be. There are no limits.*

ACKNOWLEDGMENTS

E ven though this is my second book, I'm still in constant awe that I get to write stories for a living. And this dream would never have come true without my amazing agent, Brianne Johnson, at Writers House. Bri, thank you for being by my side on this magical journey. I couldn't think of a better agent with whom to manipulate the tea leaves of my fate.

If not for my brilliant editor, Kristin Rens, this sequel would have been a nonsensical book about frogman armies and volcano-nymph kidnappings. Thank you, Kristin, for steering me right when I went left; for your love of Vika, Nikolai, and Pasha; and for helping me tell their story as it was meant to be told.

Endless thanks, too, to the wildly talented and hard-working team at Balzer + Bray and all of HarperCollins. To Suzanne Murphy, Kate Morgan Jackson, Alessandra Balzer, Donna Bray, and Kelsey Murphy for all your enthusiasm and support. To Joel Tippie and Alison Donalty for another stunning, perfect cover. To Jon Howard, Nellie Kurtzman, Caroline Sun, Rosanne Romanello, Audrey Diestelkamp, EpicReads, and the Harper sales team, you are incredible, and I cannot thank you enough for all that you've done.

I am so blessed to be a part of the YA community. Stacey Lee and Anna Shinoda, where would I be without your wacky, random texts? Probably not laughing in the middle of the grocery store with all the other shoppers staring at me. Sara Raasch, thank you for the ten billion emails and the macaroons and for sharing in my general insanity. We will totally make Pirates vs. Ninjas happen someday. Roshani Chokshi and Sabaa Tahir, thank you for your generosity and wisdom and for keeping me tethered to the ground. Monica Bustamante-Wagner, Emily Martin, Sean Byrne, Summer Spence, and Amber Hart, thank you for always being there to listen and check in. Angela Mann and the entire team at Kepler's Books, you are the gold standard of bookstores. Thank you for loving *The Crown's Game* and *The Crown's Fate* and me!

Thank you to the Tsar's Guard—what an incredible army you are! *The Crown's Game* and *The Crown's Fate* would not be what they are without you. A very special salute to the officers of the Guard: Major General Brittany Press, Captain Camille Simkin, Captain Heather L. DeFilippis, Captain Jaime Arnold, and Captain Rachel Evangelista.

Thank you to all my fans, and especially the earliest fans of this series, including: Abbi McIntyre, Ada Sandoval, Aditi Nichani, Aida Garcia, Aila Jiang, Alayna L. Olivarez, Alexa Santiago, Ali Nowac, Ali Kiki Byars, Alice at Arctic Books, Alice Zheng, Alicia Guerrero, Allie Penn, Alyson Chu, Alyssa Raymond, Amanda Perry, Amy Jo Green, Amy

Workoff, Ana Micaela Vázquez, Anelise Kim and her favorite pets Luna and Smokey, Angelique Skandalakis, Angie Cason, Annalisse, Annebelle Bosch, Anthony Acevedo, April Nichole, Ashley @ Books Buying Beauty, Ashli Wells, Aubrie Nixon, Barrie Click, Benjamin of Tomes, Berenice Maldonado, Bhavya, Bonnie Lynn Wagner, Brittany R. Cooper, Brittany Smith, Brooke Muschott, Bryanna Celeste Garcia, Caitlyn T., Candace Robinson, Carly Vaught, Caterina Cattaneo, Carina Elizabeth Zepeda, Carol Lee, Carol Tobar, Carrie Mansfield, Carrie Parker, Cassandra and Erica from BooknerdBabes, Cassidy Hess, Cassie Bergman, Catherine Ong, Celia Brizuela, Chantal Kulak, Chelsea Brooks, Chelsea Masquelier, Christina Ladd, Christina Stants, Christine Gallaugher, Cindy Da Readaholic, Cindy T. Ngo, Cindy Pon, Claire Jeanette Dizon, Cody Duffy, Cori Griffith, Cyndy DeLeon, Cynthia Akira, Dana Jan Bartelt, Daniel Shipley, Danielle Duffield, Danielle Sunshine, Daphne Chang, Denise Cayetano, Denise Wengert, Diana Laura Nava, Duane Grech, EJ Martin, Elaine Guo, Emily Crowell, Emily Gibbs, Emily H, Emily Miller, Emma Saska, Emmett Brown, Erin Arkin, Esther Saavedra, Evie Convent, Fiorella Vasquez, Frank Iasparri, Gina Scarcella, Grace Radford @ Once Upon A Teen Reader, Hannah R., Hannah Teel, Heather Ezell, Helena from Book Nerd Addicts Blog, Holly M. Bryan, Isabella Plummer, Ivey A. Byrd, Ivy Poh, Jacinda Starr, Jaime Arkin, Jaime Chan, Jaime Arnold of Rockstar Book Tours and Two Chicks on Books, Jan Farnworth, Janine Lisa Amberger, Jazzlyn Matthews, Jeff Harris, Jennzah Cresswell, Jess @ Such a Novel Idea, Jesse the Reader, Jessica from a GREAT read, Jessica Knight, Jessica Lynn Piazza, Jillian, jillian @ bookishandnerdy,

Joe Sanavaitis, John Chappelow, Jolina Cuaresma, Jordan Bishop, Joyce Goldschmid, Julia Rivas, Juniper Nichols, Kaitlin Dang, Kalista Toups, Kami C., Kamryn Blawn, Kara Wolf, Karen Jo Custodio, Karena Fagan, Kat @Treestand Book Reviews, Kate Woods, Kathie Larson, Katrina Toups, Kayla Lawson, Kayla Strickland, Kelli Avery-Ituarte, Kelly Tse, the brave soldiers currently and formerly serving our nation, KIARA, Kim Graff, Kimberly Maule, Kimi Little, Klaire Desamparo, Kricket, Kristin L. Gray, Kristi Wright, Kylie P., Laura Ashforth, Laura Gunderson, Laurel Copus, Lauren Skidmore, Lena Marsteller, Leslie Mei, Liezl Nadayag, Linda Romer, Lisa B., Lily Grant, Lilian Berner, Linda White, LizzieLovesBooks, L.M. Zachry, Lorraine R. Duran, Lucy Grace, Madeleine Michau, Maggie Brister, Mara Delgado Sánchez, Maren @ The Worn Bookmark, Maria (Netherreads), Marlene and Dan Sabo, Marlene Nuno, Mary Malhotra, Maryssa L., Maya Chhabra, Meg McGorry, Megan Mihalek, Mel @ Reviews In A Pinch, Melanie Roberts, Melissa Moake, Misty Strickland, Myranda Barton, Nathania Suissa, Nichole Elizabeth, Nicole Hewitt @ Feed Your Fiction Addiction, Nicole Lynn Hoefs, Nilun Manivanh, N.K. Traver, Núria Coe, Paige Garrison, Paige O'Neal, Perla Lopez, Rachel Bielby, Rachael Halicki, Rachel Qiu, Raychelle Steele, Rebecca Hipworth, Renee Schwall, Riley Marie, Robin Hartloff, Robyn Courtney Brodrick, Sabrina Forney, Sally Ruth Velez, Samantha Kay, Samantha Mrozek, Samara Cuaresma, Sarah Anderson, Sarah Jacobsen, Sarah Kershaw, Scarlet V. Rose, Seeing Double In Neverland, Seina Otaru Wedlick, Shana Potter, Shawn Hinkel, Shelly Collins, Sheyna Watkins, Silvia Asperti, Sondra Boyes, Sophia Life, Sophie Anne Payne, Staci Meyers, Suzanne Graf

Morrone, Sydney Medel, Tammy Theriault, Take Me Away To A Great Read, Tess Botkin, TheBookwormBrittany, Theresa J. Snyder, Tiffany Johnson, ToryAnn Stutts, Tristan Hope Poindexter, Victoria Millen, Victoria Rybalkin, Vika Kareva, Vivien, Wendy Liu, Winifred Caser, and Yet Peng.

Thank you to all my friends who stuff me with chips and salsa, show up early to help at my book events, and pester me to reveal what happens to my characters before I've even finished writing. You know who you are! My life would not be as full and joyful without you.

To Tom, for being there when the clock struck midnight and *The Crown's Game* debuted, when I found out the following week that it hit the *New York Times* bestseller list, and for all the smaller, quieter moments, too. You astound me.

To Mom and Dad, for guiding me and letting me become who I am. Your never-ending love and faith buoy me through my life, and I love you for it.

And to Reese, my favorite person in the world. Thank you for your tackle hugs and your bonus kisses and for being my number-one fan. Thank you for indulging me in my crazy moments and for pushing me to be my very best. You are made of stardust and dreams and magic. I love you, infinitely and forever.